Last Light Falling

Into The Darkness

Book II

By

J. E. PLEMONS

Published by Blarney Stone
Publishing 304 Stubblefield Lane
Suite 1402
Liberty Hill, TX 78642

ISBN: 978-1-7356623-6-7

This book is printed on acid-free paper.

This book is a work of fiction. Places, events, and situations in this book are purely fictional and any resemblance to actual persons, living or dead, is coincidental.

Printed in the United States of America

Library of Congress Cataloging-in-Publications Data Plemons, J.E.

The Covenant / J.E. Plemons. — 1st ed.

p. cm. — (Last Light Falling series ; bk 2)

Summary: In this gripping second installment of the *Last Light Falling* series, faith becomes the only escape from a relentless war about to be waged on American soil, and it's up to Arena to keep Russia from becom- ing the deterrent in an international upheaval for power. One man stands between her and a fight for survival while she risks everything to help lead a new fellowship to a permanent safe haven. While her faith wavers during this impossible quest, her sanity begins to slip, which causes her to sink deeper into a dark descent. Though the hope she embraces begins to wither, it's the difficult decisions she is forced to make that will change the course of everything.

I.Title.
[Fic] — dc22
First edition, May 2015

When the days are undressed with uncertainty, it's the fate of a man's heart that gets him through it. Tragedy is not born in the destiny of a bad man, but rather destiny born into a tragic world. If it's the lack of conviction he harbors, then it's by his selfish and prideful heart that will drive him to make bad choices. Before the end comes to pass, all men will have suffered, but only a few will survive. And it's those whose faith go unyielding, that will be given favor by their maker. So be watchful, because when the sun rests upon the day's end and its light is cast into the shadow, evil things are sure to follow.

"If the whole universe has no meaning, we should never have found out that it has no meaning: just as, if there were no light in the universe and therefore no creatures with eyes, we should never know it was dark. Dark would be without meaning."

—*C.S. Lewis*

Part I

Invasion

CHAPTER 1

In the midst of tragic suffering, we all have fallen by death in one way or another, but because of His suffering, we are given hope and a gift of eternal life. I'm still hopeful for those who still remain in this wicked world, regardless of the unleashed hell that awaits us all.

The light draws dim, and Gabe and I are forced to set camp as the sun sets behind the horizon. We find a small spot beyond a brushy field where a clump of trees stands out in the middle of nowhere. The trees are packed fairly tightly, but there is very little underbrush where we can start a fire without burning everything in sight.

"How many more days you think?" Gabe asks as he clears the ground. I brush the sweat from my eyes and gaze wearily to the east. I'm afraid Carrington won't be the same as we left it.

"Hard to say," I simply answer. Fact is I haven't the slightest clue. Nothing from this landscape looks familiar to home. I lay my pack on the cool soil and rest my swords peacefully against a gnarled tree trunk.

"You hungry?" I ask.

"Is the Pope Catholic?" he caustically answers. The sun quickly sets well behind the trees, leaving the horizon to glow.

"Why don't you get a fire started and I'll fetch us something to eat."

While Gabe dresses the ground with kindling, I venture west, anxious to hunt. Night hunting is not my forte. Without ample light, there's no telling what's lurking in the high grass that surrounds us. Although the land here offers abundant species of game birds, I fear the coyotes and bobcats will scare them away. I kneel down in the brush and wait for something appetizing to cross my path.

It's been long since Gabe and I have had a decent meal we haven't had to kill ourselves—not since before all this shit happened. Myra, our foster mom, was the chef of the household. Her roasted duck, a staple on special occasions, would have your taste buds hypnotized for days. And not many people know how to cook duck properly, but she sure did. Though she is dead along with my real mom, not a day goes by without some memory of her.

It's been twenty minutes now and not a single creature has stirred. I've impatiently waited too long to stay here. I trek further out toward a small thicket of live oak trees about a half-mile to the west.

About halfway to the coppice a small hare hops past my boots. I lunge to grab it, but catch a handful of dirt instead. I can't see a damn thing out here in this nest of weeds. My only hope is to nab something in that cluster of trees up ahead. I wade through the thick brush until the sound of heavy breathing halts my pace. I rest still and for a moment the labored wheezing stops. The sounds in the dark can be misleading, but this certainly doesn't sound friendly. The tall grass suddenly rustles, but I can't tell in what direction it's coming from. Whatever it is, it seems to be scurrying frantically all around. I know it's not a coyote, because he wouldn't be moving this much; he would cowardly wait until I made the first move. A small tree limb snaps on the ground to my left about fifteen paces. I quickly bend down and hide within the scratchy underwood. I slowly draw one of my weathered arrows and carefully place it in the string of my bow, waiting for this animal to show itself. The rustling stops and the deep croaking sound of a bullfrog echoes in the distance. That is a pleasing sound, because I know there must be water nearby and I desperately could use a drink. No frog in its right mind would hop around in this barren land without water.

It's been too long for whatever is hiding out there not to move. Just then, my stomach decides to harmonize with that old bullfrog, growling with starvation. I'm so hungry right now, I'd eat a hot dog from a gas station, but I'm not leaving this spot until I find out what's hiding out there.

I slowly stand up and walk toward where the raspy panting first started. The rustling in the grass continues when two pheasants fly out in front of me, trying to flee. I must have stepped near their guarded nest. A devilish squeal pierces the air, and two glowing eyes stare at me. In an instant, the tall grass begins to move toward me like a wave in the ocean. I raise my bow and pull the string back, but the arrow nock splits and falls from my hands. I quickly turn and run, hoping I won't be mauled by whatever is chasing me. The grass gets thicker and thicker, slowing me down, and that monstrous squeal pierces my ears.

I dart through the weeds as they slash against my thighs like stinging whips. The persisting beast moans with a hellish roar, closing in on my pace, until I finally exit the brushy pasture into a small clearing. There's not a safe enough distance between this creature and me to look back. It's fast whatever it is.

I alter my course toward an old oak tree in hopes I will climb far enough up its gnarled limbs for safe harbor. My sides ache from the exhausted running, and the muscle in my lower left calf gives in as I stumble hard to the ground beneath the old tree.

I quickly roll over, pull my dagger from its sheath, and unexpectedly recognize the beast's twisted tusks driving rapidly toward me. The moonlight shines through the clouded skies and reveals an infuriated feral hog ready to tear into my flesh with vengeance. If I falter, or lose my grip on my knife, I will be at the mercy of its sharp, bristling tusks. The savage pig bows back its hairy ears and leaps, its jowls open wide exposing its razor-sharp teeth. I swing my arm forward and thrust the end of my blade into the backside of his thick, hairy-coated neck. The hog violently flops about, squealing, not going down without a fight. I stab him again and again until the shrieking finally stops.

I lie there on the ground panting, the two-hundred-pound dead, bloody boar resting on my legs. I'm too tired to move, but the stench emitting from this fowl beast persuades me to do otherwise. Not what I was expecting to find for food, but it's all we have, and unless a nice pheasant or squirrel decides to pleasantly drop in my lap surrendering to be eaten, it's pork for dinner.

I push the hairy hog off my legs and pull out my knife. Before I slice into its belly, a small wooden cross near the tree catches my eye. It leans to the side, sitting atop a pile of rocks. It reminds me too much of my uncle Finnegan's burial that I can't seem to peel my eyes from it.

Six months have passed since Gabe and I left Finnegan's grave, and yet I still haven't forgiven myself for his careless death. If he hadn't shielded me from the soldier's bullet at the training facility, I would be the one lying in that grave right now. But my raging hatred for General Iakov caused more pain and misery to our fellowship, and it got Finnegan killed. Though Iakov has fallen with his soldiers in the facility, leaving a heavy stain on this new administration, it has broken a part of me I can't get back.

I feel less convinced of the path God has led me on with every step I take in this dark depraved place. If it is my destiny to help wipe evil from this world, it's tearing me apart, because I can feel the fragility in my faith growing now. While I wish I could go back and change things, my fate has brought me here. . . hunting in the dark for survival.

I quickly cut into the hog before the meat spoils and the blood taints our meal. There is just too much to carry back to camp, so I cut and skin what I can for the night and leave the stinky carcass for the vultures. The smell is just too repulsive to continue butchering this nasty beast, anyway. It's beyond the depths of foul. I tie up what meat I can carry with me and wander toward the small coppice where that bullfrog was bellowing. I'm sure to find water somewhere nearby.

The exposed roots twisting along the ground like a snake suggest an underground spring feeding these lonely trees. There stands a soaring cypress tree hovering over the bank of a small running creek that effortlessly meanders with twists and turns. I follow the brook until I reach the end where it pours into a clear spring. My weary eyes widen, and my dry, parched mouth salivates over this aquatic nectar.

I dunk the canteens into the cold spring water in a less-stagnate area away from the growing moss and algae. I'm so thirsty, I couldn't care less what's floating in this sweet, quenching pool of goodness. As long as I don't have to see what I'm drinking, I'm just fine. Bottoms up, I say.

The unbearable frigid temperatures of winter have finally subdued and surrendered to the fresh blooming beginnings of spring, just like this water. Unfortunately, summer has found a way to creep in, because these long hot days have been murderous. It's nearing May, I think, but I can't be for sure. I lost track of time long ago.

For six long miserable months, our weary legs have ambled through snowy drifts of white expanding as far as the eye can see. We have traveled through lifeless towns, abandoned farms, and fields of emptiness, but traveling by foot is our only way now. The roads are no longer safe. Our nation has changed into an ever-growing evil, and those who see it for what it really is have become a liability under harsh scrutiny.

The hundreds of miles we've traveled from the East Coast have worn us thin, but I feel our journey to reunite with our friends is not too far away. Texas is the only thing on my mind, and I won't be discouraged by another day of swollen feet. We haven't come this far just to give up.

There's a glowing ember in the distance and I realize just how far away I am from Gabe's warm fire. The air is starting to get a little chilly and I shiver. I make my way back to camp and find Gabe asleep on the ground in a fetal posi-tion. The egregious smell of pork smoking above the fire should wake his stomach up. Gabe has already built a spit-fire high enough above the flames to cook our meal. He's a Boy Scout after my own heart.

I'm too hungry to wait for this meat slab to hang over the fire the next eight hours. I slice off small manageable pieces to cook, skewer them on a couple of sticks, and lay them on a rock next to the fire. I wrap the rest of meat around the long piece of hickory Gabe had used for a walking stick, and secure it with some left over wire from my pack. I carefully rest the meat above the fire to slow-cook overnight. Hell, maybe the stench will evaporate from the pores, leaving us with some nice tenderloin for breakfast.

I sit next to the crackling fire and dangle the small pieces on the wooden skewers right above the flames. The rendering fat drips from the pork causing the fire to flare up. The sizzling of the fat and crackling of the tissue begins to rouse Gabe, but I don't think it's the sound that has awakened him.

"Holy mother of God, what's that smell, Arena?" Gabe says with his nosed pinched. It's quite an uninviting smell, but I've been smelling and breathing it in for a while, so I guess I have gotten used to it.

"It's our dinner," I say.

"You're kidding me. What are you feeding me, the inside of a pig's ass?"

Not quite, but damn near close, I think, trying hard not to smile. Okay, I admit the smell is objectionable, but this is all I have to offer.

"Unless you have anything better to proposition, this is our meal. I suggest you take it and fill that empty stomach of yours."

This salty meat may taste gamey, but when you are as hungry as we are, you'll eat just about anything, and my stomach can't wait until the morning to find something better. Sure I would like to have a nice juicy steak and baked potato, but this will just have to do. We both hold our noses from breathing in the smell of this wretched swine. I stomach what I can and try to dilute the taste with the fresh spring water.

Gabe eagerly falls back to sleep. I try to stay awake as long as I can to keep watch for any unwanted wild creature that may wander uninvited to our malodorous campsite. I'm pretty sure we have unintentionally attracted every wild beast for miles with the smoky scent of ass.

I watch Gabe sleep comfortably below the canvased trees while my stomach churns. The world seems so lonely. Gabe is all I have left right now, and I don't think I could bear the thought of losing him too. There were times in my life when I detested my twin brother, but I never stopped loving him, and right now, I need him more than ever.

The harsh conditions we've experience in the last six months has forced us to both grow up, but none more than Gabe. He's become a man before my eyes. His dirty blond hair drapes dingily below his ears and eyes. He's still the same brother at heart, but he's grown into something much different. Behind those skinny limbs and that frail body he used to carry, breathes courage now. We can never go back to what we were—time and history have changed, and so have we.

I want to believe there is purpose in all of this, but I'm not sure anymore what I'm supposed to do. I feel lost without Finnegan by my side. He was the only family Gabe and I had left, and now he too is gone. But his bravery will never be forgotten, and because it was his choice to follow my divine path, we've weakened a dying nation at its heart. My enemy may be dead, but my nightmares are still much alive.

I realize there is a reason for every event that happens to us, but I'm still having a difficult time accepting it. I may never fully understand my part in this world, but I will continue until I can no more. Many people left on this earth will accept their fate as meaningless acts of randomness. I believe now there is more to this world than just chaos and ruin. We were born with a plan, a purpose, and a choice. I choose to believe Finnegan saved my life to extend my fate, and I'm eternally grateful, but I wish not to endure any more humbling experiences through death.

Instead of sleeping on the padded dirt next to the fire, I nestle in between the roots of an old oak tree. I prop myself up against rough ridges of splitting bark and stretch out my legs. I grab Jacob's necklace around my neck and stare down at the worn silver cross like I do every night. I rub the edges with my fingers as if it were a nervous tick. I'm afraid I will never let go. The only boy I truly loved is gone, but his death will remain very alive in my nightmares. I fight to stay awake, but my body isn't willing to compromise. Sleep wins the battle.

CHAPTER 2

The smoke from the burning pit slowly drifts past my nostrils, stirring me from my sleep. I crack my eyes open to an uninviting ray of sunlight peeking through the nestled tree limbs. I'm too tired to fully awaken, but soon the smell of the slow-cooked sow reminds me how much I wish I didn't kill that beast. Most of the stench has either cooked out, or has settled into our camp as a part of the family and we have gotten used to it.

I rest my arm over my eyes, attempting to block the small gleam of light trying to seep through the cracks. I could really use a few more winks of sleep. It's unlike me to sleep during the morning, but our daily travels have worn me out over the last few months.

Just as I begin to fall back asleep, a cold morning breeze brushes against my skin and the tiny hairs on my arm recoil, making me shiver slightly. I really have to pee now, but I'm just too comfortable to get up. How comfortable and tired do you really have to be when you are in an uncomfortable situation? If that's not an oxymoron, I don't know what is.

Suddenly, a twig snaps followed by rustling footsteps carefully gliding across the dirt and grass. It's probably just a deer attracted to the smell of our breakfast smoking above the warm coals below. I slowly turn my head to view my surroundings. No deer.

Gabe is still dead asleep against a tree, the side of his face buried down beside the roots. The fire is still slowly burning, crackling of unburned bark popping, but the sound quickly changes to a sizzle as if water is dripping onto the hot embers. The rustling noise shifts toward the fire, and the sound of a log falling into the burning coals startles me. Out of the corner of my eye, I see small hands trying to tear off pieces of meat.

I quickly rise up, my heart pounding. Standing before me is a young girl with a face covered in dirt and a mouthful of meat. It seems like an eternity before we both engage. I take a step forward, but she is frightened and runs off into the fields.

"Wait, stop! I'm not going to hurt you!" I shout.

I hurry past the fire, nearly stumbling over the rocks surrounding it, and scream at Gabe to wake up. He is so asleep, I have to kick him in the side to get his attention. "Wake up!"

"What the hell is going on?" Gabe says, disoriented.

"A girl, she went out into the field. Help me get her."

"What girl?"

"Come on, don't let her get away."

I sprint out into the open grass field, but I see nothing but empty space. She must be hiding underneath all this brush. I quickly stop and look all around, hoping to see or hear some movement. I turn to my right and hear swishing in the grass, but it's just Gabe and his not-so-stealth self.

"Stop," I say to Gabe. He abruptly turns into a statue, waiting for my signal. "Listen, over there," I say, pointing toward the area where I killed the feral hog last night.

The sound stops, and now there is absolute silence. A couple of minutes go by and not a trace of the girl is to be seen or heard, when suddenly a small head pops up from a small clump of bushes. The girl darts out, running toward a hill on the other side of the trees.

"Come on!" I shout at Gabe.

We sprint over to her, but she quickly disappears again.

"This is like chasing a rabbit in a cornfield," Gabe says, panting and out of breath. "And I haven't had any breakfast yet."

"Shh, stop talking, listen."

"You know what I hear?"

"Hush," I assert.

"The small laughter coming from a girl who's outsmarted us."

She's smart all right. She's doing exactly what I would do, but we can't let her get away. This is the first sign of life we've encountered in a while, and it's pertinent that we find her. We could really use some shelter. I'm getting tired of sleeping on the ground.

"Gabe, stay here and don't move until I give you a signal. I'm going to flank her to the right."

"What's the signal?"

"I'll give you a whip-poor-will call. Just remember not to move until I tell you to. When you hear me call, rush her like you've got a swarm of bees chasing you."

I move as stealthily as I can around the clump of trees and the rocky bank to the west. A dry creek bed wanders on the other side of the hill and runs into a small ridge and a steep rocky wall. Twisted roots hang off the edge and protrude through the side of the limestone wall, which I use to help me climb up. When I get to the top, a plume of smoke rising in the far distance paralyzes me for a moment.

I look toward the girl's position, then back at the smoke, suddenly realizing that's where she is possibly headed. My incentive in catching this girl has suddenly increased. We may have found a place of refuge for a few days. I pull myself up over the edge and hug the knotted roots on the ground, as I slither on my belly into the deep brushy field.

I move slowly, hiding myself in the middle of the field until I see a speck of clothing swish back and forth between the blowing skirt of green grass. I've spotted my target. I feel a sense of adoration for her survival skills, but I know that fear surrounds her. She must be frightened, just as I would be at her age, but she is just a starving little girl who wanted some food to survive. I can't help but ponder what kind of life she's been dealt during these wicked times.

People in this nation have been starving since the economic collapse shattered the whole world, and even before then, it was a struggle to carry on. But they surely won't survive the chaos the government has left us with now. This girl is the product of the ruin we are left with.

She looks so lonely and desperately thin. She couldn't be more than nine or ten years old. Her tiny frame is well hidden in the brush like a rabbit burrowing in the grass. The only thing that keeps her from blending into the tan brush is her long dark hair and dingy red shirt.

Whatever has happened in these past few months has affected more than just the remote towns. I can't remember the last time we saw another person until now. We've been isolated from the rest of the world for months except for a couple of towns we drifted by. But even those appeared to be deserted, with sparse human activity.

I cautiously approach the north side of the girl's position so I can get a good angle on her when she runs. I clasp my hands together and blow into them with the whip-poor-will's birdcall, the only call that sings its song in the early mornings just right before light. It's distinctive and native to these parts, so hopefully it won't be a distraction and will meld into the natural sounds around us.

The girl slowly rises and moves carefully across the grass. Gabe sprints full throttle toward her. I crouch down and wait. She runs right toward me, but then turns to the left, as if she knows I'm waiting for her. I quickly chase her down, grabbing her shoulder and pulling her to the ground. Gabe races from the other side as I try to keep her from slipping away. I grab her ankles while she kicks and screams until Gabe finally reaches us and holds her down.

I grab her arms and hug her tightly to keep her from squirming out of my grasp. She finally gives in and collapses to the ground from the sheer rush of adrenaline that has finally ceased to flow in her body. After blacking out from the excitement for a few minutes, the girl comes to. Still frightened from the chase, she tries to wiggle from me, but I hold her tightly. I try to calm her, but she just moans and wiggles.

"Stop. I'm not here to harm you," I say as she tries to slither from my grasp. I hold her tight and look deep into her eyes.

"I'm here to help you. If it's food that you want, I can feed you." She stops momentarily, but not without a hint of hostility.

"For you and your family," I add.

She finally softens her aggression and releases her nails from my skin. I'm a little reluctant to let go of her, but I can see in her eyes that she has no choice but to adhere to my wishes. I can tell she has been starving, and whether or not she believes me, her hunger wins out over her distrust.

Gabe looks at me uneasily, as I slowly let go of my grip on her arm. She lies on the ground, staring at my feet, and begins to cry. I'm usually cautious about trusting strangers, but I feel it should be in everyone's good nature to replenish the weary and serve the needs of others. I refuse to let someone starve.

I hold out my hand to her as a friendly gesture and help her to her feet.

"Come back to our camp and take all the food you need," I say. She wipes her eyes and hesitantly looks up at me.

"I'm Arena, and this is my brother Gabe. We're just trying to survive, like you." She looks back behind us and contemplates our invitation, but her growling stomach soon decides for her.

"My name is Allison," she says haltingly, grabbing my hand.

"How old are you?"

"Ten."

"You're brave coming out here all alone." I walk her back to the campsite, keeping the conversation moving in the hopes of prodding a little deeper into her circumstance, while Gabe follows watchfully behind.

"I live with my mother," she says.

"Any brothers or sisters?" I ask. She says nothing for a moment. The silence says it all. She shakes her head as tears roll down the side of her face. Her response is a chilling reminder of what happened to Cecillia's family. I think back at how broken Cecillia was, how she didn't want to let me go before I left her with Maria and her daughter.

It seems like ages ago when I found Cecillia hiding in her house, where I tried to persuade her to come out from behind the couch. And how could I forget the gruesome images of her mom and two siblings hanging dead from the closet? So much torment has gone on, it's a wonder how much longer this world can survive. Now I wish I hadn't mentioned anything. I feel terrible, and grit my teeth with dissatisfaction because of my mistake. I quickly try to find something a bit lighter to talk about.

"Well, if you're not too much in a hurry, I can rustle up some nice pheasants to take back to your mother."

"Thank you," she says with a half-smile.

"Believe me, they will taste much better than that nasty, old hog."

Just as I say that, the lingering smell of the rancid pig drifts up my nostrils. My appetite has suddenly regressed.

I turn back to see if Gabe is still following, when Allison's hand tightens around mine, and her body comes to a complete halt. She looks intently ahead and shakes with fright.

"What's wrong?" I ask. She doesn't respond. She just stands there like she's seen a ghost. "Allison, sweetie, you okay?"

She refuses to look at me, so I bend down and notice Gabe standing very still behind her with an alarming look on his face.

With her eyes fixed and her statue-like body fighting to stay still, a deep gurgling purr answers for me. I slowly turn my head to a prowling mountain lion thirty yards in front of us, hungering over the smoked loin dangling above the warm coals.

"Everybody just stay still," I quietly say.

"Uh, I think we got that covered," Gabe says. The big cat rears back its pointed ears and opens his wide jaws, showing us a glimpse of the razor-sharp teeth that he plans to maul us with. Not too unusual to see a mountain lion in this area, but definitely unexpected. With the help of our roasting hog spreading its scent to everything that walks the earth, I shouldn't be surprised.

The mountain lion keeps an attentive eye on us while pawing at the meat. If his intention is to keep us honest, then he's succeeded. I left all my weapons at the campsite, and all I have on me is a dagger. I'm not exactly experienced fending off raging wild animals, much less the one I killed last night. Whatever his intent is, I'm hoping that the cooked loin is enough to satisfy his hunger and keeps us from being his dessert. I'm willing to extend the same respect.

He's just as hungry as we are, but I do believe he has the upper hand in this standoff. We patiently wait for this vicious feline to finish his meal, but he doesn't appear to be too interested in the hog loin anymore. I can't say that I blame him.

"Arena," Gabe quietly says.

"What?"

"He's staring right at you."

"Just stare back, and don't take your eyes off him. We can't let him know we're scared."

"Yeah, I don't think he's buying it."

"Raise your hands up high, like this."

"Why," Allison asks.

"We need to look bigger than him." The big cat growls.

"I think that pissed him off, Arena," Gabe says.

"Growl back, and louder."

"Are you insane?"

"Just do it, trust me." We growl like a bunch of idiots to show this animal our lack of fear, but it doesn't really seem to be working.

"Arena?" asks Allison, "I have to pee"

"Honey, just go in your pants, but don't kneel down," I assert.

"Why is he looking at me?"

"Just stay right here with me and don't back up."

The mountain lion recognizes Allison's frightened shivering and paces back and forth, demonstrating his intimidating nature. After a brief moment of attempting to extract fear in his prey, he suddenly disengages and leans his head down toward the ground while his back arches upward as if he's ready to pounce. He waits patiently, with the corners of his mouth stretching back like a warrior smiling with confidence upon his enemy.

Allison shivers with fear and slowly backs up behind me. I slowly pull out my dagger, keeping one eye on the cat and the other on Allison. I scream at him, trying to distract him, but there is something about Allison he wants. The mountain lion takes a few steps forward and growls aggressively.

"Allison, honey, grab my hand," I say softly.

"Why is he looking at me like that?" she worries, panting with fright.

Allison steps back closer to Gabe and cries. The mountain lion leaps forward, and charges at Allison with rage. Allison quickly runs away.

"Allison!" I scream. The mountain lion growls and screeches across the grass after her. I quickly grab my dagger and lunge toward him before he races past me, and I stretch my arm out as far as I can, slashing across his right hind leg .

He stumbles helplessly to the ground and rolls into the grass, shrieking, but his wounded leg only slows him down. He rolls back over and continues after Allison with a slight limp.

"Gabe!" I scream, trying to scrape myself up from the soft black dirt. Gabe races over and stands his ground in between the wounded cat and Allison, who suddenly stops running. The mountain lion abruptly slows down and staggers a bit before violently growling at Gabe for standing in his killing path.

He picks up an old oak limb and raises it like a baseball bat while the mountain lion arches his back. His growl painfully lingers, and his ears twitch back as I carefully walk behind him with my dagger in hand.

The mountain lion fiercely leans forward before leaping toward Gabe's vulnerable position. Feeding on pure adrenaline, I rush the lion with a fury, but my pace is quickly terminated. My boot catches the tip of a rock and I stumble to the ground. I quickly try to get up, but my feet struggle to gain their balance. The mountain lion jumps. Gabe swings the limb across the lion's body and knocks him to the ground.

I rush over to finish him off with my knife, but the persistently vicious cat quickly stammers to his feet and swings his mammoth paw across Gabe's arm. I quickly thrust my knife toward the lion's side before he can maul my brother to pieces, but I stab the black soil instead. Allison scurries across the grass and leads the mountain lion to chase after her.

I leap over Gabe and churn my feet as quickly as I can, my dagger raised and ready to strike. With the lion badly wounded, I'm close on his heels. I suddenly look up and see that Allison is nowhere in sight. I lunge forward with my knife, striking down into his ribs as the mountain lion leaps into the air and pounces to the ground on what I can only assume is Allison, who must have fallen.

I thrust the dagger into the back of its neck. The beast screams out in a fury, trying to claw me from the side, but I relentlessly stab him over and over until I hear the faint whisper dip into silence. The sharp, growling shriek finally rests, and the vicious cat retracts his claws and falls limp. Red covers my hands and arms as the warm blood runs off my dagger. I quickly try to catch my breath and push the heavy lion off Allison's small body. She is soaked in blood and not moving.

"Oh God, no, no, no!" I wipe the blood from her face and the side of her throat, searching for claw marks, but there is not physical damage I can see. I slap her on the side of the cheek, but she is unresponsive.

"Wake up! Allison! Oh God, honey, don't do this, please don't die on me." Without a hint of expression, she just lies there motionless. The sheer weight of the lion must have killed her. Pain begins to take hold of my heart as I cry out with anger. I stroke her hair and lay my head on her chest while tears pour down my face, mingling with the blood on her body. "God, what have I done? Please no, not like this." My anger may be subject to judgment, but my sadness soon overcomes as I mourn.

"Why have you abandoned me?"

CHAPTER 3

It's always disheartening to witness such a tragic and unnecessary death. Even with the nature of free will, I still can't comprehend the shock of a young child's death. But, considering the circumstances, I guess it's better than the alternative of slowly starving to death. I find it all too vexing and sad. Even the chirping songs of morning birds can't distract my sullen feelings.

Before I can lift my head from Allison's body, a slow rising movement comes from her chest as it expands with air. Startled, I quickly press my ear to her mouth. I listen closely, and suddenly, the slightest warm breath of life blows between Allison's tightly closed lips and into my ear. A sigh of jubilation overcomes me.

"What is it?" Gabe asks, startling me for a moment. I almost forgot about him lying on the ground back there.

"I think she's still alive."

Gabe carefully walks over and kneels down beside Allison. He gingerly slides his hand underneath her neck and winces. Small scratches peek beneath the tattered claw marks on his shirtsleeve. He begins to examine her head and neck area. As I watch him, I feel a hint of shame and guilt for not coming to Gabe's aid, forgetting about him in all this emotional chaos.

I look upon him with adoration and realize how much more he means to me than I do for him. My baby brother's devotion has more value than life itself. He risked his own life to slow down the mountain lion from taking Allison's.

"Are you okay?" I ask him in a sincere tone. His lack of a response suddenly seeps deep into my gut and further echoes the blame I've caused. He obviously didn't hear me and is too involved to have noticed, yet I feel the need to apologize nonetheless.

"I'm so sorry, Gabe, I—"

"It's okay, Arena," he says. He stops for a brief moment and looks up at me. "I would have done the same thing . . . it's what we do. All that matters right now is that you're alive and I'm alive, and this girl isn't going to die today."

Allison moves her head slightly to the left, and her lips relax as she breathes with more ease. Her eyes are still closed, but at least she's moving her body about. I carefully slide my hand behind her head and feel a small lump.

Her weary eyelids open, and her dilated pupils begin to wander. Gabe delicately carries her over to our camp and leans her against the large rock that is padded with his blanket. I grab some water from his bag and wash most of the blood from her face and neck. No puncture wounds from the cat's teeth are visible, and remarkably there are no claw marks on her body. I guess the blood from the dead mountain lion poured out onto her when I stabbed him.

She softly moans as the bright morning sun shines into her eyes. Shocked from the confusion, she quickly grabs the side of my arm and tries to jump to her feet, but then she woozily starts to fall, and I grab her and ease her down.

"Hey, it's okay, it's okay. Just sit back down. You're just a little dizzy from the bump on your head," I say, calming her as I softly stroke her arm. She soon notices her blood-soaked clothes and frantically searches for wounds.

"Don't worry, it's not your blood," I say.

"What happened?"

"I assume you fell down while you were being chased."

"Is he dead?"

"He's dead, but if it weren't for Gabe slowing him down in his tracks, I might not have had time to kill him before he gashed you."

She still appears to be in a state of shock, but coherent enough to acknowledge Gabe and offer him her gratitude. She slowly lifts her head.

"Thank you, Gabe," she says weakly. "I'm so sorry, I should have never run."

"No need to apologize, I would have run too. I'm just glad I was here for you," says Gabe

I ponder over what Gabe has just said. The fact that we were here wasn't an accident. I truly believe this was divine and perhaps an essential part of our journey.

"I'm sure your mother is worried sick about you," I tell Allison. She sits silently, her head lowered, and feet crossed. I reserve the effort to prod any further until she's feeling better.

"We'll take you back to her, but you need to rest here first."

I grab my dagger and bow, hoping to find some food for us all before we trudge any further. Our strength will be vital if we are to find shelter elsewhere. I grab a fully loaded mag, insert it into one of my guns, and hand it to Gabe.

"Don't go wandering off without this. You stay here with Allison while I go hunt us some food."

"Anything but pork, please."

Well, at least Gabe's sarcasm meter hasn't broken. I'm eagerly tempted to smack him in the face, but he's right. Fish or pheasant would be a tremendously better culinary upgrade.

If I was desperate and my life depended on it, I guess I would be forced to cut into the dead lion, but I'm not starving on my death bed. Its blood-riddled meat is as gamy and pungent as the sow still smoldering over the fire, which reminds me of how we got into this predicament.

I toss what's left of the loin behind the trees and grab some rope from my bag. I tie the rope tightly around the front legs of the dead mountain lion and drag the carcass as far as I can away from camp. Hopefully we won't attract any other unwanted hungry creatures.

I journey out toward the south edge of our camp where the trees are more abundant. I hope I can nab us a couple of squirrels, and if I'm lucky enough, a few wild birds. Just beyond the hillside about a quarter of a mile away, I come to a gathering of Spanish oaks. Along the way, mesquite trees dominate this area with the occasional agave cactus. I have to closely watch where I step because it's very unpleasant to bump against one of its blade-like leaves.

The deeper I walk into the thicket of trees, the more comfortable I become. I'm not much for hunting out in the open space—I feel like I'm being hunted. I find a nice soft spot on the ground behind a dead tree that has somehow sprouted a small cluster of bushes tightly nestled below it.

I lay my bow on the ground in front of me with an arrow resting on its strings. I sit back and patiently wait, and take in all the wonderful, wild sounds adorning this dense garden of green. I feel like I'm right in an educational wildlife video, listening to nature's soundtrack. This is so much more pleasing than living in the city. If I could only bottle up this serene moment and take it with me.

Without warning, two squirrels jump out to the right of me. They momentarily dance around, fighting over a half-eaten acorn before chasing each other around a tree. Their joyful playfulness distracts me so much that I've almost forgotten why I came here in the first place. My joyous grin temporarily retreats as I quietly grab my bow. The two squirrels have now split up—one has jumped to another tree and hangs onto a small branch, while the other frantically paces from one end of the tree trunk to the other. Spastic little devils they are.

They may be cute to watch, but they can be naughty little creatures. Their teeth are strong enough to chew and gnaw on just about anything from walls and roofs to car wiring. They may not mean to harm, but I'm the stronger species and I'm starving—such is life.

I carefully raise my bow and stretch back the string toward my cheekbone. I position myself like a statue and breathe in deeply to relax before releasing the arrow. Unfortunately, the squirrel on the ground won't stay still long enough for me to get a clean shot. After a few seconds, he finally stops and sits upright on his hind legs. He, too, sits like a statue, but with intense anticipation, as if something is about to happen. If it's not my arrow about to strike his head, it's something else that has distracted him from finishing off the acorn on the ground.

I carefully aim and slowly release my breath before letting the arrow fling from my bow, when suddenly an obnoxious cackling from the bushes breaks my concentration. I release the arrow and narrowly miss, sending the two squirrels fleeing deep into the woods.

"Damn," I shout to myself. While the cackling noise continues to my left, I load another arrow onto my bow with frustration and anger. Whatever is making that noise is not going to live much longer. I stand up, creep out behind the dead tree, and follow the sound with my bow aimed. The noise stops momentarily, but the manic rustling in the bushes about twenty feet in front of me doesn't bode well for this creature. Whatever it is, it's not smart enough to keep itself concealed.

I slowly walk around the bush and pull back the arrow, anxiously waiting for this thing to pop out. As soon as the head emerges from the bushes, I grit my teeth with fury, ready to strike down. The animal finally jumps out without even a clue it's being watched, much less killed. I slowly disengage the string and lower my bow. I can't help but chuckle for a moment. From a raging boar ready to gnaw my legs off to a clumsy and confused clucking chicken—this has to be God's sense of humor at work.

What in the hell is a chicken doing out in the woods anyway? Well, it doesn't seem to mind me picking him up. She's kind of cute . . . for a chicken, I guess, but she's going to look and smell much better roasted. With the chicken tucked under my arm, I hike further to the west where she was possibly coming from. Right outside the trees and down a graded incline sits a farmhouse on a lonely stretch of land. I'm going to assume this chicken belongs to whoever lives there.

I walk down to the old house and spot a chicken coop on the far right, next to a barbed-wire fence. As much as I would love to cook up this poultry goodness, it's not mine to keep, so I place the chicken back into its pen.

I'm hesitant to knock on the door because I have no idea what to expect anymore. This world has become too much of a mystery, and I just don't trust anyone in it. However intimidating this may be, I'm somewhat intrigued by the humble farmhouse, but not without a protective guard of course.

I draw my gun and peek through the screen door that's slightly cracked open. I feel inclined to just walk right in, but I quickly hold back. I don't know if these people are dangerous, but if they are as scared and timid as Allison, then this arduous disagreement I'm having with my ego is reflecting badly on my good manners. I decide to walk around to the back instead, hoping to find someone humbly ready to greet without any hostility. Unfortunately, it's as empty as the front.

Behind the farmhouse stretches acres of fenced, fertile land where cows and goats are freely roaming over patches of green grass. There's a broken-down tractor that looks as if hasn't been used for quite some time. The backyard is littered with trash and the back window by the door is broken. Shattered bits of glass lie scattered below the window on the porch as if this just recently happened. I knock loudly on the back door with my dagger in hand.

"Hello!" I shout. "Anyone home?"

The only response I get is the sound of a scrawny, mangy cat meowing at my feet. Obviously someone has neglected this cat long enough to have possibly abandoned this place. But why leave? There's enough food here to last a couple of seasons.

I slowly pull open the back door and enter the house, deciding to go against my better judgment. If there is anyone in here, they are either hard of hearing, asleep, or dead. With the dagger in my hand, I'd like to think none of the above.

The house appears to be in order and is silent. I'm inclined to think that someone may have died here. I search the downstairs for anything unusual, hoping to at least find a clue to what may have happened, but nothing strange or uncommon appears to suggest otherwise except for the kitchen area. Everything seems unblemished in this house, but the kitchen countertops. Rotting fruit and spoiled unre-frigerated food is scattered about, and the cupboard doors are wide open. Someone was obviously in a hurry or they would have kept this area just as pristine as the rest of the house.

I cautiously walk up the worn, creaky stairs anticipating the smell of death, but when I reach the top, it appears just as clean as the bottom. The air up here smells of mint leaves and fresh tobacco, unlike the staleness down below. All three bedrooms are spotless, with bedding neatly tucked into their mattresses.

A pair of reading glasses and a bottle of pills labeled, *Digoxin*, sit on the bedside table next to a note written with impeccable penmanship.

Dear Vera,
I'm going in to town to fetch a few things. I've changed the automatic chicken feeder for days only, so don't mess with it. Your new ID is tucked inside an envelope under our secret place. Make yourself at home, and be sure to lock the door behind you. I'll be back as quickly as I can. If anyone suspicious should approach the house, the small door behind the stairs will give you a place to hide. Be sure to grab the rifle behind the coat rack in the foyer. Stay safe.

Richard

I'm not sure what to think about this place or this note so I just leave. Before I step off the porch, I find myself contemplating over the chicken coop and its plentiful chickens. My stomach begins to growl and reminds me of the two other starving people back at the campsite.

I walk over to the coop and peer through the chicken wire, marveling over the plump, feathered, flapping fowls. I can just smell their tender roasted breasts as the saliva builds in the corners of my mouth. Why should we all starve? These chickens aren't doing any good walking over each other in this tightly quartered pen. Unless someone does come back, these chickens are going to die anyway. The feed trowel is low.

I carefully open the loosely wired door and see now how the chicken got out. I root around in the back part of the pen where the hens are kept and discover a large, brown, potato-like knapsack hanging on a rusty nail. I take the sack down and quickly scamper around, chasing the chickens. One by one, I grab three chickens and toss them into the sack.

Before I start my way back to camp, I find myself in a moral dilemma. Is this stealing, or am I justified in taking these chickens for the sake of the poor and starving? Regardless of the decision, I feel it necessary to at least tell the owners what I have done if anyone does truly still live here. And if this place has been abandoned, it surely would make a great place of refuge, but I'm cautious to stay here until I know Allison is safely back with her mother. I walk back into the house to find some paper to write on and tack my note to the front screen door, just in case someone does decide to come back.

I owe you three chickens. Please forgive my indulgence for food. I will repay you in any way I can.
Sincerely,
Very Hungry
P.S. I hope you will consider my honesty as a form of repayment and my selfless nature for bringing one of your chickens back . . . that I'm about to eat.

CHAPTER 4

I take a shortcut back to camp, around the trees this time. Allison is still sitting in the same position I left her in, and Gabe is swinging one of my swords around. During the last six months of our journey, it only made sense to help Gabe with his less-than-stellar physical skills, but he has surprisingly come around quite nicely. Not sure how it will translate into real battle, but he's absorbing everything I'm teaching him nonetheless. Whether he knows it or not, there's going to come a time when that may be the only weapon of choice.

Gabe's inventive skills have not gone unnoticed, but with everything else gone to shit, I don't imagine it will be of any help to us now. I really miss that boy's inventions: the tiny exploding metal bees that rained down on General Iakov's soldiers in the ominous city that eagerly engaged in human trafficking, the electrically charged wire nets that paralyzed a company of troops while attempting to seize a town, and of course his ruthless slinging saw blade contraption that diced a path of guards for us in the prison.

There's no doubt he's the brains in this fellowship, but he's out of his element when he's not behind some tool or computer screen. Now, if only I can teach him to swing a sword or toss a dagger without hurting himself.

It's evident that I was born to wield a sword, but I often wonder what might have been in another life—and would it have really mattered. But like Father Joseph said, everyone and everything has a purpose on this earth; choosing to understand it is not our mission, but choosing to accept it is absolutely crucial.

I believe everyone has a gift that should never be over-looked, and whatever career path one takes, it isn't the job or duty that we should praise, but rather the way we choose to glorify our Lord in it. That is what separates us from God. These are the philosophies my father instilled in me, and no matter how grim the world may seem or the persistent temptations that provoke my sins, I will remain grounded by these ideas.

I'm far from perfect; in fact, I'm just a broken girl trying to find my way, and no matter how many times I've fallen, it was never my faith that was in question—just my will to understand it.

Watching Gabe show off in front of Allison makes me smile. It seems like only yesterday I was protecting my brother from Derrick Maitland, the school bully. But that day our lives changed forever. As much as I fight to forget the gruesome images, my mind has been poisoned just enough to remember them. Seeing my classmates' bodies lying helplessly in the schoolyard, convulsing and expelling their insides into a panic of incomprehensible death, is an atrocity no person should ever have to witness. To this day, I still don't know exactly what it was that killed them, but it's obvious our government initiated it. And that's when it allbegan.

A war of social cultures has been on the rise, and it didn't take long for our government to dispense a nation-wide policy to tame it. The chronically poor and less-contributing classes of consumers unable to adhere to governmental agendas were all subject to immediate removal to unwanted districts or regions.

Ordered by President Kriel, officers were sent in, storming town after town, to bus families to temporary prisons. Those who refused were dragged under extreme and hostile force, some even fatal. The government's forceful relocation policy ended more than just a clash of class wars. It was the beginning of a genocide, and I'm in the middle of it all.

The government may have created civil unrest among its people, but I was the one who started this revolution. Hundreds of soldiers have already died by my sword and guns, but none more important than the leader who feedsthem.

Though President Kriel has been killed, it won't stop his malicious plans that lie ahead. An invasion on American soil has been planned for quite some time under the president's new world order reform, and if Finnegan was right about this knowledge when he worked for this corrupt government, then I don't expect it to change. The government will soon fall to its demise, and the people of this country who have risen up to fight against its malevolent rule will regrettably witness a new unforgiving wrath that will soon be upon them. I'm afraid the enormity of this war grows beyond the likes of President Kriel and General Iakov.

Whatever regrets that rest in me, there's no point in dwelling on them now—I have nothing left. Our foster parents, Myra and Daniel, who were imprisoned like many others, are dead, and Jacob, the only boy I've truly loved, is no longer on this earth. It still stings in my heart that he was shot by officers for no good reason. I don't know what's more painful—losing Jacob, or my parents being killed in a car crash when I was nine. I'm fifteen going on sixteen, and I have yet to let go of my parents' death. I wonder how long Jacob's death will torment me.

The only hope I have left is finding our friends now. I grow restless, knowing we are that much closer to them. I just hope they are still alive, waiting for our return.

Six months ago, our fellowship was severed when we reached the training facility. Although it was my choice to send Henry and Juliana back to the den where Father Joseph and Niki were waiting, I've regretfully felt my decision sting in Gabe's heart. His first true love is only a memory now, and until we can make our journey back to the den for him to reunite with Juliana, that's all it ever will be.

"How's everyone holding up?" I ask, dropping the wiggling bag of chickens.

"What the . . . ?" Gabe says, stammering backward and pointing at the sack. "Arena, tell me there's not a body in there."

"It's our breakfast, lunch, and dinner."

"What?"

"Go ahead, look for yourself."

He holds open the bag and peers inside. "Yes, thank you, Jesus. I've got dibs on the legs," he exclaims with a huge grin.

"Who the hell are you people?" Allison asks with a disturbed look.

"Chicken legs . . . as in *bawk-bawk*," Gabe adds, soothing her discouraged, pale face. She sighs with relief, as if there was ever a possibility of a mangled body in the sack.

"I've got three of them in that bag. We'll cook one for now to get your strength back and take the other two back to your mother," I say.

"Where did you get them?" Allison asks.

"Yeah, how did you find chickens out in the middle of nowhere?" Gabe adds.

I'm a little hesitant to tell them I stole them, but under the circumstances, I'm also hoping they will forgive my unexpected behavior. It's not like me to do something this irrational without first examining the situation thoroughly. As they both look at me waiting for a reasonable answer, I battle my guilty conscience for a second just to appease my own spirit even if it's not necessary. We're starving people, after all, and we should be grateful for what we have and worry about dissecting the consequences later.

"I took them from a farm about a mile that way," I say, pointing toward the west.

"That's Papa Dillion's farm," Allison quietly says.

"Yeah, well Papa Dillion wasn't home."

"So you just took them?" Gabe asks. I just nod my head, trusting they will at least extend me some grace considering our situation.

"I found one running loose out in the middle of the woods. I didn't feel right to just leave it, so I took it back to the owners, hoping to find someone there to help us. No one was home, nor did it look like they had been there for quite some time."

"I haven't seen Papa Dillion for a month," Allison chimes in.

"Really?" I say. I'm now intrigued by the possibility of maybe staying there for a few days after Allison gets back to her mother.

"He usually stops by our house twice a week and gives us some food, but he hasn't been by in a while."

"Does anybody else live there?" I ask.

"I think his grandson, but I haven't seen him either."

"You must live near here then."

"It's not far."

While Gabe rekindles the fire, I grab my sword and pull out one of the chickens from the bag. I find a nice-sized log to behead the chicken on. I've killed plenty of pheasants and small game hens, but never a bird this size before. It's a challenge just to hold down the flapping chicken while I try to cut its neck off. I ask Allison to hold down the back of the chicken's body on the log while I pin its shifty head with my boot.

I raise my sword up, then strike down on the neck, severing the head instantly. Blood sprays out, and the convulsing muscles of the chicken violently contract. Allison lets go, and I stand there slightly confused. I pull the sword from the log, and watch the chicken's body flap around in circles.

"So that's what they mean when they say, 'Running around like a chicken with its head cut off,'" Gabe says with amusement.

We chase the headless chicken around like three bumbling stooges. It staggers aimlessly between our hands until it collapses near the trunk of a Spanish oak. I grab the epileptic bird, tie the legs with string and hang it upside down on one of the lower branches. With its feet dangling from the string, the rest of the blood pours out onto the ground. I take my sharpest knife and start plucking and scraping the feathers until its pink skin is exposed.

I cut open the back end and remove the rest of the insides along with the oil gland. I grab a small flaming piece of kindling in the fire and scald the pink skin, making sure I've removed any remaining feather pieces. I can already smell the goodness of this long-awaited meal as the skin crackles under the flame.

The chicken hovering over the fire glistens from the oils, and fatty juices run off the golden-brown skin. The succulent smell of roasting bird makes everyone salivate. I just wish I had brought back some spices from the farmhouse. While Gabe fetches us some fresh spring water, I sit next to Allison to try to probe a little deeper into her story.

"So, it's just you and your mother who live together?" I gently ask.

"Yes, but she's become very ill lately."

"Isn't she worried about you being out here alone?"

"Probably, but she has no choice."

"And why is that?"

"If she doesn't want us to starve, then she will have to trust me to get food."

I'm deeply saddened by her story, which is why I'm more compelled to grow closer to Allison. I think I'm more disheartened by the fact that her relationship with her mother has come to this. Reminds me too much of my mother's nearly bed-ridden condition when I was younger.

"Isn't your mother worried you're out here?" Allison asks. I hesitate to answer, almost wishing it were my mother who was in bed, but I can't hide the pain drawn on my face. "My mother never has to worry anymore . . . about anything."

"Why?"

"She died in a car accident six years ago."

Allison's sullen face suddenly deters me from continuing, so I kneel down beside her and gently place my hand over hers.

"She's much happier now," I say to her. I don't know if I'm telling her this for her own comfort or mine, but it bears saying anyway.

I slice off a sliver of the chicken roasting above the flames. The smell is intoxicating, and I'm wavering over waiting for Gabe to return before I decide to tame my stomach's hungry growl.

I slice off a piece for Allison and hand it to her. She looks at me as if she's waiting for me to say "go," but I'm too inundated with the smell of this chicken, that I nearly bite my fingers off as I scarf my piece down.

"Go ahead, there's no shame in using your hands. Miss Manners isn't here to slap you on the wrist." She devours the first piece like a hungry lion waiting for more. I slice off one side of the breast, being sure to save the legs for Gabe as he requested. While we are on our second helping, Gabe returns with fresh water and a sweet surprise wrapped in tree bark; wild dewberries—just like the ones I picked in the ditches near our home growing up.

I almost immediately notice the surge of strength in Allison as she licks the bones clean. Gabe's face is covered in chicken juices, and pieces of skin hang off his cheek.

"Would you like me to hose you off when you're done?" I tease Gabe.

"I'll just lick myself clean, thank you."

Midafternoon approaches, and our stomachs are full after devouring the entire chicken. I just want to lie here and never move again. I haven't had a hearty meal like that since our get-together with Jacob and Juliana.

It was our first official date after just knowing each other for our few short days at school, but it felt more like our third before the night ended. Although the grand meal Myra had prepared for our new friends was delightful, the only memory my heart can rekindle is Jacob sitting next to me on the porch swing.

It's hard to believe with a full stomach that the only thing I'm reminded of is my first kiss with Jacob. I still can't believe he's gone, and the only thing that's helped displace those memories is the will to survive this treacherous world.

Though I only knew Jacob for a short time, he was everything to me—the only boy I ever fell in love with; he made me feel happy to be alive. His soft touch was innocent, but it made me shiver with delight.

I'll forever remember his deep blue eyes and his shaggy hair that tried to hide them, his sweet smile under his uncomfortable silence, and his tender heart beating after my own. What has been is no longer an idea—just a memory.

CHAPTER 5

I'm still not sure if Allison is comfortable enough bringing us to her home to her sick mother. It's not like I have pursued the subject enough to convince her, either. I've tried to stay clear from bombarding her with too many questions, hoping not to disrupt our somewhat disjointed but friendly bond we've shared in such a short time. But I'm also anxious to sleep on something other than rock or dirt. I desperately want to shower the layers of filth from my body as well. If that's not a good enough motive to move on, then I don't know what is. I would take immediate refuge in the abandoned farmhouse if it weren't for Allison's sick mother. I feel compelled to check in on her first.

I scoop dirt into the fire, putting out the last remaining flames, and grab the sack of chickens. I grab my weapons and toss Gabe his backpack, hoping to make it clear we really need to push this journey forward.

"We better get a move on and get these chickens to your mother. She's probably wondering where you are," I say to Allison, as she sits there joyfully moaning from the generous amount of food inside her small belly.

"So which way is it?" I ask.

She pries herself from the trunk of a gnarled tree and gleefully points to the south. I guess a pleased appetite can make a dramatic difference in a person's behavior. I feel a little more at ease now with Allison's rejuvenated trust as we move on.

As we head south, the terrain begins to change. The area is flat, and you can see for miles in every direction. It's a barren space with very few trees and sparse vegetation. The elevation is high enough to cool off from the constant breeze that dries the sweat on my forehead. More and more oak trees are peppered throughout the area the further we walk south, but it's the thorny-like proliferating shrubs—the mesquite trees—that dominate the landscape.

Now I know we are getting close to home, because I keep kicking up red soil hiding beneath the top layer of the ground. That's a pretty good sign we are near the Texas border. The air is becoming humid, and I spot a waterfowl flying overhead. We must be close to the Red River. After a two-hundred-yard jaunt, we come to the salty red water that divides the Oklahoma and Texas borders. The water is very low here and smells of a rotting carcass. Some places are much easier to cross without submerging waist-deep in this muddy water. We walk the banks until we find a shorter area to cross.

There was a time during this journey that I never thought we'd see this land again. But here we are...back where it all started. I miss this place so much, yet I still fear it's harboring past.

For the last three years, Texas has become the keen state for migration since the northern territories split up into class groups. The unlivable conditions created from polluted water systems also forced a mass exodus into the southern states, despite the poverty they have to offer. Texas, which stands alone among the rest of the south, makes an already shattered economy bearable, making it the desired place to settle.

Unfortunately, it's also a desired place where the federal government has established its main security outposts, flooding every city to form military facilities and national counterintelligence agencies. But I guess none of that really matters anymore. It's every man for himself. One nation dies as another rises, breeding the same result, or worse.

The demise of the United States was already pinned by a revolution long before I came. Though efforts by its dignitaries and international support keep it on life support, it's primed to fall. Unfortunately it's the people who will suffer for it. I didn't create this revolution—I just ignited it.

After about a two-mile hike just beyond the grassy plains, we come to an old, broken, but still-standing ranch home.

"Just wait out here a few minutes while I talk to my mother first. She's not very comfortable around strangers, especially now," Allison discloses.

"Sure, take your time," I say. While she's in there to sweet-talk her angry mother before an otherwise abrupt intrusion on our part, I gaze at the property

I patiently stand outside and notice the remarkable resemblance of this house's characteristics to my grandfather's ranch house. It's as if I just woke up from a bad dream and I'm six years old again, about to walk up the dilapidated stairs to the wrap-around porch, nagging my Papa for a horse ride. That's a memory I will never forget.

I can almost smell the warm cedar planks baking in the sun and the aroma of freshly ground oats for the horses to eat. Small Celtic trinkets used to hang above the porch eaves, swinging into one another, making charming, sweet music as the wind blew. The worn roof always provided enough surprises to labor over on those stormy nights as Gabe and I would collect rain droplets leaking from the ceiling cracks into Grandmother's good pots.

I feel a lonely spirit drawing me towards the house—a connection to some distant history that has yet to be uncovered. I fix my glassy eyes on a weathered plaque hanging just above the rusty-colored door that says: *May your hearts be welcome and your past be forgotten.*

"Arena!" Gabe shouts, interrupting me from my trance.

"What?"

"You okay?"

"Yeah . . . yeah, I'm good."

"Well, come on. Allison's trying to invite us in."

I walk through the door and feel a sense of vulnerability I haven't felt in a while. The musty smell from the dirty curtains reminds me of the home I grew up in. The once-varnished floors have peeled, exposing spots of bare wood, and the oil in the finish has gummed up into crystalized clumps of amber. The walls in the kitchen have been painted more than once judging by the caked-on layers of different colors showing on the edges of the door framing.

Allison takes us to an empty bedroom where she allows us to put away our things before introducing us to her mother.

"I've convinced my mother to let you stay here for a while if you want."

"We are very grateful for your kindness," I say.

"Yes, thank you," Gabe adds.

"Well you saved my life and gave me food."

The bedroom is more than adequate; hell, a barn with hay would be just as well received after spending most of our sleepless nights wrestling with knobby roots and being jabbed by pointy rocks.

I open the double doors adjacent to the bed and find a closet full of clothes that are much too big for Allison to wear. It seems as if these clothes haven't been worn in a while, judging by the collection of dust bunnies falling from them, nor do they appear to be appropriate for a ten-year-old girl.

I grab a nice-pressed shirt when one of the closet doors slams shut. It's Allison standing there holding some towels, wash rags, and soap.

"The shower is down the hall, on the left. The water is hot, but don't use it all up," she says, then walks away.

I'm pretty sure this room belonged to one of her older siblings, but I dare not push the envelope any further. If she wants me to know, she can disclose that on her own. Right now, I just want to shower the grime from my skin. After washing in river water and stagnant ponds, I fear this warm shower is going to spoil me from wanting to move on from here. Before I walk out the door, Allison pops her head back in.

"If the clothes fit, you can wear them. Just put your dirty clothes outside the bathroom door and I'll wash them," she says.

"What about me?" Gabe asks.

"You can wear some of my dad's clothes. They may be a bit big, but it's better than prancing around in a dress," she says, smiling.

"Thanks, and for the record, I wasn't even remotely thinking of the possibility."

"Good, because no one wants to see that," she jokingly continues. Well, at least the friendly banter has made the mood effortlessly change.

I clean up and enjoy the fresh warm water running over my skin. I've never felt so clean. I take advantage of the bathroom supplies and nab a razor I spotted when I first walked into the bathroom. I spend most of the time trying to shave my wooly mammoth legs. I think I caused an early retirement for this less-than-stellar razor. I finish up and grab some clothes from the closet. I must be the same size as Allison's sister, because they fit perfectly.

While Gabe showers, I wander off in to the kitchen looking for Allison. There's a large pot on the stove half-filled with tepid water waiting to boil. I glance out the window and see a headless chicken hanging upside down on an old clothesline. I walk out the back door and my face pales. Allison is bent over; her hands are bloody and she's holding my dagger.

I rush over and hover like a concerned mother.

"Are you hurt?" I ask worriedly.

"Of course not silly," she answers matter-of-factly.

I take the dagger from her and examine her hands.

"What are you doing?" she asks, perturbed.

"Making sure you're not cut."

"I'm fine, it's just the blood from the chicken," she says desperately, trying not to look helpless. "I can handle this." I refrain from coddling her and play to her strong will. I know this same carefree independence very well. She reminds me of myself at her age.

"I know you can, but with two people, this can go much faster. If you go find some pliers to pull out these feathers, I'll show you how to remove the innards." She smiles and runs off with excitement. I don't know if she's trying to test my will, earn my trust, or if she's just not content enough in accepting me as a friend. She obviously lost an older sister, and maybe she feels like I'm trying to replace her. I'll keep the boundaries wide open until she feels comfortable.

Without warning, Allison races out the back door, panting.

"Come quick . . . it's my mother, she needs you now!" Allison shouts.

I quickly follow Allison to the back bedroom where her mother is lying in the bed. A pot of cold water sits next to the bedpost and used wet rags are scattered about. Her mother's face is pale, and her wiry nest of hair is frazzled as if it hasn't ever been brushed or combed. She looks to have been bedridden for quite some time. Whatever is ailing her is more serious than just a fever. Her palms are clammy, and her forehead is ice cold.

Allison stands next to me while I hold a wet rag to her mother's forehead. I begin with small conversation, just to break the ice with my abrupt intrusion.

"I'm Arena by the way."

"I'm Meredith. Allison told me what you did for her. I'm forever grateful."

"And, I'm very thankful for your kind hospitality and inviting us into your home. My brother and I haven't seen a soul in months, so this is truly a miraculous sign of good fortune."

"Depending on how you perceive it, I guess."

"Yes, I suppose. So, how long ago did you fall ill?"

She doesn't answer, just looks into Allison's eyes and grabs her hand.

"Sweetie, why don't you go run along while I talk to Arena alone for a bit." Meredith pats Allison's hand. I suddenly feel a slight insecurity as Allison leaves the room. Being alone with this woman doesn't scare me in the least; it's the unknown that frightens me. Before she says anything that may derail this awkward moment, I hastily speak up and ask some long-awaited questions.

"Not a soul has crossed our paths in five months—no running vehicles, no thriving towns, nothing but death and loneliness is all I know. I need to—"

"I know who you are," Meredith interrupts.

I can only suspect she knows of me because of my rebellious ties with the government. The destruction we left behind in the few towns and the prison has created an unruly rumor of my existence, which I guess is unfair of me to deny, since it's true. I'm still a little caught off guard by her abrupt intrusion, but I play along and indulge her anyhow.

"And who am I?"

"You created this death and loneliness," she says with a sudden flare of anger.

I'm somewhat taken aback by her response, but because she's ill, I'll extend her some temporary grace. "What death have I created that wasn't already here?"

She looks away briefly and clenches her fist tight, then relaxes her eyes.

"I've lost more than just my strength."

"As I have too," I say crossly.

"Forgive me, but my anger is not with you."

"Then who is your anguish with that you would spew such venom toward me?"

"Why has God allowed me to linger on like this?"

"Like what? Being able to survive with a daughter who dearly loves you?"

"Survive! Is that what you call this? Living in a world of chaos and ruin with nothing to hope for?"

"There is always hope."

"Hope? I've lost my husband in a labor camp to slavery. My two daughters have been missing for six months now, and it's not that I don't believe they may still be alive, but I'm not about to cling to a sense of false hope now. I haven't the patience nor time to entertain my faith to do so." She opens up a locket around her neck and sobs over a picture of her daughters.

"Time is not your enemy," I say.

"Oh, I beg to differ."

"Look, I can help you and your daughter. I—"

"Arena!" she says, cutting me off. "I'm dying."

I kneel down beside her bed and clasp my fingers between hers, wondering why God has brought me to this place.

"I'm sorry, I didn't . . . how long?"

"I'm surprised I've made it this long. I was diagnosed with stage three lung cancer about a year ago. Without adequate treatment and necessary surgery, I'm afraid the cancer has spread beyond my control now. Just in the last couple of months have I began to fall seriously ill. Every day that went by, the weaker and weaker I got. That's about the time my two older daughters, Lily and Rachel, drove into town to buy some supplies, but to never return. We heard news about the government relocating populations, harsh sanctions, and militant revolts rising, but I would have never thought it would come to this. I can only assume my daughters were taken during that time."

She takes a deep breath and continues. "And then news began to filter through the state about a rebellion against the government that was spreading across the nation from town to town. The *Revolution Millennium* they called it. No one believed it at first, but when it was reported on the news what had happened to the president, everything changed."

The last Gabe and I heard anything about the president on the news was back at the old tavern two months after I had killed the president. All the people in the bar were cheering at the television from the false report that the president had fallen ill. Has it been revealed that the president was killed?

"Changed?" I ask, trying to dig a little deeper.

"After it was rumored that the president was murdered, every town across America started to sink deeper into confusion about the future. Government jobs were reorganized, businesses closed up, oil refineries have been shut down, gas stations closed. No trucks to deliver food to the markets in the larger communities, much less the poorer towns. Food has become scarce; it has become a luxury to dine on something that doesn't come from a can.

"I guess the rich run this nation now, and those who were already poor, well . . . they were either forced to move on or suffer like the rest of us. Anarchy aside, many people just quit what they were doing. You thought the administration was corrupt and weak before? It's absolutely in ruin now without that vile President Kriel to domesticate it. But why ask me, you know this already. It's a small country, Arena, rumors about a revolution don't get around without people knowing who started it. That blood was spilled by your hands, no?"

I rise to my feet, step back, and stare with unexpected disbelief.

"What?" she mutters. "Are you shocked that I know who you are, or are you still considering if you were justified in your actions?"

"I don't need to justify what I have done! I'm truly sorry for the turmoil that's followed, but it's nothing compared to what is still to come."

"I'm not trying to question your actions, Arena. I stand by them," she proudly states as she aggressively coughs into a tissue.

"Are you okay? Do you need some water?"

"I'm fine. There's nothing that can help me now. I feel the end is near."

"Does Allison know?"

"No, I just can't come to grips to tell her."

"I think she has the right to know."

"And what makes you the keeper of my decisions?"

"I was nine years old when I saw my mother die in a car accident. I spent the last moments holding her bloody face, hoping to hear her voice one last time, only to hear the sound of her dying breath fade. I wanted to say so much to her before she died, but I was denied that chance. Don't you dare deny Allison that chance. That is an unforgiving pain I cannot bear."

"What do you know about pain? Until you have a child of your own, keep your thoughts to yourself. I didn't invite you in my home to seek the wisdom from a girl too young to know any better," she says, recoiling back into self-pity.

I'm so stunned, I can barely open my mouth to retort, but there's too much animosity in the air for me not too.

"If the cancer doesn't kill you, the bitterness sure will."

I walk out of the room to cool off. Allison comes skipping down the hall with a smile on her face. I quickly wipe my tears away, not feeling very proud of my response.

"So, you ready to finish up that chicken with me?" Allison asks, with her bright eyes lit up.

"Sure."

While cleaning the chicken, Allison periodically looks over at Gabe as he practices with one of my swords near the shed. I can feel a sense of encouragement in my heart when she smiles at Gabe, but I'm not so sure it's Gabe she's eyeing as much as it's the sword she's enamored with—which worries me.

"Swords are made to kill and nothing more," I say, in hopes she understands the dangerous significance they bring.

"So how many people have you killed?" she asks with an ornery retort.

As I'm pulling the feathers from the chicken's skin with the pliers, I have to stop and really think. It's not something I like to think about—in fact, it's quite depressing—so I refrain from answering the question. I cut into the chicken's lower body cavity and pull out the innards, hoping to distract myself from thinking about it any further.

"Just so you know, I don't enjoy killing anything," I say, as I chop off the chicken's feet. "Here, take the chicken to the kitchen sink and wash the inside good."

Allison leaves, and I stand there watching Gabe clumsily thrash the sword around. Seeing him swing that blade reminds me of the time we were playing in Grayson Park on the playground. I guess we were about six then when our mother took us. It was the largest park in Taylor Springs, Texas, and it was easy to get lost. I remember climbing the monkey bars and watching a young boy swing a stick around as if it were a sword, just like Gabe is doing now.

Gabe walked up to him timidly and asked if he could play, but the boy just looked at him, silently swinging around Gabe as if he didn't exist. When Gabe walked away, out of nowhere, the boy purposefully swung and the stick whacked Gabe in the head, cutting his ear.

I think that was truly the first time I came to Gabe's defense with a vengeful heart. I held back nothing; I jumped from the bars, grabbed the stick from the boy, and kicked him square in the nuts as hard as I could. I didn't even ask why he did it, I just turned and socked him one. I handed the stick to Gabe, and we played knights the rest of the day in the park. I'm not sure what possessed that boy to do what he did. Maybe it was purely an accident, but I never stuck around to know. I never really felt remorseful about it untilnow.

The sun melts behind the horizon as day breaks, and the cool evening breeze effortlessly dries the sweat droplets on my forehead. I walk into the kitchen and smell the chicken stewing in the pot of water on the stove. Also inside the pot are onions, carrots, and celery all chopped up. I can even smell the spices Allison must have rubbed onto the chicken. She's quite the cook, a culinary avant-garde, especially for her age.

Allison sits at the kitchen table and watches Gabe through the window. I get the feeling our little ten-year-old friend has a crush on my brother. While the chicken stews, so do I. I walk into the bedroom and neatly lay out my weapons: two katana Samurai swords, two eight-inch stilettos, my prized scorpion dagger, and my black widow throwing knives. I lay them next to the four Beretta 92FS pistols, and clean them all the while thinking about how I reacted toward Meredith earlier.

I reach into my pocket and pull out the locket my mother gave me on my ninth birthday. The small silver heart secures a lovely picture of my mother. It's the only piece of memory I have left of her. The small vine-shaped carving etched into its face is worn, and the date of my birth on the back has been rubbed away with time. It's a painful reminder that life is fading. It's the same pain Meredith must be going through, having lost her husband and daughters. I had no right to question her decision, especially in her condition. I feel somewhat ill about my actions. It's eating at me too much not to resolve it. I must ask her forgiveness and respect her wishes. It's not mine to decide.

With some vacillation, I slowly walk toward her bedroom feeling contrite. I don't know why, but I find it hard to face her now. Hesitantly, I open the door.

Meredith's eyes are wide open. Her left arm dangles over the side of the bed, with her left hand clinging to a blood-soaked tissue. Her right hand is tightly clenched around a chain near her chest. I quickly run over, fearing she's dead, but her chest slowly expands and fills her lungs with oxygen. I remove the bloody tissue from her hand and slip another pillow behind her, propping her head up.

"Meredith . . . Meredith," I hastily say, trying to disconnect her from her somewhat catatonic state. She moans something in my ear, but it's barely audible.

She weakly clutches my arm. "Arena, you must know, I truly love my daughter. I never intended for this to happen so soon. I just hoped that I would have more time to tell her. You have to understand, this hard for me."

I feel cold inside, as if the chill of winter's eve is hovering over my shame. "I do understand, and I'm wrong for not exercising my good faith. I should have never said anything. It was not my place to judge, and I'm truly sorry. I should have given you the respect you deserve," I admit.

"Deserve? I'm a sinful creature withering away, child. Death has chosen me. What I think I deserve is irrelevant.

"You and I are the same you know. Death, yes, it will come one way or another but I choose to be free from this bondage."

"And what makes you privy to this reckless ruin?"

"A divine fate I've promised to uphold."

"So what made you want to uphold your end of this bargain?

"The only thing that can see the beauty in everything," I say, handing her a clean tissue as she coughs.

"And what's that?"

"Grace," I simply say.

She opens her right hand and gazes at the open locket in her palm she's been clinching. She coughs into her tissue once again, staining it with blood. She has very little time to live.

"Do you believe I'm worth saving?" she asks.

"I believe all men are worth saving if they so choose, but it doesn't matter what I think. Do you believe you are?"

She stares down at the locket, her mouth trembling and her eyes watering. She squeezes the locket closed and extends her hand out toward me. I'm emotionally unable to move for a moment before I clasp my fingers around hers. I sit next her on the bed, hold her hand, and lean my head on her shoulder. I stroke her hair gently, and it's all I can do to not completely break down right now.

"My sweet Lily and Rachel are dead. No mother should outlive her children," she cries. "I miss them so much."

I can't bear any more of this suffering, but I know it will soon end.

"Allison is all that I have left. Please . . . take care of her."

"I will."

"Will you tell her for me?" she asks.

It blackens my heart knowing Meredith has no intention of telling her daughter she's dying, but I can't bring myself to tell her what she wants to hear, that I will tell Allison that her mother is dying.

"Please . . ."

I'm too emotional to speak, so I agree by nodding my head. I sit on the bed next to her, trying to calm her restless spirit until both of our tears dry up. I don't know why, but I sing an old Irish lullaby my mother used to sing to me when I was sick or couldn't sleep. It was the most soothing sound to hear from my mother's voice. *Bheannaigh mo grá* was the song of choice to calm any Irish child through restless nights, and it seems only fitting to sing it to Meredith.

Loo li lai leyh
Loo li lai leyh

Lay down your sweet head and close your eyes,
fall off to sleep with splendor and delight.
And when the shadow creeps up from voices below,
may the angels guard your soul tonight.

Thy whispers from the cool blowing wind,
in the night for blessings to hold.
The shrieking of the crickets sound,
bellows deep beneath the cold.

For the road that you take will surely be blessed.
Never abandon your heart, or will.
And if your heart should seep, let the Lord be your light,
when you wander into the Wicklow hills.

Loo li lai leyh
Loo li lai leyh

In the dim weeping dawn when morning draws near,
take up your cross and kneel.
When the fog rolls in with a cold cruel mist,
let His peace keep you still.

From shades of autumn and copper fields,
to the isles of green and meadows dew.
And the thundering clouds through rainy storms,
when seasons change, I too.

Codladh Codladh grá mo chroi'
Codladh Codladh grá mo chroi'

  She pulls me close and hugs me tightly.
  "All is forgiven . . . my sweet Lily," she says, crying into
my shoulder. I have no words. Whether or not she called me

her daughter's name on purpose, I embrace her warm, forgiving, unconditional love. Though God is my refuge, He has placed me yet again next to a woman of comfort and compassion. And I know it too will not last.

I turn my head, refusing to cry anymore, and standing in the doorway is Gabe and Allison.

Bursting with tears, Allison runs over and wraps her tiny arms around her mother. I sit there for a second, slightly stunned. I quietly leave the room with Gabe so Allison and her mother can have the last moment together before God takes her.

I hover over the stewing chicken, monotonously stirring into a deep, woeful trance until I finally lose it. I fall to the floor and pull my knees up under my chin. Gabe tries to comfort me, but I just bury my head between my knees and sob. I eventually pick myself up, walk outside, and sit on the end of the porch, hoping for peace to take over my crippled state of mind.

A few minutes later, the back door swings open, and Allison stands there. Her eyes are puffy and her nose red from crying. She leaps forward and embraces me. Her arms tightly cling to me while she trembles in my lap, crying.

"She's dead," Allison blurts out.

There's really nothing I can say right now that will ease her pain, so I just hold her as long as she lets me.

Gabe carefully opens the back door and nods. "At first light, we'll give her a proper burial," Gabe says softly.

Allison relaxes her arms. "Be gentle with her," she says quietly to Gabe.

"I will," Gabe says, nodding.

I get up to walk back in the house, but Allison pulls on my shirt.

"I don't want to go back in there yet . . . stay with me," she says.

I take her hand and lead her over to an old but comfortable chair on the porch. There, we both recline back, relaxing in our own state of sorrow, and embrace one another until we both finally drift off to sleep.

CHAPTER 6

The morning light shining through the cracked roof above the porch wakes me just enough to disturb my comfortable position. But it's the unexpected cool morning breeze that stirs more than my sleep—I have to pee. Allison is curled up with me in the chair, her arms wrapped around my waist. I nudge her over just a bit so I can move from the chair to go to the bathroom.

Next to a pair of soiled shoes by the kitchen door is a trail of black dirt tracks running from the kitchen to the master bedroom. Curious enough that my bladder can wait, I approach Meredith's bedroom, but when I look in, her body is gone. Gabe comes up from behind the corner and startles me. His face is filthy, and his fingernails are caked with black dirt.

"Have you been up all night?" I ask.

"I just wanted to make sure everything was prepped before Allison woke up. There's no need to prolong this for her. I dug a grave large enough for Meredith's body to fit in and lined it with some old sheets of plywood out by the shed."

"Where's her body?"

"In here," says Gabe, pointing toward the living room.

On the couch and tightly wrapped in some fresh linens lies Meredith's spiritless body. We need to get her body into the ground as soon as possible before the smell of death seeps through the sheets and poisons the already stale air in here. I help Gabe carry her body to the grave, but because Rigor mortis has already started to set in, the stiffening makes it difficult for me to carry her, much less lifting the massive weight.

We bury the body and line the grave with stones as a marker. Allison slowly walks over, half-awake, and kneels beside the grave. Exhausted from the burial, Gabe and I watch closely over Allison while she spreads the dirt around with her palm. I'm not sure what has transpired in her broken heart overnight, but it has quickly recouped. Not a tear to shed, nor a heart to stir, Allison stares blankly into the black, clumped soil.

"I'll leave you two alone. I'm going to shower off," Gabe quietly says.

I watch her lonely eyes wander about before she suddenly becomes transfixed on something. I follower her eyes down toward my hand where Meredith's locket dangles from the silver thin chain wrapped between my clinched fingers. I had completely forgotten that I was holding it while Gabe was shoveling the dirt. I hand it to her, then walk away to let her mourn in peace.

After a long, weary morning and a much-needed shower, I spend the afternoon exploring the rest of the property. I find an old barn in derelict condition on the backside of the farm's fenced property. The inside is damp and smells of rotting hay and wet grass, but to my sweetest delight, I'm most surprised by the presence of a very familiar sound. At the end of the barn are two stalls holding the most beautifully maintained stallions.

I approach the darker one a little more cautiously, since it seems to be a little rattled by my presence. I slowly lift up my arm, stretch my hand out to its head, and gently stroke the side of the horse's cheek. After a few moments, the horse warms up to me and moves a little closer. I reach down into a bucket beside the wall, scoop a handful of oats, and feed him.

"That's Shadow, he's strong, but very gentle," Allison says, startling me.

"He's yours?" I ask.

"He belonged to Lily. The other one is Diablo. He's kinda ornery, but he follows commands. I've had him since he was born. He knows my every move, and he won't budge unless I tell him."

While petting these powerful creatures, I suddenly find our situation less troublesome. Our travels will become much easier with these horses, and it will dramatically expedite our journey back home. I feel a sudden reprieve in my heart that we will find our friends waiting for us back in the den now. As much as this place has provided a comfortable refuge, we must leave it behind, but I'm just not sure if Allison is willing to move on so soon after her mother's death. I decide to wait until tomorrow to broach the subject. In the meantime, I'm much too taken by the beauty of these animals to just let them stand closed-up in a damp, old barn.

"May I take him out for a ride?" I ask.

"Sure, he could use the exercise. Let me saddle him up for you."

"What are you two doing?" Gabe asks when he enters the barn.

"About to release some much-needed energy," I say.

Shadow is almost too tall for me to step up in the stirrups, so I climb the stall gate instead to mount while Allison holds Shadow's head down to quiet him. It's been a while since I've ridden a horse, but I still remember the basics.

I gather the reins lightly and squeeze my lower legs, carefully walking him outside the barn. After about five minutes of letting him get used to me, I hold back nothing and run the bottled-up energy he has inside. Weaving in and around the sporadic trees on the land, I maneuver Shadow effortlessly until the muscles in my ass begin to cramp. I ride him back into the barn while Gabe chuckles at the grimace on my face from the strenuous outing with Shadow. I guess certain muscles are not used to the vigorous movements of riding a horse.

Although I've worked up an appetite that won't surrender, I'm too distracted by the possibility of riding our new travel companions. While the evening looms upon us, I take the opportunity to rest my sore body on my nice, soft bed. I lie there thinking about Father Joseph, Henry, Niki, and Juliana. I try hard to believe that they are curled up right now on those godforsaken beds back in the den, waiting for us to come through those metal doors.

Perhaps Juliana is dreaming about Gabe right now, wondering how much longer she has to endure this separation. I know it was hard for Niki to let go, but it made no sense dragging my foster sister into this treacherous journey. She was better off staying with Father Joseph in the den. Oh, how much I miss her right now. I can only pray that her mental state has not been shattered from the horrendous news of her parents' death. Myra and Daniel were every bit as loving toward her as they were with Gabe and I. Death comes for us all, but the treatment they received in that prison is witness to a government that bears no mercy from my sword. All I can do now is lie here and contemplate the what-ifs.

I turn over onto my side and notice my dagger sitting on the nightstand, which was not where I left it. I turn on the lights to look for the rest of my weapons and find that one of my swords is missing. I know Gabe was using it last, but he knows to return my things. I'm trying not to overreact, but I'm never comfortable when my swords go missing.

I throw open the bedroom door and bump into Gabe in the hallway.

"What's going on?" Gabe says.

"Where's my sword?"

"I put it back with the other one last night, why?"

"Allison," I say to myself.

I walk toward her room in the back of the house, and I can already hear the sound of the blade dragging across the floor. Instead of bursting in, I quietly creep up to the door making sure there's not an intruder in here. I poke my head around the doorframe to see Allison standing beside her bed, trying to lift the sword.

I barge in and grab her hands before she can lift the sword any higher. "When you stop respecting the dangerous intentions of this forged steel, you will lose the battle with its edge. This is not a toy. You're not ready for this." I say, still clasping her hands over the handle.

"Then who is?"

"A person dangerous enough to understand its cruel intent."

"I'm not scared," she says hotly, trying to push me away. This is a formidable act of defiance I'm just not used to.

"I'm not questioning your bravery," I say. Her grip tightens on the handle and her eyes squint. "It's your intent that I'm worried about."

The scowl on her face slowly releases and she lets go of the handle. Her eyes look to the floor. All the emotion built up inside of her from her missing sisters, to her mother's death, have taken a toll on her young spirit. She collapses in my arms and cries uncontrollably.

It hurts to see her like this, and her pain will only grow colder the longer we stay here in this house. My decision to wait before talking with her about our journey back home has just terminated. There really isn't a better time to discuss this, so I just say it.

"We're leaving this place, and we're not coming back," I say, holding her head up. "I made a promise to your mother that I would take care of you, and I mean to keep that promise."

She can barely shake her head yes before burying it in my shoulder.

"We'll leave first thing in the morning."

"What have I done to deserve this?" she cries out. "Have I not been forgiven?"

Whether or not she feels atonement is in order, it's the anger that threatens to morph into hate that worries me, and shame will soon follow.

"Hey, you must believe . . . this is not a punishment. This is a cruel and wicked world we live in. We are in the dark days and many more are ahead. Your survival remains in your faith."

I struggled with my own faith when my parents died so I can attest to the bitterness and guilt, but I had my brother to lean on whenever shame began to shadow my faith. She has no one but us now. Innocent or not, it's her choice to believe the true love of God. It's up to her to accept His forgiveness, no matter what she has done in her life. I can't make that choice for her. It's hers and hers alone to make. I can protect her, but I cannot save her.

She picks herself up and stands there as stringy hairs stick to the dried tears on her cheek. She opens up the locket and gazes at the picture of her sisters.

"I still believe they are alive . . . somewhere," she whispers.

There's nothing I can say that will change anything right now. I have no way of knowing if they are still alive, and I'm not about to anchor false hope to this precious girl. She's lost too much to accept any platitudes from me. If she's harboring any ill will right now, it will only get worse if her hopes are crushed, so I leave her to believe what she wants. I would want the same. I softly place my arm around her shoulder while I lean into her fragile body and pull her close to me.

The few peaceful minutes of comforting doesn't last long. Suddenly, a wall of sound bursts through the air. The thunderous roaring horn shakes the house, rocking the swinging lights on the ceiling. I quickly grab Allison and follow Gabe out onto the porch. I can't tell where the sound is coming from, but it's so loud, I have to cover my ears.

The skies turn black and the loud bellow of deep moans roar from the clouds without ceasing. The eerie low trumpet-like sound seems to blow from every direction. The deep earth-shaking pitch slowly forms into a harmonious growl, but it's still loud enough to be completely unnerving. I fall to my knees while the noise lingers on. Both Allison and Gabe lie on the porch curled up in a ball with their hands covering their ears. Suddenly, the noise trails off, and I can hear the sound of ten million voices singing a single chord over the deep, thundering reverberation in my head. It's disturbingly chilling.

After a few minutes, all three of us slowly stand and stare into the black sky as if we are hypnotized by the terrifying shrill. The brash noise erupts into a clap of thunder, yet I can't turn from its somewhat soothing undertones. While the deep, harmonious voices continue, Gabe slowly walks toward the corner of the house as if in a trance.

I interrupt myself from this unnatural obscurity and follow Gabe, but before I can reach him, he's already on his knees praying. I race closer to the corner of the house to see what has caused him to tremble and fall to his knees. I look up, stunned with silence. Boldly erected high in the black western skies is the image of prophetic revelation—the moon, painted red as blood.

"What's happening?" Allison stutters as she creeps up beside me.

"Go in the house now," I say to Allison as I take a few steps back.

"But—"

"Go . . . now."

Gabe stops praying and feverishly looks up at me.

"This is it, isn't it? Just like in our dream?"

It was the first vision that Gabe and I shared before we were plunged into this shadowy prophecy. The frightening prophetic words from God's own mouth that war would be upon us revealed more than just our fate; the celestial signs would let us know the end was near. I wish it weren't true, but I can't deny what the sky discloses. What has and is to come isn't in my hands. The dark days are truly upon us now—it's our destiny to survive them.

"Please go look in on Allison."

"Are you not even just a bit afraid?" he asks.

"There's nothing left on this earth to fear. It will all soon be gone."

"So it really has begun?"

"War is brewing, that's for certain."

I'll never know if all of this could have been avoided if it weren't for that damn key Father Joseph sent to me in his letter—the key that decidedly opened the door to a world I never wanted to be a part of. But it just may have been that key that saved my life.

My fate was decided well before I unlocked the door to that underground lair we call the den, but it was Father Joseph, who vowed to protect Gabe and I since we were born, to ensure that we didn't turn from our destiny. That fortified bunker of weapons built below the old gas station that Finnegan had created became our only survival, and yet I chose to leave it for a journey of bloodshed.

My journey may be forever changing, but my fate ceases to turn from God's plan. Though I struggle to comprehend its purpose, my covenant to bring forth His wrath upon the evil that lingers in this world will dwell with Him until I die.

We've battled our way from town to town, hoping to save those who have been bound and enslaved by the very government soldiers that once protected us. It had all been a lie, and I wasn't going to let the heart of this administration decide my providence.

After parting from the White House with my swords resting upon President Kriel's shoulders, I've wished many times that all of this has just been a dream, but it's no more than a living nightmare. The president is dead by my account, and the nation is beyond repairable. I keep searching for a hope that this will all be over soon, but I know the grimmest days are still ahead of us.

Before following Gabe into the house to get some much-needed rest for our long journey tomorrow, I take one last gaze into the eerie sky at the blood-soaked moon.

CHAPTER 7

I never thought I would be so delighted to wake up to the air of silence; unfortunately, this morning is a far cry from that. That roaring, hellish horn noise hasn't stopped, and the vessels in my head are still pulsating. I must have been exhausted last night to be able to sleep through all this. Maybe it was those hypnotic, harmonious voices bellowing over the horn that put me to sleep. In any event, my head is pounding and I desperately need some caffeine.

While Allison and Gabe lie asleep on the floor in the living room, I scavenge through the kitchen pantry, and all I can find is a half canister of coffee grounds and a small box of chai tea. Not much of a coffee drinker, so chai tea it is.

While my tea is steeping, I take advantage of the hot water one last time. It may be the last hot shower I get for a while. I enjoy every minute of the water running down my back and the steam filling every cubic foot of space in this tiny bathroom. I close my eyes for just a moment and suddenly feel at peace thinking of home and the others waiting for us.

I turn off the water and grab my towel, but when I open my eyes, my body violently shudders, and every hair on my skin stands erect. Written on the shower door in the steamy glass is the word *Jacob*. I clutch the side of the shower walls to keep myself from falling. My hand covers my mouth and I gasp. Surely Gabe wouldn't have done something like this. What kind of sick joke is this?

I try to come to my good senses as I attempt to stop shaking and mull over the idea that I'm just seeing things. The image is too clear for this to be some kind of hallucination. I slowly get out of the shower and close the glass door with Jacob's name still clearly visible. I heatedly head for the door to see if Gabe had something to do with this, but when I turn around, I'm startled again when I see the word *Myra* etched in the steamy bathroom mirror.

Trembling, I race toward the living room, but Allison and Gabe are still asleep on the floor. I go back into the bathroom just to make sure I'm not having some delusion of grandeur. The words are gone and covered up with steam as if they never existed. Is my mind playing tricks on me? Is there some demonic rogue attempting to tamper with my spirit? Whatever malevolence is in this house, I refuse to let it break me.

Suddenly, a voice whispers through the steam—it's Jacob. Okay, now I'm frightened. I slide down against the door frame and tuck my head between my knees and shiver. For a moment, I hear the faint sound of a baby crying. I lift me head and peek into the bathroom, but nothing is there.. The steam has cleared and the whisper has faded.

Gabe walks by and startles me.

"Arena . . . you okay?"

I'm a little hesitant to say anything. The last thing I want to do is give him a reason to distress, so I decide not to bring it up.

"Fine, just uh…praying," I say.

"In a wet towel on the bathroom floor?"

"Yeah, is that a problem?"

"Chill, sis."

I know Gabe sees right through my weak attempt to hide something, because his left brow shifts upward, yet he doesn't push the conversation any further. He knows my limitations for personal space.

"I have tea brewing on the stove," I say timidly.

He pauses for a moment, opens his mouth as if he's about to say something deeply profound, then turns and walks away to the kitchen.

I walk to my bedroom, pass Allison, who is still sleeping on the floor, and change back into my freshly washed original attire. It feels good to slip back into my own clothes, weapons and all. I feel almost naked without them. I string up my bow and lock three full mags into my guns. I contem- plate giving the fourth gun loaded with a half mag to Allison, but instead I tuck it away. She's not exactly trustworthy with a weapon like this just yet, but there's going to come a time that she'll have to know how to defend herself.

With my boots laced up and my swords strapped on, I double-check the safety on my guns before treating my stomach to a hot cup of tea. Sitting in the kitchen is Gabe hovering over a steamy cup, and Allison, who's half-awake, props her sleepy head up with her elbows. She doesn't look much different than she did last night, but when I place a hot cup of tea in front of h er, she suddenly perks up.

"How are you this morning?" I ask her.
"As good as it gets, considering waking up to this," she says jokingly, covering her ears from the continuous sounds of the horn blowing outside. I pour a cup of hot tea and raise it to my mouth when suddenly the noise finally desists. Everyone sits in silence for a moment in disbelief, waiting to hear if that insufferable sound bursts into a second chorus of pain.

"Stay here," I say. With the warm cup of tea in hand, I head out the front door and stand on the front porch, observ- ing the surroundings like an eagle from its nest, but I see nothing unusual. Before I walk back inside, I spot something peculiar in the corner of my eye just to the west.

When I reach the west side of the porch, every fear, ter- ror, and anxiety I've kept bound up releases all at once. Blood rushes from my head into my heart, pumping. My teacup falls and shatters on the porch.

The front screen door swings open and Allison and Gabe come rushing through. "What happened, you okay?" Gabe asks.

The sheer shock keeps my tongue tied, as I have no response.

"We heard your . . ." He suddenly stops mid-sentence with his eyes glued to the sky. "Holy Mary mother of God."

"What . . . what is it?" Allison asks, terrified.

The dark clouded sky is peppered with paratroopers cascading downward by the thousands. Two aerial drones swiftly fly overhead, followed by a large aircraft that I've never seen before. It slowly flies behind the drones hovering over the earth below, almost as if it's floating. It's low enough that you can almost see the writing on the side of the fuselage. The blunt-shaped nose is painted with a lion's face, and the wings on the craft stretch out and dip back on the ends like a soaring eagle.

The only thing distracting me from this impressive flying beast are the two tanks protruding through the tree line to our east.

"Allison, go prep the horses," I nervously say.

"Why, what's going on?"

"Saddle them now, we haven't got time!"

Allison bursts into a sudden sprint and races around the corner toward the barn.

"Do you think . . . ?" Gabe says tongue-tied.

"Go, grab your gear and get to the barn fast," I snap. Both tanks move forward from behind the trees just outside the fence. I reach back into my quiver hoping to grab an explosive-tipped arrow, but I find none. I must have had a temporary memory glitch in the brain from the shock of what's happened, because I haven't had any explosive arrows since the training facility.

I watch closely as the two tanks slowly advance out into the open. Allison shouts my name out from the barn, and the back door slams shut. I back-pedal into the open screen door when all of the sudden the turret on the tank turns toward the house.

"Oh shit!"

I sprint past the coffee table, swing open the back door, and leap off the porch. The ground violently shakes and the house explodes into splintering fragments. Smoke and dust engulfs the air while I lay surrounded by broken planks of wood. The homestead is all but demolished except for the rickety back porch, which is about to collapse on top of me.

I scrape myself off the ground just in time and race behind Gabe to the barn. Allison, completely frightened, holds onto Shadow's reins while trying to sooth a rather agitated Diablo I throw my bow over my neck and around the shoulder, and quickly grab the bridle from Allison.

"Take Gabe with you and follow me," I say to Allison as I mount up.

I sprint Shadow out toward the back fence line where a metal gate is closed shut. Diablo comes galloping right behind me, with Gabe tightly holding onto Allison's waist. After several unsuccessful attempts at disengaging the rusty lever from the gate, I finally nudge the spring with my shoulder, dislodging the post. The gate swings wide open, digging into the dirt, and Allison exits the premise with tears running down her face.

As much as I want to comfort her, we need to leave this area as fast as we can before it's overrun by troops. I take the lead, periodically making sure Allison is still behind me. Just to be on the safe side, I slow up just a bit so she can ride up next to me, but Shadow freely gallops instead. I pull firmly on his reins again and slow him down to a canter. It's a short reprieve and not long enough to clamber. Gunshots fire into the trees. We quickly leave the wooded area behind us and exercise these thoroughbreds out into the open, threading around mesquite trees randomly spread out on the grassy prairie.

Just to my left, I spot a pack of paratroopers gliding down into another cluster of trees, and It doesn't take long for them to notice us. Within seconds, gunshots fire, zipping passed us. Trying to dodge the line of fire, I quickly steer Shadow to the right up a small grade where another line of trees meet. Before we enter the wooded terrain, gunshots fire again, just grazing my shoulder.

Diablo abruptly stops and shifts his direction. Allison falls backward onto the ground while Gabe is trying to hang onto the reins, but it's useless. Diablo is startled and throws Gabe from the saddle into a tree.

I hurry over to Allison, but she's not moving. Gabe slowly gets up and walks over with scrapes on the side of his face from the tree bark. Diablo, still startled, jumps to his hind legs, screaming and nickering. He backs up and rocks his head from side to side, looking more agitated than before. Gabe grabs Diablo's bridle before he decides to gallop away, but his unruly disorder is making it difficult. Gabe is tossed and turned before discovering a rattlesnake hissing near him.

Allison wakes up, and my heart that had sunk into the pit of my stomach has resurfaced. A sigh of reprieve and jubilation soon follows.

"Are you all right?" I ask.

"Yes, I'm fine. Diablo was just startled and bucked me off. Not sure why though."

"That's why," I say, pointing at the belligerent rattler coiled up and blending into the grass and soil.

The snake's head carefully monitors Diablo's movements, waiting to make its move. It begins to uncoil and raise its pitted head when the horse moves back into the rattler's direction. I draw one of my guns carefully, but hastily, because we still need to get out of sight before those soldiers get any closer.

"Gabe, whatever you do, hang on to that bridle as tight as you can."

"Whoa, wait a minute here . . ."

"Just slowly move Diablo away from this area."

Gabe grips the reins tight, gently pulls Diablo's head away from the snake's direction, and carefully walks him off. After about six paces, the snake buries it's head in the grass and slithers away. Gunshots fire again, but this time they are too close for comfort. We mount back up and take off through the woods to an adjacent field.

Just past the last tree, a lone paratrooper comes gliding down and slams into the top part of the tree right above us. His chute gets tangled up in the branches, and he is dangling about thirty feet in the air. He shouts something in Russian and tries to wiggle his way out of the buckled harness. He's a sitting duck, and I have no intention of killing this man while he's stuck unarmed in a tree. Of course, I'm too guarded to trust anyone in this world anyway, let alone an invading band of soldiers. I draw my gun for precaution.

The man rustles around trying to unhook something, but I can't tell what it is. Then his hand finds what he was looking for, and the tip of a gun barrel swings around. I waste no time and shoot him in the head. His gun tumbles out of the tree and lands on the ground next to a black bag that must have fallen from the paratrooper. I climb off the horse and snatch the black bag. I bend down to peer inside it when two soldiers come darting through the clearing with their guns pointed at Gabe and Allison.

Still crouched down with the bag in hand, I sneak behind the other side of the tree without being noticed. One of the men shouts aggressively in Russian to them.

"What do they want?" Allison asks Gabe.

"They want us to get off the horse, now."

"*poluchit na zemlyu! poluchit na zemlyu!*" the soldier barks.

"Get on the ground, Allison," Gabe says.

I pull my gun close up to my cheek and try to use the blade of my dagger as a mirror. I slowly extend the blade out from the tree to try and get a glimpse of what I'm about to shoot, but the steel reflection is to distorted from the dull finish. I can't make out anything but two blurry objects.

When I hear the other soldier commanding the man to kill Gabe and Allison, I swerve my body around the tree and shoot both men dead. One of the men's guns releases two rounds before falling to the ground. Then, behind us, a band of soldiers come racing through the woods.

"Go, now!" I shout.

We take off in the open field to the east, sprinting our horses over a small hill and through another wooded area until the horses are gassed. We stop near a ravine outside untilled farmland to give Shadow and Diablo a rest.

"They need water badly," Allison says.

The horses are parched, but we're too vulnerable in this open territory. The tree line behind us may be clear of soldiers, but It's credulous to believe we're safe to rest here. I gaze uneasily over the area while a calm cool breeze blows out of the west. It's a welcoming comfort except for the thunderclouds it brings with it.

"Look, down over there," Gabe says, pointing to some wandering cows.

Cows roaming next to a ravine can mean only one thing: water. If there's a source of water around here, it would be down there, that's for sure. I know it's a bit steep to ride our weak-legged horses down into that small gulley, but we take our chances anyway. I don't know how the cows got down there, or if they ever did, but I'm not going to stand out in the open waiting to be sniped.

We carefully ride next to the steep rocky incline along the edge until we safely find a passage the horses can manage. At the bottom of the stony ditch is nothing but a dry bed with a sparse of green vines growing between the jagged rocks. Not a drop of water exists in this empty trench.

The dark clouds are about to dampen our weary spirits even more. We cross over to the other side of the rocky bed and into another pasture where a trail of cattle is grazing. Smiles begin to grow on our faces when we notice the wandering cows lined up around a large watering hole about two hundred yards in front of us.

With watchful eyes, we take the horses over by the pond to quench their thirst. Things seem to settle down a bit, but our moment of rest is shortened yet again. A deep roar of pulsating blades cut through the thick air. About five hundred feet above, two black helicopters fly side by side from the north and flutter over the open field where we are resting. We quickly duck under some small brush growing near the two trees by the edge of the pond.

The choppers slowly maneuver in a circle, combing the area, and here we sit hiding like scared field mice inside a bush hoping to blend in. Allison is absolutely terrified. She grips the small branches of the bush and vigorously shakes, making the few leaves that are camouflaging us vibrate like a hummingbird's wings.

"Allison, you keep shaking like that, and they are going to think this bush is having a seizure," I say to lighten the fright on her face. She briefly opens her eyes, and the corners of her mouth stretch back. I can't tell if she fighting to smile or if she's constipated.

The helicopters finally leave the field, and the tension in Allison's knuckles releases. She held on so tight to the branches that it left an imprint in her sweaty palm. We wait about five more minutes to make sure the choppers have cleared the entire area before we mount back up and leave.

CHAPTER 8

After riding a couple of miles through this rocky soil and cactus-breeding land, tiny raindrops sprinkle on my face. Those clouds are about to drastically change our mood if we don't find some shelter quick.

We trail off down a small ridge into another dry riverbed where much of the limestone walls of the ditch have been washed out. There are dry, rotting roots protruding from the sides of the chalky walls searching for water. There must be an underground aquifer around here, because the trees have grown tall in this part. Just up ahead, there is a small cove carved into the stony sides of the ridge from years of water erosion. It's big enough to keep us and our horses covered for the night, or at least until this nasty thunderstorm passes over.

Packed like sardines in this dark, damp notch in the wall, we huddle together to keep warm from the cold breeze the storm has brought. Lighting a fire right now sounds great, but it wouldn't be smart. Attracting our enemy isn't a benefit I'm willing to risk.

The rain pours down, soaking into the dry cracks in the riverbed, and lightning sporadically flashes, giving us a silhouetted glimpse of the trees standing firm above the ridge. Allison looks parched, so I hand her my flask. She turns the canteen straight up, and I watch as the last of the water drips into her mouth.

"It's all gone," she says.

"Gone?" I ask. "The sky is begging you to fill that flask."

Maybe God knew our mouths would be parched so He brought us this rain, and maybe it was to slow down the soldiers from chasing us. Whatever the reason, I'm forever grateful. I take our canteens and hold them out into the pelting rain, filling them to the brim.

After a couple of hours, the rain finally stops and the storm passes. Even though the clouds have moved on, the sky is still dark as the evening approaches. Being cramped in this confined space has not only stiffened my knees, but it also triggers the regulation of my pint-sized bladder. I graciously uncurl my position and carefully poke my head out of the cove opening.

"Where you going?" asks Gabe.

"Nature's calling, and my bladder is answering."

Gabe rises from his an uncomfortable spot and follows me out.

"I don't need you to hold my hand to pee," I say, stopping him from advancing outside the cove.

"No, but you need someone to watch your back."

"Fine, just try not to make so much noise."

My brother's large feet dragging across the ground could attract a whole platoon. He isn't exactly one for being discreet; however, I'm the one squatting in the woods, so be it.

"Stay here, we'll be right back," Gabe says to Allison as we leave.

I bring my bow along just in case I get lonely and if a squirrel decides to scamper across my path. The ground's rough, muddy soil sinks in like a filled sponge, but it's no less inviting than the small crevice I've been coiled up in for the last two hours.

Gabe follows me until I find a nice bush to squat behind. I guess it doesn't have to be nice. Hell, it could be a rotting pile of compost and I would still urinate on it. Ah, sweet relief, my bladder is cordially thanking me right now.

Gabe's heavy footsteps rustle around behind me, but I try to ignore it. He is, after all, watching out for me. But when twigs go snapping, that's more than I can handle, so I turn around to shush him.

"Gabe, hush, stop moving your sasquatch feet."

"I'm not moving. I've been standing here the whole time."

I pull up my pants as quickly as I can and grab an arrow from my quiver. I sidle up next to a tree and crouch down. Gabe quickly lies on his stomach, hiding himself in the open. I think to myself, *It's just probably a deer*, but then I hear voices mingling in Russian as the rustling gets closer. I throw a pebble at Gabe, trying to get his attention and gesture for him to move. He slides back on his stomach and finds a tree opposite to me to hide behind.

I can't tell how many soldiers are prowling around out there because it's too dark. I suddenly hear more footsteps to my left, but they are dangerously closer. I keep the arrow nocked firmly to the string and poke my head around the trunk of the tree. One lone soldier scours the area with a flashlight, while the others are still wandering around, talking. I guess they aren't too worried about what's out here to be so vulnerably exposed.

I raise my bow up toward the soldier with the flashlight and sink the arrow into his forehead. The flashlight drops from his hands and he falls to the ground. The other two men are now talking louder where I can understand them. They are calling for the man's name, but when he doesn't answer them, they close in where I can see them.

One of the men spots the flashlight on the ground and walks toward it, while the other stays back with his gun raised and frantically looks around. Neither soldier has noticed the dead man, yet they seem spooked. I pull another arrow out and aim for the soldier with his gun raised. I strike him right in the eye, knocking him off his feet into the high brush below.

The last soldier picks up the flashlight, unaware of his comrades lying dead, and circles around. He calls out to the other men, but no one answers. Noticeably alone, he panics and spastically points his gun in every direction. He's so alarmed that he attempts to run without looking and trips over the dead soldier beside him. He points the flashlight in the man's face and shouts hysterically.

"Pomoshch! Pomoshch!"

I quickly thrust an arrow into his neck, keeping him from yelling. While the blood pours from the puncture, he struggles to keep his balance and staggers forward in my direction. I just stand there, paralyzed for a moment staring into his anguish. I don't know why, but for the first time, I feel sorrowful.

I can't bear to watch him agonize like this, so I grab another arrow to end his suffering. I lift the bow up, waiting to shoot, but the man's insistent cry for help shackles my heart. I can't seem to release the arrow without my conscience burdening me. My muscles tense up, and I fail to proceed with killing him. The man falls onto his knees about ten feet in front of me with his hand stretched out.

"Arena, what are you waiting for?" Gabe says.

I falter, considering whether or not this man deserves to die, but it matters not. The gushing blood exiting his wound will soon run out, and his cold body will fall to the earth. I can't help him now, but I can ease his pain. I say a quick prayer over him before slinging the arrow deep into his skull and putting him out of his misery.

I watch as his body falls back into a pile of wet brush. A flashing moment of Jacob replaces the man's body, and I shudder.

I look down at his face and can't help but wonder if his intentions were hostile. Was this man deceived into believing anything less than the truth? I know nothing of this man, and yet I feel deeply woeful. We are all just sheep wandering astray waiting to be slaughtered. How am I any different?

"Arena, run!" Gabe shouts.

While I try to shake off the haunting memories of Jacob, about ten soldiers rush down a small hill to the right of us. I quickly grab the man's radio that's attached to his belt and sprint behind Gabe back toward the cave.

I can hear the men racing closer behind us, slashing through the fine-bladed brush as they trod over the moist soil. The dark night and heavy thicket of trees seem to be the only thing keeping us from being noticed, yet the pace of their heavy-strapped boots does not cease.

As much as I want to stop, turn, and shoot, I'm not exactly in a position to do so, with Gabe running ahead of me without knowing my intentions. I will not put him in a compromising situation just because of my impatience, but if they spot us, one shot in the back and we're done. I quicken my pace to close in on Gabe and try to thwart his retreat in an effort to save us both.

I take a quick glance back to reassure our distance, and see a shadow of soldiers recede into the dark trees about fifty yards behind us. The only chance we have now before we run out of this small forest is to hide within the few bushes. Gabe takes an unexpected shift in direction and runs west.

I quickly follow, shouting at him to stop, but it's useless. He's too wrapped up in escaping that any noise penetrating his ears is shut off by his intense concentration. I can hear the sound of water rushing against the rocks in front of us. The terrain slowly changes from grassy marsh to rocky soil, and everything around me seems to be growing darker. I can still hear the soldiers running behind us, bumping into rotting limbs and broken branches on the ground. Gabe's body begins to blend into the foliage, and I almost lose sight of him.

There's a large tree to the left of us, surrounded by a plentiful heap of bushes that would be ideal to hide in, so I leap forward at Gabe's feet, trying to stop him before he passes by it. Gabe falls hard to the ground with my hand tightly wrapped around his ankle. I pull myself up to get his attention, but the ground beneath us begins to tremble.

"What's that?" Gabe asks.

I peer over to the side by the large tree, but the darkness has blinded me from seeing anything, until a flash of lightning reveals something far worse than the men running toward us. We find ourselves lying on the edge of a dangerously steep ravine, and the unstable ground beneath us is clamoring to break up, leaving us to plummet to the jagged rocks below.

The wet, loose rock shifts by Gabe's chest, and the soil sinks below my feet. I'm now dangling over the side of the cliff, and the only thing keeping me from sliding off is Gabe's ankle. If I move too quickly, the ground below us will collapse, sending both of us to our demise.

"Slowly roll to your right and grab the tree root," I say to Gabe.

"Slow is the opposite of what I had in mind," Gabe says, as he gently rolls over and grabs the small root.

I carefully shift my weight from the loose soil and look for something to grab, but nothing appears to be solid and stable. I look to my right and notice a coiling clump of strong climbing kudzu roots dangling from a tree in front of Gabe. I grab onto the noxious weed and slowly pull myself over the loose soil.

I almost reach the top where Gabe is holding onto the tree, but the large, tuberous roots begin to crack and pull apart, and my hands slip over the waxy leaves. I slide down the ropelike vines over the cliff until my dangling foot catches a flat, jagged rock protruding from the edge of the unsound ridge. The earth begins to shift again, and dirt abruptly falls between the tree roots, leaving a large crevice where I'm now hanging on for dear life. The only thing keeping me from falling fifty feet onto the serrated rocks is a flat, stony ledge where my toes are resting tenuously.

Gabe's grip slips away from the wet tree root, and he falls through the large opening. I quickly grab his wrist.

"Arena!" Gabe shouts.

I hold on as tight as I can as he dangles helplessly above the rocks below.

"Swing your body over to the edge next to the rocks. These vines aren't going to hold much longer, and my grip is weakening!" I say.

"I'm trying, but I can't reach!" Gabe shouts.

Suddenly, I hear soldier footsteps approaching.

"Hurry, grab onto something, now," I whisper.

He swings his body over to the side and tries to reach for a root sticking between a couple of rocks, but only his fingertips graze the edge. The men walk closer to the edge where Gabe is hanging on to my slipping hand. The men yell at one another about losing us until one of the soldiers shouts out in Russian.

"Look, look down there," he yells.

"What do you see?" asks another soldier.

My heart is racing, and my hand is slipping off Gabe's wrist. The men carefully approach the edge of the ravine. Gabe swings over to the side of the cliff out of sight, and clasps his hand around the knobby root just as I lose my grip and let go of the vine. I lean forward with my face planted into the side of the limestone cliff and claw at its rugged ridges. I find a protruding edge and grip my fingers tightly. Exhausted and trembling, I cling to the wall while my feet still numbingly rest on the narrow ridge below. The side of the cliff's curved indention barely keeps me hidden from anyone deciding to look down, but I fear Gabe's comprisable position will expose us. Right above me, a soldier's boot hangs over the edge, and the man cocks back his rifle. I brace myself for the unthinkable and begin to pray inside my head.

"Beautiful, isn't it?" the man says, mesmerized.

I open my eyes and look at Gabe in bewilderment, and just then, a shot goes off, shaking my toes from their paralyzing position on the rock. Just across the steep jagged ravine, a deer collapses to the ground and into the water.

I regain my grip with my fingers and hold on tight, but my toes tingle with pain. While the men boast over the dead doe, I look over at Gabe; the roots he is holding are pulling away from the rocks. He panics and shuffles his hand around, but there's nothing else to grab, but the jagged rocks.

I shift my weight toward him. Suddenly, the rock that my toes are balancing on cracks in two. My foot slips so I jump up and frantically search for something to grab. With both hands , I clutch the only thing I can—the soldier's boot.

The man screams for help while my weight on his leg pulls him down. We slip a few feet then immediately stop. Stuck between the roots, more than half his body hangs over the cliff.

I desperately cling to his shifty leg that is wildly kicking. Russian voices shout above, and the man's body slowly slides up. I dig my fingernails into his uniform and climb up his body like a cat. I reach the top and find two other Russian soldiers struggling to pull him up

Wide eyed, they suddenly stop and stare at me with confusion. There's a brief moment of silence before I reach for my gun and shoot. Both soldiers fall dead and let go of the man's arms. The soldier slides down and grabs desperately at the earth. Struggling to pull himself up, he reaches out his hand to me, but I ignore it. His eyes swell and he plummets to his death

"Arena! I'm slipping, I can't hold on any longer!" Gabe shouts.

I carefully rush to the edge of the cliff and reach down for Gabe. I stretch out as far as I can, but I'm much too far away to reach him.

"Arena, I can't hold on!"

"Hang on, let me find something you can grab onto."

"What part did you not understand? I'm about to fall."

I quickly grab one of the soldier's assault rifle and lower it down toward Gabe. He grabs onto the stock and hangs from its strap. I fight to pull him up halfway. The tip of the gun breeches the edge as I tug with the little strength I have left. Gabe's hand finally peers over the top of the stony ledge as I rest the gun's barrel on my shoulder. Out of nowhere, the clacking sound of a chambered bullet creeps up behind me.

"*Otpustit' yego ili ty umresh,*" says a Russian soldier behind me. I hesitate to answer him, so he repeats himself in English this time.

"Let him go now, or you will die."

If I let go, my brother will surely fall to his death, but if I don't, then we both will die. I'm betting we both die no matter what I choose, and I would never sacrifice my brother for my own life. I slowly turn my head and find a gun pointed at it.

"Now!" the man shouts.

The pressed tip of the barrel digs into my skin while Gabe still dangles below. I can't hold on any longer, it hurts.

"Grab the trigger and pull," I say in Irish to Gabe.

My muscles are bound to the rifle, but they are about to give out. Gabe finally reaches the trigger and squeezes. The bullet just grazes the skin on my shoulder, but it does much worse to the soldier behind me. The ground trembles with a thud and he falls dead beside me.

I pull on the gun's strap with all my might, and Gabe finally finds the top of the edge and pulls himself over. With my shoulder stinging, and my muscles searching for oxygen, I collapse on my back and breathe.

Gabe slithers over next to me, examines my shoulder, and says, "Next time you have the urge to pee, don't make it an adventure."

CHAPTER 9

Lying on my back to catch my breath, I stare into the black sky and notice less and less stars filling the dark backdrop of space. Just like this journey, time and space is forever changing and I know my days are numbered, but I must carry on. Gabe nestles up beside me with his head propped up on my arm. Though I'm in slight pain, I fight through it. This is a rare moment from my brother and I'm not about to squash it.

"Do you ever wonder what it would have been like as an only child?" Gabe asks.

"I don't think I would ever want to imagine anything like that," I say.

"Yeah, me either."

After a brief moment of rest, Gabe and I pick up two of the soldiers' guns and a flashlight, and make our way back to Allison—shamefully, I almost completely forgot about her. But it's moments like these I wish not to squander.

Because we deviated from our original position, the trek back seems almost twice as long. We climb down the small ridge by the cave and find both Shadow and Diablo missing, but more importantly I don't see Allison anywhere near. The small opening in the side of the cliff is empty except for Gabe's backpack and the charred remains of smoldering logs.

"Allison," I say softly, trying not to make too much noise. I search around outside the small cave for tracks when Gabe blurts out, "Her gun is gone."

"Allison," I call out a little louder, hoping she just didn't hear me the first time. "Allison."

I'm not one to usually worry or jump to conclusions, but I'm beginning to have a slight panic attack.

"You suppose she went looking for us?" Gabe asks.

Just then Shadow and Diablo come meandering out of the trees. I take a few steps toward Shadow and suddenly my heart shrivels when I shine the flashlight onto the ground.

"No," I respond with utter pain in my voice.

I bend down and closely examine the disturbing marks in the dirt. The tracks of someone being dragged from this place is all I need to see for my blood to boil and my rage to riot.

"She's been taken," I say tempestuously.

I follow the tracks that trail all the way up to the edge of the ravine and toward a small deposit of mud that's been trampled on by much larger tracks—tracks from a vehicle. Just below the swirling mud clump is a small puddle of blood.

"What is it, what do you see?" asks Gabe.

"Hop on Diablo, we need to ride now!"

"I don't know how to control him."

"Learn!"

Gabe carefully, but hastily, caresses the bridge of Diablo's nose, trying to coerce him into befriending him. Diablo shifts his head back and forth restlessly, but eventually warms up to Gabe's smell. I guess the short time Gabe spent riding and feeding him has created a cautious but genuine bond. Diablo curiously sidesteps to the right while Gabe tries to mount up, which leaves him nearly hanging from the leather bridle.

After a brief moment of frustration, Gabe finally sits upright, takes control of Diablo's reins, and follows behind me. We trace the muddy vehicle tracks through an area of sparse timbers out into a narrow but lengthy trail of black soil.

A small ember of light glows up ahead where the tracks lead, but my suspicion of trailing this vehicle to the light source may hinder our position. Instead, I lead us around the tracks, near the backside of some scattered oak trees and flank from the right of the light, hoping not to be so obvious.

We cautiously move the horses closer to the vehicle through the soft mud and discover the light is shining from an old ranch house that looks as worn as it is wet. Not sure how the gray, rotting timber keeps this domicile standing without a hint of caving in.

I put my hand up, gesturing for Gabe to stop, when I notice a black jeep-like vehicle parked on the side of the house. We leave the horses tied to some stiff cedar branches and move in closer toward the backyard. I carefully slide my hand over the cold steel of my Beretta, anxiously waiting to drive a bullet through the man who took Allison, but the spastic, thin muscles in my itchy trigger finger won't stop shaking. I physically have to stop and sit aside to calm my strenuously erupting temper before moving on.

When I rise to my feet, Gabe grabs my trembling hand and squeezes in an attempt to slow my anger.

"Hey, this isn't any different than where we've been before. Please don't lose it now. She may be scared, but she's strong. Just make sure you're accurate in your shot," he says.

We quietly and nimbly drift to the side of the gray, withered house like two alley cats searching for food in the night. Crouched down, I gradually round the edge of the house, shifting my eyes every second in every direction while Gabe watches my back. Footsteps shuffle from one room to another and the sound of water runs from the kitchen sink.

Waiting to gain my nerve back, I sit there crouched down below a large window draped in brown curtains. I draw my gun in one hand and clutch my dagger in the other. I slowly peer through the dirty glass pane. The inside of the house is nearly concealed by the curtain except for a small wrinkle in the split of the two drapes. I perch my chin on the windowsill and my eyes grow furious with rage. Allison is still alive, tied up and gagged on the living room couch.

I wave my gun over to Gabe, motioning him to flank the opposite side of the house behind the back porch. I have no idea how many soldiers are in there scurrying around. I peek through a second window that's less concealed and notice two more victims lying on the floor with their hands tied.

Just then, a soldier passes by the half-opened curtain. I quickly crouch down and away. My heart races when the window slowly slides open. I swiftly duck beneath the shadow and target my gun toward the window with the anticipation of a soldier's head popping out. Just as the black silhouette protrudes the opening, a man's voice ringsout.

"Hey, come over and help me with this," says a Russian voice inside the house.

I slowly ease back my slightly bent finger and release the half-squeezed trigger into position. I swallow what spit I had in my dry mouth and exhale a sigh of relief. Gabe's pale, relieved face illuminates from the corner light above the eaves of the house.

I carefully peek back into the corner of the open window. Two soldiers hold assault rifles. One has a black stiletto tucked neatly into the back of his pants. The shoulder of his shirt is blanketed with patches that I assume are his military ranking. The other soldier's less-decorated attire is sloppily worn, and the posture at which he stands suggests a ranking below scrub.

While they bicker over a piece of meat in the kitchen, I get a better look inside the window and check the living room to make sure no other soldiers are standing guard.

I twist the suppressor tight against my gun and silently shoot both men in the back of the head through the open window. With the men slumped over each other on the floor, and everyone else gagged, I wait patiently through the eerie silence hoping for no other unwanted surprises. I nod toward Gabe and motion him to proceed through the back door.

"I'll watch your back. Just get Allison," I say.

Gabe cautiously turns the knob and pushes open the creaky door. I follow closely behind him, guarding our surroundings. He slowly passes the rear entry closet and heads around the staircase.

I hold my position, tucked back behind the stairs, and

watch guard over Gabe. The glow in his face brightens up when he turns the corner and notices Allison tied on the couch.

"Allison!" he shouts, rushing to her rescue.

I can almost feel the jubilant reaction Allison releases when Gabe's face appears, but it quickly fades. The deathly sound of a creaking floor beside me warrants a brief moment of distress. I lean nervously around the bend of the stairs. Allison's eyes emphatically grow with fear. I pull my dagger and grip it tightly against the palm of my hand.

A soldier stands alone on the stairs and slowly raises his gun to the back of my brother. When Gabe release the gag from Allison's terrified face, the raging adrenaline streaming in my blood forces me to leap forward. Allison screams out in horror.

"Arena!"

The man quickly turns his head as I thrust the sharp tip of my blade through the tender flesh of his neck, but not without a round exiting the chamber of his gun first. It seems like slow motion when everything happens all at once. My eyes and my brain have disconnected. Time has suspended and somehow ceases to exist. Like the car crash, I strangely find myself in suspension watching every movement unfold.

I can see the casing from the soldier's gun chamber fall end-over-end to the floor, smoke still lingering from the end of his barrel, and Allison slumped over screaming. I pull my dagger from the man's neck and stare in horror as Gabe's body falls to the floor.

I race over and find an old man sprawled out next to Gabe. A pool of blood rapidly expands beneath him.

"Are you okay!?" I ask Gabe.

"Yeah, yeah, I'm fine, but I don't think he is," he answers.

The old man lies lifeless on the floor, his hands bound, and neck bruised. He isn't breathing. Gabe slowly gets up and rolls him over. Blood pours out from the man's side. With all the screaming from Allison and the adrenaline-pumping frenzy, I never noticed him. The bullet just missed Gabe and struck this man instead, deep into the side of his chest.

An old woman is nearby, tied up and crying hysterically behind her gag. By the sadness of her state, I'm drawn to believe this man, who happened to be in an unfortunate position, was her husband.

I untie the old woman and try to help her up, but she refuses my gesture. Emotionally stooped over in a ball of pain, she tarries for a brief moment before crawling and screaming toward her husband's motionless body.

With the woman's arms wrapped around her husband's limp body, Allison holds her hand, while I gently lay mine on her shoulder. Gabe sits there in silence as tears run down his cheeks.

Although Gabe is in disarray, I feel inclined to comfort the grief-stricken woman instead. My heart is confused between the remorse I share with the woman, and the sullen desire to kill all that walks the earth. I'm ashamed of my bitter disdain for life right now, and it only grows with more malice every time someone innocent is slain.

The only thing that distracts me from these ill-harboring feelings is a small lambent light shining through the front window by the door. I slowly get up and walk over to examine the strange glow, when all of the sudden light flickers from the trees in the far distance, and the humming sound of an engine gradually rumbles close. Our moment of mourning has just been cut short. More soldiers are on their way.

"Gabe, grab what you can and take Allison to the horses now!" I shout.

I manage to collect myself from panicking and search the dead soldiers in the house for anything that may be useful.

"What about you?"

"Go now! I'm right behind you."

Gabe and Allison race out the back door while I tend to the heartbroken old woman. I desperately try to convince her to come with us, but she's too upset to consciously understand the predicament we're about to encounter. The lights from the vehicles grow brighter and brighter through the front window, and my heart ticks faster and faster. I rub my hands on her back, attempting to disengage her hypnotic malaise. I gently speak into her ear and wrap my arm around hers. "He's gone. There's nothing left we can do. We need to go right now."

Her non-responsive condition labors on my good manners, and I'm forced to physically remove her from her grieving stupor.

"Come on, let's go!" I say, trying to pry her arms from her husband's dead, cold body. If we don't leave now, we're both going to die.

I tug on her body, but she refuses to budge. I'm almost under the impression that she would rather die than to live without her husband, but I don't give up. I shake, squeeze, and even pinch the back of her neck to encourage her muscles to retract, but nothing seems to work. I believe she's made her choice, and it's not in my power to change it, so I leave her be.

I rush to the back door and peer through the thinly dusted drapes while two black jeeps pull up behind the porch.

"Damn!"

I'm now forced to stay put in this house a little longer because of my obstinate behavior to unsuccessfully save a tenaciously old woman from wanting to die. Gabe and Allison have since left and are probably wondering where I am, while I'm stuck here with a heartbroken woman lying on the floor.

Two men exit one of the jeeps and walk toward the back door. I frantically look around for a place to conceal myself, but there's nowhere to hide. Right then, the front screen door opens and I stand there frozen while the woman on the floor moans in terror.

I quickly make a dash behind the stairs, desperately searching for a way out of this mess, and somehow find a small pantry-like door I didn't see before. I swiftly open the door and descend to a small basement. The darkened cellar is damp and musty, and the only light visible is coming from the small slit in the footsteps of the staircase.

I draw my gun, pointing it toward the top of the cellar door, and peek through the cracked wood in the stairs while perched on my tiptoes. The back door opens, and three men walk inside; they are shocked to find the bodies of the dead soldiers lying on the floor. One quickly draws his gun and shouts to the old woman to keep her hands up, while the other two men cautiously deploy up the stairs.

I hear the front door open and a man speaking in Russian to someone outside. I can't see the old woman, but I can certainly hear her crying hysterically. A neatly dressed soldier walks past the corner of the wall and stairs. His high-fitted black boots and fully decorated jacket suggest a boost in his military ranking.

"Anyone else in the house?" asks the Russian officer.

"Dead or alive, sir?" the soldier responds, still aiming his gun at the terrified woman.

"Preferably alive, unless it's the person responsible for this," he says, pushing over one of the dead soldiers with his boot.

The thumping of boots stomping down the stairs distracts my vision momentarily, as dust flutters in front of the small lit opening I'm peering through.

"It's clear up here, Colonel," says one of the soldiers as he clomps down on the creaky wood.

There are four men standing in the room now, three of which are toting assault rifles, and one very pissed-off colonel. The old woman is now screaming, and my patience is growing thin hiding underneath here. I can't take it anymore. I draw both my guns and prepare an all-out assault on these men. Just then, I hear the front door swing open and slam shut.

"Someone shut this cackling hen up," a voice shouts.

I recoil my guns and squint through the tiny slit to try to get a better look at who is shouting, but the man is too far away for me to see.

"Gentlemen, if you will please leave. The colonel and I have some things to discuss alone," the man says.

The men exit the front door, and the crying momentarily stops as the clubbing sound of a metal gun stock to the head silences the old woman's hysteria.

I clench my teeth, massaging my jawbone until the pain gives me a headache. I want nothing more than to just leave this basement and stick my dagger into these men's throats, but my eyes are blind to what is waiting outside. I'm afraid I'm bound beneath these stairs a bit longer. I patiently wait for the man to appear from in the living room while keeping an eye on a seemingly less confident colonel thanbefore.

The man finally enters the kitchen and is dressed in a black suit accompanied with a peculiar-looking red armband. The insignia on it is too small for me to read, but he wears the ensemble with confidence nonetheless. The tall, thin man takes a quick glance at the dead soldiers on the kitchen floor, pulls out a cigarette, and lights it. His face appears frigid and callous.

"These are your men, are they not?" hesays.

"Yes, sir, they are," answers the colonel.

"And I hear there are possibly eight to ten more in the woods that are . . . well, in the same position as these unfortunate men," he says, looking down at the dead soldiers.

"We don't know for sure that's accurate—"

"Well I do!" the man shouts.

He takes a puff on the cigarette, flicks it onto the dead soldier's head, and places his hand on the colonel's shoulder.

"Colonel, it's my job to see things better. It's your job to enforce them. How can I expect you to successfully see through the difficult tasks when you fail to entertain the simple ones?"

"Yes, sir, I understand, that's why—"

"No! I don't think you do. Look, I'm a reasonable man, even tolerant now and then to even the slow-witted, but when my agenda is hindered by sloppy engagements from seemingly top men, I feel my generosity is . . . unappreciated."

"I accept full responsibility."

"I wouldn't think of anything less of you."

The infuriated man in black glares at the colonel. The colonel swallows his pride and clears his throat. The tall man grabs a chair from the kitchen, paces slowly behind the colonel, and pulls out another cigarette. He places the unlit cigarette on the table and takes off his jacket, revealing a gun exposed in its holster tightly pressed against his waist.

"You look tired, Colonel. Why don't you have a seat?"

"I'm fine, thank you, sir."

"It's not a request, now sit."

"Yes . . . sir."

The colonel, now scared for his life, quietly sits in the chair. He tries to justify his failing actions, but the man robed in black rejects his story and paces back and forth.

"The only thing that permits me to acquiesce your erroneous behavior is the prolific leadership you displayed during the Syria invasions," says the tall, pale man.

He bends down beside the colonel's chair and kindly hands him the unlit cigarette. He brushes against his shoulder and looks deep into his eyes, but says nothing. The cruel silence is enough to evoke fear, yet send a clear message at the same time.

The man adjusts his silk tie, points his gun toward the colonel's head for a brief moment before putting on his jacket and leaves the room. Just by the sheer body language this man addresses in front of the colonel, I can see a seed of consternation and discontent effortlessly being planted in the colonel's mind.

This man is confidently in control and holds no one unaccountable for failure. Mercy isn't in his vocabulary, nor is the will to show a sign of weakness. No other man except for General Iakov could breathe such cruelty into his own men, but not even he could evoke this much fear.

It wasn't until I got myself captured at that long-forgotten training center that Iakov's confidence was overshadowed by his ego. Unlike this man, Iakov had to go to great lengths and effort to produce the same fear. Even when I was cuffed to a chair in his quarters, it was painfully obvious even to him that his threats and cruel intent were limited. It was evident that his overconfidence is what got him killed, and I enjoyed every moment of dragging my knife across his jagged throat.

But this man appears to be more threatening. There is only one conclusion I can draw from his intimidating conversation with the colonel; he must be the one they call Gorshkov—the same man that Finnegan had told me about.

He's the Russian dictator who's responsible for overseeing a shift in the world's economic rise from the ashes. For the past few years, China and Russia have dominated world affairs, but in most recent events that have involved America's political prowess, Russia has been in the forefront of global diplomacy. A one-world government was etched in President Kriel's plans, but only because it was placed there by Russian leadership, and Gorshkov is the suspected leader that is heading it. He is the real reason for what's happened to our nation, and the rest of the world that will soon follow.

The old woman must have awakened, because I can hear the hysteria continue, but it's quickly silenced again, this time from a gunshot. The door slams, and the colonel frightfully clutches his gun and begins to shake.

I'm pissed, but nauseous after having to witness the cruel death of two innocent elderly people. And I'm sure many more are to come.

The front door opens again, and the colonel quickly tries to regain his composure before the three soldiers standing outside walk into the kitchen.

"Is he gone?" the colonel asks his men.

"You must have made an impression, because he left with a smile on his face," says one of the soldiers.

"Very well then. Let's move out."

"What about the men, sir?" asks another soldier, pointing to the dead soldiers.

"Leave them; we have important things to take care of."

The men grab the guns from the dead soldiers and exit the back door followed by a nervous-looking colonel. I carefully creep back up the cellar stairs and wait until the jeeps have driven away before entering the living room. Just for my peace of mind, I curiously roll over the old woman's body to confirm she's dead. If the pool of blood surrounding her shoulder isn't enough to convince me, the bullet's large exit wound from the back of her head surely is.

I peek out the back window to make sure it's clear before racing out and catching up with Gabe and Allison. I open the door to leave, but my body freezes when I hear the shocking sound of a baby crying from upstairs.

I feel the color drain from my face. Goose bumps crawl up my arms, making my soul shiver. I hesitate to walk up the stairs, anticipating what horror it may bring, but I'm mysteriously drawn to it. With each step I climb, the crying grows louder. Why didn't the soldiers notice this baby before?

I slowly walk into one of the back bedrooms where the crying is wearing heavy on me. In the corner of the room, screeching, painful sounds are coming from with inside the crib. Suddenly, two tiny feet kick up just above the crib skirting.

I wish not to look, but my curiosity says otherwise. With my heart pounding like a bass drum, I carefully grab the roughly scarred bed railing and lean over into the crib. I shut my eyes briefly before I look down. My hands vigorously shake, and I open my eyes to a chilling awakening.

The crib is empty.

CHAPTER 10

What wicked dominion have my thoughts woken up to? Was I really imagining an infant's cry? Either my spirit has been seduced into the temptations of darkness, or something deeper is prophetically seeded that I have yet to be shown.

The old paint-peeled crib is covered in dust and filled with random junk. It looks like it hasn't comforted a small child in years and is only being used to hold the hoarded crap that's been collecting here for quite some time. I fall to my knees feeling manipulated and fooled by my own mind.

I lift my weary head and run my hand up the slat of the crib, cutting myself on a metal tag engraved with the name *Joshua* on it. I stare at the tag for a moment, wondering where the child who slept in this bed could be now. The door from downstairs creaks open.

I quickly reclaim my poise and slide out into the hallway. With my guns drawn, I quietly step near the staircase and peek down behind the corner. From outside, an arm securing a large gun protrudes past the edge of the opened back door. I immediately recognize the sleeve belonging to Gabe, so I shout out down below.

"Gabe!"

"Arena?"

"It's me, I'm okay," I say, racing down the stairs, happy to see his face.

"We waited for you, but you never came. I saw the jeeps leave and thought you were dead."

I explain to Gabe the unnerving predicament I was in when they left; the old woman not budging, the soldiers lurking, the colonel's military deficiencies and, of course, the presence of Gorshkov, but I don't mention the crying infant. It doesn't bear repeating, and it would only worry him. The last thing he needs to add to his already burdensome life is my questionable sanity.

Outside, Allison sits atop Diablo next to Shadow, whose body blends into the dark of night. Gabe hops onto Diablo, while I stroke the side of Shadow's soft face.

"You glad to see me, boy?" I say to him, gently rubbing my scent in his face before mounting up.

"Which way?" says Allison.

"South if we can. If we have to veer out of our way to avoid this kind of mess, so be it. Let's get the hell out of here."

We take off riding southwest through the night before turning eastward to avoid any more military morasses, until we have exhausted the horses. We finally stop in a low-lying valley to give the horses a rest and wait for the morning sun to rise.

Whenever I watch a sunrise, I often think of the summertime, when we were kids—waiting for Finnegan to wake us up to go fishing. The brisk and sometimes sticky morning air seemed so uneventful, but it was the sun rising in the east, peeking over the horizon that led me to realize the depths of God's beauty. The birds were singing melodies of sweet song, flying against a backdrop of morning glory and a graduation of alluring colors in the sky. The horizon would glow of ginger hues to azure blues bleeding beyond into the black space speckled with a light shimmer of morning stars. I often wish I could be a child again, not knowing or wanting to know what tomorrow may bring.

I am who I am; older, hopefully wiser, and destined to fulfill my fate. The days may change, but I will never stop basking in this beautiful moment. If only the world could just stop and take a moment to see what *is* instead of worrying what could be. I'm not perfect by any means, and even I despise my own selfish desires, but it's my will to believe God loves me nonetheless that sustains me from falling.

I tie Shadow's reins to one of the many cedar trees in these parts and scout out the area for some breakfast. Not much to hunt for in this open-range region, but I'm tired of tending to an empty stomach, so I'll eat just about anything right now.

I find an old Spanish oak that leans toward the south, its outer limbs nearly touching the ground. You can definitely tell which way the wind blows. All the trees look like they have been frozen in a swaying trance to the south. Strange how a tree can grow in one direction when it's continually forced to; kind of like a child growing up in a family with narrow minds.

I wait and wait until finally, after about thirty minutes, a gray squirrel dances around the trunk of the oak and balances himself onto a small limb hanging right above me. He's close enough that I decide to save a bullet and use an arrow instead. I tilt my bow sideways and slowly pull back on the knock and lean back. I take a few seconds to sight him in when out of nowhere, the loudest, most obnoxious sneeze scares him off.

I disengage the arrow and look with great displeasure over to Gabe, who is hunched over.

"Really?" I yell out.

"Sorry, it's these damn junipers. They're making my eyes itch and throat sore."

And I thought mesquite trees were spawned from the devil. Cedars are far worse for the allergy-prone. Its pollen production is a plague in central Texas, and has no redeeming value for anyone or anything. It's a poor source of food for animals, makes lousy firewood, absorbs all the ground water—which prevents grass from growing in its vicinity, and causes a mass exodus of allergy medicine from the pharmacy shelves.

My brother probably deserves a little more sympathy than I have to offer, but my empty stomach makes me irritable. Okay, okay, so I'm being selfish. Please don't judge me, and never deny a girl who's starving, especially one holding a slew of weapons.

I begrudgingly shuffle back to check on him when out of nowhere, something scurries across my path, parting the brown water-neglected grass. It stops momentarily long enough for me to investigate. I slowly lean over the matted grass, and there, nestled within the golden brush, hides the cutest little brown bunny.

I slide over to get a better look and notice its jerky head pop up, elongated ears standing at attention. This is no bunny, but just a young hare or jackrabbit, as we call them. Rabbit or not, he's food and we're hungry. I don't think I could have ever had a bunny for a pet. We ate so many growing up; it would have been morbidly cruel to pet him while picking the lodged macerated rabbit meat from between my teeth.

I hold my hand out quietly toward Gabe and Allison to silence their chatter and quietly pull back the arrow. I carefully aim at the hare's head and hold my breath. His tiny nose wiggles in and out. Damn, why does he have to be so cute? I close my eyes and quickly open them, imagining that he has devilish horns before I let the arrow fly into his furry, little skull.

If we had a pot of water, onions, and some tomatoes, this would make for a good stew, but I guess we'll have to be content chewing on the dry, lean meat. Gabe prepares a small fire to cook the rabbit over, while I gather a few wild cactus berries I spotted earlier. I gingerly grab the tips of the berries and shave off the outer skin with my knife, hoping to remove any unwanted tiny barbs still clinging. They are a delight to taste but a major pain in the ass to prepare.

"Can I borrow your knife?" Gabe asks.

"Sure."

Gabe digs deep into his pack and pulls out a large can.

"What is that?" I ask.

"A can of beans I stashed from the house."

Great, just what we need. If the obnoxious sneezing doesn't reveal us, it's the gaseous rumblings from Gabe's ass that certainly will. I think I'd rather massage the anal scent gland of a skunk with my nose than breathe in his bouquet of flatulent perfume.

The day grows dark like the shaded memories of past, and evening creeps up on us almost without warning. Gabe rekindles the small burning fire as we sit around and breathe in its warmth from the unusually cool summer night.

It's nights like these that give way to unsettling thoughts, but with fire ablaze, it's Gabe's outlandish musings that somehow manages to erase any uncertainties. I believe every good story deserves a little embellishment from time to time. Especially in the age we live in, when every second of life is so precious. I'll kindly invite any of Gabe's anecdotes that keep our spirits from drowning.

After an hour passes, the fire gently calms back down to a lightly burning crackle, and Allison's eyes strain to stay open. She bobbles her head a few times until she slowly rests her head on the ground and drifts off to sleep. Gabe takes first watch, while I persistently try to find a comfortable position on the crumpled dirt. The prickly blades of grass sticking into my slightly exposed lower back is annoying to the point that I give up sleeping on the ground and lean against the sap-riddled cedar tree instead.

I fix my eyes on the black sky and notice how less abundant the stars shine. In fact, I can't see many stars at all, if any, on this incredibly clear night. The only shimmer on this dark night comes from the reflected flickering of my swords resting near the fire.

I look deep beyond the burning flames, and my eyes begin to glaze over as I think back to the first time I went camping with Finnegan.

I remember those rigorous, painstaking hours of diligence—pitching a tent on my own and assiduously learning to start a fire without matches. I may not have learned those survival skills as quickly as I wanted to, but I persevered until I mastered them. I think that's why Finnegan took me camping so much during spring and summer in my early years. It wasn't so much the camping experience that drove me back and back again, as it was to conquer my frustrations and independently succeed. I really owe him much of what I've become today.

When we'd talk around the campfire, it was Finnegan's passion to share his knowledge about survival that kept me engaged. Of course the night couldn't end without a moment of awkward silence when I would ask those embarrassing questions kids usually ask their parents—like, where do babies come from? Finnegan did his best to avoid them. Aside from his lack of parenting tools, I still cherished those rare moments.

I often felt a sense of guilt knowing that perhaps my father would had loved to be the one taking me on camping trips. Even when he was home from work, he would spend countless hours in his garage instead of spending time with us. I knew he was devoted to his role as the provider for our family, and many times I wished it were him who sat next to me around those fires.

I always thought my father held a hint of resentment toward Finnegan, but that couldn't be any further from the truth. When I was eight years old during that very summer, my father had taken the day off without pay to spend time with me. He surprised me with an unexpected gift—an exquisitely handcrafted recurve bow made from exotic zebra wood and clear maple. Engraved just below the bow rest said it all: *To my loving daughter, Arena. My heart belongs to you.* All those nights he spent in his garage after a long, hard day's work was just so he could surprise me with a gift.

My heart sank with surprise and shame from any pre-judgment I may have had about my father's apparent inattentiveness. I still remember what he told me: "There are things I just can't provide for you, Arena. I would if I could, but know this: I would truly trade my job just to be with you kids, to see you grow and smile every day. You should be grateful to have someone like Finnegan around. I am indebted to his presence. I just want you to know there isn't a day that goes by that I don't wish I could be with you."

We were poor and his laboring sacrifice to work those long intolerable hours at the cement plant was his way of loving us. Without him, we wouldn't have survived. He wrapped his arms around my small frame like he never wanted to let go. I felt his cold tears on the back of my neck, but I never let him know that I knew he was crying. I had never seen my father cry until that day, and that would be the last time I ever did.

I forever respected my father for the unconditional love he showed, and for the hidden admirable qualities that sometimes love does not reveal that many of us blindly forget. I regret not having spent more time with him, and for the last six years of my life I have realized how much I need to forget how he died and remember how he lived.

I lean my weary head back on the soft tree bark and watch as the black sky unleashes a stormy wind from the far west. My heavy eyelids fight to stay open, but before they can calmly close, something erratic moving against the darkness causes me to readjust my focus. I can't quite make it out, until it finally reaches a lonely leafless tree in front of us. The pace of my heart quickens and my skin grows clammy as I watch a crow perch with his skeletal legs on the rotting branch.

I've encountered this crow before, with those same black, lifeless eyes. I should have killed him when I had the chance, but instead I left him to perch as he mocked me with that murderous stare. Nothing but death seems to creep next to this flapping creature. The wicked fowl screeches into hellish song. Suddenly, the clouds turn black, bringing with it a westerly breeze. The louder his squelch rings, the stronger the wind roars with resounding spite. I try to avoid his ominous glare, but my thoughts seem to impede me from looking away. It's not until Gabe screams and tugs on my arm that I tear away from this senseless bird.

"Arena! Across the hill," Gabe shouts, pointing to a glowing headlight about a mile from the grassy basin. I quickly kick dirt on the last of the dying flames in our fire and shake Allison awake. She's a little disoriented so I'm forced to shake more firmly.

"Allison, wake up! We have to go, now," I holler.

"What's going on?" she asks. A bit confused, she stands to her feet more alertly.

"Untie Diablo from the tree and mount up!"

I grab my things and quickly hop on Shadow's leather saddle. I take one last glance at that heartless crow, wondering if he is really made of this earth. He brings nothing to our fellowship but a forsaken hope. When the westward wind howls and the glowing lights grow closer, it becomes evident to me that this fowl was spawned from the shadow world from whence he came. Wherever this bird flies, death is soon to follow.

We ride off through the small rigid valley and into a different territory, where the terrain blesses us with softer ground and running streams of water. Through green pastures and trees a plenty, our horses gallop with determination until we are far from the lights that follow.

Hours pass through the long night, and my will to go on has ceased. The muscles that keep me from falling off this horse have exhausted, and my body is rejecting any ounce of courage I have to move forward. I'm sure Shadow appreciates my good will to stop. I don't know when the last time I had a good night's sleep was, but now is a good time to start.

We lead Diablo and Shadow into the small woods in front of us and take refuge for the rest of the night. Gabe graciously watches over Allison and me while we find a nice soft spot to rest our bodies. I find a moss-covered patch near a finely bladed grassy knoll and fall asleep within seconds of my head hitting the clover.

*   *   *

I find my thoughts surrendering to the cold tormenting images of the past, but none worse than that of General Iakov undressing me with his hateful eyes and perversely sliding his wet, calloused tongue across my cheek. My nightmare abruptly terminates, and my eyelids slowly peel back to the morning light. Half asleep, I still feel like I've been abducted back into my nightmare when I feel something cold and wet whisk across my neck.

My eyes open and the senses of reality join my body. I turn over and come face to face with a shaggy-haired mutt slobbering over me. I jump back, nearly bumping my head on a low-hovering branch, and trip over the twisted roots below it. Gabe is to my right laughing it up, while Allison tries not to smile.

"Way to go, sis," Gabe obnoxiously says, amused at my expense. I'm not overly fond of his behavior, but I'm too tired to deal with him now.

"Where did he come from?" I ask.

"Your dreams."

"Not in the mood, Gabe."

"Yeah, well that may change when you see this."

I'm not submitting to his childish games, but I have to admit, the curiosity begs me to yield. "What do you mean?" I ask.

"Come see for yourself."

I walk over and pull back the tree brush. Just beyond the hillside meadow about a mile away is a sight I thought I would never see again. The depravity that surrounds us leaves me for a moment, as my heart warms from its cold hibernation. A haven of long-awaited faces to look upon and wrap my arms around is truly within our grasp.

The once neatly painted water tower I walked past every day from school still stands erect, now rusted and abandoned like the town we left it in. I'm too excited to just stand here and wonder what's left standing. The others have long awaited our arrival, and I don't plan on prolonging this moment any further. With anxious thoughts, I excitedly untie Shadow's reins and encourage Allison to follow suite.

We race down the small sloping mound and veer to the north side, to the outskirts of town. This is the closest point to our destination without uncomfortably penetrating too deep into the city. I'm still slightly wary and unsure of the town's condition considering the unexpected escapades
we've encountered the past few days.

We cautiously keep our distance until I feel the uncertainty wear off. The last time I walked these streets, body bags decorated this town. The government had left its vile and cruel mark by killing innocent people without reason. Women and children alike scattered the lawns like rotting refuse left untouched. This city is plagued with death I wish not to remember. Buildings are still riddled with ruin, the streets are littered with filth, but no unsightly body bags are present, which gives me only a small comfort.

I search the surrounding residential area as we carefully make our way toward the old water tower. Not far from the rusty beacon lies the school where Gabe and I briefly attended. It seems like yesterday we were walking those gray halls, avoiding the likes of our personal bullies, Derrick and McKenzie. Oh, how I wish to be back there defending my brother's honor from Derrick's fist, or tweaking McKenzie and her giant ego.

The back of the schoolyard is thriving with green sprouting grass and weeds that tower over Allison from months of neglected maintenance. Strolling the empty streets, I'm almost tempted to make a small detour back to our foster house, but I know the memories will only haunt my will to press on and slow my journey. What's done is done—I can no longer go back to that place.

The old gas station looks as it was the day we left it. We tie the horses to the dilapidated billboard by the side of the station and make our way to the broken window near the back as we had always done before. The same smell, same dust, and same darkness that had graced us, brings back eerie memories, hopefully good ones this time.

The hinged metal door, rusted and all, lies attached to the floor as it did, waiting for us to enter. Just as Gabe and I had done many times before, we descend into the darkened hole beneath it where the same secret tunnel hides—the very one that Finnegan created many years ago, well before the chaos.

Walking through the long corridor to the back door of the den is nerve-wracking with every step I take. The anticipation of seeing everyone is so overwhelming, I feel a little nauseous.

The door to the den stands right before us, yet I'm too nervous to open it. My heart pounds with anxious fervor, and my hands shake with excitement, but I remain cautious and reserve my hopes until I see our friends..

Gabe turns the key, and I slowly creak the door open. The lights are still on and the den is exactly as I remember it, except it's empty. Gabe and I search every room, every closet, and secret doors, but the place has been deserted. I feel a slight sense of desperation, but I don't panic. I try to breathe calmly, convincing myself that there's a reasonable explanation for their departure.

I open the food pantry in the corner and find it well stocked with unopened rations lining the front of the shelves, or at least the assumption that no one has been consuming its contents at first glance. I'm beginning to slowly lose hope, and gradually my reasons for their disappearance become irrational.

It's not until I walk over by the door to the underground tunnels that I'm faced with a grisly reception. On the door and near one of the large tables is a trail of blood that stains the floor. There's a bullet casing below the door, red palm prints on the wall, and another reminder of the age we live in.

The disappointment is too much to bear. I feel defeated and suspended in a hopeless malaise. Though I stand here with Gabe and Allison, I feel all alone—cast from existence. Where could Father Joseph and Niki possibly be? What madness drove them from this place? Did Henry survive his condition, or worse, did he not make it back with Juliana? Too many questions to unwanted answers. My mind races with horrific thoughts.

I press my hands against the cold concrete walls and shiver with sadness. When the sting in my heart finally pierces with sorrow, I'm paralyzed with grief and loneliness. I fall to my knees and weep.

Gabe cries out Juliana's name over and over. I turn my face from the cold wall and I unnervingly watch his faith fall silently to the floor. We both stare into a desolate, lonely place with no friends, no family, no hope.

Just emptiness.

Part II

Deceiver

CHAPTER 11

Moments like these, and I feel absolutely helpless. It's not until Allison reaches out her hand to me when I truly realize my efforts have not gone unnoticed. How unfair of me to even harbor the thought of hopelessness when standing among us is a girl who's lost everything, yet she trusts in me to comfort and protect her ailing spirit.

"Take my hand," Allison says in a sweet, tender voice. I grab ahold with slight hesitation.

"They're still out there, and we're going to find them," she continues. My cold skin begins to warm with a semblance of pleasure, and any fruitlessness I held onto earlier has soon gone, leaving me with little doubt in what Allison has just spoken. Whether or not they are just words spoken from a child's lips, they are innocent and encouraging. Gabe peels himself from the floor, wipes his weary eyes, and stares intently at the wall behind us.

"What is it?" I ask. He briefly ignores my question, walks over to the shelf behind me, and grabs a piece of torn cloth stuck to the corner. He brings the piece of cloth to his nose and inhales the familiar scent as a tiny smile grows at the corners of his trembling mouth.

"Juliana." That's all he says before he reaches for a solder gun and attentively delves into a box of circuit boards. While he absorbs himself with whatever it is he's concocting, I take Allison into the knife room where I sharpen my swords and replace the blades I've lost on our journey.

"Is there anything I can help with?" Allison asks. I keenly straighten the edging of one of my swords before I hand her a box of carbon arrow shafts. I have her fix some slim-fitted nocks to the end that will fit snug, but comfortably, against the string of my bow.

When I'm done sharpening my blades, I help her attach some fletching to the arrows and cut them down to my liking. We add razor tri-tipped arrowheads to all the shafts and carefully fix a few explosive-tipped heads as well.

The painstaking task in making these custom arrows has awoken my appetite. I can see that the meticulous work Gabe has precociously created has done the same. Before I can open the pantry door to the food, Gabe is standing there with his face buried in a large can of whole pears.

While he devours the pears without an ounce of etiquette or common table manners, I grab two cans of sliced peaches and tuna fish for Allison and me. When he doesn't have his face buried in a can of fruit, I can see the determination in his eyes. It doesn't matter to me that he didn't offer us any food. His mind is solely on Juliana, and I'm okay with that. We've come too far to let hope slip from our grasp, and if a piece of cloth is the security to his confidence and fortitude, then so be it.

I'm not accustomed to this silence we share while we eat, but I wouldn't expect anything less from Gabe when he's too busy enjoying good food. Whether his silence is the result of the pain within his heart, or just the pure delight of digesting real food that blocks his sense of speech, I keep quiet.

"So what's the plan?" Allison asks. The silence is finally broken, yet I look down into the can of tuna fish, hoping Gabe will say something profound, because I haven't a damn clue what the plan is.

I wrestle with ideas in my mind while I pick at the last morsel of food in the oily can. I disengage from my wondering thoughts, and raise my head to both Allison and Gabe, who inquisitively stare at me, waiting for an answer. Though I don't have the slightest idea what to tell them, I'm suddenly stunned by an image of the old church that Henry and Father Joseph found refuge in before retreating down into the tunnels to the den. That was the last day I saw my schoolmates, the last day I enjoyed a simple life, and the last time I saw Jacob.

A pit in my stomach quickly develops. I wish to erase these memories from the belly of my conscience.

"We rest here for the night before moving on. First light, we take to the tunnels until we reach the inner city. I would like to search the old town church first," I tell them.

"Why the church?" Gabe asks.

"Just a hunch."

"Why not search for them outside?" Allison asks.

"We'll find safer passage through the tunnels. I don't know who or what's lurking out there. Besides, wherever that bloodstain leads, that's where we follow." I stare at the bloody palm print on the door, wondering who they belong to.

We finish what food our empty guts can digest until we've replenished our gluttonous appetites. Our brains seem to process at a higher intellectual level when we've had food in our stomachs, but right now, my brain and I want to find a bed to crash on. I don't care how hard, musty, or small these mattresses are, I warmly invite these claustrophobic sleeping quarters with open arms and a sleepy head.

It doesn't take but a few seconds after my head falls on the stiff pillow that I'm out like a light. I wander in and out of broken dreams that are somehow pieced together like two completely different puzzles merging into one. Nothing makes sense, and I'm forced into waking up from the constant tossing and turning on these uncomfortable beds. I think I've changed my mind. I would feel more at peace on the hard ground in the open night air than lying in here.

I toss the pillow to the side, curl up on the floor beside the bed, and lay my head on my folded jacket. I finally drift off into a deep moment of seclusion.

Into the night, I fall deep into my subconscious, digging away to what is lost or what is to come. Whether it's another vision or just some bizarre dream, it speaks to me with importance, and I can't take my eyes away from it.

Several ships pass through the east and thrust forward into the violent sea. Waves crashing into the sides spew in the air like an angry volcano. All but two ships course forward through the storm, while the other two lag behind several miles—one of which I'm standing on that is riddled with rust and grime. The other is painted solid black and appears invisible against the dark backdrop of the night sky and the thick low-lying fog. Stretching across the bow hangs a red flag and two long chains that are bound to what appears to be the captain of the ship.

There's a sound of a crying voice that's barely audible through the crashing waves, but as the storm suddenly subsides, the voice grows louder and louder. And then it hits me—it's the same crying infant sound that deceived me back at the ranch house. When the misty air finally clears, I look out and see a baby crawling on the deck toward me.

Two armed soldiers climb over the side of the bow, while the baby dangerously crawls closer to the edge. I reach for my guns, but my jacket is empty. I leap forward instead and grab the infant to shield him from the soldiers plunging toward me. I turn around, and a gunshot goes off, abruptly waking me from this nightmare.

A cold sweat sticks to my skin, while my eyes adjust to the dimly lit room. I sit upright, shivering from the cement floor, wondering how much validity there is to this dream, and if at all, what it really means.

I have no idea how long I've been asleep, but it's apparent from the numbness in my arm and leg that I've been out quite some time. There's no sunlight to determine dusk from dawn in this concrete dungeon. Regardless what time of day or night it is, my bladder's occupancy is full…again.

I head to the bathroom and notice Gabe attentively tinkering with something near the far table. Not sure if he's been up all night working, or if he's just getting a fresh start in the morning.

I gaze in the mirror and recognize right away the lack of sleep I've endured the last few nights. Whether or not these dark patches around my eyes are from sleep deprivation, the lack of rest may perpetually hinder my good judgment and perceptual cues. I can't allow myself to go on like this and risk Gabe and Allison's lives.

I cup my hands under the faucet and throw water against my face to wake me up. When I lift my head up, I'm frightened by the sudden shadow of Gorshkov's face displayed in the mirror. I nearly fall backward, clutching the doorknob to keep my balance. When I blink, only my reflection stares back at me.

Many times over have I witnessed a madness not of this world creep into my dreams; innocent blood spilled by an unseen malevolence only told in stories. But to the likeness of my fate of which I have accepted long ago, this new terror is becoming too unsettling and unnerving for the little stability I have left of my sanity.

In the main room, Allison is lying on the table next to Gabe with her legs tucked into her chest and her head gently nestled on his neatly folded jacket. She must have fallen asleep watching Gabe.

"Hard at work, brother?" I softly say, trying not to disturb Allison.

"Well, look who decided to wake up."

"Wake up? How long have I been out?"

Gabe stops what he's doing and looks at the clock on the wall before answering. "About twenty-four hours."

"Twenty-four hours! Why in the hell didn't y—"

"Relax. I thought it best to give you a sedative."

"What?"

"Look at you, Arena. You hadn't slept in days. You needed the rest."

"I'd appreciate it next time that you clue me in on what you think is good for me."

I know he meant no harm by it, but if it's the lack of sleep he's worried about, it's by my choosing. His sleeping habits may be a comfortable pleasantry, but mine can sometimes be an endless torment. I wish not to be drugged into enduring it against my will. Although I'm a wee bit pissed at his rash decision, I do, however, feel surprisingly better. I let the response of my silence soak in a bit more before continuing our conversation.

"So, what are you working on?" I ask while I look for clothes to put on.

"Tracking devices—long range. Hopefully these will keep us from getting permanently separated if that moment ever happens to present itself."

"Where the hell are my boots?"

"Oh, yeah. Here you go," he says as he tosses my boots to me..

"Whoa!"

"Yeah, I figure those old soles have walked one mile too many. They've been needing to be replaced. I made a few .. . modifications as well."

I'm speechless. The worn heels on my boots look brand new. Now I feel somewhat guilty about my stern, ungrateful response earlier.

"You're welcome," he says, responding to my dumb-struck expression.

"Thank you . . . for everything. But how did you—"

"Took them from the combat boots in the closet. Shaved, shaped, and reapplied with rubber adhesive. Quite easy really."

"Brilliant."

"Oh, and you might want to move your fingers out of the way."

I place the boots on the table. Suddenly, two serrated knife edges spring out from the rubber soles like switch blades. I'm deviously giddy as I imagine kicking my leg up and sliding the blade across a soldier's neck. I'm so awestruck by Gabe's creation, I just don't know what to say except, "I love you, dear brother."

While Gabe continues his work, I'm tempted to wake up Allison and move her to one of the beds, but she looks so peaceful curled up on the table, I just leave her be.

Standing around like this with nothing to contribute is making me want to get out of here right now. As much as I adore the weapons that grace the walls in this place, I'm beginning to feel a bit uncomfortable being immured in this claustrophobic dungeon.

I put my jacket on and wait for the right moment to slip out above ground from some fresh air. Apparently, that moment lasted less than a nanosecond because my foot doesn't even break the plane of the exit before Gabe's interrogating voice blurts out.

"Hey! Where do you think you're going?"

"I just need some air."

He just glares at me with disapproval, waiting for me to further justify my actions. "I want to check on the horses. I won't be out there long enough for you to worry. I need this, okay?" I continue.

"Fine, but at least take your gun with you."

I pull out the Beretta that I had tucked into the back of my pants. He sighs and shakes his head, but just for a moment, I can see he's trying hard not to crack a smile. His concern for me is effortlessly withdrawn when he watches me lock in the mag. He digs in the bottom of one of the many drawers behind him and tosses me a flashlight.

"Be careful, will ya?" he says to perhaps comfort his own well-being and not necessarily mine. His sincere concern has never gone unnoticed, and I'm indebted to his kindness to protect him at all costs. I get too caught up with my own conflictions, I sometimes forget how much he cares for me. I love my brother, and I don't know how I could live without him.

I leave the den and walk the lonely, white hall once again. Stuffy and quiet, it never feels short of eerie in here, especially with a few lights out now. The interior of the gas station smells musty as always, but something seems different about it. I cautiously examine the back window before climbing out. It's dark outside, but I can see Shadow and Diablo tied up. They quietly graze on the few sprouts of grass patches that have struggled to grow in the infertile soil behind the station.

I gently stroke the side of Shadow's face and lightly run my fingers through his soft mane as he moves his head close into my chest. I wrap my arms around his thick neck and rub my cheek against his warm, coarse hair.

The warm evening breeze is nothing less than serene until Shadow jerks to the sound of breaking branches and feet slowly shuffling on the dry, crunchy ground.

I slowly pull out my gun and hide behind the side of Shadow. The louder the sound grows so does Diablo's restlessness. I try calming him, but it's no use; he's not accustomed to my touch. I draw my gun toward a shadow approaching from within the line of trees and bushes covering the side fence near the station.

It's too dark without the moonlight to unveil the prowling silhouette, but it's a person for sure; there's no mistaking that. I try to conceal my entire body behind Shadow's long legs, but he's spooked and moving a lot.

I ease my way over and position myself behind the splintered pole where Diablo is tied up. The shadow creeps closer and closer to the gas station window, and I'm afraid with every movement that spooks Diablo, I'll be forced to make a hasty decision.

It's somewhat strange that the dark figure hasn't seen the horse twenty feet away. Slower and slower the shadow lumbers toward the dim-lit building; in fact, if I didn't know better, I would say the person is limping.

I brace myself behind the billboard and draw my gun forward, ready to shoot. A scream pierces the night air in the far distance. My patience is worn too thin, and I make no effort to drudge this mystery on any longer, especially now that someone screaming has been added to this unwanted escapade. I quickly leap out from behind the pole with my gun drawn and shout, "Get down on the ground, now!"

The person effortlessly falls to the ground face down, without any resistance. I shine the flashlight near the bottom of the person's tattered shoes. I examine bloodstains that cover the pant legs and gradually move up the body from what now appears to be the shape of a woman. Blood drips from her arm, and she begins to cry. I quickly withdraw my gun.

She lifts her head slightly and my heart suddenly spills into my stomach with an overflow of elation. I drop the flashlight and fall to my knees, gasping. I gently grab her hand, fighting not to cry. I can barely get the word out.

"Niki."

CHAPTER 12

There are times when you just don't have the emotional strength to move, and times when your spirit forces you to. I think I'm experiencing both, because I don't think I've ever been so elated to see such a familiar face. I pull back Niki's blond matted hair and lovingly embrace her.

"Arena . . . is it really you?" she mutters, trembling and weeping on my shoulder.

"I missed you so much," I say overjoyed with exhaustion. "Are you badly hurt?"

"A few cuts and bruises, but the others—"

"Others, where?" I excitedly interrupt, but before she can continue her sentence, the scream I heard earlier bellows out much louder and closer, abruptly silencing our exchange. Niki's eyes flash with terror and I'm almost too afraid to ask her about the others. The scream draws closer to the backside of the fence. Niki's hands tremble and her eyes widen.

"Juliana," she says, shaking. I quickly help her to her feet and through the back window.

"Stay down and hide," I assert. I race to the edge of the station and climb over to the other side of the fence. There's angry chattering and scuffling just around the corner on the next street. The beat of my heart races the closer I creep down the side street. That scream definitely belongs to Juliana.

I quicken my pace down a narrow alley when a sudden burst of light shines just to my right. Two dark images quickly pass a large crack in the fence where the light gleams through, and a roaring sound of gashing metal explodes in a nearby building. Smoke and debris quickly fills the air.

Men are yelling, Juliana is screaming, and a slew of gunshots go off. The screaming suddenly stops, and my pace emerges into a full sprint. I turn the last corner and find Juliana on the ground next to a soldier who is dragging his belly across the dirt like a snake and clenching his leg. Juliana rolls on her side and grimaces. From out of the dark, a large man hovers over her and draws his gun to her head.

I step out of the shadow and quickly pull the trigger. The man falls back into a puddle of gas that trails from a large truck. It's tipped on its side and smoldering with black smoke and burning oil.

A flaming spark suddenly erupts from the truck, and the thin trail of fuel gradually burns toward the soldier's body. I rush over and grab Juliana, pulling her away from the puddle of gas. She's alive, but badly skinned-up on her right leg, where her bloody jeans are torn. The sheer weight of carrying her is just too daunting. I briefly set her down out of the light to catch my breath.

While I lean against a chain-link fence, I keenly observe the perimeter. My vision is partially hindered from all the smoke.

Suddenly, a man waving his arms like a deranged orangutan sprints toward us from the dark street, waving and shouting Juliana's name. I quickly draw my gun. I don't recognize the voice, and the smoldering plume of blackness, which is now burning my eyes, is distorting his image.

The only thing acutely notable about his peculiar frenzy are the two soldiers chasing him. As the man gets closer, he starts to bear an uncanny resemblance to someone I know. With every bumbling step he takes, my eyes grow ever wider as I finally recognize his face.

Whether or not my eyes have deceived me, a small bit of joy beguiles my heart even if it is quite unexpected—it's Harold, the underground security guard we coerced into helping us sabotage President Kriel's White House dinner party. But it was his bravery that helped Gabe and I escape from the training facility that I remember the most. The death of General Iakov seems many moons ago.

Aside from Harold's faithful decision to help us, all I can recall from that dreadful moment was blood spewing from Finnegan's pierced side. I've never felt so defeated like that, not since Myra died in my arms. When her lifeless body was pressed against mine, I felt dead inside.

I realize now how much Harold meant to us. Without him, we may not have made it out alive. The last time our eyes met, I was burying Finnegan off the side of the road down below that steep hill. And that's when I made the painful choice to leave Harold there while Gabe and I departed on foot. It was necessary though; he wouldn't have survived with us.

I squint my eyes and carefully aim just over Harold's shoulder.

"No, wait . . . stop, stop!" he shouts. I sharply squeeze the trigger without an ounce of uncertainty in my aim, and the two men following Harold fall to their deaths. Harold quickly retreats to the ground with his hands caressing the back of his head. He gradually raises his neck, looks back at the two dead men, and is probably wondering what the hell just happened.

"Harold! Come on . . . it's me, Arena."

"Arena? Holy shit, you're alive," he says with exuberance.

A dozen soldiers come storming from a building a couple of streets over.

"Come on! Quick . . . help me with her," I say. Harold delicately lifts Juliana from the ground and carries her back to the den while I despondently stand there waiting and hoping that somehow I'll see Henry or Father Joseph running closely behind. Unfortunately, the soldiers emerging in our direction rescinds any thought I had of hoping.

I make a run for it with whistling bullets grazing the back of the fence tops. Whether it's just a pure adrenaline rush or the persuasion of the bullets ablaze behind us, the athletic fervor displayed by Harold's strength and pace is impressive. His portly figure that I had been used to seeing is no more. Either he's turned his beefy stature into a raging bull of muscle or he's hiding his broad physique behind the extra-large shirt.

While I shadow Harold's steps back to the den, my troubled mind floods with unwanted thoughts. How much longer can we truly last?

Harold carefully lifts Juliana up through the window where Niki grabs her legs on the other side. I watch intently over by the fence brush while Harold struggles to squeeze his husky body through the window. Apparently, this isn't the normal entrance he's used to. I briefly stand down my guard and help push him through.

After a slight nudge and an abrupt but successful effort, Harold slides through and clumsily falls to the floor. Before I make my way in, I suddenly remember that Shadow and Diablo are still tied up.

"What are you waiting on? Come on," Harold says to me.

"I'll be right behind you. I just need to take care of something," I tell him. I hand him the key to the metal door and rush over to the horses. Risky or not, I'm not taking a chance in letting these soldiers suspect anyone other than a vagrant is residing in this dilapidated station. As sad as it makes me, these horses need to go.

I struggle to untie the reins from the billboard post, and the sweat on my palms isn't making the situation any better either. The stomping sound of boots grows louder, and now Shadow's reins are knotted. I stretch back the reins as hard as I can from the post, but it doesn't budge. A fiery light across the fence blooms into the black sky, and a sudden shadowy reflection of Russian soldiers flicker dangerously close.

I frantically search for my knife to cut the reins, but I forgot to bring it with me. Dammit, when am I going to learn? There's no time to fidget with these leather reins, so I shoot the ropes with my gun. I promptly slap Shadow and Diablo on their rears and make a dash for the window.

The metal door is wide open and Harold's head is poking out, waiting for me. I grab a large rubber mat that covered this once-hidden door and pull it across and over the metal edging, then slip underneath and down into the hall. Harold closes and locks the door behind me, and we wait in the hopes to hear nothing but silence above.

There is a slight tremble in my hand of which I've not felt in quite some time. I can't tell if I'm still in shock from the sight of Juliana and Niki, or if my confidence is weakening.

Juliana gradually awakens, moaning and squirming on the floor before she rests her back against the wall. When she's fully conscious of her surroundings, she gingerly pulls back part of her tattered jeans from the dry blood crusted over her wounded leg. Her eyes shift to me. A moment of expressive elation briefly lights up her disheartened face before she begins to weep.

"Arena," she cries out. I gently wrap my arms around her while she leans her head into my chest and cries.

A sudden trashing of enraged soldiers scamper across the floor right above us. The rush of clatter litters the gas station, bringing down heavy shelves and God knows what, slamming to the floor. Sounds like a riot above us, and here we are, hunkered down below waiting to flee it. If we don't move soon, I'm afraid this rescue will be for naught. I feel vulnerable, yet resolute in my will to survive, and the only thing that separates us from an immediate departure for safety is this small metal barrier.

Sweat profusely drips from Harold's petrified face. With his eyes shut, and his hand firmly wrapped around the handle of the door, he mumbles under his breath a desperate but necessary prayer.

All of the sudden, a shouting match ensues among the men, and a deep thud rattles the handle of the door. I quickly reach for my gun, pull out the mag, and find it half-full. When that door comes crashing through with soldiers, I can either stand here and fight or hope that we make it to the other end of the corridor before they do. This desperate plight to stay or flee is quite obvious to me.

I return the mag to my gun, lock it, and carefully help Juliana to her feet, ready to make a run for it. The incoherent shouting above abruptly dies and the silence returns. This unexpected change of events can mean only one of two things: they've given up looking for us and moved on, or they've discovered the mysterious door in the floor. Regardless, I'm not willing to stick around to find out. Niki pulls Juliana to her side and moves down the hall.

"Harold . . ." I say. He doesn't respond, nor does he budge from his position—he just sits there on the metal steps mumbling to himself.

"Harold . . . hey, snap out of it!" I continue.

"Wh-what?"

"Let's go!"

Without looking back, we hurry down the long corridor as fast as Juliana can move. With the weighted burden of Juliana's injury, it seems like an eternity before we finally reach the den door.

I watch closely and impatiently while Harold, who suddenly forgot how to use a key, fidgets with the lock. Seeing him bumbling with a simple task reminds me of a moment I had with my father when I was seven years old.

Standing there with him in the frigid, cold December air on our doorstep, waiting excitedly for him to open the door to his thirty-fifth surprise birthday party.

Watching my father bumbling with the key just like Harold is now was a moment I'll never forget. I couldn't help but laugh when he put the key in upside down, breaking it off in the lock, while everyone inside was anxiously anticipating the door to open. We stood outside shivering, while my father embarrassingly tried to jar the knob loose. I think he enjoyed watching me giggle at his silly mistake or his otherwise inept door-unlocking skills.

It was obvious he knew about the surprise, but he wasn't one to spoil anyone's fun, so he made a valiant effort to play along. He took out his knife and jammed it in-between the frame and knob, working the lock clear from the jamb. It would have been an awkward moment if he had to ring the doorbell to his own surprise party. But it wasn't necessarily the key fiasco that made that moment so memorable in as much as it was the small, precious conversation we had before walking through the door.

"When did you get to be so beautiful?" he said to me, as my already rosy, cold cheeks blushed brighter. "You're just like your mother . . . your beauty stands out even through the most disparaging of times."

What could a seven year old say to that which she doesn't fully understand? All I could muster was, "I love you, Papa." I don't know if I fully understand how much he truly meant to me until he was gone.

My father did nothing less than what a father should or is expected to do. He clothed me, fed me, held me, and comforted me. That is the nourishment that comforts hardship. There are no boundaries to which love can show if you're willing to truly sacrifice for the needs of others without expecting anything in return. That was my father.

"You've got the key upside down," I say to Harold. When he finally turns the knob, we rush in, and close and lock the door behind us.

Allison comes dashing in, slightly distraught when she sees the condition of the others lying exhausted on the floor. She stands there shocked for a brief moment before she screams out Gabe's name and comes running over to help aid Juliana.

I help Allison take Juliana over to a comfortable chair, while I watch Harold ardently comfort Niki—something I'm not used to seeing from him the short time we've been together. Upon further curiosity, it's the warm and welcoming reaction Niki displays that has me more perplexed. Have I gone mad, or is this strange courtship a result of an ongoing bizarre romantic escapade? Harold couldn't be much older than Niki, who's pushing twenty one, but it clearly wouldn't matter anyway—they seem to be in love.

Gabe, still half asleep, leisurely dawdles into the room and gazes with confusion. Everyone stares back at him. Once he realizes Juliana isn't a dream, he immediately rushes over by her side and passionately embraces her.

Allison's recent affection for Gabe hasn't gone unnoticed. She respectfully and politely relieves herself from Juliana's side and leaves them both alone, and I notice her eyes are brimming with tears.

I can relate to how she's feeling right now. A joyful feeling fills half my heart with delight at seeing everyone back, but the other half is filled with bitterness and sadness. When I look upon Harold's nurturing affectionate relationship with Niki, and see Juliana and Gabe reunite with a tender clasp, I feel all alone.

I selfishly wish it were me to have someone to embrace, but instead, I just stand here and stew into self-pity. My pinned-up self-absorbed thoughts come un-shelved. I close my eyes with disdain. *Why am I not happy for them? Is this bitterness who I've become now? Jacob is never coming back. Why can't I just accept that? Please . . . help me. I need you.*

I open my eyes and wonder if this is truly what's left of our fellowship. No one has mentioned anything about Henry or Father Joseph, and I'm beginning to think there's good reason for it. But I'm desperate to know anyway.

"So, where are they?" is all I say, before I receive cold stares from Niki and Harold.

"Niki . . . I have to know," I mutter. A dead calm infuses the room for a few seconds before Harold finally speaks up.

"The last we saw of them was in the old church near Tillian Park."

"Why were they at the church?"

"They were being held captive before we were able to escape. The last two weeks have been hell here, you know. Ever since the town was taken over by some Russian insurgents, there has been nothing but pain and death. We were caught off guard downtown when they showed up. We were searching for supplies . . . medical supplies, anything we could get our hands on really."

"For what?" I ask.

"Two days before the Russians showed up, we were out scouring for others who needed refuge, when all of a sudden a teenage boy comes stumbling outside the abandoned market right in front of us, bleeding profusely. He'd been shot in the stomach—twice. It was obvious he wasn't going to make it, but before he died, he told us he had a pregnant sister who was being held against her will in one of the houses near the library."

"By who?"

"He never said. He just kept saying, 'They're coming, they're coming, do not believe them.' And then he was dead. Whatever madness drove him away, he was better off dead. By the looks of his face, he was definitely tortured. Jagged scars covered his back, but the most peculiar thing about the boy was the barcoded tattoo on his left wrist. Half of his wrist was either mutilated, or the skin was folded back, as if he was trying to remove the tattoo from his body with a razor blade.

"It was getting too dark, so we had to wait until the next day to go searching for the boy's sister. It's not safe to go out in the dark anymore. Aside from Russian soldiers, it's the mad men you have to avoid. They are on no one's side, raging with hate and desperate to stay alive, even if it means robbing and killing you.

"We looked for the boy's sister the next morning. After hours of searching, we finally found her chained to a bedpost, nearly starved to death. We took her from the house, and that's when we went to go seek for medical supplies from the hospital, or what's left of it."

"Arena, nothing has been the same since you left. It's a ghost town now; everyone is either dead, or a slave to someone," says Niki.

"What happened to the pregnant woman?" I ask.

Niki pinches her lips tight, and her eyes glaze over with tears. She squeezes her fist until her knuckles turn white and buries her face into Harold's shoulder.

"A small resistance group of about forty or fifty came into town looking for recruits—scouring for anyone they could persuade to join in the fight against the government's control. Very few of these groups carry any meaningful value with them. Most are made up of pissed-off hypocrites who are no better than the government controlling them," Harold says.

"They lie, they steal . . . they even whore out their women in hopes they can persuade recruits to join," Juliana finally speaks out.

I'm taken aback by what I'm hearing. Was I the cause of this chaos or was this already foreseen?

Harold lovingly rubs Niki's shoulder. "When we reached the hospital, it had already begun. Helicopters flew over, and then heavy military trucks drove into town. We had nowhere to go without being seen, so we hid in the hospital until we knew it was safe to go back, but it never was. And then it happened.

"The first wave in the battle came from the resistance. They showered bullets on the tanks, killing maybe two or three men, but it was useless. When they retreated toward the front entrance of the hospital, a shell from one of the tanks slammed into the hospital and killed them all.

"And that's when we ran out the side door and followed Father Joseph to the old church near the park. He knew that was the best chance to escape back to the den. When we entered the back of the church, we were greeted by a band of Russian soldiers setting up a radio base in the sanctuary.

"They bound our hands and locked us up in a dark room in the back of the church. For days, they starved us, beat us, even took advantage . . . of some," he says, looking down at Niki.

"For two weeks, we stayed holed-up in that musty, urine-soaked room, being interrogated about other resistance groups. None of us knew a damn thing, but on the second week, I guess they grew tiresome of our lies. They felt it necessary to remind us how valuable the truth is, so they shot the pregnant woman in the head. We knew we were next, so it was crucial to find a way out. Father Joseph knew that the room next us had a basement with a door that led to a small tunnel through the gardens and eventually to a storm door that opened near the outer part of the park.

"For days we took turns carving a hole into the sheetrock with Henry's buckle. We had to be careful not to be too loud because of the guards standing outside the door. And when we finally broke through the other side, it was all for nothing. A platoon leader burst through the door and insisted we tell them the truth or be executed on the spot. When Father Joseph looked at Henry, then turned to me, I somehow knew what was about to happen.

"Father Joseph shouted out something in Russian, and they took him and Henry out in the sanctuary, leaving us behind with the door shut and no guards. I felt sick to my stomach leaving them behind, but I knew it was our only chance to leave, and I'm forever grateful for their sacrifice. They chose to do something I don't know if I could have ever done.

"Before I left the room, I took one last look and saw Henry and Father Joseph on their knees, blindfolded and with their hands tied behind their back. That's the last I saw of them before I left."

"So they're alive."

"They were held at gunpoint . . . believe what you will, but don't misinterpret this as some kind of hope. Those soldiers are not forgiving. We were lucky to get out."

"They saved us, Arena. If they hadn't done what they did, we wouldn't be here," Niki says, trembling.

I glower with hatred while my mind painfully imagines how they died. I still can't believe it . . . and I won't until I know for sure.

"They're still out there, and I'm going to find them: dead or alive. I won't leave them to rot behind."

"Are you insane? There're soldiers everywhere out there. We barely made it back here alive," says Harold.

"We live in an insane world. Anything less would be irrational." I slam my scorpion dagger into the table. "I'm not leaving them behind."

"You can't do this alone."

"I know, that's why you're coming with me."

"Wh-what?" stutters Harold.

"You know the landscape where these soldiers dwell, and you know exactly the place you escaped from. I need you."

"Wait a minute, Arena," Niki chimes in.

"Don't worry, I'll bring him back in one piece."

"One piece. . . . how about alive?" Harold says nervously.

"Under no circumstance do any of you leave this den. This is the only safeguard we have now," I tell them. I try to avoid Juliana's eyes, but I can't. I feel magnetized to her sad- ness when she watches Gabe load a mag into his gun. I look upon his distressed face and wonder if I'm doing the right thing. He doesn't look at me, but I know he knows I'm watching him.

"Gabe . . ." I whisper.

"No," he says, raising his hand. "I choose to go on my own. You're my sister, and I'm not leaving your side again. This isn't just your fight, you know. We were in this together from the beginning, and I plan on keeping it that way."

"But—"

"Juliana will be fine. Besides, I intend on coming back."

"So do I."

Before I gear up, I find a portable welder sitting beneath the far right table and roll it over to Gabe.

"Before we leave, make sure that door is welded shut. That entrance is no longer safe. We will have to take passage through the tunnels from now on. We leave in ten minutes, so say your good-byes now."

I step into the knife room to replenish my blades, but instead I'm greeted by an unexpected sadness. Allison sits on her knees staring at the corner of the room. I fight my instincts to meddle in her privacy. It's not enough that she feels all alone, but to have to see us leave and possibly not come back probably feels too overwhelming right now. She turns and faces me with a dreadful watch.

"I have nothing now. No one to hold, no one to come home to," she says.

"Don't say that."

"It's true, though."

"Doesn't have to be."

"You know . . . Harold was right."

"Right about what?" I curiously ask.

"That boy, who was shot . . . was better off dead."

Allison's glassy eyes glaze over with tears. "And I wish I were too," she meekly says.

I hold her tightly while she cries uncontrollably in my arms. I can sympathize with her conflicting emotions, because I felt that same pain when Jacob died.

I see so much of me in her, with all that bottled-up anger and frustration, that you wish the world around you would just disappear and life would cease to exist. With both of us losing our parents at a young age and trying to survive through this wicked hell is an uncanny parallel. I see my life recklessly trodden all over again through Allison's experience, but it's not the killing that plagues my misery as much as it's the loneliness I fear the most.

I hold her close and pray. My mind gradually eases, and my voice begins to shudder as the spoken Hebrew language quietly spills from my tongue.

She stops crying, sits back on her knees, and rubs the small silver locket that belonged to her mother. I can sense an immediate change in her spirit, but there's something else that ails her broken heart. I take her small hands in mine and provoke a half-hearted smile from her face.

"You know . . . you're the only prodigious ten-year-old I've met who could have survived this long. There's much more to you than you could ever know."

"I'm eleven now."

"What?" I ask, a little confused.

"Today's my birthday."

She fiddles with the dangling hearts on her wristlet. I look down at the silver bracelet and watch her soak in the memories it brings her from the past. She must have received it for her birthday.

"It's beautiful," I say.

"My sister Lily gave it to me last year when I turned ten."

My hand searches for the silver pendent pressed against my chest. I close my eyes and allow the memories of my mother to wash over me. I shiver when I think back on my ninth birthday.

I lift Allison's chin up. "When we get back—and we will be back—we'll celebrate this special day."

"I love you," she utters with trembling lips.

"I love you too. You will forever be a part of me, and I will never forget that."

"Please come back . . . please, I don't want to be alone."

"You pray to your Father, and I promise you won't be."

"You promise?"

"Yes, I promise," I say.

"Arena," she says before I exit the room.

I turn and see a child's eyes filled with endless courage spoiled by the nectar of wrath.

"Kill 'em all."

Not something I would ever want to hear from an eleven-year-old, much less uttered from my own lips, but what's made must be unmade, and it's up to me to see it through.

CHAPTER 13

I retrieve my bow on the table and can't help but notice the happiness Harold has brought to Niki when he holds her. Standing there, caressing the end of my bow as I string it up, I ponder what would have been if I'd never opened that envelope. Would Father Joseph have pursued Gabe and I anyway, or would we have been among the many convulsing to our death on the school grounds when it all began?

Despite how this may all end, I'm grateful for every moment I can spend with the people I love for as long as God is willing to allow. I tuck my dagger snugly into its sheath, dress my quiver with the newly made arrows, and double-check my mags before we begin our arduous trek through the caverns below the city.

When I bend down to tie my boots, I notice a dry spot of blood that trickles from the tunnel door. I walk over to the splattered blood on the wall beside the door and slowly slide my hand over it, trying to understand what the hell happened here.

"Where did these blood stains come from?" I curiously ask.

"That's an interesting story," Harold says.

"Indulge me, and forgive me for being a bit intrusive when I ask how in the hell did you ever find this place?"

"Why don't you ask your brother that?"

"I told him about this place," Gabe says before his disquieting eyes meet mine. "It only felt right to.

"When?" I ask.

Gabe stands there in silence for a brief moment before continuing. "After he helped us bury Finnegan. Do you not remember when we left him beside the road? It didn't feel right to just leave him behind like that."

I have regretted leaving him, but who knows how it would have ended for him when the invasion started. What's done is done, and every step we take has already been written. Any quarrels or contemplations over what-ifs serves us no benefit. I look over at Niki, who is leaning on Harold's shoulder, and realize that everything happens for a reason whether we like it or not.

"I'm glad you're here with us, Harold, but that still doesn't explain the blood."

"About four months ago, I had no idea what to expect when I arrived to this desolate town. There was so much chaos and civil unrest, I didn't know who to trust, but you were good to me, both of you. I had nothing else to lose but to trust you, so I did exactly as Gabe instructed me to.

"I found the tunnels through a sewer grate and meandered in circles before I finally reached the underground church Gabe had talked about. It took me a day to find my way, which I know you will probably have no hard time believing. I finally came to that door on the other side, but of course I had no key.

"I banged and banged on the door until my knuckles bled, but no one answered. When I could no longer lift my arm to knock, I just sat there, leaning against the metal door, and wondered if I had made a mistake coming here. I had no idea how long I had been out, but the vibrations of the metal woke me up, and when I looked up I saw the door cracked open.

"I probably should have been more cautious before just throwing the door open and running in, but I didn't want to wait any longer in that musty, dark tunnel, so I took a chance. And I would do it all over again just to see her face," Harold says, smiling at Niki.

"And?" I ask.

"She shot me . . . in the shoulder, and deservingly so with all that's gone on outside of these doors. It wasn't until I mentioned your name when she finally put down the gun. The rest, as they say, is history."

"Lovely story to tell your kids," I say, winking at a slightly embarrassed Niki. "I'm sorry to say, but looks like you'll have to endure a little while longer in these musty, dark tunnels. It's time to go."

As Harold, Gabe, and I enter the tunnel, I pray that our companionship will long sustain when we return with or without Henry and Father Joseph. This fellowship must stay together if we expect to survive.

The quiet walk through these stale creepy tunnels makes my body anxious and my mind unsettling. I can only assume Gabe and Harold are having similar diversions because no one has said a word since we left. If there are any conversations among us, they are kept deep within, and these bleak underground channels aren't going to make it any more inviting while we continue.

It's not until we reach the old underground church where I first took refuge down here before Harold speaks.

"Seems like old times, no?" he says, breaking the awkward silence with friendly but annoying banter.

"I'll feel better when we all come back in one piece," I say. I pause for a moment and reevaluate what I just said. My negativity towards Harold's chitchat is undeserved, so I try to redact my statement. "But, yes, it does feel good to be back."

This is unfamiliar territory down here for me, and I can't tell one passage from the next. With the exception of the open room in the church, every stone-lined, grime-ridden wall looks the same. Each tunnel entrance is braced with an arch opening that trails off into different directions, and the only directional saving grace we can count on is Gabe's memory from when he and Father Joseph took passage to our house. Sure, we were smart enough to carry flashlights with us, but just dumb enough to forget a compass.

The only thing holding these old tunnels together besides decaying mortar is the quality craftsmanship of the past. They were meant to stand the test of time. Let's just hope their time isn't up, because the walls are a bit unsettling down here. Because the newer sewer system was built about five years ago, this underground water dwelling is dry, and the only thing left is distant memories.

"This way," Gabe says, pointing to the right.

For every step I move forward in this damp tunnel, I feel strangely comfortable with the task at hand, as if it were no more than a common stroke painted across life's daily doldrums—yet in terms of its dangerous consequences, it would feel like a death sentence to others.

When we turn the corner, there's a thin beam of light shining through a small opening in the ceiling about a hundred paces in front of us. I have a sudden case of anxiety as we near the light, and it's not because of the dangers we are about to encounter. It's the uncomfortable feeling of the unknown that I fear—finding them dead should be no surprise, but it's the hope that I cling to that may crush me.

I briefly muse over the last year of my life and realize how much I've changed. I feel almost completely desensitized to the world we live in now, and in that respect, I fear not death. I'm willing to fight for something I believe in rather than hold on to something I can't.

I poke my head into a shaft of light illuminating down into the tunnel and notice a large pecan branch hovering above a grate next to a lamppost. Before moving any further, I want to at least see how far away we are, so I grab onto the sides of the filthy, corroded ladder railings and slowly climb up each rusted rung.

Through the tiny jagged holes, I can just barely make out a green slide and a row of more pecan trees. This must be the playground in Tillian Park, but I'm not sure—there are three parks in the area, and all are landscaped with pecan trees.

"Well, what do you see?" asks Gabe.

"A park, but I don't know which one," I answer, trying to push the grate up. I don't have the leverage or the strength to move this iron vent, so I get Harold to climb up and remove it for me. He may be slow, but he's built like an ox, and I know Gabe doesn't possess the strength any more than I possess grace.

Harold grunts his way through the top of the grate and pushes it up and over. He pokes his bulbous head out above the opening and examines the grounds before signaling us to come up.

"See, I told you I would need you," I say to Harold, who appears to be out of breath at the moment. Though I was sure this was Tillian Park, it's not, but it may serve us better that it isn't. We've climbed through the sewer grate outside of Metro Park, which hasn't been used in a long while. It's secluded, run down, and has been fenced off from the city—but more importantly, it's just as close to the church as Tillian Park.

We are about a quarter of a mile on the east side of the church just right outside Baker's Pavilion, most of which is blocked off from the city by a twenty-foot chain-link fence. The majority of the treacherous jaunt will be through a tangled braid of wooden briar I don't care to venture through, but it's isolated from the main streets that are flooded with militant adversaries. I feel more comfortable in the woods anyhow, especially near familiar territory.

We come near the church, and just as expected, several soldiers stationed outside block the front entrance. Not that I was expecting to just walk right in unannounced, but preferably undetected. After conversing with Harold, the side door to the praying room seems to be the logical choice, but still dangerous nonetheless.

I part through the vigorously sprouting vines that are intertwined across our exit with my dagger, and find a rather small but adequate opening to the side lawn of the church. Not two seconds pass as I step through when two large trucks packed with soldiers slowly drive behind the church on Melbourne Street.

I quickly retreat back into the leafy burrow and patiently wait until they are gone. When I finally see that it's clear, I tug on Gabe's arm before I make a run for it to the door, which is surprisingly unlocked. The room is dark and cold and smells of rotting flesh. The smell alone keeps me from wanting to know what's lying around in here, so I avoid turning on the light switch and walk as cautiously as I can through the opened door in front of us.

Through the door and to the right leads to a long hall that is faintly lit. It's too dark to see if anyone is hiding in here, and if they are, it would be strangely unorthodox when there are two guards standing right outside the door.

"This way," says Harold, leading us to the back of the church. It seems way too quiet in here for any malevolent activity to be going on, and it's becoming awkwardly uncomfortable. Why would any soldiers be guarding this place unless something of value was here? It feels strangely empty in a place created for refuge.

Harold abruptly stops near a cracked door and carefully opens it.

"This is where they had us kept," he says, staring at a puddle of blood near the corner of the room. I watch him gaze with a sadness I haven't seen from him, and it troubles my soul knowing what he had to witness. I try to get his attention, but he seems too engrossed in the red stain to hear me.

"Hey . . . come on, let's go," I say, tugging on his elbow. I'm not sure what transpired in this room, and I don't feel the need to ask. Enough pain has passed our way, and it won't get any easier from here on out. Whatever it was has tragically changed him.

There are two other rooms to the right, one of which is locked, and the other with the door unhinged. I take a quick scan of the open room before my flashlight burns out; it's beginning to glow dim, and I don't have a backup. The room is bare except for a few dead mice shriveled up in the corner. One seems to be moving, but upon closer review, it's not alive. I've seen enough dead creatures in my life to know it's nothing more than maggots crawling around the inside of the rodent's belly.

I take a quick peek up ahead through a small corridor that reaches no further than twenty paces. The walls appear clean, almost pristine, covered with framed tapestries with the Holy Scriptures embroidered on them. This dark hall feels lonely and untouched, yet I feel uneasy as screaming voices incite the thoughts inside my head.

While the flashlight flickers, I struggle to find my way, bumping my boots against the uneven wooden planks in the floor. The light finally fades to black and I'm left to clutch the walls to help me see through the blackness. I carefully whip my arm back to search for Harold and Gabe, who are walking so close they're nearly upon my heels. There's an eerie quietness in the air except for a faint scratching sound scuttling against the dry, rotting floor.

Every time I step, a crackling and popping sound discharges from underneath my boots that feels kind of like granola. I stop for a moment and bang on the flashlight until it softly glows for a few seconds long enough to reveal that the floor is infested with a scurrying battalion of Texas-sized cockroaches.

Disgusting creatures, but nothing I'm not already accustomed to seeing, until one the size of a potato chip rears back its brown, waxy wings and takes flight. My walk quickly turns into a canter until we reach the end of the hall, where a small emitting light glimmers toward the left. I take a deep breath and draw my guns close to my chest.

Just around the corner from where we are standing leads to the main room of the church; an asylum that once was, but is no more. It reeks of carnage and a slow whispering of death now. This is no sanctuary—this is but a tomb filled with tragedy and misery. In here lies nothing of what I'm looking for, and if Henry and Father Joseph truly are dead, I'm forever indebted for their sacrifice.

While I carefully walk between the broken pews, I become drawn to the unusual light near the corner, where a large, black drape shades the bizarre lonely lit space. Shining above the black cloth, a low wattage floodlight spotlights the floor below.

Harold takes to the right of the pews, and Gabe wanders to the left while I stand grounded in front of the mysterious light, perplexed by the oddity of the situation.

Something just doesn't seem as it should. A cold shiver crawls up my spine, and I feel like I'm being watched.

Harold and Gabe slowly approach the light when suddenly I hear a small brushing sound slide against the floor followed by a strange, muted murmur.

"Stop!" I say before they move any further.

"What is it?" asks Gabe.

"Stay out of the light."

"What do you see?"

"I don't know, but—"

"But what?" asks Harold.

I quickly race around to where Harold is standing and move toward the back of the dark draping fabric that's shielding whatever is making the sound. I draw my guns forth and blindly, but cautiously, aim into the darkness. A flash of shadows intermittently sway back and forth behind the black drop.

I pull out the flashlight and twist and knock until the flicker sustains long enough to shine on what 's moving in the background. A desperate gasp of air inhales into my lungs. With hands bound, mouths gagged, and hanging from thick, braided ropes, Henry and Father Joseph dangle in agony.

CHAPTER 14

"Henry! My God, what did they do?" I say, disturbed by their condition. I lift the light up to get a look at the rope that has them bound and notice the long, raised abrasions running across their bare backs while blood drips down to the floor.

Their faces are barely recognizable from all the floating dust sticking to their sweat-soaked skin. The only thing not stained red or covered in filth are the rags partially stuffed in their mouths. Their bare, dry, cracked feet are covered in blisters and barely touch the roach-infested floor.

"My God," I utter under my breath, wondering what kind of man of such callous hate would do this. I move toward the edge of the drape to help get them down, but Henry mumbles hysterically underneath the wadded rag in his mouth and frantically shakes his head.

"Gabe, stop!" I say before he walks any further to cut down Father Joseph.

"What?" he asks.

"I don't know, something doesn't feel right." I look back at Henry's face to try to decipher his body language, but I'm bewildered by his intense expression. Then he nods his chin over his left shoulder and shifts his eyes in the same direction.

I follow his eyes, and when I peer over to the back corner of the wall, I notice two small, glimmering, green dots. These nearly invisible low-power lasers are the only thing separating us from getting to Henry and Father Joseph. It's a trap, and they're the bait.

I bend down to see if there are any other low-lying beams to cross, but nothing else appears to be flickering from the corner.

"What is it?" Gabe asks.

"Come over and see for yourself."

He kneels down beside me and assesses the ridiculous setup. This just doesn't make a whole lot of sense. It seems absurd to think someone wasted their time with this poorly made mousetrap, if it wasn't purposefully made like this. Either it's borderline stupidity or mysteriously clever.

"What do you make of it?" I ask.

"Seriously, this is what they came up with? We'd be better off killing the two guards outside and walking out of here through the front door," he responds. Dangerous, but he's right.

"Exactly my point. Why go through the arduous production of setting up these ridiculous lasers when they could have just as easily secured the area with cameras or guards."

"Can't you just blow some dust on the beams to see them glow?" Harold pipes in. His contribution to this puzzling dilemma is just an affirmation that his skills are best suited elsewhere. I've been around Finnegan, who was a highly trained special ops leader, long enough to know that the movies conjure up on-screen fallacies to spice things up. I admit it's fun, but it's pure horse shit nonetheless.

"Even if you were to use dust, it would have to be used on visible-frequency lasers, and it would scatter too much energy, setting the alarm off anyway. Besides, unless there's been a recent technological advance in magically invisible reflectors, these so-called lasers are reflecting nowhere," Gabe explains.

"What do you mean?" Harold asks.

"He means they're a decoy . . . a fake. They would have had to pass through where Gabe just walked."

"So, what are we waiting for? Let's just cut them down and leave. If they're fake, then there's nothing to be alarmed about."

"Yeah, that's what scares me. They went out of their way to make it look like a trap for our benefit. I think they want us to rescue the others."

"Why?" asks Harold.

"They're watching us," I whisper to him.

"We are of no value to them."

"Perhaps, but maybe there's something else they are looking for, like resistance leadership," I respond.

"Or maybe they are just looking for you," says a lone voice in the shadow behind the drape. I quickly jump to my feet, pull my gun, and raise the flashlight into the dark space next to Father Joseph. It doesn't work.

"Damn it," I say. I throw the flashlight down, walk past the phony beams, and tug firmly on the side of the drape until the corner rips from its hinged end. The black cloth falls gracefully to the side, hanging by one corner and revealing a clearer image of Henry and Father Joseph, who have been severely beaten.

Hidden in a darkened alcove is a young man displaced on a strange wooden plank with his hands bound with zip-ties. He's fully clothed and looks unharmed except for the rigid plastic digging into his wrists.

While Harold and Gabe cut down Henry and Father Joseph, I get a closer look at this man's face. Nothing seems to be out of the ordinary if you consider ordinary to be a complete cluster of chaos in this age. While he squirms in agony, pleading for me to cut the ties from his scabby wrists, I gawk over his broad shoulders, stout chest, and muscled stomach. He's obviously a strong and fit individual, but when my eyes carefully move over his distinguishable face, the brief moment of human desire is short-lived.

His chiseled jawline and high cheekbones remind me too much of Derrick, that senseless slow-witted bullying asshole from school. I suddenly become slightly less intrigued.

"What the hell are you waiting for? Untie me from this splintering contraption," he shouts in my face. I place my dagger underneath his throat; I'm in no mood to be barked at like some rabid dog.

"What did you mean when you said that maybe they were looking for me?" His pupils suddenly grow large and the jagged lines in his face relax. "You want to get out of here? Then answer the question," I continue.

"I know who you are," he says, trembling. I tighten my grip on the blade and press a bit firmer into the rugged, prickly hairs beneath his square chin. "They know who you are too. Why do you think they're stationed here . . . coincidence?"

"How do you know this, and don't you lie to me. I'm pretty good with a blade."

"Because they told me when I was being interrogated."

"For what?"

"I'm one of the leaders of the Northern Resistance!"

"There is no Resistance."

An untamed and unorganized rise in rebellious behavior sparked an underground cultural spin against government rule several years back. It was during the first wave of the new government's harsh regulations on gun control, which eventually turned into a feeding frenzy of political control. All guns were completely outlawed and stripped from civilians harboring them. That is when a new resistance was born.

They first called themselves the Patriotic Protectors, but that soon died after a brief civil unrest on the capitol steps turned into senseless bloodshed. A threat to the government's agenda brought on a massive murder spree that killed nearly every member of the rebel group. Since then they have stayed hidden in the desolate northern territories, where the government ceases to exist, hoping to build and prepare for an all-out war against our nation's leaders once again. Many believe that a much larger and more effective group of rebellions reside somewhere in Texas, which is conveniently referred to as the Southern Resistance, but no one knows for sure if it really exists.

I relax the knife from his neck and hold it near his crotch.

"I swear it to be true," he pleads.

"What is your name?" I ask.

"Nic."

I slide my arm around his waist and prepare to cut the plastic restricting ties with my knife before I have a sudden urge to question his name.

"What is that? Short for Nicolai?"

"What, are you implying I'm Russian?" He seems too quick to jump at the accusation, triggering some doubt. I'm probably better off to just leave him here, but part of me feels pity. After I cut him loose from the knotted wooden board, he rubs his sore wrists, and looks upon my face with a harmless shy smile, making me feel uncomfortable but slightly flattered.

"It's short for Nicholas, and I'm from Chicago," he says, grinning while he expands his broad chest out like a bird puffing his undersized breast during a mating ritual. He looks maybe twenty-five or so with blondish hair, blue eyes, and a muscular build that's nothing short of stout. I feel the need to apologize, but I still don't trust him, no matter how charming he may appear. Standing there like he's just won my approval, I leave his besotted grin and quickly help the others.

I want to hug Father Joseph, but he's much too weak to endure any physical affection. His back is badly scarred, and his dry, blistered lips are cracked from dehydration. Both he and Henry's neglected condition is nearly overwhelming, but surprisingly, they can still walk. It's a miracle they can even stand, much less move around without falling over.

"Arena, I'm forever glad to see you, but you shouldn't have come back," Henry whispers. I carefully hold his calloused hands.

"I had no intentions of ever leaving you behind . . . dead or alive. My hardened feet have traveled too many miles to just give up now."

"They're watching you," he says softly, while his eyes slide upward. I nonchalantly take a quick but subtle peek above the wall behind them and notice a large but craftily hidden camera.

"Is that the only one?" I ask softly while shielding my mouth with my hand.

"No, there's one above the front door."

I pause for a moment to think before motioning to Gabe and discovering the truth that I so doubtingly wrangled from Nic.

"Do they know who I am?"

Henry doesn't say anything, and looks down, dejected for a moment, then just slightly nods his head. I explain the situation to Gabe and Harold, and after a few convincing words, they readily agree. I look at both Henry and Father Joseph and say, "You both are getting out of here alive today."

I chamber my Beretta while Harold and Gabe position themselves next to Henry and Father Joseph.

"Get ready," I say.

"What's going on?" Nic asks.

I raise the gun to the camera above the wall and attempt to get an immediate reaction outside. Nothing happens as I expected.

"It's now or never boys," I say as I lower my gun. Then I grab the back of Nic's neck and press the end of my barrel against his head.

He quickly falls to his knees and put is his hands up in the air. Right then, the front door bursts open and two guards charge through. Unfortunate for them, they are quickly greeted by two bullets from my gun's chamber.

"Go, now!" I shout to the others. I quickly take out the camera on the wall and above the front door before pressing my gun back against Nic's head. The others rush to the side door near the hall and down into the basement, while I have a hasty, interesting chat with Nic.

"Any second now that door is going to be flooded with soldiers. You better explain to me what the hell is going on, because apparently someone doesn't want you dead."

"I swear to you, it's the truth. I don't know any more than you do."

"You sure? Because I'm beginning to feel a little used, Nic." I press the gun deep into his crotch and slide my dagger beneath his belly button. "Do you know what happens to a person when they bleed to death, Nic? They slowly wither, not like you see on television when they die, no. It may take hours of agony. I'm going to take just enough off your gut while your organs slowly spill out from the seam, and you'll frantically try and shove them back in without tearing. You see, when blood decides to exit, your body tends to compensate and restricts the flow in the vessels, which causes blood pressure to increase until they rip open, but your empty, pathetic heart will beat faster and faster until it ruptures or until you decide to just let go. Either way, Nic, in three seconds, you're going to have to endure two hours of hypovolemic shock . . . and, for good measure, without your penis. One . . . two . . ."

"Okay, okay! Like I said before, I'm one of the Northern Resistance leaders. That wasn't a lie, but they want me alive so I can lead them to a much larger Southern Resistance camped along the southern plains of Texas near Houston, but then you came into the picture. I guess they wanted two for the price of one."

"And what was the price?"

"My life."

"Why shouldn't I just cut your throat right now?"

"Because I can help you."

"How?"

"The Southern Resistance group is much larger and more prepared to take on the size of this new regime, and I can lead you to it. You'll find a safe haven with this group, and I'm sure they'll want to see you. You started this revolution, after all. You can lead them."

"The revolt started when people like you turned your convictions into hate. I made a covenant, not a war." I briefly withdraw my gun and pick up my bow.

"They're coming for you," Nic says.

"Who's coming?" Nic withdraws to say. "Who...who dammit?"

"You really don't know what's happened."

I shove my gun beneath his chin.

"Who's running the government, no bullshit Nic...so help me God—"

"The Russians! It's always been the Russians."

His answer is no surprise. I believe him, but I certainly don't trust him.

"If you wish to live, then you better open the front door." While Nic nervously walks over by the door, I load my bow with an explosive-tipped arrow. When he opens the door, about fifty soldiers storm out of two gray-and-black military trucks. They are heavily armed and run toward the church, firing aimlessly at will.

I draw back and fling the arrow about twenty feet, just short of one of the trucks. The explosion ripples the earth and sends most of the soldiers to the ground, while others drag their limbless bodies.

It was a favorable shot, but not completely successful. About a half-dozen men who survived the explosion are sprinting with rage, and I only brought one explosive-tipped arrow with me. I slam the door shut and make a run for it to the basement, with Nic leading the way.

Before we can even get to the side door, two soldiers passing through the left hall greet us with two beautifully manufactured AN-94s, a very quick and nasty gun. Hell, even I'm enamored by its crafted beauty.

They angrily shout at us in Russian to drop on the floor. Nic seems surprisingly calm for such an intrusive and unpleasant little greeting.

I slowly raise my hands up while I kneel on the floor, but I'm not going out like this, especially to these two buffoons. The one standing in front of me doesn't even have his finger on the trigger, and the other pointing his gun at Nic still has the safety on.

With a rare opportunity like this, I waste no time and take maybe the only chance I have to escape from this sticky situation. I thrust my hand upward, shoving the end of soldier's barrel into his nose, and quickly draw my gun, striking the other one in the head. I pull the AN-94 from the soldier's arm and slice my dagger across his throat.

The front door bursts open, and before I know it, Nic has vanished downstairs. I squeeze off a few rounds through the opened door with the automatic rifle, and three Russian soldiers fall dead. I make a break for it downstairs to the basement while the front door is momentarily blocked by the piled-up bodies.

I quickly search around and find the metal door to the tunnels closed tight. I try opening it but it's useless—it won't budge. That bastard Nic locked me in, and now I'm trapped down here with God knows how many pissed-off Russians about to recklessly plunge through that door.

I feel sick as I desperately search around for an alternative before I'm forced to stage myself for an all-out battle. Without another exit to flee or anywhere to shield myself, I quickly dump the idea and run back up the stairs to face my enemies.

A sudden rush of blood seems to flow away from my head, making me a bit dizzy as I ascend halfway up the stairs. I grab the stair rail to keep my balance while evocative images of Allison race through my mind, reminding me the promise I made to her.

I stop swaying from the rail, my eyes come back into focus, and I convince myself that I'm not going to die today. I draw both guns and wait. The door swings open, and I release a fury beyond even my control, recklessly emptying both mags.

Several soldiers drop dead in front of the basement door, while I maneuver away from a few others who unexpectedly take a tumble down the stairs. Feeling somewhat woozy from the surge of adrenaline wearing off, I step carelessly over the pile of bodies and fall against the side of the wall. I slide down to the floor, smearing red down with me against the dingy wall.

Some blood must have splashed on my jacket, because my arm is covered in it. It's not until a rush of excruciating pain soon replaces the numb nerves in my arm that I realize it is my blood. I've been shot, and it feels unbearably unpleasant. I press down on the bullet wound to help clot the blood from exiting, but my need to rest here a while longer is temporary.

Two more soldiers come sprinting through the front of the church, firing toward the wall. I jump to my feet and take off down the hall where we first came in. Bullets zip past the corner of the wall and into the framed pictures hanging in the hall. They are so close, I can actually feel the air push past me, one of which harrowingly grazes the side of my neck, close enough to sear the skin.

I sprint back through the musty halls leading to the side door that we came in, and hurry out through the wooded briar without being noticed. I pull out my dagger and swing aimlessly at the thorny vines devilishly dangling in front of me, but it's unworkable without a machete. I'm doing more harm slicing up my hand on these sharp, green barbs, so I use the front of my bow to barge through. Without looking back, I trudge forward, running as fast as I can. Every few steps, those prickly thorns whip across my body like bee stings, one of which lashes alongside my cheek.

The tiny razor-like cuts on my body painfully throb, and my sides begin to burn with pinching agony. I finally exit the wooded nightmare and reach the fenced park, but I'm too exhausted to move any further, so I collapse onto the moist grass to catch my breath.

While I lie there for a couple of minutes to regain enough drive to press on, I decide to channel my energy into anger. I look upon my bloody cut, my hand pressing against my sore, wounded arm, and boil over Nic's lies and abandonment.

My breathing finally calms to a relatively normal pace, and my sides stop cramping. My boiling rage settles to a slow simmer, and I curse myself for foolishly trusting him. Although I'm deeply curious now about the Southern Resistance camps he spoke of, when I see him again, he's going to feel more than the scratch on my hand. For all I know, it's all a lie. Truth be told, it's hard to believe that a rebellious militant group would settle in Texas—not with the government's handprint all over it.

I guess there are some advantages though, like miles of uninhabited territory and sea ports for escape. Still, it would be foolish to come here unless you are willing to accept defeat. Of course nothing appears to be senseless in this apocalyptic nightmare. This is the world I live in now; crazy no longer exists.

The sound of a heavy tank suddenly rolls past one of the buildings across from the fence. I quickly jump to my feet and race over to the opened sewer grate that Harold had previously pushed through. I hurry down the dirty bricked tunnel, chomping at the bit to reunite my fist with Nic's face, but more importantly, I'm committed to look upon Allison'ssmile.

I feel as though I've abruptly left her in an unusually unstable state, and I owe it to her to be there if anything were to ever happen. Very few times in my life have I been able to erase my own discomforts to embrace someone else's, and running through these dark channels beneath the ground bears no exception. Though my hands are cut and my wounded arm drips with blood, I'm able to extinguish the excruciating pain just to see her. I'm willing to sacrifice my life for hers.

A sudden warm glow of elation showers over my body when I turn the corner. A small sliver of Christ's silhouette hanging from the cross peeks through the side tunnel that enters into the church from the northeast. I pull my sore arm tightly against my stinging ribs, and sprint as fast as my tired legs will allow.

When I'm ten paces from the entrance, Harold, Gabe, Henry, and Father Joseph slowly limp into the church from the north tunnel. I shout out at them to let them know I'm here, when I notice Nic running behind them.

Anger churns through me. I ball up my fist and jump out to a full-on sprint, lunging my knuckles into Nic's jaw. He falls hard to the ground and rolls over in pain. Adrenaline or not, that hurt, and I don't mean his face. My hand throbs in agony. I think I just broke my hand.

"Arena! What the hell are you doing?" Gabe shouts.

Blood drips from Nic's nose and I reach for my dagger. I guess I'm a better aim with a gun, because I missed his jaw.

"Arena, stop!" Father Joseph yells.

I ignore them. I press my dagger against Nic's throat just beneath his unusually large Adam's apple. I'm ready to fillet his skin.

"You son of a bitch."

"What are you doing?" he hysterically asks.

"Arena, stop and put the knife down!" Gabe yells.

"You left me back there to die."

"I don't know what you're talking about," Nic nervously says, as I slowly begin to slide the knife across his tender skin.

"Stop!" Gabe shouts and runs over to me. "Arena, give me the knife."

"He locked the door to the tunnels, leaving me to fend off all those soldiers, and I was shot in the arm."

"What?" Gabe asks, confused.

"I swear I didn't know it would lock. I was scared, so I ran," Nic says, pleading once again for his life.

"You swear an awful lot, Nic."

"Arena, let it go," Gabe says.

"Arena, even you sometimes make mistakes in the heat of the moment. Please don't make this one," Henry says, who's hunched over and leaning on Harold's shoulder.

I glare at Nic, my jaw clenched, then tighten my grip around the blade and push it firmer against his neck. No matter how the others feel about his inexcusable actions, I still don't trust him, but it would behoove me to lay low for a while until I can convince them that I'm not insane.

"The next time you decide to cross me, this blade will be the death of you," I say, pulling the knife away from his neck. I shove his head back to the ground and walk off. My temper is flaring too close to a fire I desperately need to put out, and the only chill that seems to dampen my flame is from the cold stares I receive from the others.

My skin must be made of flame-retardant cells, because I'm burning mad right now. My anger has spoiled any desire I had for Father Joseph and Henry's homecoming. I snatch the key hanging around Harold's neck, and I fume with a hatred I hadn't felt since I was strapped in a chair, enduring the foul breath spewing from General Iakov's wretched mouth. My resentment for Nic gradually subsides as I watch two men nearly beaten to death slowly trudge behind me.

Has it come to this, that I've put myself before others without even a hint of mercy? I feel ashamed and unworthy to my friends who've trusted in me to lead them, yet I've allowed my anger to linger.

The one thing that I've learned to lean on and hold close to me through bitter times, the one thing that would put a gleam of light on the darkest of unsavory days are my friends. As we reach the den door, I watch the only two men left in my life who ever gave a damn about my own suffering struggle to lift their feet across the pitted floor.

I stand there questioning the integrity of my soul and the motives behind my actions. How can I let my empty heart be filled again if I continue to let misery and rage dictate my unwarranted behavior?

While they wait on me to open the door, I just stand there and lose my composure. All that has been tucked deep into my emotional state freely surrenders. Tears discharge from my eyes faster than I can wipe them away, and my body shakes. I open my arms wide and quickly wrap them around Henry, apologizing for my sordid behavior and my lack of compassion.

I feel a sudden warmth placed upon my back from Father Joseph's hand, and a burden of unforgiving pain released.

"Forgive me for my lack of sympathy," I say.

"No worries, you have a lot on your mind," Henry says.

"I don't expect every decision you make to be perfect, but . . ." adds Father Joseph.

"But what? I rudely interrupt. "You didn't intend for us to come get you? You didn't intend for this to happen? Well, it did, and my heart has been spilled too many times to endure anymore of your painful advice," I say with a resentment that's somehow spoiled my true nature. What's happened to me?

"Arena, wait . . ." he says softly.

"I didn't ask for any of this," I interpose with rejection.

"Arena," he says, trying to calm me down, "but I still trust in you, and I will follow you to the end," he sincerely adds.

"I just want all of this to be over," I cry out, clinging to him.

"I know . . . I know."

CHAPTER 15

When we enter the den, Allison is sitting on a metal stool, digging into a mound of rice. She looks up in utter shock and struggles to speak, nearly choking on a mouthful of food when she notices me. She drops her fork and runs to me with open arms.

I hug her tightly, wincing in pain as my arm squeezes around her small, frail body. While the others limp through the doorway, I quickly head to the storage room and grab the first aid satchel. My injured arm begins to hurt even more, and after hugging Allison, blood runs freely down my sleeve. I pull back the tattered material and see that I've reopened the wound.

I hurry back out to help the others, but I'm incapable of walking more than a few steps before I slowly lose my balance and collapse to the floor. My face feels flushed, and my dizzy eyes start to wander. The only thing I'm able to see through the fading daze are blurred images of Niki and Juliana running, and Allison crying on the floor, before I completely black out.

*   *   *

I feel shut off to the world, suspended in limbo, yet I seem strangely comfortable with it. The dark space surrounds me with splendid allure. I feel a peaceful, almost serene moment cover my heart and empty my pain. My thoughts escape me, and nothing I speak flows from my mouth—only floating memories that comfort me.

I lie there wondering if this is what death truly feels like—trapped in a prison of emptiness. Out from the vast blackness, a soft whisper calls out to me. I'm suddenly afraid to answer what I can't see, and even if I could, my lips restrain me from uttering a word. After a brief moment of silence, the muscles in my mouth finally relax, and I dare to speak up.

"Am I dead?"

"No, your time has not come to pass, for many things are yet to be done in this world," the voice whispers in my ear. Have I come before God in my death, or is my mind playing tricks on me again?

"Who are you?" I dare to ask.

"You know who I am. The same that was, and is, and will ever be."

"Father?"

"You are not alone, and all is not what it seems."

"How much longer must I endure?"

"Time only exists when you are counting the seconds. You must carry on."

"Where?"

"When your broken body is healed, you will leave this place behind and never return."

"How will I know...where will I lead them?"

"I will guide you, but you have to trust your instincts. Do not be deceived."

"Why...why me?"

"It's your destiny."

"Am I going to die?"

A long pause weights on my heart and surrounds me with silence. I search deep to find an answer, but I'm instead troubled by what my mind sees. Whether it's my sanity I've questioned, or the dark that deceives, I feel what is ahead and keep it tucked away. What I may know seems impossible, but I must believe.

A flickering trail of white seeps through the dark canvas pulled over my eyes, and a sudden rush of blood flourishes throughout my body. The black gradually fades, and a dimly lit hanging lamp slowly sways above my head. When my eyes eventually adjust, I find myself lying in one of the beds with Allison and Juliana sitting next to me.

I try getting up, but it's too much too soon, and Juliana gently lays my head back down on the pillow.

"Easy cowgirl, no rodeo for you just yet. You lost a good amount of blood."

I feel a slight cool sensation on my left arm, and when I look over, I just now notice the needle that's stuck in my bruised vein. Coiling from the end and running up the side of the bunk post hangs an IV with a half-filled expired bag labeled "normal saline."

"How did you . . . ?"

"My mother use to give IV infusions to in-house patients. I watched closely," Juliana interrupts.

"But," I say, pointing to the expired tag on the bag.

"Don't worry, they've been properly stored and sealed, and it's better than nothing. Most of the bags stored in the first aid cabinet are just normal saline and Ringers Lactate solution anyway. They can last for years."

I look deep into her eyes with sincere gratitude and extend my hand in thanks.

"Thank you so much," I say.

"It's what I do," she responds softly while gently holding my hand. I wince in pain when she touches my bruised knuckles.

"Sorry, are you okay?" she asks.

"It's a little tender."

"I've got something for that. Be right back."

I think back at slamming my fist into Nic's face and wonder if I did the right thing. I'm not as easily apologetic to those I loathe, but I guess he deserves the benefit of the doubt. I can't prove he purposely left me back there, but I'm sure as hell not going to trust him.

Juliana comes back with a bag of frozen peas to place on my sore hand. She's become quite the caretaker for all of us, but more importantly, she has been an inherently divine blessing in Gabe's life. While she leaves the room to check in on the others, I ask Allison to stay next to me.

"So how long have I been out?" I ask.

"A few hours. She stitched you up, you know."

I was so distracted by my dazed-and-confused surroundings that I completely forgot about my gunshot
wound. I carefully pat the gauzed area covering the stiches
and realize that the back of my arm is also stitched. I guess
after the initial shock of being shot, I hadn't noticed that the
bullet went clean through my arm.

"Sorry about your birthday."

"It's okay, I'll have plenty more, right?" Allison says
with uncertainty. I wish I could say yes, but even I'm not so
sure anymore, so I just smile.

"I wish I had a present to give you."

"Are you kidding? Having you back here safe is the
best present I could ever have."

I'm so beyond touched by her sincere remarks and
unconditional love that I vow to myself to enjoy every precious moment I still have while she's here on this earth. I
found more than just a friend in her; I've found a younger
sister, and I will protect her at all costs.

"I tell you what, you go pick out anything you want in
the knife room and it's yours to keep. It may not be what
you've always wanted, but it's all I have to give."

"Well, I've kind of had my eye on that black dagger you
carry."

"Consider it yours, but be careful. Respect can go a long
way when handling a blade like that," I say like a concerned
mother. With her vibrant smile stretching from ear to ear, she
nearly stumbles from her chair before leaving the room all
giddy.

I manage to pull my head up from the pillow and gently sit on the side of the bed. With the cold bag of peas resting on my sore knuckles and my body replenishing with
fluids, I feel the sudden urge to relieve my somewhat
swollen bladder.

Just as I adjust my weary legs to stand, the IV catheter
in my arm tugs against my skin. I groan.

The door creaks open and Father Joseph walks in. I still
feel a little uneasy about how I left things between us back in
the tunnel, and I'm not sure if I've forgiven myself yet for

speaking to him that way. My feelings of culpability keep me from making direct eye contact with him. I fidget with the bag of frozen peas to distract myself from his presence, and press it on my bruised hand as if I'm too busy to chat.

"You need some help with that?" he asks.

"No, thanks, it's fine. Just a little bruised."

"I expect some man's face feels differently," he says with a smirk.

"Yeah, well, he had it coming . . . Is he okay?"

"You mean other than the broken nose, discolored cheekbone, and battered ego, I suspect he'll live," he says, smiling.

I'm still pissed, but feel a little less convinced I did the right thing. I guess my motives may have been slightly irrational.

I tilt my head down toward the floor and avoid looking upon what I can only imagine is a concerned face, or at the very least, one of reverence.

I can't help but wonder how this will all end, and for the first time, I'm beginning to doubt whether I can continue on like this. Are the voices inside my head whispers from wickedness, or am I deceiving myself into thinking God is truly speaking to me? I'm so emotionally shattered that I'm still questioning my sanity. I just don't know anymore.

I do know that the truth surrounding my emotional stability can no longer be hidden from Father Joseph. He sits on the bed next to me. He doesn't need to see the tears dripping from my cheeks to know what troubles me, so I just blurt out my frustration anyway.

"Am I crazy?" I ask, looking up at him through swollen eyes. He smiles, probably wondering if I'm joking, but then his eyes wander, searching for an answer.

"I see an innocent girl who's hurt—a pain that I cannot heal," he softly says.

"I don't know myself anymore."

"Well, I know you. I know that you're a strong young woman who has been thrown into a fiery hailstorm that no man on this earth would ever want to endure. I know you have the will to stand when the time comes to wield a strong conviction, a faith that stands to hold no differences, and a passion to do what is right . . . and I'm not the only one who feels that way."

"Then why do I feel like the whole world is crashing down on me?"

"There are things I just don't understand, that only God can answer. But know this—you were born into this world for a reason, whether you believe that or not. We were meant to experience all feelings and massage every emotion, but it's the heart that we must tame before we are called," he says with glassy eyes.

The fortitude that had been with me from the beginning seems so long ago, but this intimate moment bolsters my will to continue with this fight even if I feel defeated.

With my jaw resting on the palm of my hand, I glance over and notice a Celtic cross tattoo peeking out from his unbuttoned sleeve.

"So what kind of priest marks up his arm with ink that he's too ashamed to expose behind those hiddensleeves?"

"One who doesn't judge."

"Touché," I retort, while he buttons up his sleeve and smiles. "So, are you going to tell me, or do I have to beg?" I continue.

"Another story for another time. You need to get some rest now."

He pats my shoulder and persuades me to lie back down before he leaves my side.

He slowly walks to the door and stops for a moment before turning back around and says, "You're right . . . you didn't ask for this, no more than I was asked to help you see it through, but I can only follow you if you are willing to lead."

He closes the door, and I lie there gazing deep into an empty room and questioning my true intentions before I eventually close my eyes and fall asleep.

CHAPTER 16

It's the first night in a long while that I haven't had a dream, or at least one that I can remember. I wake up in the same empty room and realize with immediate disappointment that none of this was just a wild and crazy reverie. It's not that I think that all of this is just going to magically go away, but a little of me believes that perhaps a day will come when I wake up in another body and in another place.

There's a slight tingling in my left shoulder as I stretch out my arms, and the only thing that has changed in this room is a small bandage placed on my upper wrist where the IV was inserted. The gauze around my arm has been replaced as well, and I can only assume these were dressed by the gentle touch of Juliana's nurturing abilities.

I know I needed the sleep, but I didn't realize I was that tired not to notice someone coming in here to change my bandages. My arm still feels sore, but at least I'm able to make a fist again without wincing.

Before I venture out in the main area, I try pulling my tangled hair up and out of my eyes to avoid the obvious bedhead look, but nothing seems to work. I finally adjust it with an old, dry, rotted rubber band I found near my bed, but before I reach the door, it breaks, leaving my abysmal hair to hang like a used, dirty mop.

Oh, screw it, who am I trying to impress? I leave the matted, greasy strands to dangle in my eyes. I walk outside to wash my hands and to relieve my overextended bladder that's about to open up like a broken dam once again. Everyone is sitting at the far table consuming a morning feast of canned fruit . . . again.

You would think after a constant diet of fruit and small grains we'd all look like super models, framed with those disgustingly protruding skeletal features that no man could possibly find remotely attractive. Well, at least we'll have healthy and flourishing colons.

I baptize my hair underneath the lukewarm water in the sink, trying to extract the dirt, oil, and whatever else that may be clinging to my dark locks. I twist the long ends of my hair, squeezing out as much water as I can. When I look up in the dingy, chipped mirror, I'm reminded how much I truly resemble my mother, except for the long, flowing hair.

We both share the same pouty bottom lip, oval face to which our bangs curve around its edges, and lemon-shaped eyes that are glazed with a mixture of caramel and green. If my skin wasn't browned by the sun's heat and a fine layer of grime, you could see the milky-white glow that's hidden beneath.

Have you ever felt the need to do something spontaneous without having to justify why you did it just so you could know what it's like to be free? Well, this isn't exactly a life-shattering moment, but I feel the sudden urge to make a dramatic change to my hair.

Not sure why. Maybe because I'm tired of chewing my hair when I eat, or washing out dried-up blood matted between the fine fibers. Or maybe I just want to look more like my mother.

I search the bathroom until I find a pair of scissors. Unfortunately these poor, rusty shears have seen better days, and I can't imagine they were ever useful even when they were new. They may have to do for now, but I can't count on them to do the bulk of the work, so I fetch my sharpest knife.

I cut the majority of my hair in the back, leaving it free of my shoulders. I let the front of my hair flow down the sides of my jawline just so I don't look too much like a boy. The blunt bob I've created isn't something I would normally choose to do on my own, but I think I like it. It's bold, different, and most importantly, practical. I'm not one to primp vainly in front of the mirror, but I'm beginning to feel more like a woman who's breaking out of a tomboyish shell.

I take a nice long, hot shower before joining the others for breakfast, and ponder over what our next move will be. I haven't really thought this far ahead about what we are supposed to do. Just a day ago, I thought my friends were dead. Thinking back to the first time I planted Derrick's face to the floor with my boot, I've realized that I've relied too much on my own instincts instead of waiting on God for direction. But this time feels very different. I'm absolutely convinced that the prodding thoughts invading my consciousness under this warm sedating water are extremely important, and I believe that there's something special about the Southern Resistance that will play a vital role in our fate.

While I dry off and change into some freshly cleaned clothes, it becomes apparent to me what God wants me to do. I think it may be in everyone's best interest if we just lay low for a while and heal our broken bodies before leaving the den and moving south. Whether it's just whispering thoughts or an inception planted by God, our journey will continue on to the Southern Resistance camps. I can't believe I'm saying this, but Nic was right. That is our safe haven, a refuge where I'm to shepherd some lost sheep.

I reapply a bandage to my wound and join the others at the table. I'm greeted with drifting glares and slightly confused expressions. I act as if nothing has changed, so I grab a plate and go about my business as usual. Of course, the men just stare with their jaws aligned as if they had been dressed with a dog muzzle. Not exactly the reaction I was looking for, but then again, men aren't exactly wired to articulate their thoughts into words.

They just sit there and stare with their mouths half-open, like a train furnace waiting to have coal shoveled into it. It's not until Juliana speaks up that I was almost convinced that I had walked in on a mute convention.

"I love it," she says, springing from her seat.

"You are so beautiful. Makes you look much older," adds Niki. I look for a place to sit down while Niki, Allison, and Juliana give up their seats for me, and the men just sit there, continuing to stare and stuff their faces.

And just when I thought all the men in here were gallantly inept, I'm startled by the generous gesture from Nic, of all people. He pulls my chair out for me, attempting to mend any hard feelings I might have harshly shared with him yesterday, and politely offers to seat me like a gentleman.

Nice as it may seem, I'm still harboring some ill trust with him, so I respectfully reject his unexpected generosity.

"No, thank you," I say, grabbing his wrist away from the back of the chair. "I'm capable of seating myself."

"Arena," says Niki with her nose crinkled, and nudging my arm as if I had just pulled the man's heart out from his chest. Juliana's eyes grow big as she grits her teeth and motions for me to retract my demoralizing reply. It's obvious they disapprove of my response, so I begrudgingly allow him to continue with his courteous, but curious, gesture.

"My apologies. As you can see, I'm not used to being around a gentleman," I say, clearing my throat and glaring to the other men sitting around the table, scarfing down their food.

"Forgive me for being insensitive to your kindness," I continue with a hint of sarcasm as I wink at Juliana for approval.

While Nic pushes my seat in, Juliana smirks at me like a little schoolgirl, relishing my awkward attempt to hide any traces of flattery I may have for him. I admit his somewhat chiseled face brings a slight glimmer to my eye, but it's no more than just a faint attraction that I can simply switch off when he opens his mouth to speak. I don't know what it is, but there's just something about him I don't like or trust, no matter how nice he may seem.

I finish my breakfast and follow Gabe back into the sleeping quarters, where he's on the floor, looking under one of the beds.

"Lose something?" I ask.

"My shoes," he replies.

"They're over behind the door."

"Thanks."

"Hey."

"Yeah?"

"Do you trust me? I mean, do you truly believe I'm capable of making the decisions when it counts?"

"Of course, and I'm not just saying that to give you peace of mind. I trust in you just the same as you trust in me. We're family, and nothing changes between us," he says while he puts his shoes on. He carefully closes the door to make sure no one can hear us before he continues.

"Look, I'm not here to question your actions against Nic, or the erratic choices you may make in the heat of the moment. I don't want this any more than you do, but you can't expect to be the only one in pain," he says, looking into my eyes with deep concern. "You're not the only one who's hurting, or who wishes they could escape all of this without some kind of guilt. Whatever baggage you own, I'm carrying it too."

I quickly tear myself away from his eyes. "I'm so sorry," I say, as I wipe the tears from my cheeks.

"Look at me, Arena," he says as he grabs my shaking hands. "What's in the past stays in the past. What matters is that you're here now... alive. We may not be identical twins, but we were cut from the same cloth. We're connected in more ways than you realize."

"I understand."

"No, I don't think you really do. I feel your pain inside of me. I know the sadness that continues to shadow you. When you cry at night in your sleep, my heart aches with you. I know the unsettling whispers that mock you, trying to strangle you with a wickedness you can't see. Do you think that I don't hurt, that I'm somehow oblivious to grief and sorrow? There's not one day that goes by that I don't think about losing Juliana out there."

"It's just so hard sometimes," I say.

"It was never supposed to be easy, Arena. Mom and Dad are dead, and Myra and Daniel are dead. Whatever pain that's dwelling inside of you that's keeping your memories of Jacob alive will only distract you."

I stare at the wall blankly, only to be haunted by images of Jacob smiling in the classroom doorway. I rest for a small moment in the words that Gabe has spoken until I become suddenly annoyed and restless by such a notion.

"So what are you suggesting? That I just forget about everything that's so dear to me? That somehow I'm just to supposed to stop remembering what it was like to be in love?"

"No," he says, shaking his head, his eyes sloped downward.

"Suppose it was Juliana who died—would you remember her, or would you just magically wipe it from your memory until she ceased to ever exist?"

"I'm not asking you to forget, Arena."

"Then what are you asking?" I angrily shout.

"Stop hoping to bring them back."

The burning of my cheeks can't describe the pain and anger I feel inside, but it soon goes away like everything else, because what he says is true. I have to accept it and move on, or my feelings will be the death of us all.

I stand there in silence until I nearly lose control of every emotion penned up inside. I collapse into Gabe's arms, sobbing.

I eventually lie on the bed, while Gabe sits beside me for my well-being, and I search deep inside my thoughts for direction.

My tears finally wane and my body stops shivering.

"We mustn't leave the den right now. It's not time."

"I concur," he agrees.

"We'll stay here for a couple of weeks to heal and prepare."

"So where are we going exactly?" he asks, unsure of my response.

"Southward. I want to know if the Southern Resistance exists or not, because if it is real, then these provoking thoughts swimming around in my head are not my own."

"I hope you know what you are doing," he says, slowly walking to the door.

"There isn't any other way and you know it. We can't stay here forever."

"Why not? No one even knows we are here."

"Gabe, the tunnels have been compromised and we've practically trapped ourselves down here. How long do you think we will last? The food is almost gone."

"So is this your gut talking or—"

"We're twins, would it matter?"

"I just want to know that your thoughts haven't been deceiving you."

"Well, if they have, I'll be sure to let you know first."

"I hope you're right about this, I really do—"

"Do you trust me?"

Arena, there's not—"

"Do you trust me?"

"Yes." Gabe's stony face gazes silently for a moment. "You haven't given me a reason not to since we've been in this shit storm." He smiles as he open the door.

"Hey," I say before he leaves the room.

"Yes?"

"Thank you."

"Yeah, sure . . . are you going to be okay?"

"I'm fine," I say, standing and balling my sore knuckles.

"You know, none of us would be alive if it weren't for you," he says. As grateful as I am for his kind words, I struggle to graciously return a smile.

"I wish it weren't up to me."

The only thing on my mind right now is keeping this fellowship together and unharmed.

"Seal the tunnel door. The tunnels can no longer be safe, and no one leaves here until it's time," I firmly add.

I bite my tongue, restraining myself from telling him the real reason, but I suspect he knows. The little time I've spent in here has stretched my reliance thin with Nic. He cannot be trusted among us. Whether or not we believe he's telling the truth, he's still a stranger to our group, and we know nothing about him. Even if he was under forceful persuasion, he did make a deal with the Russians after all, which makes him a liability now.

CHAPTER 17

We've been holed up in this place nearly two months now, much longer than I wanted to, healing our broken bodies. It has been anything but enjoyable. I'm beginning to understand the qualms that surround a prison inmate's unstable psyche. My skin's itching to break free to the outside world, no matter how conceivably dangerous it may seem. Being cooped up in here for this long with the likes of Nic is more detrimental to my health than my safety out there.

While I'm stuck in here, which was apparently a unanimous vote, Gabe, Henry, Father Joseph, and Harold have taken to the surface an hour ago to scout the area for a possible escape from this place. It's the first and only contact with the outside we've attempted in the last few weeks, which is making me even more anxious than the obnoxiously overconfident courtship Nic has been so gallantly failing to flatter me with.

I've been finding myself less detached toward the others. Having Juliana and Niki around has been the best thing for me right now, and it can only make my relationship with Allison that much stronger if we are to survive this living hell.

If it weren't for the women down here, I would be more distracted and distressed over the men risking their lives outside, which is where I want to be. But some distractions just simply go unnoticed, especially when you have a lean, well-cut man with an ego bigger than his pecks sauntering around with his shirt off. I'm not generally attracted to men like this, especially ones who vainly flaunt it, but my hormones have not been suppressed either. While some girls may have a pitter-patter thumping in their heart, I'm not as easily impressed.

I can appreciate a nice, well-fit man, but it's his ego that proves he's less than a great catch. And for that reason alone, I'd throw him back.

I'm growing rather fidgety again, wondering why it's taking so long for the others to come back. Since we had both doors sealed, they had to exit up the stairs to the secured garage where Finnegan's Camaro is parked, which should have made it easier to take a quick peek outside.

I look around for something constructive to do to keep my mind off things, but I've sharpened all of my blades . . . twice. There's really nothing else for me to do except practice with my bow at the target range at the other end of the building.

I dress my bow and pick up a small quiver of arrows that Allison recently made for me. They're quite nice, light, streamlined, well-balanced, and perfect fletching—custom arrows tailored for my liking that no professional could design. Allison has a true calling.

I flex the newly twined string, priming the bow's flexibility to ensure it has adapted to the new cord. I stretch the bowstring back to my cheek while I warm up, practicing with phantom arrows to get a good feel of the tuned bow.

I prep the bow and place one of Allison's arrows in the knock, ready to shoot. Not as enamored with these incredible arrows, Niki and Juliana sit at the far table, gawking as if something has them in a trance.

From afar, it looks as if though their faces have been turned to stone, but close up, they are no more than just two giddy girls with gallivanting eyes transfixed on a sweaty man doing pushups on the floor.

I don't think I can bear anymore testosterone flowing in this den any more than I can bear to see my girlfriends ogle a predictably small-brained man-child desperately trying to impress.

"Really?" I ask, looking with disappointment to Juliana and Niki.

"Hey, just looking, not lusting," Niki whispers.

"Seriously? If you stare any longer, your eyes will cross."

"Come on, Arena, you have to admit, he may not be much on conversation, but he's cute," Juliana says.

"Sure, if you like the shallow, vapid, narcissistic type." Not that I'm mad at Juliana or Niki for watching, but I have to admit, I'm a little surprised and somewhat disenchanted by their will to not look away, but then again, who am I to judge? My willpower has been anything but firm.

Nic stops his flirtatious exercising and walks past me without saying one word, as if I'm invisible. He wipes the few beads of sweat rolling down his glistening chest, and proceeds to sit next to Juliana and Niki, who suddenly appear to be less impressed with him than before. Not sure what changed with them, but I'm in no mood to intrude while Nic is still sitting there. Whether it's because he snubbed me, which I can't blame him for since I've been ignoring him for the past month, or if they've finally seen right through his transparency.

I don't know what has come over me, but I suddenly feel a tad bitter about the whole thing, and I think for the first time there may be a hint of sprouting jealousy that's been tucked deep inside an emotional wedge. Not that I would ever entertain the idea of returning Nic with playful blandishment, but a part of me misses being courted, by the right guy, of course. I suppose Jacob never really had to pursue me that hard, because I was already taken by him the first day we met.

I try hard not to show any interest in this dramatic charade Nic's attempting to lure me in with, and keep as though nothing has changed. I pull back the arrow and fling it toward the target just slightly off my normal mark from this distance. I hate to admit it, but this childish pretense is much more distracting than I can stand.

I quickly draw another arrow, but my hand begins to shake just a little. Nic leaves his chair and walks over to me. I try to ignore his presence, but I can't help noticing out of the corner of my eye at his repellent, smug grin painted deep into his face. There's nothing more I would love to do than to rearrange that cynical smirk with my knife.

I hold steady, trying to keep my eyes focused on the target, but I'm too distracted by his heavy panting and bare chest hovering next to me, like I'm being tested. It's unlike me to be this unfocused next to someone I find disenchanting, for the moment anyway . . . I think. The balance of my bow shifts in my hand, while I struggle to restrain myself from looking at him. The muscles in my arms begin to weaken, and I have to withdraw the arrow from its perch.

"Do you mind? I'm trying to practice here," I curtly say.

"I'm sorry, I didn't know I was being a distraction," he says while he attempts to impress me with a subtle twitch in his pectoral muscles. Little does he know, I'm about two tweaks shy of grabbing a very sharp dagger and slicing that pompous ripple from his chest permanently.

"I should leave you alone. I just couldn't help but notice what beauty you possess with such a callous weapon," he says in a soft but confident voice.

Wow, really? Did he come up with that all by himself? I think I just threw up in my mouth a little. His amorous intent to woo me doesn't change a damn thing between us, and I'm pretty sure whatever else spews from that treacherous mouth of his would truly be anything but sincere.

"I know we don't see eye-to-eye on things, but I just thought this would be a good time for us to make a clean slate. Can we start all over?"

"Uh . . . sure," I say, shocked at the notion he could say anything remotely genuine. Wow, maybe I was wrong about him.

"You are so beautiful."

"Thank you—"

"Even with all your flaws," he continues.

Okay, I was wrong about this guy. What a douchebag.

"Uh, pardon?" I ask.

"You're pretty and all; you just have some issues that are not so attractive."

"Really now? Please enlighten me. I'm so intrigued by someone who's brave enough to share suchdelightful things."

"Well, for starters, you're a bit moody."

Huh, just what a girl wants to hear. Well, if this is his idea of trying to court me, his ship is sinking quickly. What an abrasive, outspoken asshole. What is *moody* anyway? Code for *bitch*?

"Shall I go on?" he dares to ask. He would have done well to shut up the first time, but I can see being observant isn't one of his better qualities.

"Do you really think that's in your best interest, Nic?" I ask, resetting the arrow in its knock, "because something is telling me not so much."

"I'm just trying to be honest."

"Honest? Ha! I can think of a better name for that. You might want to move . . . I would really hate to mess up that pretty face of yours," I say, drawing back the arrow. He abruptly grabs my arm before I can release, and the arrow rattles the belly of the bow and slings erratically to the side, nearly striking Juliana in the head.

I swing my bow back into his face and twist my wrist out of his grasp. I quickly pull the dagger from the strap on my thigh and shove it close beneath his testicles.

"You ever touch me like that again, and you'll wake up with a gender crisis." I slowly lower the handle of the knife, keeping the sharp point tethered to his pants. His insidious smirk has remarkably disappeared, and the muscles in my arm seem to have regained their strength.

Juliana and Niki cautiously remove themselves from this nasty scene, while Nic stands there like a defenseless statue.

"Look, I didn't mean anything by it to hurt you," he nervously grovels.

"Yeah, you're a regular Cyrano de Bergerac."

My gut tells me to shove the blade up as hard as I can, but I can't afford to be wrong about this guy again. I'm trying to regain any trust I may have lost with the others, as well as my sanity.

"I'm sorry," he pleads.

I'm still not sure about him, and I'm feeling more and more resolved about his deception, but I must usher in a little sympathy right now to convince the others I've changed. Well, just a little.

I rapidly pull back the dagger and slide the sharp steel tip across the bottom of his crotch and split open a small seam. The incision is close enough to induce a fear he desperately needs, but without breaking the skin to remind him I'm still in control.

He jumps back, floundering about, and shouting colorful epithets while he secures his crotch with his hands.

"Jesus Christ, Arena!"

"Your words can be just as sharp as this blade. Be careful how you choose them, Nic," I say as I place the knife back into its sheath.

"You're one crazy bitch, you know that?"

With the dagger in my hand, I walk toward him while he's bent over examining his junk.

"Call me crazy one more time. I dare you," I say, pulling the knife halfway out.

"Easy, I was kidding."

"Arena, don't!" Juliana shouts as she and Niki watches from a distance.

I pull the knife completely out, and my mind races with a repressed memory of General Iakov grabbing at my breast. I'm besieged with a fury I just can't seem to control, and when I get close to Nic, who is fearfully backing away, I suddenly disengage.

The door slams open near the wall, and the others finally return from the surface. I look down at my shaky hand holding the dagger. I'm not myself. Nic is nearly backed into one of the side tables sweating with fear. I quickly slide the knife out of sight as Niki and Juliana look at me with concern.

Gabe rushes in to hug Juliana and immediately senses an awkward moment among us. Henry, Harold, and Father Joseph proceed to sit at the table in the middle of the main room. They're unaware of what may unravel in the next few minutes, but to my surprise, an unexpected turn is taken.

"Is everything okay in here?" Gabe asks with uncertainty. He wavers before suggesting there might be some conflict between Nic and I. Juliana quickly grabs his face and kisses him, reassuring him that everything is fine.

"Everything is good. No problems. In fact, Arena was just teaching me some . . . interesting combat moves," Nic says.

Niki quietly sits back down at the table, while Gabe scans my face one more time for assurance. Juliana and Nic may think they have convinced him, but I know my brother better than that. Gabe is extremely smart and intuitive, and not for one second does he believe I would be generously helping Nic with anything.

Juliana's reaction to all of this isn't really a surprise to me. She's a nurturing and caring girl who desires companionship and restoration. She would rather cover the truth than to see this group give way to a petty rebellious resentment. And exposing any unnecessary conflict to our situation that would hinder an already broken fellowship wouldn't benefit anyone.

I'm more shocked by Nic's unanticipated response. For someone who is so abrasively blunt and self-absorbed, he seems genuinely concerned for the well-being of this group. I'm not sure if it's for the benefit of the group or himself, but I hate to admit that I begrudgingly go along with his act nonetheless.

"No hard feelings," he says, winking at me with his hand extended.

I can't believe this guy. I want to carve up his genitals and disfigure his pretty-boy face, but I can't seem to sever my pity for him. Maybe it's that deep-planted seed of loneliness tucked in the back of my head that struggles to resist the rare and charming moment of chivalry he sometimes offers.

Damn this guy. I hate to love him and love to hate him. Regardless of the tension, I shake his hand and call a truce.

As much as I despise giving in like this, it's best for everyone.

I let myself get so caught up in the drama of teenage hormones, I almost forgot about the others being back from the surface to give us a report. Gabe looks distracted by Juliana's affection, while the others bicker among themselves on how to move forward.

Apparently, everything in the city is in ruin, but more importantly, its barren dwellings are free of roaming soldiers. The town has been cleared of barricades and armored vehicles that once flooded the streets nearly a month ago. There seems to be no sign of life left among the place I used to call home, and it makes me sad and lonely inside to know that we started this journey right here.

The memories I've taken from this place are like all the rest—they will eventually fade but never be forgotten. I lean into the table to intrude in on the conversation, and everyone except Gabe seems to agree that holding onto this place for as long as we are able would be best served for everyone, but I vehemently disagree.

"We leave this place as soon as we can," I firmly say, interrupting their conversation. The immediate silence is a strong indication that my words sting. It's so quiet and still, I can hear my heart beating.

"What makes you think that's a good idea?" Harold asks.

"I'm not saying it's good, and it's not entirely my idea. My tone in this matter is not of arrogance or pride, but rather faithfulness to my covenant. I would gladly stay here and ride it out as long as I could, but that simply will not do. This place will soon be overcome by the Russians and I won't allow us to be here when that happens. God is the only reason we are still alive, not me. If you all want to survive, then our only chance is to find the Southern Resistance. That is our safe haven. Isn't that right, Nic?"

"She's right," Nic agrees, "It's the only way. It won't take the Russians long to fill these tunnels with troops. Welding the doors shut won't keep them out."

"What do you know about this Southern Resistance?" Father Joseph asks.

"It's not a rumor, I assure you. In fact, not only does it exist, it's stationed in the south Texas territory. When I led the Northern Resistance in the last revolt, word was given by my superior to lead our group towards Texas and pull our forces together. Very few of us lived to see its fruition. I'm told it harbors enough men and weaponry to defend against this regime. Believe what you will, but Arena is right. I don't want to be here when those doors fail and flood this place with soldiers."

"Okay, I'm on board, but why leave now?" Henry asks.

"I don't expect any of us to understand why, and I don't wish to debate it. All opinions aside, it's not what you want for this group or what I think is best. When God speaks, I lis- ten, and come first light, we move on from this place," I
firmly answer.

"And you're sure of this?" Father Joseph asks with uncertainty in his voice. I can't blame him. I've cast enough doubt to cause me to question my own judgment, but this time is quite different.

"I've never been more sure in all my life."

"I hope you're right," Niki adds, unconvinced.

CHAPTER 18

The stillness in the air harbors a discomfort that Allison pretends to hide while we lie next to each other in her bed. I can see it in her eyes and on her frightened face. I'm in no way eager to unmask the terror that awaits us on the outside, but I can't lie, and if she does ask then I will have to reveal the truth.

However, I vow not to fill the little time left spent in the den with undesirable thoughts, so I try to comfort the unpleasant ones instead. When I try to get up from the bed, Allison refuses to let me go and cries for me to stay. I wait until the worry on her face placidly relaxes and her eyes close before I leave her to rest for the night.

I walk back into the main den where Niki, Gabe, and Father Joseph are quietly discussing the peculiarities of Nic's previous engagement. The tone of their conversation diminishes when I enter the room, and their eyes conveniently avoid mine when I pull up a chair to join them.

"So, do you believe Nic's story?" Father Joseph bluntly asks me, knowing I've undoubtedly heard every word spoken so far.

"Well, I was taught to trust no one, so my opinion in this matter is irrelevant."

"But you do have an opinion."

"Then no," I immediately say. "He is supposed to be some leader of the Northern Resistance? Not likely, but there may be truth to some of his story."

"The camps are stationed in the south?" Gabe questions.

"If it is true, would we find our own resistance along the way?" Father Joseph asks.

"I guess we're going to find out."

"So, we're just going to leave this place based on a hunch you got from Nic?" Niki asks.

"It's more than just a hunch. You're just going to have to trust me. I think he knows more than what he's leading us to believe. And I'll be damned if I have to spend another day in these closed corners with that egotistical Neanderthal." Gabe tries not to crack a smile at the expense of my nauseating revulsion for Nic. He knows my true feelings, and I know he wasn't at all fooled by our playful confrontation earlier.

"Pack up as much as you can of what we absolutely need—food, clothes, whatever's necessary to survive," I say to Niki.

"How are we supposed to carry all of this stuff on foot?" Niki asks.

"I don't plan to."

"Well, we certainly can't cram everything and everyone into that death trap of a car."

"Death trap? It was that car that saved Juliana and Henry from being stranded. Besides, the Camaro will seat at least four."

"And what options do we have for the others?"

"There are always options," I say as I look over to Father Joseph's fatigued facial expression, "right?"

"Perhaps there's a solution," he says, looking to Gabe.

"And what might that be?" asks Niki.

"We did find a few vehicles that appeared to be in working order, but I wouldn't get too excited. We'll have to siphon every truck and car out there to have enough fuel for this journey," Gabe says.

"Well, giddy up, little brother," I say as I pop a fresh mag in my gun. "Let's go fetch some gas."

"Whoa, wait a minute. I think I better come with you two," Father Joseph says.

"No, we got this. I need you to stay here and keep a close eye on Nic. Besides, you look like you could use the rest."

"But it's too dark outside."

I'm used to the dark. Besides, I really need the fresh air. I was beginning to think I would never see a tree again."

Because both doors have been securely sealed from the outside, Gabe and I take the stairs up to the garage, behind the only door left that hasn't kept us completely closed in to this dungeon. Seems like ages ago, but I can remember the first day I set my eyes on this place. I was so enamored by the technological beauty displayed on the walls that I immediately fell in love. And now, it's all I can do to keep myself from going mad hoping to escape this claustrophobic prison.

The wide mechanical metal door in the garage creaks open wide enough for Gabe and I to slip through without exposing anything important in this grease monkey's lair. I nearly get tangled up rolling underneath the door in the underbrush that has taken over the ground. Just on the other side, a lattice of vines braids the roof green and coils down the corners, attaching to anything with a crevice.

From the outside, it looks nothing like a garage. The concrete walls are nicely camouflaged with dirt, sweeping brush, and whatever other green climbers that are attracted to it. Rusted car parts and trash litter the sides of the nearly invisible structure helping it blend in to a less desirable place to snoop around in.

The streets may seem empty, but I'm not taking any chances. I draw my gun. Gabe nervously walks ahead, trying to remember the location of the vehicles while I follow behind. You can learn a lot from someone's body language, and right now his is telling me he's terrified.

I can tell when Gabe is stressed. He responds with these erratic tics when something has him on edge. His head jerks like a chicken, and he jumps into a full-body twitch even at the slightest sound or movement. Every critter scurrying across our path right now has him dancing with alarm.

Paranoid or not, he's come a long way to want to venture out on such an eerie, still night like this. He's had to overcome more internal pain and personal affliction in a year than most people have had in a lifetime. I've never known Gabe to initiate bravery, but he has always stood his ground in his beliefs. I think that's what makes him strong during the weakest hour, what gives him peace to silence the chaos, and a will to abide courage during a time of suffering and the malice of evil men. He is my blood, my confidant, my brother, and I couldn't bear to live a day without him.

While we walk the vacant streets, we are bitterly reminded of the kind of terror that has scorched this town clean, tormenting souls, and ravishing the innocent from their meekness. Buildings have been burned, lives have been severed, and families have been broken. And for what?

There's nothing left here to start anew. It will perish like the world around it and soon be forgotten. A cold chill crawls up my spine when Gabe stops just short of the Bowie street corner and gasps with fright.

Just around the corner, and lying partially decomposed, is the old man who owned the cleaners where Jacob had lived. Judging by the ashen color of his skin, he's been dead for some time now. His body is riddled with gunshots, and his chest has burst open from the distended gases trapped inside. His face and neck have turned grayish-white, and the ground beneath him has painted the concrete a red-brown stain.

I look away for a moment, desperately trying not to think of Jacob. It seems like no matter where I go there's always a memory left for me to painfully hold.

Gabe quietly walks away. I let my thoughts settle, leaving me to absorb a minute of mourning, but unfortunately that's not all that's being absorbed. The smell is too wretched to stand near the body much longer, so I leave.

Just as I walk away, a sudden flash above moves across the dim-glowing streetlamp. Descending from the dark skies, a shadowy bird glides down toward the body. Once it reaches the old man and comes into the light, I immediately recognize the menacing black fowl as the same feathered squelching horror that has followed me this entire journey.

Those same deep, cold eyes stare through me with dead calm until I try to disengage from his piercing gaze. A sudden cry calls out to me from his pitted beak with that malevolent squawk I've come to detest.

This time I'm in no mood for a standoff. The only thing I engage in with this blood-soaked crow is the barrel of my gun pointed to his head. While I watch him feed on the insides of the man's bulging gut, I gently squeeze the trigger.

The bird is quickly knocked from his perching carnage and drilled into the side of the brick wall. The crow is thrown on his back and pieces of feathers float down on top of him. I turn away for a moment and wonder if what I have done is borderline crazy—letting some bird manipulate me into thinking I'm mad and hoping to tempt my anger to rise above me.

Gabe walks over and gives me a hug, as if to assure me I'm not at my wit's end. I can't help but to think that my brother may be the only one in the group who truly understands my struggles and realizes the inner strife that has bled me dry.

"We're all scarred by something . . ." he says as his words softly trail off. Before he can finish his sentence, a popping sound behind me abruptly captures his attention. I follow his eyes while he alertly looks over my shoulder, and when I turn around, the crow flies away into the deep dark skies.

"I think you're being haunted by your our own personal hell," he says.

"Well, that's comforting, dear brother," I sarcastically retort.

"I wouldn't worry about it too much. It beats the alternative though."

"Yeah, and what's that?"

"Instead of a two-legged feathered annoyance, it could have been a four-legged beast with teeth. Bird . . . lion," he facetiously says, pretending to use his hands as an invisible scale to weigh the options.

"Yeah, that's really not helping at all."

About two streets over, near the corner store bakery, or what's left of it, sits an abandoned GAZ-3950 Tiger, a light armored Russian military vehicle. The tread on the tires has been shredded beyond repair, and the only thing that might be of use on this assault machine is an empty ten-gallon fuel container attached to the rear door.

Gabe unlatches the small tank from the metal trunk and opens it to make sure it's empty of any contaminated diesel. Most of the wrecked cars and trucks in the area don't run on diesel, and if we are to siphon any gas, this container needs to be cleaned.

Gabe jogs over near the end of town square, pointing with excitement.

"Over here," he says, straddling over a damaged wrought-iron fence. Two cars are parked curbside into each other, one of which is missing the right rear wheel. The other looks less damaged on the outside but has been badly burned on the interior.

"This is it. This is what we need," he says, trying to open the dented driver side door.

"Really, out of all the fuel-efficient cars in the area, and you choose a gas-guzzling SUV."

"It has enough room for everything we need, plus it's the only vehicle we've found that still has the keys in the ignition."

"It's a piece of shit if you want to know the truth."

"Yeah, well it's our piece of shit now."

It may be a ridiculous choice for a vehicle in an apocalyptic world, but in our case, it's the most logical. When he turns the key, the truck struggles to turn over, gasping for the right mixture of air and fuel, until it finally fires into a growling rumble with black smoke emitting from the exhaust.

Since its been stranded here for God-knows-how-long, he slowly pushes the throttle inward, giving it a nice, steady flow of gas to warm the engine up and exercise the lubed parts again. All the gages seem to work properly, and after a few minutes of idling, Gabe turns the engine off.

"She sounds rough, but it'll do. She's got about a quarter tank left in her," he says as if he suddenly manifested into a mechanic.

"Her? Who is she, your mistress? Are you going to give her a name now?"

"Yeah, well at least I don't sleep with my knife," he replies. Okay, so he's got a valid point. I wish I had something witty to retort with, but I don't.

"Stay here with your sweetheart then, but don't get too attached. We still need a hose." I was so anxious to go outside for some fresh air that I completely forgot to grab something to siphon gas out with. Luckily, Mason's hardware store is still standing without any severe damage, but whether or not there's a garden hose in there is anybody's guess.

Though the town is a barren wasteland, the quiet streets still give me an unsustainable comfort. There are a few bodies scattered along the curbs that smell of sulfur and refuse, many of which have been burned. The charred remains are beyond recognition, except for one that is the size of a small child with his or her arms stretched out, as if they were reaching out for help. It's a shocking and sickening display of cruelty.

I avert my eyes the best I can as I walk around to the front of the store. It's a disturbing reminder of the wickedness still left on this earth. The door to the hardware store has been jarred open, and most of the glass-paned windows are shattered or completely missing.

I enter the store with extreme caution, praying nothing falls in on me. The ceiling is still intact, but it's just unstable enough that it might just suddenly cave in. The shelves are bare and left with nothing but a few rolls of twine hanging on an end cap.

Of course there would be a surplus of garden tools hanging on the walls and no garden hose. I'm pretty sure cultivating crops wasn't exactly a priority when this place was ransacked. If this was a zombie apocalypse, at least I 'd have an arsenal of head-chopping tools at my disposal.

I wander through the back of the store where piles of rubble and refuse decorate the aisles. I dig through the trash, but find nothing except a door barricaded behind the debris.

I open it and find a storage room hiding a frightful stench—the smell of a rotting corpse. If there is anything useful in here, it's too dark to see it. I turn the flashlight on and nearly piss myself. Someone is standing before me. Feet askew, I jump back and gasp with fright.

I quickly pull my gun and shine the light once more, but upon a closer look, I find that it's just my reflection in an old mirror. Below it drips a leaky faucet attached to an old, gray water hose. Its end is too corroded and rusty to unscrew. I pull out my knife and cut the hose loose. Suddenly a door next to me creaks open a few inches. I quickly shine the flashlight by the corner of the opening when a very large sewer rat comes racing out.

"Shit!" I shout.

Attached to the front of the door is a sign marked, *Bathroom*. If for no other purposeful reason to enter this room, my curiosity is piqued by the sudden scurry of a creature leaving it. I slowly push the door open with my boot to see what has him frightened. A whiff of stale air suddenly emerges like a punch in the face. The smell is so putrid I have to cover my mouth to keep from gagging.

I slowly graze the inside with the light until I realize I'm about three feet away from a rotting corpse. Startled, I drop the flashlight and push myself out of the bathroom door. I calmly reclaim my nerve and shine the light once more over the victim's face, only she's not a victim. At least not in the sense of the term most come to expect.

I carefully examine the body's posture, sitting tightly against the wall with her head leaning against the side of the toilet. There's a trail of blood on the wall that leads down to the back of her head, and a smaller gunshot wound, black in color, is slightly offset to the right of her forehead.

Still firmly grasped in her hand is a .45 magnum pistol that apparently aided in this self-induced death. I can only imagine what horror drove this poor woman to these extremes. With what we are dealing with, I wouldn't be surprised to see more of this.

I quickly roll up the hose and hurry back to Gabe, where he's tinkering with the engine. We siphon what we can from the two wrecked cars directly into the SUV's fuel tank and nearly fill it full.

We take the SUV deep into the littered town, roaming street by street until we find enough vehicles to siphon gas from. Most are bone-dry, but we manage to get enough fuel to fill eight of the ten gallons the container will hold. Before heading back to the den, we unexpectedly decide to make a small detour to our house.

My mind's not exactly in a place where I plan on ruminating in this house too long, but I want to at least take advantage of the small window of freedom we have left to gather some personal belongings.

The air in the house is musty, but it looks just the way it did before we left nearly a year ago. Avoiding any heart-wrenching memories hanging on the wall, I race upstairs and grab a purple box beneath my bed. I fill it with a few things that have the most sentimental value to me, starting with my mother's book of poems and a picture of her.

I grab a few pieces of jewelry in my music box, and a charm bracelet that once belonged to Niki's younger sister, Grace, who was shot in a violent accident. Myra had given it to me the first day we were taken in as foster children. I don't know why it touched me so dearly, but it was one of the few things that gave me a sense of peace during that transition. I had no idea that it belonged to her daughter until Niki told me a few years later. It still gives me a warm feeling inside when I look at it.

While Gabe scavenges through his messy room, I take one last look around before leaving. I walk over to my bed, close my eyes, and recall all the times Niki gave me sisterly advice, loving on me when she didn't have to, and comforting my deepest despairs when I needed it the most.

I open my eyes to find a moment of serenity breathing within me, until I gradually break down and cry.

"Are you ready?" Gabe asks, standing at the door watching me.

"Yeah, just give me a minute," I say quickly, calming myself from an emotional moment. Gabe avoids looking me in the eyes. He uncomfortably stands there, stone-faced, and says nothing. I'm not sure if he's trying to think of something to say or if he's waiting out the awkward silence.

In any case, my brother isn't normally one to let a quiet moment linger if it makes him uneasy, so he blurts out the first random thought that comes to him.

"The fish are dead."

It's random all right, but it does loosen the muscles in my jaw and makes me chuckle.

"Yeah, I figured," I say, patting him on the cheek. "Come on, we better be getting back."

While we walk down the creaky steps, I feel an unsettling sense of sorrow brewing.

"Arena?"

"Yeah?"

He pauses a few seconds and stops halfway down the stairs. "We're not going to live through all of this, are we?"

My feet slow to a crawl before my body comes to a complete halt on the steps. I meditatively stare down at the railing and choose not to answer what I don't know because I've often wondered myself. I'm not sure what he wants to hear, as it will never change his fate, but I can only tell him what I do know.

"We're going to live as long as we are supposed to."

CHAPTER 19

Everyone in the den is asleep, except for Father Joseph, who stayed up waiting for Gabe and me to get back. As much as I need the sleep, there's still too much to do before we leave this place tomorrow. I grab as many fully loaded magazines as I can fit into my pack, while Gabe takes a thorough inventory of all the tools and electronics he may need to take with us.

Displayed on the wall behind me are a slew of weapons, ranging from semi-automatic short-burst firearms to fully automatic assault rifles. Buried beneath a blanket, a large box holds a variety of grenades and shells, some of which were made specifically to be shot with a launcher.

With the flood of guns at our disposal, I suddenly feel a bit disconnected from my swords. As odd and disturbing as it may sound, I feel more comfortable killing a man with sharpened steel than I do with a bullet. I can't remember the last time I've had to use them. Seems sort of silly, but I miss swinging them about.

But if we are to be smart with our resources, we must choose our weapons wisely, and not every gun that wants to be held can be carried with us. However, there is one in particular I'm not leaving here without.

Packed tightly in a black case sleeps a beautifully designed CheyTac M200 with effective range of two thousand meters, .5/7 round feed system, and a detachable box magazine. This is pure self-indulgence, but it's coming with me.

Gabe and I pack the trunk of the Camaro full with our wonderfully dangerous toys before going to our quarters to sleep. It would behoove me to get some rest, but I'm too anxious about tomorrow. I take advantage of our last night here and soak under one last hot shower.

I close my eyes to submerse into reflection under the steamy water, and as the warm water massages my body, I fall into a deep hypnotic slumber.

I hear the bathroom door slowly creep open, and a blurry shadow moves past the translucent curtain. I quickly turn off the water and cover myself with a towel while the silhouette is standing right outside of the shower.

"Gabe, is that you?" I ask nervously. After a few seconds, I call out again, but there's still no response. A shiver of fright slides up and down my spine. The beads of water cascading down my skin turn frigid, and my toes begin to curl. I quickly look around for something to defend myself with, but there's nothing.

The vinyl curtain suddenly slides open, and standing on the other side is Nic pointing a gun at me. I knew it from the first time I saw his face that he was a detriment to our fellowship. I should have cut him when I had the chance, but now I stand here helpless without anywhere to escape, except from this world. I feel draped with defeat, and all I can think about is how Allison will cope without me if she isn't already dead.

"Wait," I plead, "you don't have to do this."

"Oh, but I do. Did you honestly think you expected to leave here alive?"

"I've obviously expected too much of everyone, and you were no different."

"My part in this is trivial; there are much bigger things to worry about."

"Put the gun down. There are ways around this where we can both get what we want."

"I'm in no mood to make a deal."

"You really expect to get away with this? When that gun goes off, Gabe and the others will be all over you."

"You're actually making some sense now," he says, pulling out a suppressor from his pocket and screwing it on to the end of the barrel. "This is what you would have done, and when they see the gun in your hand, they won't have to question your sanity anymore. They already know you're actually crazy enough to do it."

"Wait!" I scream before the gun goes off. Suddenly, my eyes open, and I jerk my head back, clutching the slippery tiles. The warm water has gone, leaving me to shiver underneath a cold shower and a horrendous nightmare. I turn off the freezing water and wrap the warm towel around my quivering body.

I take a quick peek where Nic is sleeping just to assure myself it was only a dream, but I know in this world nothing is completely impossible. I shudder to think there's always the possibility that any disquieting dream can turn into a living nightmare.

I wonder what may come of this journey, with the potential threat Nic poses to this group. I've never been one to be overly paranoid, but tonight I sleep with a gun underneath my pillow.

*　*　*

I wake up feeling a little nervous about the decision I've made to leave this place, a decision that may jeopardize everyone's safety. I wipe my eyes, look around, and find that I'm the last one to climb out of bed.

I quickly dress before joining the others to help them pack, but when I walk out to the main den, everyone is standing around and ready to go. I'm a little bitter that no one had the decency to wake me, but then again it was probably better for them that I hadn't. I'm a crotchety, grumpy person when I've had a lack of sleep.

I look at everyone waiting and wonder how many of us will be left standing when this journey is over. A new fellowship has been bound, and it's my responsibility to keep it from being severed.

"I know many of you have had second thoughts about leaving, and regardless of what happens out there, I assure you that this is the right decision."

Niki walks up to me privately while the others make their way up the stairs. "Arena, sister to sister, I love you, and I will honor any choices you make. I will stand with you and fight as long as I'm able."

"And the others?"

"They all believe in you. Some may show it differently, but deep inside they know who to follow. We've been through a lot, but what you have created has made us all better for it. I guarantee you when the time comes, they will have given their life for you."

"Thank you," I say as she hugs me. "You're going to make a great mother someday."

While Niki ascends upstairs, I take a moment to think about how this place has served and done more for us than we could ever know. And now we leave it just as I first saw it, to never return again. I whisper into the air a few words of gratitude before turning out the lights and heading outside.

Everyone is standing around as if they're waiting to receive some kind of revelation. If it's direction they need, it's direction they're going to get.

"Allison, Juliana, Gabe, and I will take the Camaro; the rest of you follow behind in the SUV. We'll stick to the highway unless something forces us to do otherwise. We should be able cover more ground that way. Just remember, if you see anything remotely threatening, don't hesitate to pull over and bail. The trees may be our only friend. The Resistance will most likely be kept hidden deep in the woods and away from the main thoroughfares."

I grab the door handle of the Camaro, when Gabe presses his hand against mine.

"What do you think you're doing?" Gabe questions.

"I beg your pardon," I respond with a little vigor.

"I don't think so, Arena. You've never driven a car like this before."

"I've watched Finnegan handle this car very closely. Besides, Henry has been letting me practice driving the past two years at his place. I have more experience driving a stick shift than you do. I know what I'm doing, now hand me the bloody keys."

"I'm sorry, but I can't do that."

"If you weren't my brother, I'd slap you into a coma."

"I can do that for you," Juliana intones.

"Look, I've been shot, stabbed, slapped, punched, spit on, fondled, and nearly raped. I don't know how much longer I have on this earth to live, but I'll be damned if I die before I get this one and only chance to know what it's like to drive a car like this. I'm nearly sixteen and I believe I've earned the right to learn how. I'm leading this pack. Now give me those damn keys before I twist your testicles into a pretzel."

"Buckle up everyone," he says, smiling, and hands me the keys. I ignore the nervous tension in the car and concentrate on the stiffness of the clutch. It's slightly different than Henry's car, but the concept is the same.

I push the clutch in and turn the key to a roaring sound of pure adrenaline. I shift the beast into neutral and tease this angry lion as it growls fiercely when I press slightly into the accelerator. While the others load up in the SUV waiting for me to take the lead, I try to get a feel for the pedals.

I know this is probably an inappropriate moment to scream with joy, especially during a depressing age of global turmoil, but sometimes it's what you have to do to keep the little things that remind us of who we are from completely dying.

Gabe closes his eyes and prays underneath his breath while Juliana and Allison nervously double-check their seatbelts. Geez, it's not like I'm flying a plane here, at least we're grounded . . . for the most part. I awkwardly shift the car into first gear and ease the beautifully purring machine slowly out of the opened garage, pressing ever so slightly on the gas.

If I didn't subconsciously look in the rearview mirror I wouldn't have noticed the frightened look on Allison's face.

"You can do this, Arena. I trust you," Juliana says kindly. Although I think she is just reassuring herself, I'm trying to keep things in perspective here.

I'm a little jerky with the shifting, but after a few turns down main street, I get a better feel of the stiff clutch. I'm able to punch the gas around the last turn, sending Gabe's face pressed against the window.

I stop at the ramp entrance and wait for Henry to catch up with me. I'm so giddy at the idea that I'm actually driving that I'm going to let loose everything that has ever slowed me down.

I mean, really, who am I to leave behind the only chance I'll ever have to drive such a beautifully engineered machine? The desolate roads are begging to be driven on, and here I am, just inches away from the accelerator, waiting to feel free again, even if it is short-lived. I owe it to myself to let go of everything.

"Enough pussy-footing around. Hang on to your asses back there, we're going for a ride," I say before I punch the gas. The sheer torque of the engine sends the car jerking forward, and everyone is glued to the back of their seats. The smoking tires' friction with the road is a marriage of rubber and asphalt.

I can't tell if it's the squealing of the tires mingling with the warm pavement, or Allison and Juliana screaming. I'm much too excited to look back and see, but after a couple of seconds, it doesn't really matter. The Camaro quickly propels us forward, with its sprinting muscle like a rabid cheetah, and within seconds, the ramp entrance and SUV are left behind in a cloud of dust.

I shout with excitement as I fly through the gears until I have to downshift around tight bends in the highway. But when I find a long, flat piece of real estate to exercise this engine on, there's no holding back. I milk the gears on the long stretch of highway until the force pushes my back firmly against the seat and every gear has been exhausted.

The performance behind this muscle car is relentlessly terrifying, and if you lose respect of its power for just a split second, it will turn on you without remorse. It's fast, dangerous, and unfathomably commanding of the road—it's exactly as I'd hoped for.

I can't say that about the others. Gabe's eyes are nearly rolled back in their sockets as he clutches the side of the door and the back of his headrest. Juliana and Allison are screaming in unison demanding that I stop the car, but I'm so enthralled with being in control behind the wheel that I shut them out. The trees along the sides of the highway are a solid blur of green, and the white dashes in the center of the road are passing by so fast, it looks like one solid line.

My heart races faster and faster with exhilaration while the engine rumbles louder and louder, but like all things that are good, they must soon come to an end. And this ride is no different. The thrill of the drive is short-lived, but not because of the incessant screaming in the back of the car, or my brother's ridiculously dramatic carsickness.

Just over a small hill, there's a wreckage of cars spread across the highway about a thousand feet in front of us. I immediately slam on the brakes, screeching rubber across the pavement, and sending everyone nearly motionless in suspension. The G-force of us slamming against the seatbelts is horrific. My ass is out of its seat, and Gabe looks as if he's floating in space.

The distance from the wrecked cars is barely enough for me to get this churning engine to come to a complete stop. We're just inches away from ramming the side of an RV. When the dust settles and my eyes fully adjust, I look through the clouded windshield and see a carnage of twisted metal. It's an unsettling sight to behold.

"Ride's over."

"Sweet baby Jesus, Arena! There's a reason you don't have a driver's license. I think you just stunted Allison's growth," Juliana says.

"I think I'm going to be sick," Gabe says, leaning over and holding his stomach.

"Go right ahead, I think I swallowed mine earlier," Allison says.

Gabe sits back, adjusts his neck, and turns to Juliana. "You okay back there, babe?"

"Yeah, but I'm pretty sure my boobs are a cup size smaller than they were five minutes ago," she answers.

"You're lucky. I think my nuts forgot they were attached, and I'm pretty sure I lost my tonsils somewhere on the dashboard."

"Arena, give those keys back to Gabe—you are officially fired from driving," Juliana says.

"No problem," I mutter as I look upon the grisly sight. "I don't think we will be driving any time soon."

I get out of the car and slowly approach the mass wreckage with caution. The smell of the Camaro's scorching tires is enough to make me nauseous, but it's nothing compared to the stench that's before us.

The smell of decomposed flesh soon filters through the burnt aroma and punches me in the face with extreme prejudice. The rotting, gaseous pile of sick permeates into my clothes. My belly suddenly begins to churn, and it's not enough to cover my mouth and nose with my hands that I finally lose whatever my stomach has refused to digest.

Gabe drags his shoes close behind me while I try to recover. Allison and Juliana slowly walk toward the wreckage.

"Allison! Don't come over here. Stay with Juliana by the car," I shout.

Bodies after bodies lie comatose on the pavement, decomposing in the warm sun. Men, women, and children have fallen to something I just can't explain. As I wander through the carnage to examine their deathly state, I shockingly see no gunshot wounds or any signs of fatal scarring. Many look like they just fell asleep, while others tried to flee into the woods, only to be stopped in their tracks by something that was equally horrific—ravaged by wild animals.

Surrounded by a sea of corpses, my eyes glaze over with a sadness I cannot fathom. What kind of reckless hate is among us that would do such a thing? My eyes are fixed on a shocking display of wretched and vile devastation. I just don't understand why so many people are being killed and some are being imprisoned. What's the point to all of this?

I walk closer to the ghastly sight and see a woman curled up with her eyelids closed, unlike the other bodies that lie beside her. My teeth grind with revulsion. I'm so distraught by the horrific image, I'm forced to turn my head away.

Still wrapped in her arms is a distorted slice of innocence—an infant buried into her mother's chest. I stand there, cold inside, and stricken with grief. This is beyond the scope of transgression. This is an abomination.

I wipe my eyes and make my way back over by Gabe, carefully stepping over and in-between the rotting figures.

"What are we to do, Arena?" Gabe asks.

I'm too emotional to respond when I walk past him, and yet far too determined not to give him an honest answer. I climb up the ladder that's attached to the RV and look out beyond the line of wrecked vehicles from the rooftop.

"We travel on foot from here," I say in a stern, bitter voice.

The highway is painted with rotting corpses and wrecked cars as far as my eye can see. Thousands upon thousands lie scattered alongside the ditches and peppered throughout the tree line where they failed to retreat.

My mind is completely and utterly numb, and I would do best to keep my heart from following. I climb back down to wait for the others to arrive while Gabe keeps Juliana and Allison far away from this massive gravesite. I try to understand why God would have led us here. What purpose could this possibly fulfill?

Maybe it's just another small reminder of what's to come. Whatever this represents, I will no longer take the following days of our journey lightly. No matter the scrutiny or ridicule I may receive for my decisions, I will not falter from God's path.

I pace back and forth behind the camper and wonder how the others are going to feel about my decision to move on foot.

I rest on the back bumper of the RV and lean my head against the door that is slightly ajar. The back of my head gently vibrates, but I ignore it. It's the sudden buzzing inside the camper that garners my attention. I carefully stand up and put my ear against the vinyl door. The humming chorus grows louder.

"What is it, Arena," Gabe curiously asks.

"I don't know."

I'm too curious not to open the door so I draw my gun and peek inside. Within seconds, a swarm of angry wasps exit the RV like a stream of fighter jets.

"Run!" I shout. I sprint away from the RV and head to the car. Juliana and Gabe stand fixated on my retreat while I'm getting bombarded by these kamikaze bees.

"Get in the fucking car, now!" I reiterate more firmly.

I swat the back of my head, jump into the passenger side, and slam the door. Juliana and Gabe race safely in the back seat, but Allison doesn't. Instead she runs away toward the ditch.

I open the door and shout out at the top of my lungs, "Allison!" She's too hysterical to listen and stumbles to the ground, frantically screaming.

"Juliana, stay here. Gabe, come with me," I assert.

I quickly run to her side and try to pick her up, but she refuses to move and clings to the earth. Gabe picks her up and carries her to the car safely. I stroke her arm and hold her hand, but nothing works. She's unnerved to the point of catatonic limbo. I try shaking her back from an altered state of consciousness but she doesn't respond. The back of her neck is swollen and red. She must be allergic to the bee sting.

I pick up her limp body and hold her against mine as I cry out. I can feel her breathing heavily and her eyes begin to twitch. She's hyperventilating.

Her breaths shorten, but the trembling has subdued. She appears to be completely unresponsive and is falling fast into anaphylactic shock. Her face is sweating, and the skin on her chest flashes red. Gabe and Juliana stare helplessly not knowing what to do, while I desperately try to find an escape from all of this. I'm lost, and totally unprepared for the fact that Allison's life may be taken away from me in an instant because of my stupidity.

I feel absolutely helpless.

CHAPTER 20

I can remember a time when the warm morning sun would soothe my face, but now it only pains me. Just once, I'd like to wake up one morning and know what it's like not to feel sad.

Allison's body falls into my lap as lifeless as a stone unturned. The violent shakes have passed, and her erratic breathing slows to a whisper of air until she begins to gasp for every breath.

Suddenly, the SUV pulls up and then it immediately dawns on me—the first aid kit Niki has packed is carrying a stash of epinephrine. I ask Juliana to hold Allison with her head up while I sprint over to the back of the truck. Everyone is nervously standing around, wondering what's going on.

I frantically dig through clothes, blankets, and food, but I cannot locate the first aid kit. Terror nearly overcomes me, knowing that Allison's death is near. If I can't find the adrenaline to relax her chest muscles, her lungs will soon collapse.

Nearly at my wit's end and falling under desperation, I know nothing else to do, so I scream, "Where's the damn first aid kit?"

Niki rushes over and pulls out one of the backpacks where the kit is zipped up. Allison is barely breathing. I open the case, pull out an EpiPen, and inject it into Allison's outer thigh.

After a few seconds, she begins to jerk. Her pupils grow large, and the short breaths return to a normal deep pace. The redness in her neck goes away, and she gradually becomes more responsive to my voice.

"Allison . . . Allison, can you hear me?" I tenderly ask. She squeezes my hand for the first time and looks up at me with those groggy eyes. She finally speaks. My heart stops racing, and the anxiety suddenly releases from my body.

"Arena? What happened?" she asks as she pulls herself up.

"Honey, you were stung by a wasp. You had an allergic reaction." She sits up and leans on my shoulder.

"Are they gone?"

"Yeah, they're gone." She slowly gets out of the car and fixes her eyes on the carnage in front of us. She stands there as if she's in a trance.

"Allison?" I softly call out. She ignores my voice and slowly moves toward the dead. There's an eerie silence as she inches closer to the pile of bodies. Everyone just stands there and watches. Not a word is spoken. I'm not sure if the shock has completely worn off her or if a new one is beginning to set in. I go after Allison, but she stops, trembles, and falls to her knees.

"We're all going to die," she cries.

I hold her tight and rub her back to soothe her anxiety. I know comforting her can only last so long before she looks upon the bodies again, but I try nonetheless. She needs to be convincingly reassured.

"Look at me! Allison, look at me! That is not you. You are here with us and alive," I say as she starts to shake again. I hold her tighter and become more authoritative. "Hey! Look me in the eyes, Allison. Don't look over my shoulder. You're not going to end up like them, do you understand? I will not let that happen."

"You don't know that," she says, rejecting my assurance.

"There are many things that I don't know, but this I do," I say, wiping the tears running down her cheeks. "You have my word." She leans her head against my chest and hugs me tightly for a moment before she feels convinced that she's safe.

"I trust you," she says.

I feel a moment of reprieve, but I have to be honest with myself too. I'll admit I'm scared that she does trust me, and when I look over to the pile of bodies, I briefly try to assure myself as well. From this point on, we're all in this together, well, except for maybe Nic. I still don't know where he stands in all of this.

While Gabe tries to explain to the others what the new plan entails, I return to the trunk of the SUV. By the looks on their faces, I can tell no one is exactly thrilled about the idea, but we really have no other choice.

The smell of the warming corpses worsens by the minute, and there's nothing we can really do to avoid walking through them. Bodies lie scattered within the woods on both sides of the highway, so walking around them isn't really an option, especially if there's a vehicle possibly waiting on the other end of this deathly trail of carnage.

We're going to have to make some makeshift masks to at least filter some of the smell out. Everyone is gagging at the pungent aroma. It's too much for any of us to endure.

I dig through the pile of clothes and search for a couple of old T-shirts to cut up. I'm willing to sacrifice a few clothes to get through this hopefully short excursion. I pull out my knife and cut one of the shirts into long strips.

I search through Niki's bag to find some perfume of any kind to soak these strips of cloth in, but I can't find anything but a half stick of roll-on deodorant. I guess it will have to do. I roll on one side of the strip with the deodorant and wrap the shirt piece over my mouth and around my head. I may look ridiculous, but at least I can get through the smell without vomiting.

I take the remaining shirt strips to the others, making everyone a crude version of the filtered mask. I walk over to Allison just to make sure she's coping with all of this.

"Hey, I want you close to me, okay. Don't leave my side," I say, hoping to relieve any future anxiety that should pop up. She nods her head, but by the look in her sloping eyes, I see a resilient, young girl trying to survive.

"Don't let your eyes wander, just try looking forward and follow my footsteps," I add.

Everyone takes pause, lifting their grief-stricken faces

ahead. The dark clouds in the west begin to fill the skies, and the mid-morning light slowly fades. The warmth of the sun is intermittently shaded by a mysterious haze above, but it will be the storm brewing that's going to dampen our spirits if we don't hurry.

"Take only what is necessary. We may be on foot for a while," I tell everyone.

"Arena, what about the weapons?" Harold asks.

"Take what you can, but don't carry any more than your body is willing to handle. We may have a long journey ahead of us, and those woods aren't going to be pleasant."

"I was a Boy Scout once; I think I can handle it."

I abruptly grab Harold's arm as he reaches for a rifle. "You think this is a picnic? Some outdoor sleepover with the boys? The second you walk into that green thicket and you decide to disrespect her, she's gonna give you a hell of lot more than a frightened rabbit to chase after."

"Easy, Arena," says Gabe, "he just wants to be prepared."

"You better not take this lightly," I say to Harold.

"I got it, okay!" he shouts, pulling his arm back, "but you needn't worry. He looks over at Niki, who is gathering supplies. "I'll protect her."

"Yes, but who's going to protect you? This isn't summer camp in the park. These woods aren't as forgiving as the city, and you better damn well be by her side."

"Geez, Arena, give him a break. What's with you?" says Gabe.

I don't know what just came over me. I feel a sudden rush of hatred flowing from me.

"Sorry, I just . . . be careful is all, okay? I love my sister."

"So do I," Harold says sternly. He walks away with a cold, bitter stare before I can reach out to him to truly apologize. My callous remarks may have hindered our relationship, but I meant what I said. Yes, it was a little harsh, but everyone needs to understand that from this moment on, nothing will be short of hostile and unpleasant. We all need to be on our toes.

I finish gathering and separating our weapons from least to greatest importance for this journey. Although, there's no need to lunge around with a sniper rifle, I break protocol, contradicting my own advice I'd given to Harold.

I take it apart and place it in a soft carrying case for easier transport. It's too much for me to carry. I have enough already, so I ask Henry to take it with us.

The clouds slowly grow darker as we walk through the tangled bodies. It's not enough that everyone is trying to avoid the stony, lifeless faces beneath our feet, but it's the eerie silence among the dead that sends shivers about. The only conclusion I can draw from this unsightly grim affair is that a deadly poisonous gas killed these people.

We scavenge the abandoned cars along the way, hoping to find anything that might be beneficial. I try to put empathy aside while I sift, but it's sometimes too emotionally painful to rummage through someone else's personal belongings. No matter how many innocent deaths I come across, I don't think I will ever be desensitized to this kind of cruel atrocity.

While everyone has their own system for searching, I keep it simple—look straight ahead and avoid any cars or trucks with children in them. It takes us nearly an hour to wade through the dead and delve through the vehicles, but I can finally see empty road up ahead.

Unfortunately, the last vehicle has been tipped over on its side and is surrounded by a sea of dead about a quarter mile from the open highway. And to make matters worse, a light drizzle begins to empty from the sky.

This wrecked SUV was destined to be found, and while those driving it desperately tried to escape, they left it filled with a large amount of camping supplies. The cargo carrier that had broken free from the luggage rack is open, spilling out its contents. Finally, a moment of fortune has turned to us.

Inside are several tent sacks, two sleeping bags, and a survival bag filled with matches, ice packs, eye wash, hydrogen peroxide, latex gloves, burn-free pads, vice grips, rope, a folding shovel, and strangely enough, a bottle of vodka.

Before we leave the truck, I take one last look through the broken rear window and notice a half-opened bag with white protruding from the top. I knock out the remaining shards of glass to get a closer look, and suddenly my bitterness turns to joy.

"Oh, please let it be . . . oh please, oh please, oh please," I say to myself. I pull the drawstrings back and look inside to find a large pack of toilet paper, but below that is the mother of all bonus survival items that has me giddy—a large box of tampons, thank you, Jesus! This is one bag I'm not leaving here without.

I pull the drawstrings tight and carry the sack over my shoulder, while everyone else gathers the rest of the camping supplies. A sudden loud crash of thunder rumbles above, and the drizzling rain comes down a little hard now, forcing me to lead us into these beastly woods for cover.

The trees are heavily dense in this area, but it makes for a natural covering from the nasty drizzle. The morning sun has slowly dissipated into the black skies and the towering foliage that surrounds us. The tranquility of the rain droplets bouncing from leaf to leaf is the only thing keeping this trek through the woodlands reasonably inviting.

I can tell that the group is anxiously waiting to stop and rest, but I forge ahead anyway. I understand they aren't used to hiking long distances, but we need to be as far away from the dead as possible. The smell will be far worse than it was before when the clouds break and the sun decides to pop back out and warm those rotting, wet corpses. I certainly don't want to be anywhere downwind of that unforgiving stench.

Hiking with this group is quite the challenge, and I know I'm not going to win any favor over them by exhausting them on the first day, so I stop. Besides, the thunder is growing louder, and the rain is beginning to come down much harder. The tall timbers can only shield so much water before we find ourselves drenched without any cover.

"It's about time we stop. You're going to bleed us dry out in this wilderness," Nic whines. Of all the people, I would have expected him to be the last to bitch and moan. I guess I failed to give everyone else some credit.

"You'll live," I respond.

"Yeah, but how about the women? They are no more geared for this than . . . you are at having sex with a man," he obscenely spouts right in front of Allison.

I immediately throw down my pack and grab his shirt, digging my nails into his chest.

"There is still hope riding here among us, and you will keep a civil tongue if you wish to stay!" He surrenders his vulgar mouth momentarily before he attempts to offer a feeble apology.

"Damn, PMS much? I'm sorry, meant no harm by it."

"Just keep your tongue in your mouth."

I estimate we've traveled a good five miles at the point we left the highway. The men quickly set up the tents in a small clearing before the punishing storm blows in on us. I take a little jaunt through the woods up ahead to scout out the environment for any unwanted entanglements that may dampen our evening.

I find a nice, beefy tree with plenty of branches to climb up on so I can get a better view. I climb near the top and immediately notice a plume of smoke trailing into the sky to the south of us. I can't tell exactly where it's coming from, so I pull out the scope I snatched from the sniper rifle to get a closer look.

About two miles away, a small ranch home sits nestled into a small coppice of trees, but the smoke isn't coming from the home. It's blowing in from the west of the property, and I can't see beyond the hill to know what is causing the smoke to rise behind the rain.

I'm eager to know, but I can't leave the group, not like this, anyway. I need to stay close to camp, especially for Allison's sake. I made a promise to her, and I aim to keep it. I climb back down from the tree as the rain pounds the side of the bark.

The sky roars even louder now, chasing every rodent on the ground out in the open back into their burrows, and it's exactly where I'm headed. I come back to the camp and find three tents firmly tied to the ground, one of which houses Allison and Juliana. While Father Joseph, Henry, and Nic occupy the second tent, Harold and Gabe share the other, which leaves the third tent for the women.

I'm not in any way against the idea of sharing a tent with the men, but I refuse to sleep anywhere near Nic, and Gabe's feet could knock a buzzard off a sewer truck. Besides, I really need to stay close to Allison—she needs me, and I desperately need Niki and Juliana.

Through hours of pouring rain, howling wind, and thunderous rumbles bellowing above, the storm churns with a force wreaking havoc on anything in its path except for the small area we decided to stop and set camp.

The storm passes, and the evening approaches, leaving one dark sky for another. It's too risky with this group to travel by night, though I'm eager to move on. I'm still a little uneasy about stopping here to camp, so I rest myself up in one of the trees above the tents and keep a keen eye on things while the others eat.

I'm so worried and anxious about tomorrow's travel that my appetite has escaped me. There are many miles between here and the southern plains. I find a nice forked branch to rest my ass on while I lean my head against the soft bark. I look up between the waving branches against the evening sky and notice just a speckle of stars gracing us tonight.

It's such a peaceful moment after a storm, and tonight seems even more serene, despite the cruel images still swarming in my head.

I sit up here suspended in peace overlooking God's world from above, when all of the sudden, the tree begins to vibrate. Climbing like a clumsy-footed bear rather than a nimble cat, my intrusive but caring brother decides to join me.

"Need some company?" he asks.

"No, not really," I answer honestly.

"Good," he says, climbing up anyway and sitting on the opposite branch to me.

"So what's on your mind?" I ask.

"I'll be honest, Arena, I don't really know how the others are going to handle the daily travel. It's a bit of a load for them."

"I know, but we can't slow our pace now."

"Nor can we keep it like this forever."

"So what are you suggesting? We just sit around twiddling our thumbs until someone finds us?"

"No, but it wouldn't hurt if you showed a little bit of compassion when you lead."

"Excuse me? Of all the people to speak to me about compassion, you're the one person I would expect to understand. We are of the same blood and carry the same wounds—or have you forgotten?"

"By blood we are the same, sure, but we are still very different."

"The only difference I see is that you have someone to love, and I'm alone."

"What is this obsession with you? Why can't you just let things go?"

"Because it's all I have," I say softly, trying to hold back my tears.

"You must move on from this. It's been nearly a year that he's been gone. I know it's hard, but—"

"Do you? What do you know about losing someone?" I brashly interrupt. I pause for a quiet moment before I realize I've completely forsaken my brother's compassion. My selfish pity conveniently forgot that they were his parents too. I can't control the tears from my eyes anymore, and my lips begin to tremble.

I reach out to Gabe for forgiveness, and bury my face into his shoulder while I let loose my frustrations. "I'm sorry."

"It's okay . . . it's okay."

"When will this ever end?"

"I don't know, but I do know you have friends down there who love you very much and would do anything to make it all go away," he says, attempting to amend my self-pity.

I stare down to the others while they are eating and realize this group has survived more turmoil than they probably should have. And I know deep in my heart I wouldn't have survived either if it weren't for them.

"Shall I bring you some food?" he asks.

"No, thanks, I'm fine. I'll be down shortly, I just need a few minutes alone up here." He looks at me and smiles, but doesn't respond. He knows my intentions are justified, and he fully respects my privacy, so he quietly shuffles down the tree.

I lean back and gaze out in the space between the fluttering branches, wondering if I'm truly the person who is capable of leading, because my brother seems far more suited than I. Just as I get comfortable against the branches, my short moment of serenity is once again interrupted. Not by someone per say, but from a familiar clamor that is spitefully shrill.

A lingering ghost, or wicked spirit, it haunts me with extreme persistence. This crafty crow that shadows me is becoming more and more irritating. His black, mangled body rests with sinful delight perched just behind me on a small, fragile branch.

Though his negative presence is felt, I covet to be in the company of my Lord. The plume of smoke that had risen high in the clouds earlier has faded into the evening sky, just as my weary heart fades into a place of solitude. I shelter it against the mocking evil that flaps his oily wings, and pray into the night that no more hidden demons prowl within me. The vindictive squawk soon fades away into the night.

CHAPTER 21

Waking up to the morning light flickering within the flowing branches is always enjoyable; however, lately those moments have been rare. The delight of waking up this fine morning though comes by a startling gunshot echoing in the woods.

"Arena!" Gabe shouts from below.

Apparently, I had fallen asleep in the tree. It's a wonder I didn't fall out and break my neck. I quickly climb back down and find Gabe crouched down behind a rotted tree stump.

"What's going on?" I say with panic in my voice.

"Don't know. Just a few minutes ago we were eating and breaking down the tents when this huge buck comes running through the camp, frightened. Didn't think much of it until a gunshot followed."

"Where are the others?"

"Behind me a little ways, hiding over behind that brush."

"Stay here and keep an eye out," I say before I race over to the others. Everyone is stooped underneath a canopy of kudzu and a freshly dense pocket of invasive Mimosa leaves. Allison is shivering in Juliana's arms next to Niki, while Harold, Father Joseph, and Henry stake the perimeter of the covering. Everyone is accounted for except for Nic, which doesn't surprise me.

"Hey, where's Nic?" I ask quietly.

"I don't know. We all just took cover when the gun went off," Henry says.

"Where's the sniper rifle?"

"Sitting over there by the tents, but the scope is missing," he says.

I quietly pull the scope from my jacket and hold it up in front of Henry before I silently make my way over to the gun.

I slither on my belly once I'm close enough and carefully open the case to assemble the rifle. I attach the scope and slowly peruse the outer perimeter in a stealthy effort to locate a possible intrusion to our camp.

I gradually move the gun from one side of the woods to the other, viewing through the scope until I finally spot Nic resting his back against a tree about fifty meters away. Suddenly, four heavily armed soldiers approach from the west side where he's standing.

I watch carefully as Nic slowly moves around the tree when he notices the men coming his way. They get dangerously closer, and Nic has no idea that one of them peeled off to the left to flank him. I still don't understand why the hell Nic would run off like that. He's putting not only himself, but all of us in danger.

I quickly load the rifle with a fresh mag and follow the flanked soldier moving in closer behind Nic. He's about ten meters away from where Nic is hugging the tree with his back. The closer he advances, the less Nic moves.

Nic just stands there like a statue, not even realizing the compromising situation he's in. Just a meter away, the stealthy soldier closes in with his gun raised, yet Nic doesn't know the soldier is approaching.

I shift the safety off and carefully press my finger against the trigger, waiting for the right moment. I need to be accurate and fast, because I have no clue where the other three soldiers are roaming. My sights are directly pinned on the immediate threat.

Suddenly, the soldier stops in his tracks, then turns behind the tree where I now have no clear shot. Nic is exposed and looks like he's about to shit his pants. For whatever reason, Nic leaves his statue position and moves to the right, exactly in line where the soldier moved. "Nic, what are you doing, you fool?" I say under my breath.

Not a split second goes by when the soldier jumps from behind the tree and holds Nic at gunpoint. With Nic's hands in the air, I can't get a clear shot of the man. "Come on, Nic, just move over a bit," I mutter. He slowly lowers his hands and takes a step to the side. The Russian soldier lowers his gun and proceeds to talk with Nic as if they know each other. Nic hands the man something, but I'm too far away to see what it is. This is beyond startling and a disturbing reminder of why I didn't trust Nic from the beginning.

So this is what it has come to—my sanity in question against a living lie who fooled everyone.

The rancorous voices bellowing inside of me tempt me to shoot them both, but I have no way of proving to the others that my intent is just. I already have a strained relationship with Nic that makes my emotional condition a liability to the group. This would only cause further questioning of my trustworthiness and leadership. I must wait for a time to expose him in front of everyone.

I wait for Nic to move to the side. When he slides over in front of the tree, I take a clean shot to the soldier's head. In an instant, the man falls dead, leaving a shower of blood sprayed across Nic's face. His terrified expression is priceless.

I quickly search through the scope for the remaining soldiers, but it's pretty evident they scattered like mice when their comrade littered the ground with his brains. I finally spot one running north in a clearing, but before he can reach the dense trees, his escape becomes fatal. I pop him in the back of the head, which sends his body fluttering into the bushes.

It's extremely quiet now; not even the wind blowing through the tall brush makes a sound. I examine every area within fifty to seventy-five meters, but no soldier is visible. I guess they got wise and dropped to the ground. It's only a matter of time before they make a mistake and expose themselves.

After a minute of silence, and a long thorough view at ground level, I finally spot the third soldier hiding in a low line of thistle weeds and honeysuckle vines. The top of his helmet peeks over the vines and uncovers a clear shot. Without disturbing his comfortable hiding position, I leave him lying just as he is with a bullet to his head.

I don't feel any more comforted that only one soldier remains out there somewhere. I've exhausted every nook and cranny with the scope and can't seem to locate him anywhere. Unless he comes to me, this one is going to have to be waited out.

I refuse to leave my position, hoping he will make a mistake, but this one is much smarter than the others are. Gabe, who's still hiding behind the tree stump, points emphatically to my other side.

Just then, twigs snap, and suddenly I've conceded my position. Just behind one of the tents, a scurrying of footsteps heads toward me. I race to the back of the tent.

The soldier comes rushing around the corner, and I nearly trip on the ground and lose my footing. I'm forced to roll and pop a round at point-blank range in the man's chest. His gun falls from his hands, and he immediately clutches his chest before he drops to the ground. I have to slide out of the way to keep from being crushed by his falling body.

Gabe comes running over to me, screaming my name over and over, until I finally catch my breath to respond. I poke the man's body with the blunt point of the rifle just to make sure he's dead.

Henry and Father Joseph relieve their spot to see me, while the others remain hidden underneath the covering. Henry looks concerned for our safety, but he doesn't say anything that would otherwise disrepute my decision to leave the den.

"Everyone okay?" he asks.

"Yeah, but not so much for these guys," I respond, pointing at the dead soldier. Gabe turns the soldier onto his back and searches for clues that might help us understand their unexpected presence. Although I know why, I don't say anything. I can't seem to get the words to come out of my mouth about Nic's betrayal.

"Are you sure that's all of them?" Henry asks me. I hear his voice, but I don't listen. I need to find Nic.

"Arena," he says, trying to get my attention, but I fail to meet his eyes or respond to his voice.

"What did you see? Are there any more?" he continues to ask. Again, I'm totally oblivious to what he's saying. I hear nothing but the woods calling me. I'm too troubled by the revelation of Nic's purpose that I keep my eyes and ears glued to the woods instead, searching for his absence.

"They're dead, what other proof do you need?" says Gabe, speaking on behalf of my silence.

"Wherever there are soldiers, there's trouble," Father Joseph says.

"I'm not too worried. These aren't going anywhere," Gabe answers.

"What concerns me is what is to follow."

Suddenly, out from behind a blend of dense briar and browning reeds, Nic appears. Half his face is still covered in blood, but it can't hide the dejection glowing from it. I closely watch every step he takes while Niki and the others finally emerge from the kudzu to join us.

When Nic finally reaches a clearing close enough for everyone to notice him, they meet him with open arms, but I stay back. I keep my distance so I can patiently plot my vengeance.

While everyone joins in the elation of his survival, I look upon him with reproach. Not until his eyes finally meet mine does the glow he once had immediately flush from his nervously stricken face.

Whether he knows that I'm aware of his deceit, he will play along in the lie until I call his bluff. It may seem unorthodox for me, but it's in my best interest to solidify my case to the others by building a fortified stronghold of proof before I can make accusations.

But if something does go awry and threatens the safety of everyone else, I won't hesitate to slit his throat. I'm so full of rage that I'm close to just cutting him right now and deal-ing with the consequences of the group's loyalty later.

Nic comes dangerously close to my personal space before stopping and gazing at the dead Russian soldier lying on his back.

"Not bad for a girl," I say, intently searching his face for a weakness. I clamor for his discomfort when he's around me now. I want him to know who's in charge in this cat-and-mouse game.

"She's the best shot I've ever seen," Henry adds.

"I'm grateful for her that I'm still alive then," Nic says.

"Yeah, I bet you are," I say.

"Is the whole Russian army after us?" Harold asks, examining the soldier's uniform.

"No, I think this is just a scouting party," I say, looking up at Nic, "but it's a guarantee they'll be back in greater numbers. What do you think, Nic?" I say to plant a little ambiguity into his head. If there are strings attached to this role-playing, then I better damn well be the puppet master.

"Yeah, I agree. I think we need to move, now."

Everyone quickly grabs their gear while Henry privately walks over to me.

"Are you okay?" he asks.

"I'll be better once we're out of here."

"You seemed a little tense back there."

"Well, nothing is ever as it seems."

"So, how do you suppose they knew we were here?"

"Well, it wasn't by luck, that I'm sure of," I say as I walk off.

During the arduous trek through the wooded acres, I keep a sharp eye on Nic. I bring up the rear of the group with Allison next to me, making positively sure there are no unexpected surprises from our Russian deceiver. He's not stupid enough to try anything foolish now, especially since I leave him out in front of the pack without a weapon. I will be damned if I let this fellowship sever because of a lie.

Just up ahead, past the dense timbers, lies an opening to a less populated area of trees. The smoke from yesterday is all but gone. There's just a hint of smoldering ash on the other side of the valley, beyond the tight ridge of piney foliage.

Behind the last sparse line of towering white pines is a grand view of golden prairie fields and grassy pastures of green. Horses of all kinds pepper the verdant fallows, grazing and sauntering about.

The tall, brushy, well-managed acreage is bordered by white fencing that is beyond the means of a less-than-wealthy individual. As far as I'm concerned, this is inherited royalty. It's perhaps the most beautiful equestrian farm I've ever seen. Truthfully, it's the only one I've ever seen.

Allison's eyes grow with delight, and a smile that's been hidden for quite some time springs from ear to ear. Although it was under unforeseen circumstances, the idea of leaving Diablo and Shadow behind still eats away at me. I can't imagine how hard it must have been for Allison, who had raised them.

Just across the fields behind the ranch house, a suitable but humble paddock sits between a barn and a grand Victorian cottage. Beside the barn is an elaborate nest of stables, which is teeming with beautiful Arabians and Friesians.

Though the grassland bears a tailored lawn, no sign of life exists outside this equine complex. Regardless of the nature of this serene place, I draw my gun anyway.

"Gabe, Nic, come with me. The rest of you wait out here." I wouldn't normally want Nic coming with me, but this is the only way I can keep tabs on him. While everyone nervously waits on the veranda, we wander toward the back of the house. I peer through one of the uncovered windows, but see nothing to suspect that anyone is home.

The exterior looks extremely well cared for and untouched until we find broken glass shattered from one of the rear windows, and the back door is marred from being pried open with something meatier than a crowbar.

I offer Nic a slice of tolerance by allowing him to enter the premise first.

"Ladies first," Nic says craftily.

"Lady?" Gabe chuckles.

"By all means, only a gentleman would make sure it's safe before the lady enters," I say, nudging my gun forward toward him. I may not be the ideal lady, but he sure as hell isn't a gentleman. Gabe gives me a subtle look of confusion before he follows behind Nic, but I just smile and pretend that this is nothing more than a course of friendly banter.

The interior smells exactly like the farmhouse where I had taken the chickens from, but this time we're not alone. Just to the right in the lounge area, an older gentleman lies slumped over a French settee with a bullet wound to his head.

His face is pale, and his arms are greenish in color, but the body hasn't started to smell too bad yet. This must have just happened within the last two days, because the bullet wound looks fresh.

The back of the house appears to be untouched except for the library, where countless books are scattered on the floor, and papers of all sorts have been sifted through. The desk has been turned upside down and the walls are torn into. Whatever they were looking for, they were certainly determined.

The living room carpet is covered in bloodstains, and the walls have been littered with gunfire. There's an opened bottle of brandy and a broken glass sitting on a small table next to a leather chair. In the chair sits a manila envelope that's marked "classified."

The mysteries that lie within these walls smell of corruption and deception, but more importantly, the curiosity that's nestled inside the envelope is nothing short of peculiar. I can't leave this place without at least knowing why this man was killed.

I look inside and find photos of him, the former president, Chinese delegates, numerous classified documents for Russian military operations, an affidavit of candidacy for one Clarence Dillard, and a multitude of classified files pertaining to the United States' involvement with Russian leadership.

Deep within the papers are personnel files for Clarence Dillard, coincidentally the same man who's lying dead on his own sofa. After burying my face through the files for a minute, I rest my eyes on a startling discovery.

This man was obviously of high importance. Born in Volgograd, Russia, he was a former agent for the KGB that was reformed in 2020. He moved to the United States permanently while he became a member of US Congress from 2033 to 2045 and the director of operations for the CIA. And perhaps the most disturbing piece of information: as an adversary of American democracy, he was handpicked by Nikolai Kriel as his advisor and successor, unfortunately under further evaluation, his true credentials were exposed. According to this file, his unexpected ties with the Israeli government was a detriment to future power. I can see where there was cause for concern. This man was a friend and foe to a common enemy.

After reading through all the bureaucratic secrecy, I look up and I'm startled to see Nic staring at me with a sinister smirk.

"You going to read that all day, or are we going upstairs to check things out? Not that I'm trying to rush you or anything, but I am here to help in any way I can," he says, hovering over me with a smile on his face. The tactical move on his part to somehow coerce me into doubting where his allegiance lies is belittling. I'm not convinced in the slightest; however, I continue to tread lightly on the subject to make sure he knows I'm oblivious to the truth.

Overwhelmed by Nic's foul breath blowing in my face, I manage to peel myself away from the folder and move toward the staircase. The house interior is simply divine, but the elaborate intricacies in the woodcarving around the banister are absolutely stunning. While every inch of the house has an individually unique touch to it, the owner spared no expense with this gorgeous staircase.

The high ceilings on the first level nearly brings us up sixteen or seventeen feet to the second floor, where everything is made of some kind of exotic wood. The champagne-colored walls in the hall are fully decorated with large canvased paintings from Monet to Pissarro, but none reveals an eccentric or charismatic side of this man until I turn to the other side of the hall.

There, boldly hanging slightly away from the wall, are some of the most famous prints by Wassily Kandinsky, a Moscow-born abstract artist. I'm no art connoisseur, but I do remember seeing these prints in a book I read in the library once. It's only fitting that they would be displayed in this house.

I creep down the hall a little ways, passing by a large great room filled with opened boxes, and just for a moment I hear the faint sound of music playing. I can't tell if I'm imagining it or not, but when I immediately turn around to Gabe, he answers it for me.

"Music?" he says with a shrug.

The last door at the end of the hall is closed, but the closer I get, the louder the music becomes. I'm almost too scared to open it, but the curiosity forces me to anyway. I slowly turn the knob and push the door, but what I witness is even beyond my comprehension.

Gabe is even less prepared than I am when he walks through the door. Nic stands there speechless, wavering to leave the scene almost immediately. Every ounce of morality I've come to accept in my life was absent in the individual who could have done this.

While the music plays on a radio sitting in the windowsill, my heart fills with wretchedness I can't comprehend. Spoils of debauchery and cruelty cover the stained bed sheets.

Three young girls, all of about thirteen years old, lie dead in a pool of their own blood. Hands bound to the bed, and stripped, I can't begin to wrap my brain around a death so horrifying. The slashing abrasions across their bodies add to the unmerciful cruelty. It's evident that the horse crop lying next to them was the weapon used to lash them beyond imaginable extents.

I stand there, reeling, demanding an answer to such malice, trying to peel my eyes away from three innocent girls, but it's the world we live in now, and nothing will change until it's gone.

I turn my eyes away briefly from the depraved scene and wonder if this could ever happen to Allison. Gabe and Nic retreat quietly back into the hall. I grab a tattered quilt hanging over a rocking chair in the corner and stare gravely over the girl's faces. With an inescapable sadness, I cover their bodies, turn the music off, and close the door behind me.

"This isn't for anyone else's eyes to see. None of this will be told to anyone," I say firmly. "Do you understand?" They both solemnly nod in agreement. I'm sort of taken aback by Nic's response to all of this, but I guess even he has a soul, regardless of his wicked ties.

I rush back downstairs, grab the folder, and head out to the veranda, where everyone has been patiently waiting. Everyone but Allison, Harold, and Niki, that is.

"Where's everybody else?" I eagerly ask.

"Allison took Niki and Harold over by the stables to show the horses," Henry says.

"I think Allison got the horse bug. She hasn't stopped talking about them," Juliana adds.

"Good, because we need to get the hell out of here as soon as we can."

"What's going on?" Father Joseph nervously asks.

"Nothing yet, and I certainly don't want to be here waiting around for it."

"Are we in danger?"

"We're always in danger."

"What did you find in there?" he says inquisitively.

"Nothing to see here. This place is dead," I say abruptly to end the conversation. "Looks like Allison is going to need some help saddling these horses."

While Juliana, Father Joseph, and Henry head for the stables to help, Gabe, Nic, and I scour the barn, but before Father Joseph gets too far, I say to him in a soft voice, "Father?"

"Yes?"

"Let her choose the horses. She'll know them better than anyone."

The front barn door slats are sealed shut from the inside, so we are forced to go around to the back. The back doors are chained, and the only other way in is through a small window at the top of the barn's loft.

I search around the side of the barn for a piece of metal to break the chains, but I find something even more useful: an old, rusted sledgehammer. I'm not strong enough to wield this cumbersome tool with finesse, so I hand the heavy piece of iron to Nic to break the chains off.

After three swings of the hammer, the lock pops off and the chains loosen. When the large doors slide open, the warm, rotting air escapes like a carbonated explosion. The smell is horrific, no, putrid. For once I would like it if my curiosity would take a vacation.

Now I know why the large house is so empty. The rest of the guests are hanging from the rafters like a meat locker. The only thing missing from these human meat steaks is the stamp of approval from the USDA. There's nothing in here that we didn't already assume, and nothing surprising either after what we just witnessed upstairs.

Nic and Gabe immediately close the barn doors to contain the permeable odor. Nic leans against the barn with his head down, and with a sober glaze painted on his face, he looks to me and says, "Why do so many innocent people have to die?"

A sudden shock of disbelief overcomes me for a moment to hear those words spew from his mouth, but I stay grounded from his efforts to weaken me emotionally. Though I'm cautiously aware, I briefly give in to his remorseful reaction. It's almost painful to watch him conjure up a single tear, but my delusions of sorrow for him are quickly lost. Suddenly, from over the hilltop, a large jeep with a fifty-caliber cannon attached to the top comes rambling toward the house with a vengeance.

If this was a deliberate attempt to win my trust, then I applaud Nic's resourcefulness, but I will not be convinced of his innocence, nor will my judgment be patronized like that. His tears conveniently dry up, and a look of fear quickly replaces his solemn face when I unfold the limbs on my bow to string it.

"Get to the horses, now!" I shout. I sprint over to the corner of the house, out of direct sight from the vehicle barreling down, and I pull the only explosive-tipped arrow I have left from the quiver. This is a one-shot deal, and I better not miss.

I pull back the arrow and steady my aim, waiting for the soldiers to get closer, but the gun atop the jeep erratically fires into the stables, forcing me to release early. The arrow falls just short of the jeep and sends the earth rumbling with explosive debris just in front of the front axle.

The jeep lunges forward upside down and rolls several times before everyone is thrown from the windows like ragdolls. Black smoke ejects from the jeep's underbelly, and a discharge of flames suddenly burn. The driver is pinned by the steering wheel and is unable to exit the jeep.

One of the soldiers manages to awkwardly rise to his feet, stumbling to help his fellow combatant, who is still pinned. I draw another arrow to put both men down, but the jeep's fuel tank ignites and explodes, saving me the effort.

I race over to the stables, where everyone is already mounted and ready to flee. Allison walks over an exceptionally muscular, well-maintained Arabian breed that resembles Shadow and hands me the reins. I quickly hop on and lead the group galloping out of the stables toward the southeast corner of the farm. Through the daunting wooded passage, I ride closely with Allison, knowing the dangers following this fellowship have just begun.

CHAPTER 22

We sprint our horses past the pine wood valley and into an open grassland where trees sprout scarcely in the wide-open space. I look back to make sure everyone is accounted for, especially Nic, but I don't stop until my ass is numb and the horses are spent.

Once we reach the end of the brushy basin and into another pine grove, I stop to let the horses catch their breath. These beautiful creatures were bred to run, but they also need fuel to restore their exhausted muscles. There has to be a source of water around here for these horses, or we aren't going to get very far.

I notice an abundant cluster of aggressively growing river ferns dominating most of the ground foliage, which leads me to believe we're not too far from an underwater stream. These plants grow naturally along creeks and ditches in this area. I should know, because I can remember bringing them home to my mother whenever I went craw-fishing with Gabe.

I hop off the beautiful, black thoroughbred and pet the side of his face, carefully stroking his silky hair. Allison was right about how attached you can become with your horse, and this one is no exception.

I'm so admired by his loyal temperament toward me that I secretly give him a name to personalize our new rela-tionship. I shall call him Storm. It's the only name I can think of that would fit the physical attributes for this magnificent creature's strength and agility.

"What do you think?" Gabe asks me.

"It could be a stretch, but I think we'll find some water around here."

"How much further you think before it's safe?"

I pause before answering, deciding whether or not I should confide with my brother.

"It's never going to be safe as long as Nic is with us," I say softly so no one else can hear.

"What do you mean?"

I look over to the others waiting patiently next to their horses before I decide to take this conversation privately.

"Come with me," I say. I ask that everyone stay put until Gabe and I get back from scouting up ahead. This is the only opportunity I have to reveal the truth to the only person I can trust.

We walk through an extremely dense growth of ferns until we reach a mossy passage that leads through the thick invasive greenery. The winding path proves to be one obstacle after another as we sink ankle deep into the undergrowth. Just on the other side of a small patch of blackseed needlegrass is a slight declining ravine filled with flat, mossy rocks and overran by wild lovegrass, prickly weeds, and a few sprawling mesquite trees woven into the rocky soil.

Twenty yards ahead, the ditch ends, but just on the other side flows an abundant creek waiting to quench our thirst. Gabe begins to scale the ditch, but I stop him so we can finish our private exchange about Nic.

"Do you trust me?" I ask. He turns his head and looks at me as if he's about to receive some bad news.

"Of course I trust you . . . you know that."

"Then what I tell you can only be between you me. Okay?"

"Sure, okay."

"Nic is not who he appears to be."

"Yeah, I think you've established that earlier in the den."

"No, I don't think you understand. He's working for them."

"Look, I understand you don't like the guy, hell, he even creeps me out a little, but to make these claims because he scratches you the wrong way without any evidence is uncharacteristic even for you."

"I have proof." With a little more curiosity, Gabe quickly quiets and walks back down from the top of the ditch.

His eyes engage mine. "What proof?"

"When you were crouched down hiding behind the tree stump, I was able to get a good look at our comrade hiding behind a tree through the scope."

"So, and by the way, I wasn't hiding. I was waiting for an opportunity."

"Yeah, so was Nic."

"What do you mean?"

"I mean he knew the soldiers were approaching. One of them stopped right before him with his gun withdrawn and made an exchange."

"Exchange?"

"I don't know, but the point is, they let him go without an ounce of hostility. They knew each other. It wasn't a coincidence, it was planned. And by the shock on Nic's face when I shot the soldier in front of him was more than enough evidence I needed."

"What?" Gabe says, surprised.

"How do you explain them finding us in the middle of nowhere, and then conveniently tracking us again at the farm?"

"That son of bitch, I'm gonna kill him," he shudders. His face burns red, as he angrily stomps away.

"Wait," I say, holding him back, "not like this. You're going to need more than my word for reason to convince the others. I'm not exactly sound of mind these days."

"Are you crazy? There's a killer in our company."

"Crazy, well, that's still up for debate, but killer, no. If he wanted us dead, he would have done it already. No, I believe they want you and me alive, but you damn well better believe that everyone else is expendable."

"Then why didn't they come after us in the den?"

"Whatever they're using to track Nic isn't detectable underground, or at least in the den."

"I guess Nic really did mean to leave you back at the old church, then. Arena, I . . . I'm sorry, I—"

"No worries. I probably wouldn't have believed me either."

"I guess when they failed to capture you then, they moved on to plan B."

"Whatever deal he struck, there's something out there of more value to the Russians than just you and I."

"You really believe there's a Southern Resistance?"

"I don't know, but he sure seemed to think so. And if we somehow lead him to it unscathed, then the Russians can claim two victories. He becomes the hero and gets promoted, and we become slaves."

"If they want us alive, then why did they try to kill us back at the farm?"

"I've been asking myself that ever since we left. Maybe they only want me alive, maybe there isn't a Southern Resistance and this is all a lie, or maybe someone else is leading this army and we just happened to be in at the wrong place at the wrong time. I really don't know, but I'm not about to tell the others that the Southern Resistance may or may not exist. They need hope to move on. . . wherever that may be."

"So what do you suggest we do? We can't keep Nic with us."

"And I don't plan on it. If we're being tracked though, we'll have to ride on as far as we can toward the southeastern woods before setting camp. We can at least make it hard for them to get to us to buy us some time. There we will get the truth out of him."

"And how do you suppose you're going to do that?"

"I'm working on it," I reassuringly declare.

"I say you cut him now and worry about the consequences later."

"Believe me, there's nothing better I want to do than to—"

Suddenly, the woods crackle and leaves rustle above the ravine. Out from behind a puny maple, Harold's head pops out and looks down at us.

"Just making sure you guys didn't get lost."

Lost? Really, is he serious? This coming from a man who would get lost in his own bed.

"We're fine, but we did find a nice creek bed just beyond that ditch for the horses. We'll have to cross downstream to avoid the steep incline," I say before climbing up to him.

"Something wrong?" Harold asks me. I guess the concerned look on my face is a little transparent, even for him to see, but if anything is going to make it apparent that there's a problem, it will be Gabe's irritated behavior. I'm not exactly Mary Poppins when it comes to dealing with a snake in my own backyard, but if Gabe feels he's being crossed, especially if it jeopardizes Juliana's life, you better know he's out for blood.

"Everything is good. Just go get the others ready to move. We'll be there shortly."

"Are you sure?" he readdresses.

"Harold—"

"Got it, I'm going."

Gabe approaches me with fire nearly breathing from his nose.

"Hey, calm down," I say.

"How can you just stand there and not do anything?"

"Believe me, it has been stewing for quite some time. I had a chance to do something back in the tunnels, if you remember. Now you know how I feel."

"We need to go, we're wasting time."

"Just keep it together, okay?" He brushes against my shoulder, fuming, but I quickly grab the back of his jacket before he can advance any further.

"Hey! Calm yourself," I say firmly. "They need to know that nothing has changed." He avoids looking at me, but the muscles in his jawline ease temporarily.

"Look at me," I say calmly. With his head down and his fists clenched, he closes his eyes tightly. I can only imagine the dreadful things his mind conjures for the displeasures that may follow. I, too, have felt the weight of uncertainty, but I won't allow him to share the same torment.

"Gabe, please look at me," I say, begging with a stillness in my heart. "I won't allow anything to happen to the others. You have to trust me."

"I want to," he says quietly.

"Then follow my lead."

With everyone dismounted, we lead the horses by the reins through the dense green underbrush until we reach a clearing near a large waving willow tree. The half-exposed roots creeping into the water allow the broad sallow to stretch its weeping branches and give shade from the blistering August sun. Here the small, pebbled bank descends into the clear, flowing water where the horses quench their thirst.

When I plant my cheek on the side of Storm's neck while he drinks, I notice Gabe angrily glancing toward Nic, but no one else recognizes his glare. After the horses take a brief rest, we mount back up and head across the other side of the bank. We ride alongside the small riverbank until we reach a clearing to pass through.

A three-and-a-half hour journey across the eastern grasslands and piney forests on horseback will give anyone a numb ass. The distressed look on everyone's faces is all I need to see to cut the ride short. I lead the others through a safe, secluded passage deep into the woods, where the ground is cool from the sun, but not cluttered with wiry thistle weed or annoying clover.

I know Gabe is anxiously waiting to spill Nic's lies to the others just as much as I am, but I remind him to stay calm and wait for the right opportunity.

While I search the area for a water source, Harold and Henry ready a fire for an unexpectedly cool evening. A storm must be developing to the north, because a crisp northern breeze suddenly changes the sultry interior of our wooded campsite. I'm okay with the sudden weather change. I haven't had a shower in days, and the sticky, warm air doesn't exactly invite a bouquet of goodness to the situation.

I don't wander too far from camp, knowing Gabe is eyeing Nic's every step—I'm still feeling uneasy about his tracker. I have very little luck finding a water source until I reach a plateau on the edge of the tree line. It's not much but a trickle of water scooting around a rocky bend.

I follow it, hoping to find a larger pocket of water, but there's nothing more than a small oxbow of stagnant liquid resting against the side of the rocks. Just a few yards up ahead, a dam of twigs and branches keep the water from flowing any further. The horses can drink from here, but I'll be damned if I soak my mouth in this algae pool of filth.

Not that I don't trust my brother, but his position on Nic has me more than concerned. I'm not sure I've seen him this angry before, but it's enough to make even me worry.

I quickly make my way back to camp. Everyone but Gabe is huddling around a healthy-breathing fire cracking into the crisp, cool air. I lie on the ground and lean my head against Gabe's pack while I nervously search around out of the corners of my eyes for him. I'm so tired right now, but I can't sleep until I know Gabe is in sight. My eyes begin to glaze over and my lids start to weaken. I struggle to keep my eyes open. Just as I give in, Gabe comes popping out from the woods, smiling.

"Whatever you do, don't go over there," he says, pointing toward a few scraggily bushes. "I think I just fertilized someone's habitat."

You would think the lack of cordial manners would have changed since having a girlfriend, but nothing seems to have staunched his sophomoric humor. Not even an apocalypse could hinder my brother's uncouth behavior. Nice to know his plumbing is working properly, so now maybe I can get a little sleep.

"Is anyone else fighting off the mosquitoes as much as I am?" he asks, swatting at his arms and scratching his genitals. "Well, they better stop because if they suck any more blood from my nuts, they'll be raisins."

Wow, that's just a grotesque misadventure I want no part of. Leave it to my brother to ruin a moment of decorum with this group. Juliana gets my praises for putting up with that. I can't bear to listen to any more of my brother's crude annotations for the night. My eyes and body aren't willing to suffer through anymore sleepless nights. I waste no time, leaning back with my eyes shut, while my body relaxes.

I doze off into a deep seclusion of darkness, until another nightmare reaches my internal sleep, where I find myself bound to a metal chair. Everything around me is covered in blood except for a shiny silver case that sits in front of me on a table. The room closely portrays my bedroom back home, but there are no windows or doors.

I suddenly feel a breath warming against the back of my neck. The room closes in tighter and tighter, and the breathing becomes hotter and hotter. Because I'm bound tightly to the chair, I can't free myself. Finally, out from behind me, a man appears, but his face is covered by a black mask.

He holds a knife in front of my face and slowly slides it down toward my chest. I shake violently, trying to break free of the chair, but to no avail; there's no chance of escaping. With a fiery rage, the man unmasks a hellish squeal spewing from his darkened face and slices open my shirt.

He brings the silver case closer to me and taunts me with his knife before revealing what's inside. Slowly the case opens, and sitting on a piece of charcoal foam is an object covered in a black pillowcase.

The walls begin to bleed from the ceiling, and the ties binding my feet and arms to the chair begin to melt and loosen. The man grabs the ends of the pillowcase and asks me, "What keeps you bound to this world that you cannot have?"

My heart fills with a burning wrath bursting to free itself, but I cannot answer, because I wish not to know. The man breathes into my face the words I do not want to hear, only to torment me into further insanity. "You do not answer because you already know."

The black pillowcase is swiftly pulled off, revealing Jacob's severed head. I scream with rage. I pull my arms against the loosened bindings with every ounce of strength my body can yield until I finally break free.

I grab the knife from the man's hand and lunge forward with fury, but I can't seem to move any further than the wall, and the man eventually disappears. I scream like a savage until my voice goes silent and everything turns completely black.

I immediately wake up near the fire with my knife in my hand, while Henry, Harold, and Nic are holding me back from jumping into it.

When I finally realize where I am, I stop fighting and relax. Everyone is staring at me as if I were a mad person. I drop my knife, while my eyes wander against the troubling glares, and I slowly back up away from the fire.

Nic tries to hold my arm as I walk away, but I rip my elbow from his grasp and hastily shove him back.

"That will be the last time you touch me," I vehemently say with a wicked lingering in my eyes.

"Arena . . ." Gabe says, approaching me.

"No, I'm fine. It was just a nightmare, that's all."

"But, I just want to—"

"Just . . . please let me be for a moment. I need to get some fresh air for a bit. I'm fine, really." I'm still shaken up from the horrific terror in my sleep and I just want some time alone to pray.

I venture off back toward the small broken creek and climb up to the top of a hill where a large, rounded stone rests. I sit on the rock and pray for whatever wickedness that's following me to leave me at peace. No more do I want to dwell on the loss of Jacob. No more do I wish to continue this journey with my heart in dismay.

I fervently pray for what's best in God's plan, but I simply desire what's best for this fellowship to stay alive, and tonight, we sever a piece from it. I walk back to the camp with confidence brewing over the revelation of Nic's deceit, but the sound of voices arguing in the distance distracts my poise.

I slow my pace down when I hear my name mentioned in the conversation. I slowly sidle behind a clump of trees away out of sight, but close enough to where I can still see the fire burning and hear the voices clearly. I've just walked into the middle of a peculiar discussion about me.

"She knows how to survive the woods better than anyone. I trust her with my life," Juliana says.

"I'm not questioning her survival skills. I just want to know that her head is clear in all of this," Father Joseph says.

"Whatever happened to her, it's in the past now. Look, far be it from me to play therapist here, but she's my sister, and I know her well," Niki says.

"Then you know she tried kill me back in the den," Nic spouts.

"Oh, for God's sake, you were being an asshole, Nic."

"Stop!" Father Joseph shouts, trying to bring the conversation back down to a civil tone.

"It doesn't matter who provoked who. If she is to lead this group, then we better damn well follow, because when push comes to shove, I don't know if there's anybody else I'd rather fight next to when bullets come firing down like rain," Gabe says. "I will never leave her."

"No one is leaving anyone. We survive as a group, we die as a group, but know this: if we are to get through this, our mental stability will be challenged," Father Joseph demands.

"Then we should be praying instead of debating my sister's emotional condition," Gabe chimes in.

"Mental breakdown or not, I think she's allowed to express a little emotion considering the hell she's been through. Most of you wouldn't have survived what she's gone through," Niki expresses.

"It's not where she's been that concerns me now; it's where she's headed that worries me," Father Joseph says sadly.

CHAPTER 23

I wait until the conversation dies down before I walk into an already uncomfortable scene. Not a stir in their voices move when I enter the camp, but I do find it peculiar that Allison is the only one wearing a smile on her face. It's the one thing that fills my heart with the warmth I so desperately need.

I walk over and sit beside her, while everyone else hovers around the fire, trying to keep from prying.

"Tell me, what's so amusing that it should put a grin on your face?" I ask, smiling in return.

"Just happy to see you come back," she says with that sweet, little voice.

"Come back? Where was I going?"

"A place where even you are afraid."

My smile briefly withers, because I now know what she's referring to. We all have demons hiding within us that we often shelter, but if there is an evil rooted deep inside of me, I want nothing more than to see it die.

"I can see it your eyes," she continues.

"See what?"

"The same girl who saved me."

Instead of reaching for another question, I wipe the only tear rolling down the side of my face, and I embrace her with a love I wish I could sustain forever.

I dig deep in my jacket, searching for something only she could appreciate—the bracelet I took from our house, the one treasure that Grace wore before she tragically died. It was never meant for me to wear—just a token to hold onto for a much more humble suitor.

I place it around her wrist and clasp the ends together. The joy on Allison's face is priceless, but I can only imagine the smile it brings to Grace's spirit right now. Niki watches the exchange of endearment and decides to join our company. The lasting memories of Grace harboring inside of Niki reflects from the silver bracelet dangling around Alli- son's wrist.

She looks upon Allison's face, reminiscing the presence of Grace and her contributions to the world. While she shares stories about her with Allison, I gradually sneak away to a corner where I'm isolated from everyone. I sit alone and gaze into the hot coals, searching for a moment of clarity.

I'm mesmerized by the glowing fire, as the orange flames dance alongside a blush of scarlet in crackling unison. I clutch Jacob's cross necklace that I haven't removed from my neck since I last saw him. I dangle the cross from the chain out in front of the fiery backdrop and rub the sides against my fingers as I do every night, until they become raw.

"Why do you hope for something that is not there?" a voice asks beside me.

I tear away briefly from the blazing trance and look over to see Nic standing brashly against a tree.

"You couldn't possibly understand," I tell him, hoping to impede the conversation.

"Since I've met you, I've watched you stare at that cross for hours on end . . . and for what? To painfully search a broken memory you can't get back."

"Watch your tongue," I sternly say. I turn my head away; I don't want him to see my tears. "You know nothing of what I feel or what I see."

"I'm not here to hurt you, Arena. I'm here to help you."

"Help me from what?" I turn around to face him. It's too late to cover up the tears running down my cheek.

"The misery that escapes your face," he says, walking closer toward me.

"Leave me!" I can't bear to listen to any more of his sympathetic deceit. Whether he's right or not, I choose to dwell in my own memories, and moreover, I just don't trust him.

"There's no shame in being afraid," he says, continuing the pointless banter.

"There's nothing here I fear."

"Everyone fears something, even you," he says, prowling next to me.

As much as I hate being tormented by his words, he's right. If there is anything I fear, it's the one thing that has kept me captive.

"Loneliness," I answer.

"What?" he says in a shocked tone.

"Yes, I fear being alone. Does that satisfy you?" I say, trying to summon a fake cry. He stands there with a dumbstruck expression knowing that he may have pushed too far.

"I didn't mean to—"

"Why are we always trying to hide things, Nic?" I ask.

"What do you mean?"

"When you're looking for that special someone out there, you always try to hide the truth because of expectation, but once you find them, it's the disappointments you try to mask to keep from losing them. You'd think at some point you would grow and mature in your relationship when you plunge into marriage, but you don't. Because now it's the sins that you hide. Those very sins that have kept you imprisoned. The same ones you brought to the relationship that you were sure would magically disappear once you found who you were looking for. It's a vicious cycle."

"But it can be broken?"

"People don't change because they want to, Nic. They change because they get caught. The lack of discloser will forever be your enemy. As long as man is around so will there be secrets."

"So what's your point in all of this?" he asks with those shifty eyes abating.

"I've unwillingly shared my personal secret with you. It's time to uncover yours. What is it that you're hiding from me?"

"I have nothing to hide," he assuredly says.

"Fine, then come have a drink with me. If we can't deal with our secrets, we can at least bury them for a while." He's precariously stunned that I would even suggest spending one moment with him, let alone willingly sharing a drink with him.

I grab the bottle of vodka from Niki's bag, two small plastic cups, and I discreetly place the dagger I had dropped earlier back into the sheath attached to my hip. Gabe paces back and forth wondering what I'm up to. I give him a subtle nod of assurance that my plan to extract Nic's lies in front of the others has just begun.

"What are we celebrating?" Henry asks, looking at the bottle in my hand.

"The truth," I say softly under my breath while I stare intently at Nic.

"What's that?"

"Life," I quickly say, trying to recover.

"I'll drink to that," he merrily says.

I fill Nic's cup and happily hand it to him. If it's the raw exterior barricading Nic's lies, then the seduction of libations may just be the cure. He downs the double shot like it was water to try and impress me, but I can see in his eyes it's burning his insides.

"Now you," he says.

I pour a double shot into my glass and swing it back. The burning fumes singe the walls of my nose as I exhale a gasp of fiery demons. I feel like the breath of a dragon has just escaped my mouth, but I do everything I can to hold it together just to match his poise.

"Impressive."

"Well, I'm Irish, you know. This is a sport where I'm from."

Father Joseph walks by and when Nic turns his head to talk to him, I take advantage of the brief exchange to spit the vile fumes from my mouth when he's not looking.

I fill his cup once more, and again he slams the vodka down without a sting in his throat. At this point, everyone is becoming a bit more curious about what I'm doing.

"Now you, little Irish girl," he eagerly submits.

"Ah, just one for the lady, but I can see that your man enough not to back down from another drink," I say, toying with his masculine ego. He asks for another shot, as I knew he couldn't resist, and I fill cup after cup until the bottle is three-quarters gone. He nearly falls backward from the log he is sitting on, laughing uncontrollably.

"What do the Irish know about drinking? I was born with this flowing in my veins."

"More than you know," I say to myself.

Unentertained by Nic's obnoxiously humorous state that I coerced him into, Father Joseph walks over to me and demands I end this insolence. "Arena, stop this. I believe he's had quite enough."

"Maybe so."

"And for that matter so have you."

"You don't understand."

"I understand someone in your state shouldn't be drinking at all."

"What's that supposed to mean?"

"I-I'm sorry, I didn't mean it like that."

"Look, I'm not here to get into some inane moral debate. I have my reasons. You're just going to have to trust me on this one."

As instructed, Gabe walks Father Joseph to the side and explains to him my agenda for Nic's behavior. The others gather around each other, shielding Allison from the embarrassing spectacle Nic is now displaying.

The only thing left that's keeping me from ascertaining the truth about Nic's existence is hiding beneath those drunken eyes. But, I must hear it from his own lips if I wish to convince the others I'm not totally irrational.

Nic stumbles by the fire, chanting random passages from Tolstoy's *War and Peace,* until he awkwardly stumbles on a log and falls to the ground, laughing.

"For Mother Russia," he screams out into the trees.

While the shock of Nic's radical loyalty is exposed, I continue the witch-hunt, prolonging my efforts until he's fully revealed. I sit down beside him and slowly rub my hand on his thigh, just close enough near his crotch to get a reaction. Sometimes seduction is the best interrogation tool for a job like this, and I'm willing to sacrifice my better judgment if I want to break him.

"So, you still want to help me?" I ask in Russian.

"Yes," he responds back in Russian.

"When do you plan on returning to the Motherland?"

"I will, as soon as the Americans are compromised."

Suddenly, his eyes grow large and his smile flattens. He just realizes the mistake he's made. I quickly grab the top of his hair and swing my knife around toward his neck. Gabe immediately draws his gun to Nic's head, while I slowly slide the tip of my blade into his neck, breaking the skin ever so slightly.

"I should have spilled your guts when I had the chance."

"Holy shit, he's one of them," Harold shouts.

"Where the hell is it, Nic?" I ask.

"I don't know what you're talking about."

I dig deeper into his neck, releasing a trickle of blood, but he clamps up and continues to deny what I have asked.

"Arena, enough," Henry says, interrupting my not-so-subtle interrogating approach.

I tuck my boot behind Nic's leg and lift the tip in front of his crotch. I eject the blade protruding from my boot and press it deep into his scrotum.

"Where's the tracker? We know you have it on you."

"They've been tracking us this whole time?" Juliana finally realizes.

He stubbornly sits there and just laughs.

"Take off your belt and shoes, now!" Gabe carefully examines the belt and shoes, but finds nothing that would indicate a tracking device was planted.

"You're wasting your time," he says, laughing. "You'll never find it. It's buried deep within me."

I push him back to the ground. "So be it," I say. I pull out my sword and press it against his neck.

"Arena, wait! Hasn't enough blood been spilled? Bind his hands and feet, and tie him up against the tree," Father Joseph says.

"It matters not. They've locked into your location an hour ago. They will find you with or without a tracker," Nic boasts.

Henry and Harold immediately put out the fire, while Gabe and Father Joseph secure Nic tightly to the tree. I stare deep into Nic's devious eyes one last time, while everyone quickly mounts up to ride.

"Was it worth it? Falsely living in abandonment and bound by the very peers you lied to?"

"I only told you what you needed to hear."

"The southern camps, the resistance to the south? Was that all just a lie too?"

"Only a rage of Texans would herald such camps from its eighteen minutes of glory, and yours are almost up," he drunkenly spews. Not sure what the hell he's talking about that makes any sense, but I'm too angry to ask.

"Valor has no place for a man like you," I say to him with disgust.

"I've since moved on from chivalry to self-preservation. It's the only way to live. You should know this well by now. We are much the same you and I."

"There's nothing of you that is like me in any way."

"Oh, but there is. You just don't see it yet. Just like you can't see past the death of Jacob, who got what he deserved."

I backhand him across the face. "You're un-fucking believable. You mock me in the presence of the grace that was undeservingly extended to you." I draw my knife and press it hard against Nic's neck.

"Arena, no. It's not worth it," Father Joseph urges. I look back to make sure everyone else has left the area, especially Allison. This isn't a state I want her to see me in.

"Well, I've changed my mind. I'm not in the business of extending grace anymore."

I slide the razor-sharp blade across his neck, ripping open a fold of skin. Blood freely exits, and Nic's dead, cold eyes can see me no more.

I bend down, grab Nic's shoe, press it into the soft dirt, and script the word "WEST" with his heel. I hope this subtle message will be effective enough to detour whoever follows.

Father Joseph looks at me but says nothing as I walk by and hop up on Storm. He just nods with a sorrowful expression that I cannot explain. Though it isn't for Nic's death; it's for something that has died inside of me instead.

Part III

Lost in Ruin

CHAPTER 24

There's a bitter taste in my mouth after slicing Nic's throat, but I'm more concerned with the stony glower on Father Joseph's face. I'm much too enraged right now to feel guilty over his disappointment with me, though it does pain me to see it carried with him.

When he mounts up on his horse, I notice a sudden sporadic flickering of light flashing beyond the woods up toward the northern tree line. Nic was right; they knew where we were, and this time judging by the rows of lights, they've come in greater numbers, as expected.

Father Joseph and I quickly lead the others through the dense woods to the south about a quarter mile until we reach an unfortunate barrier. Another lambent of light flickers behind the southern tree line, forcing us to dramatically alter our course.

We race eastward alongside the thick rows of kudzu that shields us from the southern troops. Because I delayed our escape while arguing with Nic, we just make it over the next hill unseen before they pass by, avoiding a costly mistake.

I can only assume they are headed straight to the tracker, but I don't look back, not once until I reach a point where I feel we're comfortably safe. The only thing those soldiers will find at the campsite besides another dead man is another frustrating failure. I wish I were there to witness their defeat. I would have been more amused by their frustration than Nic's death, but it's imperative that I filter this sick enjoyment from my heart before I sink deeper into the dark depths of hatred.

After a few miles on the run, we are forced to rest for a bit—just enough to catch our breath and regroup before heading another ten miles away from the pack of soldiers. We've traveled more east than what I wanted to, but we had no choice. Plans are inevitably going to change when you're running for your life.

I slow my galloping horse to a sauntering pace when I discover a familiar terrain up ahead. Gabe quickly rides beside me and looks with the same expression as we both suddenly recognize a childhood memory.

A wooded spectrum of yellow pines, cherry-bark oaks, and sweeping wildscapes accompany a very resourceful bending river with plenty of fish to flounder. The open grassy meadows rolling toward the southwest is a sight I would never forget. It's the very region I came to embrace when Finnegan took us camping during the summer.

And now, the very area we became so acquainted with as children is right in front of us. It's a joyful moment to see, but I'm quite frightened that it will soon become a haunting memory in my sleep.

I slowly stroll into the oak-wooded forest, and suddenly I'm flooded with memorable events of Gabe and Finnegan. An unusually large tree stump catches my attention, so I stop. It's the same stump I used as a table to eat on when we camped. I remember it like it was yesterday. I spent hours of my childhood around this poor, forgotten tree, jumping on and over it.

I tie Storm's reins to a small branch and bend down close to the gnarled stump, counting the rings one by one like I used to when I was eight. One hundred three, the same as it was the last time I counted.

Finnegan would often tease me about how each tree had their own different personalities. And I remembered being saddened by the thought of this one felt nothing because it was dead. He told me that though it was dead, there's still something about it that gives it life.

I remember placing my ear down on the tree's severed trunk to listen for a heartbeat, but all I heard was the vibrations of the beautiful sounds of the forest. I knew Finnegan was just pulling my leg, but I didn't care. I wanted to hear the tree, and I swear to this day that I heard it crying.

Whether it was true or not, it has been a long, lasting memory that I will never forget, and has made me appreciate and respect God's bountiful gift. Just as I did when I was eight, I press my ear to the ashen wooden table and rub my fingers across the cracked splitting rings.

This is a place I can truly hold onto and never let go. It's a place of tranquility that covers me in the moment, but outside of here is a world I want no part of, and yet it's a world I will have to face.

I've become so completely inundated with my childhood memories that I forget that I'm not alone. I turn around and everyone is staring at me curiously. I can't hide behind my glassy, joyful eyes anymore, and I don't know if there's anything I can show them to make them understand how I feel, so I utter the only word I know that will.

"Home."

Juliana climbs down off her horse and walks over to Gabe, who is now standing next to me by the tree. "Is this where you grew up?" she asks us. I just nod my head, as I stare transfixed on the twisted roots running from the tree's base.

"We spent half our lives here," Gabe says.

Father Joseph slowly walks over to me, but doesn't look me in the eyes. I'm not sure how our relationship may have changed, but my heart stays slightly shielded now. I feel like I should explain myself back at the camp to mend any scars, but I just stay quiet in my own personal serenity.

"This area doesn't look familiar to me, as maybe it should," he says.

"Why is that?" Juliana asks.

I clench my jaw, swallowing the unwanted memory.

"During a different time in my life I often came near here to look upon their mother. Their uncle Finnegan and I were close friends."

"We'll set camp here," I abruptly say.

"It's mid-morning," he quickly responds.

"Which is exactly why we're going to stay here. We've been riding through the night completely exhausted. None of us has gotten any real sleep. We should take advantage of it." He pauses for moment before he continues the debate.

"We've veered quite a bit off course. I suggest we move south now while we still have the chance."

Everyone can feel the intensity between Father Joseph and I, and it's becoming awkwardly pointless to continue, but my stubbornness doesn't allow me to give an inch.

"We stay, and I don't want to debate it any further."

"Hey! Arena, what's gotten into you?" Gabe asks.

"I suppose it's not far from here, is it?" Father Joseph says.

"What's not far?" Juliana asks.

"The house we grew up in before our parents died," Gabe whispers.

"About three miles," I answer Father Joseph.

"I thought our plan was to move south," he continues to hound me.

"If it's south you want, then there's your horse. Take what you need and go!" I say irritably. At this point, it's too late to hide what's been building up inside, and everyone quickly takes notice.

"I'm not here to hurt you, Arena. I'm here to protect you, as I always have—"

"Then why do you treat me as a leper?" I quickly interrupt.

"Nic? Is that what this is about?"

Annoyed by the exchange, I try to block it out, hoping he will ignore it too, but it's hopeless. I'm in this too deep with my belligerent comments.

Father Joseph sighs. "If this is about him, then—"

"It's more than that!" I pause for calm. "The argument you had about me back at the camp when I left—what is it that you don't trust about me?"

"Trust is not my concern. I will always trust you. It's your intent that troubles me, and there's a dark road I don't want to see you go down. There's a hatred you are beginning to possess, and a heart you've sheltered from the demons within, but you're standing too close to an evil that casts shadows on both. When the time comes, will you be able to discern your feelings from God's word?

"You were purely and wholly made from God, and born into this world for one purpose. That alone is enough to keep my guard up from the evil that persistently tempts your heart. I love you like a father, Arena. If I've treated you unfairly, then I'm truly sorry, but you must understand my position."

I slowly stand, now doubting my own intentions and determining if my purpose has been hindered by my self-interests.

"But it's home."

"Home is more than just memories. It's where family and friends dwell in your heart. We have followed you, mourned with you, and comforted you. We are your family, and we are your home now. You can hide, avoid, and shield me, but you can't keep me from abandoning you."

A slight tremor of unwillingness moves within me, but I'm much too sorrowful not to exchange my gratitude for him. I cage my pride and walk into his arms.

"Forgive me, Father," I ask as I weep. He holds me like my father would have whenever I did something wrong or displeasing.

"And as far as Nic is concerned, I'm glad you did what you did, because I didn't have the guts to do it myself," he whispers in my ear.

Shocked by his response, I disengage from the embrace.

"If you trust me, then at least just allow me to see it one last time. All I'm asking is ten minutes and not one minute more. It's been nearly seven years, Father. Allow me to leave this behind, my way."

He places his hand on my shoulder and pauses before he gives me a good gesture of accord. He knows it's a risk, but I know he doesn't want to blemish an already mending relationship between us.

"If you go, we all go, and that's not up for debate," he says, smiling.

I quickly hop back up on Storm and lead the others through our wooded sanctuary with Gabe and Allison at my side.

Memories flow in and out of these woods, especially when we pass by the old, gray Spanish oak Gabe and I used to climb as kids. We used to call it the Tree of Life, because of its ornately twisting branches and roots sprawling in and out of each other woven into a web of wooden knots.

This budding green forest stokes more memories than I can recount, but my gaze is beyond much of these trees here. I've already pinned my curiosity to a place I feared I would never see again. Perhaps I was meant to part from these memories.

With each step closer to home, a cold chill shrouds my body with goose bumps. I feel excitement and horror. I'm just not sure what to expect, and I'm beginning to have reservations about my decision to go.

Just up ahead lies an old road bending around a tight corner that leads into the town I grew up in. I only recognize the road from its pimply paved surface and the same rigid divots in the sides we rode our bikes over. It looks just the same as it did nearly seven years ago, except that the grassy ditches have been taken over by tall invasive weeds, bluestems, and other shrubby wooded species.

Without any hesitation, I completely avoid taking the old road back toward our house. The last thing I need to conjure up are haunting images of the crash site. It's already enough that I still struggle with the disturbing memory lingering in my nightmares. There's no need to perpetuate it.

Instead, I lead the group through an open field about a half mile to the railroad tracks, where we cross over into yet another wooded area. It's at least half as dense as the others we've traveled, which makes it much easier to walk through without dodging low-hanging branches trying to smack you in the face.

I slow Storm into a small ditch that's infested with a thick trail of bastard cabbage, a very intrusive weed that has flourished in this area. About a couple hundred yards through the ditch, we pass by a small row of poverty-stricken domiciles, most of which have been overrun by weeds, pine needles, weathering rot and the like from severe neglect.

The last house on the end of the row is sheltered by two trees growing into the side of the roof. We approach its back-yard and see perhaps the only defense that this town may have to offer: three malnourished Rottweilers slowly grazing the sides of a rusted chain-link fence that holds them in.

Before we move any further, I open up the gate to free these withering animals. Whether it helps them or not, I can't bear to see these poor dogs suffer in these conditions. Should they wander off and die, or find food and survive, they should at least be free to roam to make those decisions.

Much of the invasive plant growth in the area paints a very different image than what I had growing up here. It feels eerily different, as if our presence is unwanted in these parts. Our house lies just beyond a lengthy stretch of land covered in black soil riddled with small, rotting maize stalks.

As we approach the front side of the property, my heart begins to pound, and my eyes brim with tears. I hold them back while I mutter to myself, disdaining my decision to come back here.

The far right side of the house has been badly burned, and the roof is nearly caved in. The porch, or what's left of it, has weathered severely, and the fertile ground, which seem-ingly has given birth to an aggressively growing weed, holds the rotted boards together.

Gabe stands next to me with his hand on my shoulder while we stare at the front door for a few minutes.

"Are you sure this is what you want?" he reverently asks.

"No, but it's the only way I can move on."

We step up on the creaky steps to the door, and by the grace of God, we don't fall through the battered planks. The door has a padlock on it, and the windows have been boarded up. I pull out my gun to shoot the lock off, but Gabe has beaten me to it.

I carefully open the door to a dark, damp house that smells of mold and cedar. Our home was modest at best when we were kids, but it's less than desirable to look at even now. The only light exposed in this shadowy room comes from a small hole in the roof where it's dangerously close to caving in.

We abandon our plan to rummage through memories until we are able to see where we are walking. I tear the curtains off windows while Gabe dislodges the boarded windows with an old lead pipe he found on the porch.

Soon, the rooms brighten from the peeking sun, and suddenly I feel a cold stir shivering in my body. It's not what I was expecting to find after all these years, and I'm less than anxious to open them now.

Of all the memories left here, all I can unwantedly recount is the last day I would see my parents alive. Our ninth birthday could have been a special day, but it turned to tragedy by one phone call. If the hospital could have delayed but thirty seconds more to contact my father of his dying mother, these memories would be forgotten as would my nightmares. Instead, it resulted in an unforgiving impact from a cement truck striking our car, and ending my parent's lives.

Not until now have I wondered if perhaps it was meant to be in order for my destiny to be carried out. Who knows, my parents may have ended up like Myra and Daniel.

When I walk into the kitchen, I'm surprised to see a few items that were left behind. The house obviously never sold and was left to rot.

Tucked away in the empty kitchen are a few boxes still packed and labeled with some of our belongings and memories I'm not sure I want to rekindle. I'm just still in shock that this house has not been occupied by anyone other than perhaps a wandering vagrant the past several years. I guess no one in the family felt the need to move on from this, or knew how to. Finnegan was gone, Aunt Angela was too busy caring for us and battling her own emotional illnesses, and no other immediate family members were alive to know about it.

I leave Gabe's tender curiosity in the kitchen while I wander toward my old room, or what's left of it. I carefully open my door; it's still covered in stickers that have yellowed over time, and I immediately peer into the corner of my room with surprise.

My first bow ever leans against the wall unstrung, and it's still exactly where I had left it before the day of the crash. With the emotional chaos, I guess I was too distraught to go back and retrieve every sentimental belonging. We only stayed in the house a few days before leaving with Aunt Angela. I can't believe I left behind the bow my father made for me.

I gently hold it in my hands as if it were made of glass, and carefully wipe away a layer of dust. Underneath all the grime it still gleams of cherry and golden honey stains on the marbled exotic woods carved into a perfectly crafted masterpiece.

If there is any memory I want to take away from this place, it's going to be this. The rest of the room looks exactly how I left it, as far as I can remember. The unmade bed, probably infested with a colony of mites and lice, the tiny pin holes in the wall from constant dart throwing, and the nasty rat-nested shag carpet that smells like goat piss and hamsters.

Despite the condition of the house we grew up in, I was always content, but I guess as a child, contentment is indicative of your happiness without garnering expectations.

My eyes wander with reminiscing delight, as I touch everything I can, recalling memory after memory. When I put my hands on the dresser mirror, something from behind the wall suddenly slides down to the floor. I bend down and reach behind the dresser and find a rare photo of my entire family standing on the porch at my grandfather's ranch house.

I sit on the floor for a while and hold the picture to my face. I close my eyes and soak up the lasting memories of my childhood while I try not to cry.

I hear Gabe softly weeping in the kitchen. The rarity of my brother crying stings my heart deeply, but I know him well enough that he would rather be alone. I'm just not comfortable sitting here, considering where we are, to leave him grieving alone this time, and unless he is physically hurt, this painful scar he's been carrying forces me to leave my room to be by his side.

I walk to the kitchen and see an open box placed to the side of the other boxes without a label written on it. Behind the counter, Gabe sits with his hands wrapped around his knees and his head dangling in his lap. Next to him on the floor is a package wrapped in bright-red paper.

My heart sinks a little as I identify his sorrow. The box he opened is filled with our unopened birthday presents—the very presents we waited to open after we were supposed to get back from the hospital to see my dying grandmother. But like all uncertainties in life, three people died that day instead.

I sit down beside him, but there's really nothing I can say to ever heal his pain. Instead, I just lean up against his shoulder and mourn with him. After a few minutes, he lifts his head from his lap and stares into the box. He picks up the present and searches over it with his hands, deciding whether or not he wants to open it.

He grabs the corner of one end and begins to tear the paper, but I quickly stop him from opening it. While he peers into my eyes with a sadness only I can uncover, I shake my head, discouraging the temptation to open another wound. I carefully let go of his hands, and he gently places the present back in the box and closes it.

It may seem unfair on the surface to neglect him of those unopened memories, but I know it will only further the pain we desperately need to leave behind. I hand Gabe the photo of our family hoping to soothe the discomfort, and we let our eyes take in one last look before departing.

I hesitate to walk out the front door with my father's bow in my hand, knowing I'm only perpetuating the same pain left on my brother's heart. Just as another chapter in my life that's been harboring deep in my soul closes, I turn the page to start a new one. I gently rest the bow against the wall and close the door behind me.

CHAPTER 25

We travel back to my childhood wooded playground
before the night drapes over us. While the sun begins to
burn behind the clouds, the evening sky shades before twi-
light. I feel comfortable enough to leave the others to set up
camp while I hunt our dinner for the night.

Everyone has been less than impressed with our food
pantry of late. I'm pretty sure stale pretzels and canned vegetables are the last things our salivating mouths are craving.
At the very least, I can nab a few pheasants to entertain our
less than exotic pallets.

I carry Gabe's knapsack with me to humor my overconfident hunt, hoping that more than a few birds will fill it.
I would really hate to come back to this group of already disappointed faces empty handed. It would be in the group's
best interests if everyone gathered some food. Niki, Harold,
and Juliana search for wild berries while Father Joseph and
Allison tend to the fire. I send Henry and Gabe in the west
woods while I scour the east. If I'm going to forage these
grounds for something other than squirrels, I'll need a
change of scenery.

Not much in these woods is worth fetching, or at least
not worth the wait if I'm wanting some good game bird.
Pheasants don't much prefer the wooded areas as much as
they shelter themselves near belts of tree fence rows or outside the edges of sparse timber. I try my luck out in the open
fields to snatch a few ringnecked pheasants, but the scarcity
of these birds are so limited, I have to settle for a few bobwhites instead.

Just when I start to give in, the sound of wings fluttering against the dry brush drives me to continue. About ten

yards in front of me nestled in the tall grass whistles a nest of doves. Their soft sustaining calls sound like lamenting songs.

I draw closer, careful not to disturb the cooing calls to one another. I lean over to get a glimpse of the nest and notice there's more than one sharing the brushy ground. The female is caringly hovering over the twig-burrowing fixture protecting her eggs, while the other one dresses the nest.

Most doves like to occupy unused nests of other birds highly elevated in the treetops, but sometimes being grounded seems less of a hassle, which is why I leave this young family unharmed. It's not worth laboring over a few bites of meat, anyway. Whether it's my eyes deceiving me or my starving stomach growling, I need to think bigger.

I bypass the doves and search near an old pecan orchard for something meatier. I'm beginning to think that the three bobwhites rolling around in the knapsack gracefully died as an hors-d'oeuvre, but I'm willing to wait a few more minutes before heading back.

I sit on a split cedar log and gnaw on the end of my bow to pass the time, when suddenly out of nowhere, a slow sharp cluck echoes from within the trees. I can hear its staggering feet strutting against the fallen leaves. *You've got to be kidding me.* Did God just read my mind, or was the interpretation of my gurgling stomach a clue.

The distinct cackling sound grows louder as does my stomach, and it becomes quite apparent that I'm in the presence of a wild turkey. While he yelps with his short, staccato purr, I hear him waddling behind a thick growth of briar, but I can't see him. His brown-spotted feathered canvas blends too well into the foliage of pine needles, cherry bark, and rusty blackhaw shrubs.

It's quite easy to be invisible in this upland vegetation, especially if you're native to these parts. The only thing keeping this unusually stealthy bird from being completely cloaked is his uniquely echoing chatter. I spend nearly five minutes just trying to position an arrow on the bow rest without revealing myself or disturbing the turkey's mating ritual.

I carefully kneel behind the cedar log, resting the arrow knock between my fingers. I patiently wait for the strutting bird to expose himself in the open while I relax my burning, exhausted eyes.

At last, the turkey arrogantly peeks out from behind the shrubs, sauntering and fluttering his colorful feathers like a horny teenager. It's quite the scene. Too bad I have to cut his romantic evening short. I quietly pull back the arrow, waiting for him to turn around to get a clean shot at the backbone.

He stops before turning his head, but it's not enough to get a good shot. My arm muscle is starting to twitch, and I'm forced to let the arrow go anyway. It sinks into the side of him near the lower part of the neck, but not enough to bring him down. He runs off, squawking back into the woods and flapping erratically. Damn, that's one tough bird.

I jump to my feet and quickly run after him, trying not to lose sight, but he's so fast, I get confused to which way he took off. The only thing preventing me from losing him is his cackling call for help.

I quickly load another arrow and stand upon a tall tree stump to get a better point of view. I spot him about twenty paces to the right of me. The turkey charges forward as do I, dodging broken limbs and bushy obstacles. I finally reach a point where the bird is trapped in front of a thick briar barrier.

He hesitates just long enough for me to close in and stick him in the back of the neck. He struggles for a few seconds before he finally falls limp to the ground. This bird better taste better than he was to hunt, because he isn't exactly your plump Butterball grocery-bought turkey. In fact, the only thing worth saving on the wild game is the breast meat. I stuff the bird in my bag and head back to camp before anyone unethically decides to practice cannibalism. The only thing I regret about hunting this bird is my lack of patience waiting for its mate. I'm so hungry, I could devour this whole thing by myself.

Sitting on a rock next to the fire lies two dead squirrels, skinned and skewered. Gabe and Henry didn't have much luck, but it's better than nothing. Niki places a handful of wild black berries in an empty soup can and hangs the two squirrels over the fire.

While everyone else digs into the few cans of vegetables, I pluck the turkey's chest and bypass gutting this labor-intensive cleansing. The legs are too scrawny for eating, so I cut away the breast meat only, and skew them with sharpened hickory twigs over the nice fire that's been built.

I finish cleaning the three bobwhites and hover them over the fire until they are nice and crispy. With a half-bag of stale pretzels, several cans of green beans and corn, and my bag of game, I'm pleasantly surprised that none of us will go to bed starving.

I curl my knees against my chest and stare into the glowing flames while I sit and reflect over Gabe's emotional episode in the house earlier. I wonder to myself if I've made the right decision denying him the opportunity to rekindle our ninth birthday. But seeing him snuggle up with Juliana with a smile on his face makes my anxieties fade.

If there's any disappointment to be had, it comes from my own self-neglect. If I wanted to stay in the house longer, I could have, but I made the choice to leave it behind with the rest of the memories. I feel a sudden disconnection from my past, but I know this is the road I must travel to secure my fate.

The burning white flames of the fire dance before me. I suddenly become worrisome over the fact that everyone is counting on me to lead us to a safe haven. I feel lost.

"You look troubled," Gabe says, sitting down next to me.

"Just in deep thought is all," I respond.

"Thank you, by the way."

"For what?" I curiously ask.

"For what you did back at the house," he says while drawing in the dirt with a stick.

"Look, I'm sorry if—"

"It was for the best," he says, "for the both of us."

"I was afraid you would be angry with me."

"You know, sometimes it hurts so much, and then sometimes I'm just too numb to feel anything. And I don't know if that's really a bad thing."

"I prefer to stay numb, but at least now I know from my own eyes that I can move on. I just wish I knew where that was," I say.

"You really believe the Southern Resistance is out there?"

"I don't know, but we can't keep this up much longer. Look at them," I say, staring at their exhausted bodies as they fearfully try to sleep. "They've put too much hope into someone who isn't ready to lead them like this."

"Whether you feel ready or not, it's the trust that's keeping this group alive. And they will follow you wherever you lead them."

"Well, I hope we find something soon, because there's a lot of land to cover. Besides, whose crazy enough to establish a fort in Texas anyway?"

"I'll tell you who's crazy enough, a bunch of pissed-off Texans, that who," Gabe answers. And then it suddenly dawns on me what Gabe just said may not be far from the truth.

"What did you just say?" I ask with revelation.

"A bunch of angry Texans. Hell, I'm one of them. Why?"

"That's it!"

"What's it, being pissed off?"

"No. The camps. Nic. He was right."

"Okay, you're not overwhelming me with specificity here."

"Back at camp, where Nic was tied up, he said something that didn't make any sense to me, but he was trying to tell me something."

"Tell you what?"

"It was a riddle, but how—"

"Bloody hell, sis, get to the point."

"He said 'Only a rage of Texans would herald such camps from its eighteen minutes of glory.' So riddle me this,

Mr. Texas History aficionado. Texans, crazy, eighteen minutes, where do you think we're headed now?"

Gabe's eyebrows raise with a revelation. "San Jacinto."

"Damn straight."

On April 21, 1836, the Battle of San Jacinto was probably the most important battle during the Texas Revolution. Less than a month after the sacrificial defeat in the Alamo, the Texan Army caught General Antonio Lopez de Santa Anna's Mexican army off guard during a siesta in a grassy field, slaughtering the enemy. It lasted just eighteen minutes and paved the way for the Republic of Texas to become an independent country.

Not only did it transform a nation, it changed sovereignty forever. Today, the San Jacinto battleground and memorial park rests just outside of Houston in La Porte, Texas. And that's exactly where I intend to lead this group.

"And you trust he was telling you the truth?" Gabe asks.

"There was too much about Nic I didn't trust, but in that moment, there was just something different about him. I don't think he had any reason to lie other than to piss me off."

"I'd say he succeeded."

"Still, I think he knew something he was keeping from everyone else. Whether he found this information working inside the northern camps or not, he was on to something. I just think he lost sight of knowing I would be a better catch for his comrades. I believe you and I were his ticket to a promotion in the Russian military. Maybe it was his knowledge of the Southern Resistance that would provide him the needed proof for such a step up in the ranks."

"At least we have some direction now," Gabe says.

"How far away you suppose we are?"

"I'd say a hundred fifty miles or so." Gabe has a keen sense of direction and can judge long distances more accurately than I ever could. He's a regular human GPS.

"That's about a five-day travel on horseback. You had better get some sleep. We got a long day ahead of us."

Before he lies back down beside Juliana, he picks up his backpack and pulls out a matchbox-sized case and hands it to me.

"I almost forgot to give this to you back in the den. I know our birthday isn't for another few days, but I figure . . . you know, just in case."

A sense of trepidation comes over Gabe's face. It's as if he knows something terrible is going to happen. Quite honestly, it's something I wish not to dwell on before I go to sleep.

I open up the case with a mild eagerness, expecting anything but a sentimental gesture from my brother, but I'm wrong. Wrapped in a piece of parchment is the photo of our family I left behind in the kitchen of our old home. I could cry right now, knowing my brother does have a sentimental side to him.

"It's better suited with you," he says.

Underneath the photo is another picture Myra had taken of Gabe and me on our first day of school. I'm utterly speechless.

"Where did you get this?" I ask.

"I've been carrying it around with me ever since we left the first day. I just thought I'd have something to remember you by if we ever got separated."

I've been carrying around a rage of anger and guilt within me, while my loving brother has been carrying anything but. I'm nearly in tears now, trying to forgive myself when I unfold a piece of embroidered cloth. *Arena Deniel Power born August 30, 2038* is stitched into the bottom of the laced edges, and an embroidered Irish prayer is sewn at the top. It's the baby blanket my mother swaddled me in.

I've completely misjudged my brother. I know he loves me, but this is simply beyond what I had expected from him.

"I figure, there's no reason to leave everything behind. What good does the future hold if we can't take a little of the past with us to remember who we are and where we came from."

I press the cloth against my face and try to soak in a memory or two of my mother. I close my eyes, willing myself to hold on to this memory. I squeeze my brother with a gratitude I could never repay.

"Thank you so much for this. I couldn't have asked for anything better."

"Well, I figured if this wasn't enough, I would go with plan B."

"What was plan B?"

"You'll have to look in box number two to find out." He delicately hands me a second box for me to open, and I emphasize delicately. He abruptly holds my hands as I shake the box.

"Gently! This isn't really the kind of present to shake or disturb."

"What is it, a mouse?"

"Just open it, carefully."

I open up the lid of the box and find it lined with rubber and stiff charcoal foam. I lift the top portion of the foam and see two large-ridged metal cones. Each cone has a tiny switch near the bottom.

"These thermal explosive tips can be attached to your titanium arrow spines, but be very careful. There's enough explosive materials packed in there to put a hole in the side of a skyscraper."

"And you decided to give it to me, why?" I say, lowering the box as if it were armed.

"When you need to use one, just remember to slide the switch over to arm it. Detonation will only occur when struck firmly at the tip."

Okay, this is the type of present I was expecting to receive from Gabe, but damn, I don't know if I want to accept it. Having this box jumble around in my pack isn't very comforting.

"You sure this is safe to carry around like this?"

"It should be."

"Should be?"

"Of course it's safe. I wouldn't give you anything knowing it may kill you."

"Thanks . . . I think."

I set the box down far away from the fire. Gabe curls up next to Juliana, while I curl up with my soft baby blanket next to my cheek. I rest my head on a pile of soft crabgrass and smile.

*   *   *

The dark enveloping foliage swaying against the sun in the morning breeze casts dancing shadows across my face. I awaken to the trembling light moving over my eyes, and the cool breath of the sky blowing chills up my arms. While the wind wishes to blow where it may, I wipe the morning dew from my hair and wake the others.

This forest brings a peace I wish not to leave, but now that I know where I'm going, I will not cease until I get there. My anxious body springs with an energy I haven't felt for a while. I become so restless to leave that I start breaking down the camp while everyone is still trying to wake up. I roll up sleeping bags and cover the dying fire with dirt, while their bitter faces stare at me.

I look over to Father Joseph praying near the foot of a tree and suddenly realize that my anxious heart will go no further until I fill it with the patience it should desire. I put down my pack, my sword, and leave my anxiety for a moment in prayer.

I wander toward the Tree of Life and kneel below its grayish-scarred trunk. Its gnarled, pallid branches hover over me like the arms of an old, withered man. I rest between the sprawling intertwining roots sinking deep into the earth and lean my forehead against its knotty bark to pray. There I give my heart, soul, and mind the food it needs to prepare for this journey.

While I wait for the others to pack up their gear, I notice Allison sitting alone in the corner nook of a pecan tree. Her head rests on her knees.

"You okay?" I ask softly as I walk over. She doesn't say anything for a moment until I place my hand on her shoulder.

"Everything seems so different now," she mutters.

"I know exactly how you feel."

"The last time I saw Lily and Rachel, we had an argument before they went into town. I keep replaying it in my head over and over," she says regretfully.

"I'm sure whatever it was about, it had no bearing on how much they love you."

"When mother passed, I gladly accepted it. At least I know she died in peace. But it seems like ages now since I've seen my sisters," she says mournfully. I nearly forgot about her siblings.

Gabe walks by with a small, innocent smile, and I suddenly realize how devastating it would be to lose him. I rub my fingers through her chocolate-brown hair and tuck it behind her ear.

"How can I truly know if they are still alive?" she asks.

I clench my jaw, searching for words.

"I guess it really doesn't matter anymore . . . because we're all going to die anyway," she morosely continues.

Stunned to hear such depressing thoughts being uttered from her innocent lips is troubling. All I can do is hug her.

"Do you think I'm pretty?" she asks.

I stroke her hair and smile. "Oh, honey," I say, wiping away a small patch of dirt from her forehead with my baby blanket, "even with a little dirt on your face, you are absolutely gorgeous. Why is an eleven-year-old so concerned about these things?"

"I don't want to die alone."

I'm suddenly stunned with a numbing pain and a fear I'm all too familiar with. The misery of dying alone without Jacob belongs to my internal demon, and I'll be damned if I' let her imprison herself with that same agony.

"Look at me. You are not going to die alone, ever. You will always have someone around you. I promise."

"How do you know?"

"You're just going to have to trust me, okay?"

"Okay," she says.

"Hey, and you know you don't have to settle for the first guy you lay eyes on, agreed?"

"Agreed," she says, smiling now.

"Arena, we're ready to go," Gabe says, trying not to intrude in on our private conversation. I nod my head and help Allison to her feet.

I hop on Storm and take him out in front of the pack with Allison riding next to me. The others ride close behind each on their own horse. Since Nic is no longer part of our group, we have an extra horse to lead. The cool morning crisp in the forest air is left behind as we ride out into the open grassy fields toward the southern plains.

CHAPTER 26

We travel as far as we can during the cool morning before we are hindered by the scorching sun bearing down on our weary backs. The humidity is almost unbearable to endure, and the only saving grace we have from this sinister heat is traveling through the most prolific forest areas in Texas.

The towering timbers stretch their fully decorated branches over us like an umbrella, shading us from the intense sunrays. I can only estimate we have ridden maybe thirty miles from our last stopping point, and I suspect only another twenty miles will be all these horses can take for a day's worth of travel, not to mention the painful muscles in my aching body.

We stop just short of the end of the tree line, where a major highway passes by on the other side. It's as desolate as all the other roads we have traveled by, but this one seems to be a bit more intriguing to me. It's a highway I recognize, which gives me a better sense of direction to where we are headed. More interestingly, we just happen to cross near an exit ramp next to a large green road sign that reads: *Rest Area.*

Whether anyone else in this group takes this as a sign from God, literally or figuratively, I'm not going to question it either way. And depending on your metaphysical resolve, a sign is a sign no matter how you read it.

Without any hesitation, I take the lead, crossing over the highway and through the ditches over to a narrow road that winds behind the trees. Sprouted throughout the area off the path are a few covered concrete picnic tables, and near the end of the winding road is the rest stop's abandoned facility.

Inside this run-down structure gleams a more glorious contentment than its derelict exterior—indoor plumbing. You would have thought the war was over, seeing their faces light up at the restroom entrance. I'm more interested in the drink machines in the corner of the building.

I get Henry to help me pull the machines from the wall and hope to find a way inside. Unfortunately, it's completely sealed, and the steel lock on the front looks to be impenetrable.

I pry the sides of the front door with my knife until it finally budges, but it's not enough to fully open it. Frustrated and annoyed by this stupid drink box, I've finally had enough. It pisses me off to the point that I'm willing to waste a couple of bullets on the steel latch. I weaken the front two slides on the lock just enough that I can use my knife again to pry the door open.

The door swings open, and packed tightly against each other are bottles of water ready to be purchased, or in this case, taken. Ah, the sweet nectar from the heavens. No more will I have to boil the bacteria out of pond water, at least not for a while.

Since the electricity has been out, the water isn't cold, but I couldn't care less. I stuff my bag with as many as I can, and encourage everyone else to do the same before we leave. The air in this building is so hot and stuffy I feel like I'm going to suffocate. The salty sweat begins to drip from my forehead and into my eyes, stinging them with an annoying pain.

I wipe the sweat from my face and make a quick exit outside into the little breeze that's blowing in from the north. Around the back, the horses graze under the large pecan trees. They scour for any green forage that's protected beneath the shade and eat whatever little crabgrass is left that hasn't been singed brown from the sun. While I stroke the side of Storm's neck, I notice a red-splattered fence leaning into a small ditch behind one of the picnic tables. I walk a little closer and discover that the fence is painted with someone's blood. Right below the ditch lies a mangled body that's been picked apart by every living creature who's crossed its path.

I wouldn't normally be worried about another dead body lying around considering what we've gone through, but what concerns me is how fresh the blood on the fence looks. The skin on the person doesn't show any signs of decay as far as I can tell.

Maybe I'm reading into this too much. I look down and notice very distinct boot tracks pressed cleanly into the dirt that haven't been tampered with. They look as if they were just made within the day. I'm suddenly bothered and feel a sense of eagerness to leave right away.

I rush back to Storm and eagerly hasten the others to leave this place without any mention of what I've discovered. It's not that they couldn't handle it, but for once, it's nice to see smiles on their faces regardless of how weary they may feel inside. They certainly don't need any more unsettling news that may blemish their lively spirits. This group desperately needs to experience a sense of hope.

With Allison by my side, I lead the others away from the rest stop and try to keep my distance from the road. I mainly stick to the woods for seclusion, but I also want to keep a sharp eye out for any possible dangers we may cross, and the highway would be the only logical means for the enemy to travel.

We pass by a few abandoned trailer homes in the middle of nowhere, but there is nothing of value to keep us from stopping. I'm guessing we've put in a forty-mile trip today, and it's bearing down on us quickly. The smiles earlier near the rest stop have all dissipated, and the annoyance of sitting for so long on the backs of these beautiful creatures have taken their toll.

Before we decide to stop for the evening and set up camp, I take a quick view of our surroundings. Just to the west, I notice something in the distance glaring bright blue between the trees. I nearly fall off my horse stretching my neck around the branches to get a better look.

I ride over next to Henry and ask him to pull out the sniper scope from his case. I peer into it, focusing through the scope's dials until I discover something more surprising than the enemy at our feet. It's a huge neon-blue sign flickering: *Carl's uck Sop*, which I can only assume it would normally read *Carl's Truck Stop* if the neon eyesore was properly maintained.

I'm stunned with nervous excitement, and it's not because of the possibility that this truck stop may have working showers, but more shocked that the electricity is still on. Have the soldiers taken over this area? Seems a bit strange that a place like this in the middle of nowhere has electricity.

I rub the muddy sweat from my dirty face and realize the opportunity to clean myself of this filth is just a quarter-mile away, but it also could be the last of this journey. I don't know if I should jump for joy or flee like hell. I cautiously consider the former and do my best to persuade the others to follow.

I hand the scope back to Henry and lead the weary but hopeful faces across a broken path of diseased-ridden pines toward the direction of the truck stop. As we get closer to an opening near the road, the bright-blue neon burns brighter than ever. Only a few of the exterior lights around the building are on, but they are working nonetheless. There are a few broken-down stores in the same area, none of which show signs of life inside. They are crippled with darkness and abandonment.

I draw my gun forth and approach the back of the truck stop with extreme caution, while everyone else except Gabe follows at a safe distance. This just seems too strange for a building like this to have its lights on in the middle of rural Redneckville.

I tie Storm's reins to a concrete pillar and slowly make my way to the front of the store. The lights inside are turned off, but guard lights near the corners of the store are still on. I grab the handle and pull, but it's locked. Gee, what a surprise, this just keeps getting stranger by the minute.

I dig into the keyhole with my knife and press deep into the crevice with the tip of my blade, but the pins won't budge. I nearly break the point of my knife off before Gabe not so nicely shoves me carefully out of the way.

"You're just gonna damage the lock doing that," he spouts.

He pulls out a metal contraption with two thin cylinder posts at the end and shoves it into the lock. He releases a lever while turning the device and successfully unlocks the door.

"Well, that would have been nice to know back at the rest stop," I say with slight annoyance.

The store is dark and musty, and smells of spoiled meat and sour milk, which is incidentally what the warm refrigerated storage units are holding. The shelves have been riddled by looters who've taking just about everything except for a random selection of packaged candy and nuts.

Besides the rancid lunch meat and spoiled milk left behind to rot, it appears to be unanimous that even the gas station sandwiches are better suited for the shelves rather than in someone's stomach. You know the food at a truck stop is a risk when even the deli snacks have been rebuffed during the apocalypse. I'm pretty sure there's no good marketing strategy to recover from this. It's quite obvious this place has been abandoned for some time now, judging by the black, moldy, shrunken bread still growing a bacteria farm in its tightly sealed packaging.

Gabe and I walk to the back of the store, where we pass an open entrance that leads to a small, quaint restaurant, which is much too dark to venture into. There are restrooms to the left of us, and a long hall that leads in two different directions. At the end of one hall is a door for personnel; the other wing leads to two separate metal doors, one of which has a sign dangling atop its gray metal frame that reads: *Public Showers.*

There's a keypad right above the door handle, but it apparently has been disabled, because the door opens with no problem. Unfortunately, without light, it's too difficult to see anything in here, and Gabe forgot his flashlight. The only glimmer of light we have is coming from a small fluorescent bulb flickering from the hall ceiling, but it's enough of a glow to see the light switches by the door entrance.

I flip all six of them one by one, only to receive the same unsuccessful result—darkness. I feel a sense of dejection right about now, and my hopes for a warm shower have just been crushed. I lean my forehead against the wall and slam the wall with my hand. It is then that I accidently stumble on a different set of switches about a foot away from the others.

Accepting the same result from the other switches, my expectations are low, but deep inside I'm praying for just a flicker of light. I grab the first switch pleading inside, *please, please, please let there be light.*

I flip the switch on, but nothing happens. I want to scream, but then a buzzing sound fills the air, and the ceiling in the back begins to glow bright. It flickers momentarily before it glows fully bright, like an old engine starting.

I've gone from complete misery to jubilation in less than five seconds. I'm so excited about the small ray of light, I nearly forgot about the other switch. I quickly flip it on, and just like the other one, it glows slowly until the corner of the room is illuminated.

There's still not enough light, but it's enough to see the showers, and that's all I really care about. Gabe watches the door while I meander my way over to the shower floor. At this point, I don't even care if the water is cold—I just want some running water that doesn't reek of sulfur and pond algae.

I carefully turn one of the knobs, and water hesitates to come out right away. The air in the lines causes it to chug and gurgle for a few seconds before it flows like a cascading spring. I don't anticipate any hot water, but I turn the other knob anyway just to appease my curiosity. It takes a while, but a gradual stream warms the water until it starts to create steam.

"Thank you, Jesus!" I shout within the echoing concrete walls.

"I'll go check on the others while you get cleaned up. We'll watch the perimeter while you girls shower first," Gabe says.

While the water is running, I look around for something to towel off with, but there is nothing available except for a half-open box of paper towels. Well, it's better than nothing, and I didn't even expect that.

I quickly undress and soak my filthy body under the hot water. It feels so good, I don't want to leave. The flowing warmness rains down on my back, massaging every inch of my skin until I nearly fall asleep.

I close my eyes to let my mind wander in this rare moment of happiness, and I don't know for how long. I'm enjoying this too much to care, but then suddenly the sound of broken glass reminds me that I probably should. I quickly open my eyes and realize I'm still alone in the shower. I see no signs of Niki, Allison, or Juliana, and I begin to worry.

I quickly turn off the shower and stand there dripping wet in silence.

"Hello? Gabe, is that you?" I say nervously. I quietly step out of the shower, but there is no one there. If there were, I wouldn't know because it's still too dark in here to tell. I walk over by the wall that separates the main part of the store where the box of paper towels is sitting.

While I nervously dry off, I hear a sudden crash just on the other side of the wall. I drop the wad of paper towels and put my ear up against the wall. My heart fretfully beats faster now, when I hear the sounds of voices arguing followed by a gunshot.

I quickly scurry around for my clothes in the dark, but I'm too tensely frightened to find them. Suddenly the door to the room creaks open. I quickly drop to the floor and crawl out of the light.

I quietly make my way behind a concrete pillar in the middle of the room, trying not to panic. I know for sure it's not Gabe or the others, because I can hear Russian voices whispering outside in the hall area.

Now I'm glad that none of the other lights are working, otherwise, I would be totally exposed . . . in more ways than one. I frantically search around and remember my clothes lying on the floor next to the shower entrance. My weapons are sitting on a wooden bench next to my clothes, but I'm too far away to reach them from here.

I quietly crawl on the floor toward my gun that's sticking out halfway off the bench, but I'm forced to recoil back behind the pillar. The two men standing at the door are now walking toward the shower, and I have nowhere else to hide. I have no weapons, I'm scared, and I'm completely naked.

CHAPTER 27

With my back pressed against the concrete column, I hear footsteps slowly approaching. I begin to shake, feeling absolutely vulnerable without knowing if Gabe and the others are still out there hiding, or if they have been caught.

I can't tell how close the soldiers are to me until one of them stumbles into the bench and knocks my gun to the floor. My heart pounds deep with frightful verve, and my frigid body begins to tremble.

The light in the corner near the wash area flickers, and steam filters out from the shower room. One of the soldiers whispers to the other that someone is still in here. I can hear them going through my clothes and discovering the weapons on the bench. Suddenly, the light stops flickering and goes completely out.

I turn my head ever so slightly and notice one of them moving into the darkened shower area. The other pursues ahead with his gun drawn toward me. I stay frozen as I can, hoping he will either pass me or take another direction.

The sound of his boots draw closer, and I'm in no position to move elsewhere without getting caught. He's so close I can hear him breathing near the column. I try to inch my way around the pillar and avoid him, but when I do, my knee bumps into a metal stand that begins to fall over.

I quietly but quickly grab the top of the stand with my right hand before it topples to the floor. I have nowhere to go. The soldier slowly advances forward, but then stops. I can see his left boot and the end of his gun barrel sticking out in front of the pillar.

I hold my breath to keep from making even the slightest noise. When I see his boot move forward, I don't know if

I'm prepared to take him down like this. I ball my fists and brace myself for the unexpected, and that's exactly what happens.

"Hey, come here and take a look at this," the soldier in the shower calls out. The man unexpectedly stops in mid-step, turns back around, and I find my inescapable predicament suddenly change. My mind races as I go over every scenario, but I'm not sure what to do next. I'm too terrified to think straight, so I do the only thing I know I'm capable of doing. I carefully stand and quietly sneak up behind him, because I know this is the only chance I will get.

I jump on his back, pin my arms around his head, and forcefully snap his neck as hard as I can. He gracelessly falls to the hard floor and slumbers forth with a thud. I struggle to unhinge the gun strap from his shoulder, and I can hear the soldier in the shower moving about in my direction.

I can't budge the gun from the sheer dead weight of this man's arms, so I'm forced to grab another weapon before I'm exposed. I quickly snatch one my knives that's sitting on the edge on the bench and race toward the darkened corner unseen. I would have grabbed my own gun, but the other soldier took it. He's still in the shower and is oblivious to what has just transpired, but the sudden change in his voice tells me he suspects something isn't right.

"Viktor?" he says, waiting for a response. A few seconds later, he pops his head out and searches through the darkness until he notices his comrade slumped over. The shock on his face is immediate. He swings his rifle forward and cowers behind the bench. I stand quietly just a few feet behind him in the shadow with my hand firmly wrapped around the handle of my knife. He eventually crawls his way over to Viktor's body and examines him, while I stay secluded.

Stunned by his comrade's death, he begins muttering curses in Russian, *"vot der'mo, vot der'mo."* He timidly shuffles his feet back toward me. I hold my knife tight and wait in the shadow behind him. Suddenly, another soldier scuffles outside the door, shouting. I'm left with no choice but to slit the man's throat immediately.

I drop down next to his body, searching for my gun while his bloody throat gurgles.

"Ivan, are you in here?" says the soldier standing out in the hall. He steps through the door while I frantically look for my gun.

"Ivan," he says once more. I run my hand up the side of his jacket and finally find it tucked away on the inside. The soldier, now with his gun drawn, moves deeper into the room and is dangerously close to recognizing the two dead men. Without any hesitation, I turn and shoot him in the head.

Suddenly, a fire of multiple gunshots echo outside the walls. In a panic, I scurry along the floor searching for my clothes. I quickly dress and grab my weapons, while the gunfire continues in a frenzy of chaos. I cautiously make my way through the dark room and out in the hall, when all of the sudden the gunfire ceases. An almost-inaudible Russian voice intermittently murmurs from the dead soldier near the door, followed by the sound of static.

I crouch down to turn the dead man over and find a very weak signal humming from his radio. I take the radio and hold it close to my ear. I can hear the outside ambiance fluttering from the radio, and a man frantically whispering and breathless, but I can't quite make out what he's saying.

The strength of the signal grows gradually the closer I make my way down the hall. It's evident now that the voice on the other end is desperately calling out for help. I cautiously round the corner with my gun drawn and take a quick peek into the main store.

Broken glass litters the floor, and a small trail of blood is smeared in front of one of the aisles. I carefully walk toward the red-stained tile while the voice on the radio continues to breathe heavily. I follow the bloody track around the corner of the aisle and find a soldier face down in a maroon puddle.

I slide his head over with my gun and perch my foot on his shoulder. His eyes are wide open, but he's not breathing or moving. This man is obviously dead, but the voice on the

radio is apparently still alive. Every breathless plea whispering from the receiver becomes clearer and clearer the
closer I walk toward the entrance.

While the left side of the store's front windows are completely shot out, the right side leaves a more gruesome
image. Pinned helplessly through the window lies a soldier
whose chest has been impaled by a shard of jagged glass.

I lower my gun but approach with caution, notwith-
standing his grisly position. When he sees me, he struggles
to reach his gun with his left hand while his right is still
firmly attached to the radio, his finger still pressed tightly
against the talk button.

"Help me," he says, gasping for life in the radio, "the
bitch is here."

My eyes suddenly grow with fear, and the pit of my
stomach refutes in agony. He calls out once more on his
radio for help, but is greatly disappointed when I pull the
other radio from my jacket and hold it up in front of him.

I toss it on the floor while he curses underneath his
breath. I become slightly distracted from the sudden sparkle
of hysteria showering from his mouth with laughter.

"You can kill me, but you will still be a whore like your
mother," he spews with vile intent.

I'm feeling beyond the realms of rage right now, and
the discomfort of my twisted thoughts bears no remorse for
what I'm about to do.

I draw my sword and slowly slice open the skin just
under his belly until his guts bulge from the fleshy seam. He
screams in agony and tries to reach for his gun. I pick up the
gun and secretly empty its mag and chamber. I discard all
the bullets except for one, which I firmly hide in my fist. I
turn to him and give him an opportunity of redemption.

"I don't care about your unseemly past, or the defiling
things that have scarred you," I say to him in Russian.

"Fuck you," he venomously ejects.

Whether or not he surrenders his heart to God and suc-
cumbs to his death, he will eventually have to submit to one
authority or another. Though he doesn't deserve it, I allow
him one last chance.

"If it's mercy you want, then you shall have it," I say, pointing my gun directly to his head.

"May you be raped a thousand times over, you bitch," he vulgarly replies. I hand his gun to him and smile as he pulls the trigger to an empty chamber toward me.

"Fine, you want a way out of this pain, then you're going to have to dig deep within your soul to find it," I furiously say. I show him the bullet in my fist, and I lodge it into the slit of his belly. He winces in misery. I shove it deep into his guts with the end of his own gun before I walk out the door.

Outside there are two more bodies next to a very large military vehicle painted with markings I have yet to see before. I quickly hide behind the back of the truck, waiting for another string of gunfire, but instead I'm greeted with a voice shouting my name.

"Arena!" Gabe yells from the distance. I can't see him, but I can hear his voice echoing in the dark near the back. I sprint around to the rear of the building where I left Storm tied up, but he isn't there, nor is Gabe. I hear his voice shout to me once more, but it's not until I notice Harold waving me over that I find them crouched down next to the dumpsters.

I race over to the metal bins where another dead soldier, whose jacket is riddled with bullet holes, lies stretched out onto the ground. Gabe is bent over, panting with exhaustion, holding onto Storm's reins, while Harold stands and gives me a quick hug.

"We thought we lost you in there," he says with relief.

"I'm so sorry, Arena. They got here before I could return," Gabe says with guilt seeping through his voice.

"I'm fine. Where's everyone else?" I ask.

"They're hiding far back in the thicket. Don't worry, they're safe."

"So what the hell happened back there?" I ask.

"While you were in the shower, I went back to check on everyone. That's when Henry spotted movement up the road. It was a convoy of some kind, I'm not sure, but it was moving fast. We were hoping that it would pass, but one of the last trucks peeled off from the group and decided to stop before we could reach you. There was no chance of getting into that building without being caught. Our only option was to wait until we could flank them. And from there, it was an all-out fire fight until we were forced to retreat because of that crazy asshole," he says, pointing toward the dead soldier on the ground.

"I thank you, both of you, but we really need to get the hell off this road, and fast." I hop on Storm and race up over the wooded knoll and into the dense forest where everyone else is still hiding. Their bleak faces elatedly renew when I approach, but it's apparent that our safety has been threatened, because they are still overwhelmingly frightened.

I gather everyone together and lead them southward through the piney reserve, far away from the main roads. Though our bodies are exhausted, we all agree to travel through most of the night to avoid the possibility of another mishap.

A cool northern wind blows through, and the sultry forest air soon dries. The night draws colder with every step, and my muscles cramp within my frigid body. A sign of change is in the air, and it forces us to take shelter for whatever night is left in the clouded skies. Whether it's morning, noon, or evening, planning ahead is trivial. Time has no bearing anymore in this world—it's our survival that drives us.

Our food supplies have dwindled down to almost nothing, and everyone is becoming disenchanted and irritable. Couple that with the lack of sleep, and you have the ingredients for a dangerously petulant fellowship.

As the mid-afternoon sun approaches, I'm suddenly awakened by its bright, unforgiving smile. The little sleep I've surrendered to has caused serious delusions as I wander from my dirt bedding and squat behind a bush. As my urine waters the ground, smoke rises and ashes sizzle. I must be half asleep because I suddenly realize I'm squatting over the dying fire instead.

The only saving grace from this humiliating moment comes from a few chuckles and a succinct comment from Gabe.

"Well, that's one way to put out the fire."

"I see you in a whole new light now, and I rather wish I hadn't," Harold adds.

Okay, I admit what I have done was inappropriate at best, and maybe offensive to a lesser degree, but I believe it has very diminutive effect on my leadership skills. I think I need more sleep.

I gather my things and rustle up the last of our food before we leave here. Every can of fruit and vegetables has been emptied in to our hungry stomachs. The last two cans of tuna are equally divided among us, and not one morsel is wasted. It's enough to sustain us for a little while, but sooner or later, this group's low blood-sugar is going to turn ugly. Oh, how I wish I were tearing into a hot, steamy roll with a glob of melted butter dripping from the inside, or fresh buttery biscuits smothered in bacon and peppered gravy.

My hunting skills are just good enough to supply us with the needed protein, but without carbs, our energy levels are going to plummet. It would behoove us to gather as many berries we come across. The sweltering heat from the sun is enough to put me in a foul mood, but my growling stomach is adding insult to injury

As we ride into a barren pasture, our pace slows through the clay soil. Our hopes are becoming trodden with exhaustion, but it becomes short lived when we spot a rooftop just above the trees on the other side of a grassy meadow. The gloom on everyone's faces begin to lighten, and when we exit the field into a fertile grassland of trees, they brighten even more.

We resignedly stumble with humble hearts and hungry stomachs into an orchard of plum and peach trees. This fruit has suddenly secured a place in my heart, but more importantly into my hollow stomach.

Like Charlie gazing with wonder in Wonka's Chocolate Factory, our mouths water with satisfying splendor. We all wander from row to row, grabbing what we can like a kid in a candy store. I pick plumb after plumb and peach after peach, eating as I go and filling my pack until I no longer can zip it shut.

With smiles on everyone's faces, fruit is plucked from branches left and right and immediately shoved in their mouths until the pit of their stomachs are filled with fermenting gratification.

While everyone takes hold of this rare opportunity of enjoyment, my curiosity broods over what's beyond this grove. If there are rooftops visible from here, then there surely must be a town that follows. And wherever there's a town, there's always the possibility of people like us, trying to survive, if the enemy hasn't already extinguished them.

I turn away from my curiosity for a moment and watch as the others relish in their delight. It's the little things in life that preserve our contentment. It's unfortunate that we have to be reminded through humbling circumstances, but I guess that's what makes us stronger.

I hop down off Storm's weary back and walk out to the middle of the orchard. As I look out among the entire grove in awe, I somehow gravitate toward the only peach tree that has bared no fruit. In fact, it's not only bare, but its branches are discolored and brittle. Out of all the colorful fruit trees, I'm strangely drawn to this one.

Compared to the other broad trees whose plentiful fruit surprises, this lonely outcast is a far cry from springing forth life just by its lack of beauty, yet I cannot look away. I'm mesmerized by its imperfections and dazzled by the way it proudly stands at the center of the orchard without being disturbed.

My heart pounds and my mind drifts into seclusion, far from reality. My eyes draw back, and I become deeply drowned in a dreamscape. The light becomes dark, and the dark becomes clear. My thoughts briefly rest on a great temple not of this earth. Its pillars stand mighty, towering over the land, and its walls lined with grapevines and olive trees shine bright white. The front doors open like the broad gates of a city, and fleeing from a dark abyss inside the vast depths of this sanctuary comes a black horse with a rider whose face is unseen.

Suddenly, the earth trembles for a minute, and my eyes refocus back on the poisoned tree. The gnarled branch I'm holding snaps off, and blood begins to pour from its broken vein.

I step back in shock, and while everyone runs over to me, the horses race around with madness. The tremor in the earth has shaken all the fruit from their trees, and not one piece left hangs from its branches.

Suddenly, a deep bellowing rumble pierces the skies like a choir of a million French horns singing. The clouds break, and the sun's blazing brightness slowly falls into shadow. While the deep-driving horns fill the air, the moon crescents the light of the sun until it has fully eclipsed, and the sky above blackens like a storm in the spring.

The silhouetted trees casting down their shadowy branches slowly fade into darkness. The deep sounds of misery singing above finally stops, but the ringing in my ears has not. Allison is on the ground crying, Juliana is nestled in Gabe's arms, and Father Joseph is kneeling in prayer. Harold, Niki, and Henry are fighting to calm the frightened horses. And here I stand with a prophetic gift that I cannot share. I'm bound to my Father's words to keep content and hope among the group.

The cantering horses slowly withdraw and return to a peaceful calm. Allison walks over and clings to me, shaking with fear. I rest my hands on her head and leave her to cling until she's ready to move on.

Everyone's eyes transfix with bewilderment, except for Gabe, whose stony, cold gaze reposes before me. While everyone frantically huddles, or prays, he peers into my eyes with an understanding of my thoughts, and he knows what the future holds for us all.

For the past six years, this world has experienced a string of catastrophic events that could rival the Dark Ages. Those still left living in desolation have been endowed a new beginning, if they can survive its tribulation. No one among the wicked will be given favor. As for the rest of us, our survival lies within a covenant to God—to believe, to love, and to hold the truth sacred for those who choose to accept it. The malice and cruelty to which men have poisoned this world has reached heights beyond horrific, but soon it will witness a plague of misery and despair like no other age in history.

266

CHAPTER 28

"We're going to die, aren't we?" Allison asks.

"Everyone dies," I say with resolve, "just don't forget what you're dying for." I leave her with an honest answer to an honest question.

Surprisingly, she says, "You know, I've never had the chance to taste a peach before in my life until today. This is a moment I'm going to savor forever. Thank you." If it's the taste of a peach that brightens our mood, then I warmly invite moments like this anytime.

Niki brings over two of the horses that appear to be in a rather quieter state than before. Harold and Henry are still trying to wrangle the rest that are wandering around, while Storm gobbles the fruit that has fallen to the ground.

With the full eclipse, my eyes struggle to readjust to the dim skies. I look out toward the edge of the orchard and notice one of the rooftops we saw earlier, hiding within a blend of post oaks and shortleaf pines. Just above a sparse canopy of scattered dogwoods, an erected church steeple leans. It looks as though we may have stumbled across a small town in the middle of bumble.

I hop on Storm and pull him away from the fruit to join the others. The horses have finally been wrangled, and everyone anxiously waits for me to lead them out. With our bags filled with fruit, we need to stay no longer. Our destiny lies beyond this grove, and if there's any chance of seeking anymore survivors, we may find it here in this town.

We cross the edge of the fruit orchard and into a place that's far from inviting. The leaning steeple from the church is close to falling in on its burned structure below. There's nothing left but the frame, and it doesn't look safe.

Two houses to the left of us have sunk into the ground a few feet, and their yards have been invaded by thorny sticker weeds. The few other abandoned dwellings on this street are littered with rotting trash and broken glass. The smell is quite offensive, and it has apparently attracted every fly in the state to make this their home. The scarcity of housing in the town may be the only bright spot because down the street is even less charming.

The town square is peppered with rotting corpses. Shattered windows, broken doors, and crumbling mortar must be the theme for every store's exterior décor.

From far away these bodies appear to be in the same deathly state as every other corpse we've encountered, but upon closer look, it becomes a grim sight that I have yet to see until now. Their bodies are covered in boils and scars that resemble that of the pox. If there are any survivors left, they'd be crazy to stay here. I'd take my chances in the woods before I live among these diseased-ridden bodies.

I've witnessed too many places like this, but when I see children face down in the dirt, calm is hardly the word I would use to describe my emotions. These disturbing images make me feel sick and broken. I'm too distraught to linger anymore in this town, so I hastily click Storm's sides and gallop away from this disturbing sight.

When we reach the end of the square, I'm burdened even more with a sickness I cannot control. Just beyond the road on the other side of the railroad tracks is a bloody field of bodies piled on one another. It's a twisted wreckage of human carnage whose deaths were ignored and forsaken. There must be thousands of dead here.

"What pestilence has taken this place?" Father Joseph gasps.

There are too many bodies to count. Suddenly, out from behind the pile of the dead, an older woman wanders aimlessly toward us, screaming vulgarities and senseless drivel. She is obviously not in her right mind; in fact, she may have sprung someone else's, the way she is talking.

Her eyes roll back a milky white, and her teeth, stained with blood, chatter behind her grisly gums. She stops short in front of us, demanding we help her, but then continues to shout curses underneath her venomous breath. I'm not sure which personality is leading this conversation, but it's evident she's possessed with something, or just downright insane.

Father Joseph immediately raises his hand toward her and begins to pray, hoping to expel this malevolent preternatural sprit. She falls to her knees and rocks back and forth until her body eventually finds stillness. She stays in that position like a zombie until she begins to tear into her own flesh with her fingernails. Allison weeps beside me with her hands over her eyes, while the others huddle together far away, behind Father Joseph.

A demon of the underworld has taken this woman under possession, and there's nothing any of us can do to change her. Either she has betrayed her fellow brethren, or she has been innocently held captive by this malicious force for reasons unknown.

The sickness this woman carries is beyond troubling, but I do not fear what has fallen possessed in front of me. I have been called to serve God on all accounts, and this is no exception.

Gabe slowly creeps beside me while this women stares into space and sporadically convulses.

"You know what you have to do," he says.

Even prayers to undo her suffering will not help, for God Himself has already whispered into my mind to end the demon's call. It seems strange to have to put someone down like a rabid dog, but like Gabe said, it's what I have todo.

I draw my gun and mercifully fire into the woman's head to end the torment. Whether it was for her own good or for everyone else's, I leave nothing to further plague us.

"What have you done?" Father Joseph is shocked in horror.

"I've freed her soul."

There's an evil among us that can't be cleansed. Not even God would allow such vile and wicked malice to go on freely forever. The sanctity of this town has been replaced by an evil that I fear will continue, and the suffering that has driven these poor people mad is only the beginning.

Suddenly, out of nowhere, the skies bellow with a disturbing clamor. The chiming cry of bells ring over us and they aren't coming from what's left of the burned church. The bells ring deep and loud, and in between each brass clang breathes an eerie silence. Seven times, they ring, one louder than the next. I believe Hell has just awoken.

I've had quite enough of the disturbing sights and sounds, and by the distressed look on Allison's face, she has too. I waste no more time here and lead everyone into the woods. It seems to be the only place where our troubles are minimal. If our problems are reduced to sleeping on the hard ground or complaining about mosquitoes, then I gladly accept it. This town has no place among this group's hopes.

We travel through woods after woods until we are met by a path we cannot avoid. Without a gradual decline, the forest abruptly ends at another road that has cut a path through it like a line in the sand. My guard is on alert, and I'm well aware of the dangers these roads possess now. I don't take any chances squandering our time out in the open like this, in anticipation of another debacle.

I keep my good judgment and survival instincts closely appended this time. Before we prematurely cross over to the other side where the woods continue extending southward, I closely observe the road through the scope, looking far up ahead as I can to make sure it's clear.

I look down the opposite end and notice a green road sign that reads: *Houston 73 miles*. Finally, a sign with hope. I was beginning to think we were traveling slightly off course, but with this marker, I can actually enjoy a little peace of mind, knowing we're at least heading in the right direction where the Southern Resistance may be. It may seem strange that our hopes lie within a band of rebels, but I know God would not lead me astray now—this is a part of our journey I will not flee from.

I take one last glance up the road through the scope before signaling the others to cross. The next twenty miles is an arduous undertaking. Treacherous ravines, densely covered foliage, and rocky trails have made it too dangerous for the horses to travel. The strain on their calf muscles hinder our pace, and we eventually become too exhausted to move any further.

We decide to stop and settle for the evening. Although with the sun's light shadowed by the moon, it seems like the evening started hours ago. The small valley where we set camp is beautifully decorated in a pre-fall motif of spectacular change in color. Sweet gum trees are beginning to peek through with orange highlights, and the semi-yellow oaks and red maples prematurely dapple the evergreen pines. Though they aren't fully changed, the hint of an early fall delights me.

I take a quick snapshot of our surroundings before choosing to make my bed underneath the mammoth pecan tree that covers us from the dark skies. I prop myself against the tree with my gun in one hand and a peach in the other. I sink my teeth into the warm, fuzzy flesh of the fruit, and the juices run down my chin while I reminisce my childhood.

It brings back memories of my grandfather's farm and the cherished moments hiding in the barn to steal a taste from grandmother's fruit bin before dinner. I remember lying on a bed of hay in the old barn, eating a bucket of apples until my face flushed pale and my pooched stomach soured with regret. It was an ill-advised adventure, but a happy memory nonetheless.

While everyone else dozes off into dreamland, I stay wide-eyed and alert, sitting tucked between the pecan tree's finger-like roots, but it doesn't last long. My eyes struggle to focus, and my muscles fail to hold me straight against the tree. I shake my head a few times and give myself a slap to the face, but nothing seems to work.

When I look over beside the tree and notice Gabe and Father Joseph are still awake and whispering to one another, I decide it's useless to continue this nonsense. I lean my head back against the tree, and without any struggle whatsoever, I fall fast asleep.

* * *

Suddenly, my arm begins to tingle, but I can't decide if it's part of my dream or if a bug is crawling on me. I'm too tired to wake up and care, so I change my position. I nestle against one of the roots and relax my thoughts right back into a deep slumber.

Then, my shoulders are shaken, and I force my eyes to open, thinking it's some wild animal trying to ravage me. It's just Henry gently nudging my arm to wake me up. The lack of sunlight normally puts me in a state of confusion. When I see everyone cleaning up the gear, I realize that it must be the start of a new day, and if it weren't for Henry shaking me, I wouldn't have known it was morning.

The stillness in the woods prevents a breeze from blowing dry the morning dew still trapped in my hair. The dim morning must have confused the birds as well, because I have yet to hear one chirping song spring from them. In fact, it's as quiet as it has been in these woods. Not even the stirring sound of a chattering squirrel, or the fluttering of the leaves dancing into one another high above the branches have I heard since we stopped here.

I wipe my eyes and stretch my arms wide until they pop, when suddenly our quiet woods are disturbed. A cracking branch echoes to the left, followed by unsettling footsteps scurrying into dense shrubbery. Everyone quickly stops what they're doing and freezes for a moment. I immediately draw my gun and scan the woods from left to right until I spot the leaves on a bush shuddering.

I signal Gabe to flank to the right while I take the left. I crouch down and sidle around the trees, trying to step on the soft spots of the earth just as if I was hunting for wild game. I stop for a moment and quickly drop to the ground when I hear footsteps slowly move forward.

I slither on my belly like a snake in the grass across a carpet of clover and through a thick jungle of aralia plants. I'm beginning to grow impatient until I notice a trail of green stalks laid broken to the ground and shoe prints pressed into the soft, black soil. I'm much too restless now to let this person go untouched and threaten our group, but it's too difficult to see anything hiding in this erratic-growing ground cover.

I follow the broken stalks until it stops in front of a cluttered area of bushes. A pair of black shoes stick out behind one of them. I carefully draw close without disturbing the ground, but apparently unwanted noise isn't in Gabe's DNA.

I briefly look over to my left shoulder where Gabe is crushing pinecones with his heavy feet while he tries to hide behind a tree. I turn back around, and in an instant, the shoes that were sticking out are now gone. Why does this always happen to me?

I quickly race toward one of the bushes and peer through the tiny leafy branches. I spot an older boy maybe all of eighteen hiding behind a tree. I quietly ease my way around the bushes and carefully approach the boy's back without a peep, but then he does something I wasn't expecting.

He walks directly into our camp, revealing himself, but says nothing. Everyone is standing around in shock, wondering what this guy is about to do. He seems quite peculiar just standing there unarmed, waiting for someone to respond.

Of course, there's always the possibility he's just playing coy with them until he's given the right opportunity to attack. I don't get it. Is this guy a mute, because he hasn't said a word. I can't imagine this guy being scared to say anything; he did, after all, come to us, and boldly I might add. Maybe he's just reaching out for a peace offering. Oh, hell, who am I kidding, when does that ever happen? Nevertheless, he's a total stranger to us, and we know what happened the last time we took in a stranger.

I slowly make my way from behind the tree and watch as he raises his arms up in an attempt to surrender. He seems strangely different, but more than not, strange is just a decoy for psychotic. I'm not taking any chances with this guy, and he's going to have to earn his trust.

As he steps toward Henry, I sneak up behind him and push him forcefully. He falls hard to the ground, squirming until I roll him on his back. I sit on his chest with the point of my blade sticking into his neck while he pleads his case.

"Arena, wait!" Henry shouts.

"If you got something to say, you better say it quickly," I tell the guy.

"I'm not here to hurt anyone," he says nervously.

"Unless you decided to beat one of us over the head with this empty water flask, I'd say you'd be foolish to."

"Please, I'm just trying to survive like you."

"Wandering around in the woods with an empty flask and nothing to protect yourself with? Survival? Stupidity is more like it."

"Arena! That's quite enough," Father Joseph shouts. Gabe comes out of the brush and gives me one of his austere looks. He reminds me so much of our father.

"Well, get off of him already," Gabe says.

I rise to my feet, hovering over him like a hawk waiting to nab its prey. He reaches his hand forth expecting me to help him up, but something in me just suddenly snaps. I feel a sense of déjà vu remorsefully stirring inside me, and I'm sadly reminded of the first time I met Jacob.

I remember knocking Jacob over with the door on our first day of school and feeling absolutely horrible. I stood over him, trying to help him to his feet and felt my heart stir instantly with adoration. Looking into those beautiful, blue eyes underneath that shaggy, curly hair was the first moment of love at first sight I had ever experienced. And suddenly now I wish I could go back and never relive another moment.

I stand there dazed in solitude for a moment before Gabe abruptly steps in and helps the young man to his feet.

"Geez, Arena, why such a hard ass?"

"Wh-what?" I say with confusion.

"Don't mind her, she's still working on her manners," Gabe says to the young man.

"You'll have to forgive us. We've been through too much to really trust anyone right now," Henry says.

"Yeah, the last stranger we took in wasn't who he said he was, and it nearly cost us our lives," Juliana adds.

The memory of Jacob's face fades, and I'm welcomed back to reality with a slight sting. I wish I had the power to suppress these feelings. But now I need to focus.

"What are you doing out here in the middle of nowhere?" I ask him. His hands slightly tremble, and the fear painted on his face tells me more than I need to know.

"I'm actually with another group a few miles from here—"

"What other group? How many survivors?" I ask impatiently.

"There's about three hundred of us camped just south of here."

I look at Gabe and Henry with surprise. This is the first news of hope we've heard since the skies were flooded with Russian paratroopers gliding down at Allison's house.

"Are you part of the resistance?" I ask.

"Resistance? No, we're just weary travelers trying to survive."

"Family, friends?" Gabe asks.

"Strangers mostly, from all different parts. Our group was much larger before the man in the black robe came."

"What man?" I ask.

"Just a peculiar stranger who called himself the 'Messenger of Peace.' I can only assume he means God, but then again, there are a great deal of insane people these days, wearing strange robes no less. No offense, Father," he gestures to Father Joseph sincerely.

"So what did he want?" I ask.

"He offered us safety. Said that anyone who wished to receive peace would have it if they surrendered to his will and followed him into the foothills for sanctuary. He told us that protection would only be granted for us if we submit to him as if he was some sort of king. It was ridiculous, but strangely many bought into it, at least a couple of thousand."

"So why didn't you go?" I ask.

"Look, I'm not saying I don't believe in God, but any man can go around dressed in a black robe spouting off irrational promises, again no offense to you, Father. The only thing more intriguing than this man's words were the two soldiers standing beside him. Either people genuinely believed what he was saying, or they were too scared not to believe him."

"And those still with you at your camp, they feel the same way as you?" I ask.

"From what I can tell, yes, but you can never be sure anymore. Most of the group isn't harboring any ill-will if that's what you mean, except for maybe a few crotchety old men."

"So why are you wandering out here away from your group?"

"Three of us were sent to go out on a food run. About a mile from camp, we stumbled upon another party doing the same. They all got into a heated argument over the territory and tried to drive us away. The other two men with me didn't seem to like where it was going, so they started fighting. That's when we all heard gunshots from the road. Suddenly, I look over and two men are lying on the ground shot in the head, so I just ran. I got lost, and that's how I ended up here. I'm just glad I found you before they found me."

It may genuinely appear that his empathetic behavior is comforting, but a pretty face can only go so far before the exposure of his true nature is a wrenching disaster. I think I'm willing to give him the benefit of the doubt though. Besides, there's an uncanny resemblance to Jacob, so how bad can he be?

"How long ago was this?" Gabe asks.

"A few hours ago maybe," he recalls.

"Shit! Everyone mount up, we're leaving now. And you're going to take us to your camp," I say to the boy.

"Wait!" he exclaims, "there's more."

"What is it?" Father Joseph asks. The boy stares at me for a moment as if he's searching for something.

"It's you who they are after," he says.

"What do you mean *they*?" I ask.

"Everyone who's made a deal with the Russians. There's a bounty on you. I didn't realize it was you until now, but you're her, the one in the picture everyone's been talking about. Look and see for yourself," he says, unfolding a piece of paper with my photo on it.

I swipe it from his hands and recognize the street from the snapshot. It was the first big city Henry, Gabe, Finnegan, and I came to during the time of the government's relocation policy. That city was riddled with all kinds of obscurity. The town was filled with strangely dressed wealthy civilians, who all had been marked with inked barcodes on their wrists, while others were involved with sexual slave trading. All I can remember is wreaking havoc with my swords, slicing and dicing through evil men partaking in such devilish and wretched vulgarity. Looks like one of the cameras must have gotten a shot of us coming out of the library of that partially gated city.

"And this bounty . . . you're not part of this, right?"

"How could I be? You're the one who saved me from the prison."

I'm stunned to even hear about the prison, let alone meet a survivor. All I can remember from that misery is Myra's torment, and the raping hell Juliana went through before we rescued them. I guess some good did come of it.

"What's your name?" I ask.

"Matthew," he replies.

"Everyone grab your gear. Matthew, you're riding with me." I mount upon Storm and grab Matthew's hand, swinging him up behind me.

"Put your arms around me and hold on tight, but don't get too comfortable back there," I say with an innocent wink.

I follow Matthew's directions toward the camp, while I try to keep an extra eye on our surroundings. If what Matthew told us was true? This could make for an even more difficult journey than it already has become.

CHAPTER 29

I'm not sure if it's just pure loneliness, but the warmth of Matthew's hands wrapped around my waist is strangely comforting. I don't want to get in over my head here, because I still have trust issues, but it's nice to finally be embraced by someone other than a memory.

Whether or not Matthew resembles Jacob, his presence seems genuinely real. I find myself feeling slightly fond of him. I can't know if he has any true affections for me, nor if I really have any for him. This may all just be a misguided substitute for my pain, but if there were any fondness between us, I'm surely not going to reveal it. I have bigger things to worry about.

I feel a bit nervous knowing I have many enemies hunting me. I can't stop thinking what may happen to this group if I'm caught. I still have faith in Gabe that he will protect everyone, but I'm worried for Allison's emotional state if I'm not here.

It feels like we've been riding for hours. The difficulty in finding a clear path through the dense brush has made the journey slower than I would have wanted, but on the bright side, it has given me the chance to get to know Matthew.

Come to find out, he and I attended the same school. I feel slightly embarrassed that I never recognized him, but then again, we were never in any of the same classes together.

He transferred from one of the schools in Houston with two of his younger siblings—a brother, one year younger, and a sister my age. They were separated from each other during the government's relocation decree and haven't been heard from since.

Both his parents, Gloria and Steven, were killed during the first raids that occurred two months after the president's death. Apparently, a revolt in the eastern regions caused a widespread revolution that ended badly for everyone. Government control had been spearheaded temporarily by military forces, forcing martial law to quell the country's chaos.

I can tell by the tone in Matthew's voice that he doesn't much like to discuss it, so I pry myself away from the uncomfortable conversation and try to inject some lighter dialogue to pass the time.

The camp must not be far now, because I see a glow from the fire peeking through the trees up ahead. Before we enter into the camp, Matthew instructs me to approach these people with kitten gloves.

"Let me do the talking," he says with a nervous tone. "Some of these people can be a little unsavory toward outsiders, especially when they recognize that you are the girl in the photo."

"So should I expect a hostile engagement?"

"You mean like the one you gave me?" He smiles.

"Sorry," I bashfully apologize.

"No, most in the camp stay guarded and just keep to themselves, while some of the more eccentric ones may question you. But there are just a few that may find your . . . aggressive nature a threat. Let me deal with them."

"Aggressive nature? Look, if this is about the knife in your neck, I'm—"

"No, no, it's not that. I completely understand; you had to do what you had to do to keep your people safe."

"Then what is it?"

"Well, for starters, you're not exactly dressed for an evening ball. Is there anything less threatening attached to your outfit? How many guns and knives do you really need? No offense, but you look like you're riding in here as the executioner, except you're much more attractive . . . actually you're quite stunning," he shyly says.

Okay, all I heard was the word *stunning*; not sure what the hell else he was mumbling about.

"Stunning you say?"

"Are you listening to me? Some of these people are going to find you a threat and may try to expel you, and I don't want you forcefully engaging them until we all sit down and have a civil discussion. Your guns alone will startle them. Unless you're the enemy, or an advocate to the resistance, guns do not exist to us, and I don't want to ask where you got yours."

"So you really think I'm stunning?" I reiterate, still smitten by his earlier comment, though judging by his frustration within the deep sigh, I don't believe he really cares what I'm saying.

"Don't worry, I'm harmless," I say, patting him on the thigh with resounding conviction, "trust me."

Gabe butts in with his usual intrusive self. "You just take care of your group, and I'll take care of my sister," he says with that cocky grin I've come to detest. I'm not at all amused by his brash comments, but if it makes Matthew feel better, then I guess I should too.

We proceed through the last of the thick brush and into the open campsite, where a crowd of people immediately gathers. Most look no more ragged than we do, still wearing the same clothes for weeks. Well, most—some aren't wearing anything, which makes for an unsightly visit. If I didn't know any better, I'd say we just stepped into some kind of tree-hugging hippie gathering, but at least they're not hostile, I'll give them that.

Just then, a crowd of garishly dressed onlookers pop out near the front, uninhibitedly waving their arms and chanting God knows what. These are definitely not hippies, just a strange oddity sticking out like a sore thumb among this group. It a sight to behold.

While Matthew addresses the crowd, explaining our situation, I find myself bored and inattentive. The only thing keeping my interest right now is the excessive amount of make-up these people are wearing. Who the hell dresses like this and finds it important enough to glamorize their face during a time like this?

I'm mesmerized momentarily until I recognize strange markings on a woman's exposed wrist. It's the same barcode that was tattooed on the anomalous people back in that strange city where my photograph was taken. These aren't strangers at all; they're just the same wealthy, uninformed, and indoctrinated consumers the government has been pawning for invested interests. For years, the rich have been fed government propaganda telling them that they are making the country better by promulgating their wealth among the people, when in fact it has been pocketed by politicians. It's a sad state of affairs to know that people like this were once innocent before they were integrated into a governmentally corrupt system and pandered to their every whim. Now that our government has been nearly abolished and replaced with a new enemy, all they have left is a false sense of hope that one day a new government will provide for their well-being. This couldn't be any further from the truth, but how am I to convince them otherwise?

I'm now less distracted by these once-wealthy socialites and have become enamored by the abundant wildlife flying back and forth just above the camp. Two meaty pheasants swoop down near one of the many tents in the camp, and I can't take my eyes off them. I carefully grab my gun, but I immediately stop when I see one of the women staring at me. I'm briefly reminded what Matthew said to me about keeping my cool, but hunting for food isn't hostile—this is for survival, and I'm hungry for some protein.

Don't get me wrong, the peaches are wonderful, but if I eat another piece of fruit, I think my colon is going to cleanse itself in my sleep. Protein deficiency is just not an option for this grueling journey, and I'm not just going to sit here while dinner is waddling away.

I ease my gun from my jacket while Matthew continues to talk to the crowed. I wait just for the right moment until the birds creep out away from the tent before I shoot. *Boom, boom!* Twice I sink a bullet into both pheasants. The crowed screams with fright, and a sudden shout deepens from Matthew's voice. I completely forgot to attach the suppressor to the end of my gun, and the noise from the shots startle everyone into a rabid frenzy.

I jump from Storm's back and race over to the birds to make sure they are dead, while everyone else quickly retreats back nearly fifty feet. Children are screaming, and women are fleeing back to their makeshift shelters.

Meanwhile, Matthew, who looks very upset and displeased with me, tries to calm everyone down. A few minutes into the pandemonium and the chaos eventually returns back to a normal calm.

The people return from their tents and gradually huddle back toward Matthew, who is fuming. He rubs his hand across his face with frustration and walks over toward me. Gabe quickly steps in between us to intervene, hoping to suppress any further anger.

"Are you out of your fucking mind? These people are gun-shy enough. They don't need any more help," Matthew barks. I'm a little hurt that he would scorn me like that, but I certainly won't allow him to know that it bothers me.

"Excuse the hell out of me. All I did was fetch us a little dinner for the evening. Forgive me for caring."

"I thought you were going to contain her?" Matthew irately says to Gabe.

I pick up the two dead pheasants by the neck and hold them up. "What's the big deal? I harmed no one . . . well, people, that is."

"It's not your intent I want to hold back, it's you lack of good judgment that stymies you." If he wasn't so damn cute, I would have ripped his nuts off by now. I'm angry, but I can't help but look upon his warm face, brown shaggy hair, and into those deep baby blue eyes just like I use to do with Jacob and feel slightly intoxicated by his innocently charming looks.

"A lack of judgment?" I softly say, searching his face for an apology, "for you . . . yes." I take the two pheasants and walk away, annoyed and hurt.

"Arena, wait," he faintly sputters. I keep walking without looking back, hoping to rid some of this embitterment.

Suddenly, two women dressed in the most gaudy attire I've ever seen approach me with stricken grief. One has tears running down her face while the other's overly dramatic voice expresses her deepest sympathies for the two dead birds in my hand.

"What have you done to these poor creatures?" the woman who's crying asks.

Oh geez, it isn't enough I have to be ridiculed by Matthew, but now I have to deal with this ridiculous drama.

"They sacrificed their lives for us," I facetiously say as I join them in fake sorrow. If I could conjure up some fake tears to go with it, I would, but it's hard enough to keep a straight face in front of these two oddities.

"They did, really?" one of the women says.

"They flew here just for us to help keep our bellies full," I add with a bit of sarcasm.

"Then you must be special. You were sent here just for us, like these two birds," the woman says sincerely. Oh, what have I done?

Suddenly, I feel my conscience calling for me. I begin to feel guilty carrying on like this with these two women. They're completely harmless, and I should be ashamed for teasing them. Their inherited eccentric behaviors and conditioned responses are no more different than my own abnormalities. I'm no better off judging these good women no matter how bizarre they may seem. I guess I feel somewhat sorry for them. They've been fed so many lies from the government that they don't know how to express themselves any differently.

I look over the birds one last time before handing them to the two women. "Here, you take them. They should make a good meal tonight," I say.

"Oh, no thank you, silly girl. We just wanted to see the birds up close. Never seen anything like these before. Besides we're both vegans."

Wow, just wow. Vegans trying to survive an apocalypse is like an actor trying to survive without attention. They desperately need this meat, way more than I do. If their corsets were constricted any more, their spines would crumble.

So be it, then. I take the pheasants back over by Storm and grab some peaches from my bag. When I give the fruit to the two women, I swear I heard one of their stomachs grumble a thank you. They immediately express their gratitude as their faces are lit with joy, but it doesn't stop there.

Suddenly, more and more people begin to cautiously meander over until they realize I'm not a threat to them. I don't know if it's from the lack of nutrients or not, but they all seem to be in some state of delusion. The only expressions they seem to know are joy or fright. Anything else is borderline hypnotic. I feel like an alien in some foreign country who's just stumbled across a village deprived of modern culture. It's a bit creepy.

Juliana, Niki, and Allison bring their filled bags of plums and peaches over and dump them onto the ground. I feel like I just landed in a starved third-world nation as hundreds of hands sprout from the crowd, nabbing what they can. It's an unorganized, undisciplined way to feed these people, but seeing their excited faces makes it seem well worth it.

I notice a young boy no older than six watching this starving frenzy from a distance in his tattered, soiled clothing. I grab a few peaches before they are completely scavenged over and bring them to him. He's a bit standoffish at first, but he soon warms up to me when I hand him the fruit.

It's too difficult for me not to display a motherly instinct and wipe some of the filth from the little boy's grimy face. I spit on the baby blanket that Gabe gave to me and wipe clean the dirt atop his forehead.

He devours the peaches while he begrudgingly allows me to give him a spit bath. Oh, the joys of motherhood, only I'll never get the chance to know what it's like. I run my fingers through his tousled hair and remove some leaves knotted in his curls.

"I'm Arena, what's your name?" I ask in a pleasant voice. He says nothing, but grins with juice running from the sides of his mouth. I can attest to his response—eating is overwhelmingly more important than speaking, especially if you're starving.

But if he did respond, I wouldn't know it unless his words somehow secretly seeped through the peachy flesh. He finishes three of the peaches, leaving the last two in his hand to savor for later I suppose. He wipes his sticky hand across his chest and grabs mine, trying to lead me away from the crowd with a persistence I'm all too familiar with. It was the same persistence I used with my mother and father to garner their attention—grab first, talk later. Very effective.

I'm not sure where he's taking me, but it's quite intriguing nonetheless. He walks me over to a nearby tent while he happily sucks on one of the peach pits. I'm quite charmed by his eagerness to trust me like this, especially with my knife dangling near his little hand. He drags me inside the tent where a woman, whose back is turned from me, is humming some strange incantation and waving her arms about.

She's sitting in what I can only assume is some sort of yoga position, but you can never tell with this special group.

"Excuse me," I say, interrupting the woman's chanting. She abruptly stops in the middle of the chant, throwing her arms out wide in a gyrating fury, and flops her face violently into a pillow in front of her. Oh, Lord, is she dead? Did I just give this strange woman a heart attack? If she is alive, I can think of a less harmful way to meditate.

The only sign of life from this woman is the mild pulsating breathing that's moving her head up and down. This is just too bizarre for me to handle. I thank the little boy for his kindness and kiss him on the head before I leave this strange musing performance.

Suddenly, a scream of excitement bursts from the woman's mouth as she wakens from her reflecting stupor. Her startling voice sends my heart jumping into my throat as I fall, tripping forward to the floor of the tent.

I turn around to a woman whose painted face closely resembles that of a clown. If she were wearing any more makeup, I would think I was inside a circus tent.

"Please come sit, friend," she bubbles, with a smile that looks as if it's been permanently drawn on her face.

"No, no thank you, I really need to be getting back to my group," I say, desperately trying to figure a way out of this conversation.

"But you just got here."

"Yes, well . . . I, just wanted to . . ." I say, stumbling to find an appropriate response without offending. The little boy holds out the two peaches, and with the help of his kind gesture I continue my thought, "to bring you some fruit."

"How delightful, thank you."

"Is this your son?" I dare to ask, extending this conversation any further than I really want to.

"Oh no, but I've taken him in as if he were. We found him hiding in the back of a car about thirty miles from here."

"He doesn't say much," I add.

"He hasn't spoken a word ever since we found him," she whispers to me in a saddened voice. Finally, I witness an emotion in this camp that's honestly revealing. Not to take away from the joy that gleams from their faces, but I'd rather deal with the truth than filter through the façade that's displayed here.

"Does he have a name?"

"I can't get anything out of him, so we've been calling him Digby."

"Digby?"

"Yeah, that was the name of my sweet precious Pomeranian. Oh, how I miss him so. He was just the cutest little thing you've ever seen. He had the sweetest little nose, and oh, his puffy tail was adorable. Oh no!" she says, gasping.

"What is it?" I ask worriedly.

"Here it comes again."

"What, what's coming?" I say, grabbing the handle of my gun.

"I think I'm going to lose another tear. Oh, my precious Digby, sweet poor Digby," she cries into her pillow.

Oh, for the love of God, shoot me now, please. What kind of feverish drugs did the government infuse into this lady's diet? Lord, bear me the strength before I lose it. I think I'm more afraid of this woman's eccentric behavior in here than I am of the soldiers out there.

I look into the little boy's eyes and they immediately widen. He shrugs his shoulders in confusion to the woman's obnoxious outburst and grins. I gracefully pull him to the side and try to tear myself away from this disturbing conversation, but I can't seem to distract this lady from talking about her damn dead dog.

"Did you know that of the nine dogs on board the *Titanic*, the only two that were rescued were a Pomeranian and a Pekingese?" she excitedly shares.

"Yeah, yeah, that's wonderful," I say, trying to pretend I actually care.

"They make the best watch dogs too. Nothing will get past them without them barking to alert their owner," she annoyingly adds.

"Yeah, well in east Asia, they will gladly eat them," I say, hoping to put an end to her small talk. She abruptly stops smiling—from what I can tell on her permanently marked face, and freezes into a statue. I think she's about to start crying again. Lord, what have I gotten myself into? I take advantage of her cold-stone silence and turn back to the little boy.

"You do have a name, don't you?" I ask him. He shakes his head, and I'm now intrigued to know what it is. "You think you can you spell it for me in the dirt?" He bashfully shrugs his shoulder as I hand him my dagger.

He puts the point of the dagger in the dirt and begins to slide it across, drawing the first letter then another, until he has spelled out the word *LUK*. I say it to myself underneath my breath, thinking he probably means Luke.

"Luke?" I ask more freely. He nods his head up and down with a big smile and hands me my dagger back. I feel much better knowing his natural-born name rather than addressing him under the allusion that he's been reincarnated from some pompous show dog.

I would stay here longer for Luke's sake if it weren't for Gabe suddenly shouting my name. I run my fingers through his curly hair and kiss him on the head before I leave. I feel terrible about leaving this poor child in the hands of this woman, but I guess it could be worse.

CHAPTER 30

Gabe stands next to Matthew with a distraught look on his face. Normally I would be concerned, but something else has piqued my interest beyond the trees to the left.

"Arena, we got problems," Gabe says.

"Yeah, and what's that?" I numbly ask as I continue to concentrate on the trees.

"These people have gone without food for days and barely have enough water to survive for another."

"I can solve their food problem right now."

"And how's that?" Matthew asks.

"If you quietly hand me my bow and can keep your chatty group's mouths shut for more than ten minutes, I'll show you."

"What is it, Arena?" Gabe inquires.

"A nice, big buck about sixty yards past those trees waiting to feed a few hundred people."

"You . . . you're going to kill this creature with that?" Matthew says with disbelief.

"You have a better plan? For someone who's named after a disciple, you sure have little faith."

"We have two hunters in our party, but without any real weapons neither one has bagged anything larger than a squirrel since we departed."

"How the hell have you lasted this long?

"Before the others in our group left with the man in the black robe, we had plenty of food, but they took it with them. It's been three days since we've had anything meaty to eat.

"Well, have your men ready to gut a deer, because tonight we dine on venison."

"If you kill that, you're more amazing than I thought, but I just don't see it."

"Then you better learn to love the taste of crow, because I just might bag one of those too, just for you," I say with wink.

Gabe grabs my bow hanging from Storm's side, while Matthew quietly calms the crowd's lingering voices. It's a miracle a deer this size would ever tempt grazing this close to a somewhat noisy and distracting campsite, but I'll take it.

"Henry, Gabe, you two come with me, but don't follow too close. Give me some time to track it alone. I calmly and patiently make my way behind the trees to get a better view. Without disturbing the ground's foliage, I slowly and methodically maneuver across the soft patches of grass and soil to keep from making even the slightest bit of noise.

After about fifteen minutes of silently tracking this buck, I come across a path that's not in the cards to pass. There's too much rough terrain and ground clutter to risk losing this deer in my sights. I hug my shoulder against the rough bark of a Spanish oak and raise my bow up to the sight line of the deer.

I'm a good thirty yards away from him, but two trees are blocking me from striking him high into the neck or head area. I patiently wait until he moves a few steps into the clearing for a decent shot.

A sudden rustling to the right of me stirs the woods loud enough for the deer to nervously pop his head out. Damn squirrels playing in the leaves are going to ruin this opportunity. I quickly brace myself and pull back on the arrow, but the deer suddenly takes off before I can set my aim.

I hastily slide my fingers from the string and prematurely release the arrow, but with a shocking result, I somehow manage to tag him behind the head as he runs. I rush over, weaving in and out of the trees, and find him lying on the ground just behind a small bush. I approach the young buck while his warm breath slowly exits his mouth. I've never enjoyed the suffering of any animal no matter the circumstance, and this is no exception.

This poor creature has sacrificed for the starved and should be treated with respect. Slitting its throat and waiting for the deer to slowly bleed out in agony is a cruel and insolent method. I instead quietly approach the deer where he can't see me so it can die with a last image of its beautiful landscape instead of me cutting into him. I plunge my knife deep into the back of its skull right above the first cervical vertebra for an immediate death.

Now the laborious task of dragging this beast of a buck back to camp. I field-dress the animal as quickly as possible, emptying the entrails and any other extra weight that's hindering. The insides aren't going to keep this meat any cooler, and it should weigh considerably less while we drag it back.

Henry and Gabe grab the buck's hooves and struggle to carry it up the ravine and over the rocks. It's too cumbersome to carry it the whole way, so they slide the deer across the floor of the padded earth the rest of the way until we reach an opening into the camp. I take a deep breath as a crowd begins to develop around us. Matthew quickly runs over , and his eyes grow large with surprise.

"I don't believe it," Matthew says with this stunned look. "I just don't believe it."

"Crow is going to taste mighty fine for dinner," Gabe says to Matthew with a hint of sarcasm.

After I catch my breath, I help Gabe and Henry carry the deer with my salty blood-covered hands. Before we can drag it any further, two men kindly step in and take the buck from us for a thorough cleaning and butchering.

The crowd slowly recesses back, and Matthew is left standing next to me with an embarrassed smile. I can tell he's waiting to say something, but Gabe, who's still standing in front of us, keeps Matthew from expressing any words. The shy awkwardness he portrays in front of me is a warming moment I playfully adore.

I know Matthew isn't Jacob, but it's nice to feel this way again. However, I would greatly appreciate if Gabe would leave us alone, but he seems to never get a hint. I have to nonchalantly bob my head to get his attention for him to leave.

"I guess I'll go check on . . . Juliana," he awkwardly says, making the situation just as uncomfortable as it was before.

"I guess I owe you one," Matthew says bashfully.

"Actually, that's two now."

"How so?"

"Did you somehow forget the tip of my blade resting on your neck?"

"Yeah, thank you for not killing me by the way," he says with a smile.

"It would be a shame to waste such a pretty face." Our flirtatious banter isn't at all engrossing, but I enjoy it nonetheless.

"I'm sorry for doubting your hunting skills."

"And I apologize for jumping on you."

"No worries, I quite enjoyed it," he rattles with a smirk.

"I assure you, it's not a habit I'm willing to compromise." I think his insecurity has faded, but I still hold a favorable intimidating presence in this budding relationship.

"Come here, I can show you where you can clean up," he says.

"Why, does a little blood on my hand bother you?" I respond with coy intent.

"If I want to hold it, yes."

Wow, that was bold and unexpected. I must say, if he's trying to court me, then he's succeeding. I think my heart just suddenly warmed, because this tingling burning sensation around my chest is exhilarating. Either that or I just have heartburn from the peaches.

Matthew leads me across the opposite side of the camp and into a small thicket where I instantly hear running water. The tight, steep ravine leading to the aggressively flowing creek below is covered in jagged, mossy rocks that seem to be strategically placed for a rather uneasy descent.

Matthew steps down first and purposefully lodges his shoe between two rocks, while reaching his hand to help me down. Though I've scaled much more treacherous environments than this, I lead him to believe I haven't and take advantage of his kind chivalry. He's a gentleman after my own heart.

I make it down to the bottom with no problem and rinse the dried blood from my hands. I can sense Matthew's smile glowing over me as I wash, but I'm too besotted by his respectfulness to look up and share the same reflection.

Instead, he crouches down next to me and gracefully grabs my hands out of the water. I can't tell if he's examining them or if he's taking a rare opportunity to hold them with affection. I'm too enamored by the warmth of his hands to care. I've never felt so nervous in front of a boy in all my life.

"Your hands are freezing cold," he says with a serious look.

"Yes, but they're clean now," I say, hoping that he will honor his earlier request. He stands and gently takes my hand. I return his grasp by clasping my fingers between his as he gallantly helps me up the steep ravine.

We return to the camp while a fire is being prepared for a feast of venison. Matthew leaves my side for a moment to help out just as Niki and Juliana walk up with gleeful smirks.

"What?" I say as if I don't know why they are grinning.

"Oh, come on, Arena, like we don't notice you following him around like a little puppy dog," Niki says.

"We're just friends," I assure them. Instead of delving any further into my personal relationship with Matthew, they walk away, smiling. I don't know why I suddenly feel so inclined to deny my affection toward him. Maybe it's because I have yet to sever the memories of Jacob. If I'm still not fully comfortable moving on with my life by now, I don't know if I ever will.

The dim skies begin to lurk in shadow as night falls upon us. The smell of fire-roasted venison covers most of the camp, but strangely I haven't the appetite tonight. A sudden feeling of despair draws from my heart and sours my stomach. I don't know why, but something just feels out of place in this camp.

Niki and Harold huddle around the fire next to Gabe and Juliana, while Henry and Father Joseph converse with a few elders in the group. Allison, the one person who worried me the most on this journey, seems to be doing just fine talking to a young boy about her age. Meanwhile, everyone else in this unconventional group mingles around the divine smell of meat as I stand there, all alone once again.

While everything may appear to be sound on the surface, something much more disturbing dwells deep within this group. I look around and watch these people carry on with lifeless smiles like programmed robots. Maybe there's something more to these barcodes marked on their wrists I don't know about. It's quite creepy. They act as if they haven't a clue of what is truly going on in this world, except for maybe a few who haven't lost touch with reality.

If there is true emotion to express in this camp, it has been caged for a long time. It's all balled up into a means of forced jubilation, false enrichment, and regimented spontaneity. Truth be known, when all of this is uncovered, it's just a hollow pantomime. I truly feel sorry for them, but I can't hold myself responsible for changing these people. I can only hope and pray that their lives are pardoned from the terror that awaits them. To be quite honest, I feel safer alone in the woods than I do among these people.

Just when I think I'm all alone, I notice Matthew sitting by himself on a flat stone away from everyone else. I'm not sure if he's waiting for me to sit beside him, or if he purposefully wants to be alone. I risk invading his personal space and grab one of the pheasants hanging above the fire to share with him. He sits with his hands tucked away and says nothing when I sit down.

I'm not sure what's changed since our last encounter, but it feels awkward and uncomfortable sitting next to him in complete silence. I'm afraid I've done something wrong or said something earlier that may have offended him, but I can't imagine what. I badly want to say something, but I also want to respect his privacy.

Obviously, he doesn't want to talk to me, and I suddenly don't feel like it either. I place the cooked pheasant beside him and get up to leave.

"Wait, don't go," he says before I completely walk away. I stop, but I can't turn around to face him, because I don't want him to see how hurt I must look. I don't know why I'm feeling this way. It's not like we've known each other for a long time. We've just met, and already I'm gripped by his gentle voice. Whatever has possessed me to feel this way I wish it would stop, because I know it will only bring misery later. I don't know if I'm destined to hold on to love again without it slipping away.

I turn around. He's holding a wild yellow rose and I gladly accept. He stares at me with those beautiful, blue eyes before he finally embraces me with an affection that I have longed for the past year. He brings his arm around my shoulder and pulls me close to him where I happily lean against his chest.

I've felt scared and tormented by the loss of Jacob for too long, but I'm beginning to finally close that chapter behind me. We just sit there enjoying the rare moment of peace that both of us had hoped would still exist. He lightly, but warmheartedly rubs the back of my neck and combs my hair with his thin fingers.

This unexpected engagement has progressed much faster than I'm used to, but I'm too happy to really care. Deep down I know I can trust him with my life, and if this is the beginning of promising relationship, I will not tear myself away from it.

Our conversation remains light and somewhat superficial, but it's the friendly affectionate exchange that makes it worthwhile. If I was lost before, I have certainly found my way with Matthew, sitting here with his arms wrapped around my shivering body. Our conversation slowly dwindles into silence, but I realize now that with moments like these, talking is simply overrated.

After an hour of absorbing such pleasant affection, our short time together is briefly interrupted by a stir in the crowd. Father Joseph converses with coarse criticism to one of the elders in the group. Shouting begins to ensue among three men while Father Joseph and Henry try to calm everyone down. I can't hear exactly what they are saying, but I suddenly recognize my name being mentioned throughout the conversation.

I walk closer to the crowd with Matthew when out of nowhere I'm approached by three oddly dressed ladies, one of whom is the same woman in the tent where Luke took me. They tug onto my arm, trying to lead me into the heart of the elevated argument.

I nervously walk through the congested crowd near Henry and Gabe. One of the men arguing with Father Joseph shouts and points at me with false accusations that I have hindered this group. Matthew stays close by me and fervently defends my honor by pushing the man back from my face. I grab the handle of my dagger, ready to draw it forth, but Henry quickly lays his hand on my shoulder gesturing me to stop.

"You, you are the heretic among us, and you've brought nothing but evil with you," the man spouts with harsh indictment.

"She's no more evil than you are a gentleman," Matthew retorts.

"You cowardly fool. She's even possessed you," the man says.

"What has she done to deserve these remarks?" Juliana angrily chimes in.

"She did this to us. She's responsible for the unmaking of our living souls. This devil child has made us wander in fear, leaving us homeless and childless. She's the root of what causes all of us to fall into waste. See for yourself," he shouts with venomous intent. He holds up a piece of paper with my photograph on it, the same one Matthew was carrying in his pocket.

"So what does that prove?" Father Joseph asks.

"A Russian colonel handed this to me. He said that if we want our lives back then we must destroy the one who perpetuated this hell. So it proves, Father, that our fate belongs with her, and until she dies, we will never live."

"It only proves the stupidity of man has once again shown its ugly face," I say. Like a lonely cricket wandering in a garden spider's web, these men have all been deceived, and they will not stop until death takes them.

"This girl has been nothing but helpful to us. Why should we believe otherwise?" asks another woman in the crowd.

"You will see the destruction she brings. We should have left with the man who granted us freedom when we had the chance," the man says wildly.

"Freedom? If it's freedom you want from this hell, then you should be on your knees praying to your Lord. And if there is any more destruction or death to be had, it is not by my hands but by the will of God," I zealously reply. I push through the congested gathering of people out toward the center where I can be seen to everyone.

I feverishly address the crowd, "For those who believe in the Christ, they will be rewarded for their persecution, but be known for those who deny His grace will forever perish in deep suffering. I can only hope to protect your souls; I cannot save them."

Several women walk through the crowd and stare at me for a moment before they begin to kneel at my feet and begin to chant.

"Stop this madness," I shout.

"But you are the chosen one to deliver us," one woman exclaims.

"No, she is the very angel of God whom He has sent," another replies.

"Stop it! For the love of God, stand up. I'm no angel, and I'm certainly not your messiah. I'm no different than you. We're just damaged people born into a broken world. If you want to see something different, fine, but don't put your trust in me. I'm not your savior… just a messenger trying to survive like you."

Suddenly, a deep roar echoes beyond the horizon, and a quick burst of light glows white behind the trees to the north. My heart pounds with a thundering pulse, and my mind races with worry. How am I to keep these people out of harm? There's no safe escape from here except through the daunting passages into the forest, where hopefully many will survive.

"If you are a messenger from God, then surely you have a message for us," says one of the women, who's completely oblivious to the soldiers who are about to attack.

"Message? You honestly need a message to see what's about to happen?"

"Arena, hurry, we need to get out of here now," Gabe shouts. Niki and Allison quickly gather the horses, while everyone just stands around like zombies waiting to be instructed. I don't know what's wrong with these people, except to say that it's complete madness. It's as if common sense has been stolen from them, or at least simple logic.

"What are you doing just standing around? Do you not see what's happening?" I yell.

The lights grow brighter from the north, and two large military trucks slowly drive down the rough terrain. If not for the obstruction of the trees, these people would be dead by now. The only other obstacle that may pose a risk for their vehicles is the steep rock-bedded creek that's impossible to cross, but I'm not going to wait around to find out.

Matthew scours the camp making sure no one has been left behind sleeping in any of the tents. I gather my weapons and quickly hop on Storm, while these people are still standing around waiting for God-knows-what. They're like sheep aimlessly wandering without their herder. I look for Matthew, when suddenly dozens of soldiers exit the trucks and begin running through the trees.

"Arena, come on!" Gabe shouts.

I'm so confused on what to do. Matthew is missing, my group is about leave me, and these people are waiting for a bloodbath. I frantically look around for Matthew until he pops out of one of the tents.

"Matthew!" I scream. He holds his hand up, gesturing for me to wait one more moment, but we do not have another moment to spare. The soldiers are moving danger-ously close, and I'm not about to lose another man in my life. Just then, Matthew comes out of another tent, but this time he's carrying Luke who must have fallen asleep.

"Allison!" I shout in a panic. She's the best rider among us, and the one person I trust to take Luke to safety. He rubs his little eyes open and finally wakes up. Matthew sets him down, and his groggy face brightens when I yell for him. Before I can turn Storm around and grab Luke, the same crazy woman clutches the side of my leg, insisting I divulge my purpose.

"I know you were sent here for a reason, please share your message with us all," the lady persistently stresses.

I've had just about enough of this crap. Soldiers are coming, Matthew is still looking in tents, and now Luke is a sitting duck out in the open. I angrily push my boot against the woman's arm and yell for Luke to run.

"Okay, sure. You want a message, I got a message from God. He's telling me to tell you to get the fuck out of here or you're all going to die! Is that clear enough for you?"

"Wh-what?"

"Run, now!"

Suddenly a blaze of bullets shower from within the trees, and people run screaming in horror.

"Arena, come on, we have to go now!" Juliana screams.

I look desperately around for Luke in all the hysteria. I spot him running from a thick patch of grassy brush and thrust Storm full speed toward him. Bullets graze past my ear, and Luke falls lifelessly to the ground.

"No!" I scream in agony. I rush over to pick him up, but he's not moving.

In a quick instance, my rage turns into a sigh of relief when Luke pops back up. He had tripped and fallen down from a root sticking out of the ground. A bullet has grazed his arm, leaving him with a slight wound but nothing a bandage can't fix. I don't know how much more of this emotional roller coaster I can take.

"Are you okay?" Allison says, panting.

"I'm good, he'll be fine. Take him with you and get in the woods as fast as you can. Join the others and don't stop moving until every breath has run out, you hear me?"

"What about you?"

"Don't worry about me, I'll catch up. Just go," I say, slapping her horse on the backside. There's no way I'm leaving here without Matthew. And even if I had to, I don't think I could live with myself, wondering if he' s dead or alive. I race over by the tents and hide myself from the second wave of soldiers scouting the grounds.

I search in each tent, but they all seem to be empty. I enter one of the last remaining tents on the end, but it's empty as well.

Before I can exit the tent, a shadow near the entrance draws me back in. Flustered for a way out, I pull my knife and sidle up next to the open flap. I wait there, sweating myself into a rabid frenzy, anxiously ready to plunge my knife into this soldier's neck. But when he enters, I have to do everything I can to keep the knife from sinking into the side of Matthew's throat.

"Dammit, Matthew, I could have killed you," I angrily say with a slight tremble in my voice.

"We need to move now. They're approaching to the west of the tents," he says.

We step out of the tent and wait until it's clear before we race over to Storm. I hop on first and grab Matthew's arm, trying to pull him up, but a gun fires and strikes Matthew in the shoulder. He loses his grip from my hand and falls backward.

"Matthew!"

I jump down to help him to his feet when a soldier barrels out between the tents. I push Matthew out of the way and quickly draw my gun, shooting the man dead.

I carefully grab Matthew's wounded shoulder to elevate it while he hoists himself onto the back of the horse. I hop on and thump Storm's sides with the edge of my boots, while shots are raining from the tents as we head into the woods.

I can tell by the weak grip of Matthew's hands feebly wrapped around my waist that he has lost a good amount of blood. I push Storm as hard as I can to put some distance behind me, but the low-lying branches make it difficult to maneuver. I can still hear a faint gunshot or two, but it's far enough behind us that I don't panic.

I feel Matthew's head weighing downward at my side and his grip loosening from my waist. I hold the reins with one hand and slide my other across Matthew's arm to keep him from falling back, but the weight is overwhelming. I nearly bump into a tree trying to handle Storm with one hand and manage Matthew with the other.

I grab the reins with both hands for a brief moment, and direct Storm away from the dense growth of under-brush. Matthew's hands suddenly slide from my waist. I turn around to grab his hand, but the sheer weight of his body takes him off the side of Storm and into a pile of brush.

I turn back around to stop Storm, but before I can pull back on his reins, the top of my head tragically meets a thick low-hanging branch that kicks me from Storm's back and onto the ground. I lie there wondering if Matthew is still alive, as my vision struggles to refocus on the blurred image of Storm riding away. The ringing in my ears and the sting-ing pain in my head leaves me in great agony. And it's not until I slowly lose complete consciousness that the pain begins to fade and the little light left in the woods turns com-pletely black.

CHAPTER 31

Isolation from cognizance seems painfully endless when your brain is suspended in a dark, blank canvas. I feel trapped in a horrific hallucination that seems to repeat over and over, and I can't escape. It's not until the pain in my head subtly returns and the light from a fire creeps into my eyes that I realize I've woken from one nightmare only to learn that I'm living in another.

My eyes fully widen with horror when I awake all alone with my mouth gagged and my head resting against a tree in some small camp. I feel a tingling sensation hampering my wrists to which I look down and notice that both hands have been chained to a couple of metal rods hammered deep into the ground.

To my right is a large tent covered in gray cloth and netting, and directly in front of me is a burning fire crackling beneath a hanging pot. An off-road motorcycle with no markings sits against a tree behind the fire, and various metal boxes are scattered throughout.

I can't see beyond the tent beside me because I'm severely restricted from moving, but it's evident that there's more than just myself imprisoned here. I can hear whispering and crying coming from behind the tent. Inside there's inexorable moaning, and not the kind I would address as pleasant. I recognize a soldier's jacket neatly folded over a stone near the fire and realize I've been taken to a temporary Russian camp.

Suddenly, I hear the faint cry of my name being whispered, but I can't tell where it's coming from. The voice deepens, followed by coarse coughing. I twist my body around to my left where I see Matthew tied up against a tree.

His face is pale, and his head weakly rests to the side. His left shoulder is completely soaked in blood from the gunshot wound, but he's still alive, barely.

Out from his agitated voice, I can hear Storm nicker just behind me, but I can't turn around enough to see him. Only in the shadow as the fire flickers can I see the silhouette of his reins tied to a limb.

Two men suddenly approach from behind the tent, one dressed as a simple soldier, and the other outfitted in higher-ranking attire. His stern, cold face emits a foul and alluring malice that only the devil himself would delight in. Following close behind saunters a large, muscular soldier whose shirt is soiled with sweat and his arm speckled with blood.

"So, you're the dirty, little minx who propagated the misfortunes for her people," the colonel says in an arrogant voice. All I can do is mumble curses behind this gag; otherwise, I would spit on him.

"What, no retort? Cat got your tongue, no?" he continues to mock. He nods his head toward the soldier and picks up a piece of white-hot metal from the blistering ash in the fire. The soldier leaves.

"You should be thankful I found you when I did. The wild beasts in this area aren't as forgiving as I am. Nothing that a wild . . . how do you say, coyote . . . would rather do then to tear into your sweet, young flesh. I'm the one who brought you back from purgatory."

I furiously wiggle my body and try to pull the chains back and forth from the metal rods to loosen the soil.

"Don't be so hasty, my flower. There's plenty of time to thank me. We'll discuss how you will repay me later. For now you can sit back and enjoy the reaping of your nation."

Right then, the soldier comes back with a man who's been severely beaten. His hands are bound behind him and blood runs from his ear. The soldier throws the man down to the ground onto his knees and forces his head toward me.

"Do you know who she is?" the colonel asks the man. He can barely lift his battered face to shake his head no. "It matters not. She's no interest to you, but what does interests me is this Resistance I've been so fondly reminded of. They cower in seclusion, yet they somehow wreak havoc on my men. You wear their colors, so you must know where they are hiding."

"I know nothing, I swear it. This isn't my jacket," the man says.

"Of course it's not, that would be formidable to explain, wouldn't it?"

"I found it to keep warm during the cool nights."

"Unfortunate for you, but somewhere in this is truth. Care to take me to it?" the colonel says, holding the glowing hot piece of metal to his face.

I didn't notice the jacket before until now. Its black color mingles effortlessly with the shadows, but the unique white painted X below the lapel is remarkably noticeable. I'm convinced that the Southern Resistance does exists, and by the tone of the colonel's interrogation he believes it too.

"I found it in the streets . . . on a dead man," the man explains.

"More American lies!" he shouts as he slaps the man across the face. "My patience is growing weary with this drivel. You leave me no choice. Sergeant!"

"Yes, sir."

"Bring the little ones."

"No, please no, they have nothing to do with this," the man cries.

Two children, a boy and girl, are dragged out of the tent by their bound hands. They are placed on their knees in front of their father. He cries and pleads for the colonel's mercy, but the colonel doesn't respond. He paces back and forth behind the children who are absolutely terrified.

He walks over to the one of the metal boxes and pulls out a black stiletto.

"You love your children, yes?" the colonel asks.

"Yes," the man cries. "Please don't hurt them. Take me instead," he pleads.

"And why is that?"

"I'm the Resistance, not them."

The colonel showers him with a cold, stony stare. "Why don't you tell me where they are, and this can be easily avoided," he says as he places the knife underneath the little boy's neck.

"Please, they know none of what I've done. They are innocent. I'm the soldier you want." The colonel slowly slides the blade across the boy's neck, breaking the skin just enough to where blood is drawn. I'm twitching hysterically trying to escape these chains, but the metal rods are just too deep in the ground for them to budge.

I scream with rage from behind the gag in my mouth, and tears begin to swell up in my eyes.

"South . . . it's about thirty miles south from here," the man cries out. "Please let them go, I've told you everything," he pleads.

"You know, nothing in life is really free, is it. There's always something, or someone, that has to pay a price. You are a threat and an obstruction to a greater cause. And for that, you must pay. I'm not the evil man you think I am. I get no pleasure from doing what needs to be done, but life is a cruel reminder that you simply have no control over it. I want you to take a good look upon you children once more, for it will be the last your eyes will remember."

He callously slides the blade against the boy's skin and slits his throat. The man screams, crying in anguish and torment, just as I am right now. And if it's not enough for the man to endure, the colonel does the same to his daughter.

My blood boils beyond the dispelling of forgiveness. I fear I have nothing but hate growing inside of me now after witnessing such vile and wicked filth.

To continue with his merciless cruelty, the colonel plucks out the man's eyes with the knife so that his last memory of his children can linger into the shadow of his mind, or until he finds the opportunity to kill himself.

The colonel's cold stony stare meets mine in a heated standoff of hatred.

"What?" he asks, "do you think I really enjoy senseless killing? You should be grateful it wasn't you. I'll let you thank me later."

Headlights suddenly flicker from behind the tent, and the sound of a sputtering engine follows with it. The front of a jeep pulls just slightly past the tent where I can only see the hood. A soldier exits the vehicle, but when he observes the shocking display of carnage, he immediately hesitates to walk any closer to the colonel.

"Private," the colonel nods.

"Yes, sir," the man answers, saluting.

"Take my prisoner back to base, bound and unharmed. I don't want to see one scratch on her young body until I've thoroughly examined it for myself. Is that understood?"

"Yes, sir, but what about the other one?" he says, pointing to Matthew.

"Leave him be. He's going to die soon enough on his own."

I can't peel my eyes away from Matthew's pale face and limp body. I feel helpless watching him die like this until he raises his head to me and smiles.

"Don't give up on me, you hear," he says softly.

When the private turns to unchain me, his eyes grow shockingly wide, as do mine. I can't believe it's him, and here he stands before me wearing a Russian uniform. His chiseled frame and arrogant face looks just the same as it did in school, but something seems oddly different about him now regardless of his ties.

He bends down to unlock my chains and replaces them with handcuffs. There's enough hate in my eyes right now to disfigure his face. The last time I saw him, my hand was firmly attached to his crotch bringing him to his knees with a deserving thud after bullying my brother. I give him a cold stare of condemnation, but he doesn't look back. Instead, he whispers from the corner of his mouth while the colonel and the other soldier are talking.

"Arena, you must know I'm not part this. I've been forced into this. If I don't follow orders my life will be taken. They've already killed my family," Derrick says. I lift my hand from the chains and try to grab his gun, but he quickly stops me.

"Not now," he says, holding onto my arm. "Just play along, I'll get you out of this mess."

I may have never liked Derrick for what pain he put my brother through, but I have no choice but to trust him this time. I can see it resting behind his pallid face that he's telling the truth.

He cleverly cuffs my hands in the front and pulls me up from the ground. He casually points to his gun with his finger and coolly nods his head before he turns toward the jeep.

"Wait right there, Private," the colonel says just as Derrick tries to grab his gun. "Sergeant, radio the base and let them know that we have a threat in custody that isn't to be touched."

"Yes, sir."

The colonel rubs his fingers over my cheek and pushes the hair behind my ear. He grabs my waist and gropes my ass while his repulsive breath scorches my nostrils.

"You know, Private, you deliver this beautiful specimen unscathed and there may just be a promotion in your future," he says with a perverse smirk. "Oh, and, Private—have them bathe her twice before she's brought to my quarters. Even beauty has its imperfections."

When the colonel turns his back, Derrick reaches for his gun and angrily snaps in a prideful voice, "That may be a problem, sir."

"And why . . . is that?" he says stunned, as he turns around to a gun pointed at his face.

"Because you aren't going to be in your quarters."

"Backup! Backup, we need backup now!" the soldier in the car shouts into the radio. Derrick squeezes the trigger, putting a bullet directly into the colonel's head, and quickly turns to do the same for the other soldier, but the gun is empty. The soldier throws down the radio and races over to his gun that's lying on the ground. Derrick scampers after the man and lunges on his back just as the soldier picks up his gun. They roll around trading punches until the soldier has Derrick pinned on the bottom with his neck constricted.

I leap on the man's back with my cuffs thrown around his neck, then I pull back his head. I squeeze the chain against his trachea as hard as I can until the muscles in his body relax. His last breath gasps as he releases his hands from Derrick's neck, and he falls wilting over to the side.

I collapse back with exhaustion, while my bruised handcuffed wrists bleed. Derrick grabs his neck and massages his windpipe, choking blasts of air.

I unravel the chain that's restricting my hands from the soldier's neck and extend my arms toward Derrick in an exchange for freedom. He stares into my eyes for a moment before lifting the keys from his belt.

"Why did you save me?" he asks.

"Because you're not like them," I answer. He unlocks the cuffs from my sore wrists and holds my hands.

"Thank you," he humbly whispers with sincerity—a side I haven't seen from him. If there's a time when someone deserves a second chance, then this is the moment.

"Come with us and be free of this madness."

"I can't go, not now."

"They don't own you."

"It's my choice to stay, and mine alone. Now go before they get here."

"You don't have to do this."

"You have your fate to deal with. I have mine," he says hardheartedly.

His persistent absurdity is immunity to remediation. It's much too irritating and frustrating to understand. I'm convinced that stupidity among men will never go unchanged.

"So, that's it, then. You're just going to fold up and let them decide who you are? They are the murderers, not you. This is a genocide you don't have to be a part of."

"I never meant to hurt anyone."

"I know that," I softly say with understanding.

"I'm not a saint by any means, but I'm no stone-cold killer either. Too many people have died for nothing. I've lost my family and my friends. They've taken everything from me. I'm not going to allow them to do that to you. Now go while you have the chance. I'll hold them off as much as I can."

It's useless to try to convince him. I can only know my path and leave him to choose his own. I grab my weapons lying beside the tent and untie Matthew from the tree. His weak body nearly collapses in my arms before I'm able to help support his wounded shoulder.

I delicately place his arm around my neck and walk him over by Storm. He has just enough strength to grab the saddle and pull himself halfway up until I have to shove his legs the rest of the way. I hop up and sit behind him this time with the reins wrapped around his waist for extra support. I'm not letting him go.

Derrick holds his post next to the jeep with a gun in one hand and a grenade in the other. I can't help but wonder who else from my school may still be out there alive. Though my bitterness for his obstinate behavior idles, I'm grateful for his valor all the same.

"May God be with you, Derrick," I say before riding away.

"Hey," he says, "if you see your brother…tell him I'm sorry."

I turn around wondering what would have been if Gabe and I had never run into Derrick at school. I don't know how my fate would have changed, but I do know I wouldn't have been able to see a different man standing before me.

CHAPTER 32

I don't know how long we've been wandering these woods, and I'm not sure if we are going in the right direction. I have no compass and no sense of time anymore. The best I can do during this endless eclipse is to find some moss growing on the north side of the trees, and even that's not always the case with the recent loss of sunlight.

My body feels exhausted beyond repair, and my mouth is parched under extreme dehydration. I stop for a minute and reach into my bag to find the last bottle of water. I take a few sips to conserve for the journey until I can find us another water source.

I hold Matthew close to me to support his unstable body, and I offer him the rest of the water. He doesn't immediately respond until I have to shake him a bit. He mumbles a few words, but I can't understand what he is saying while I'm sitting behind him.

I carefully hop down and help him off the saddle. He can barely stand straight and his hands feel cold. I walk him over by a soft patch of grass and lay his head in my lap. I hold the bottle to his tender lips while he drinks. His eyes begin to open slightly wider than before, and he smiles.

"I don't think I could open my eyes to a more beautiful face," he kindly says. My heart stirs with an adoration that I once had before, and my feelings for him have come to a pinnacle to which I can hide no more. I carefully raise his head from my lap while he peers into my eyes, and I lean in close to his face. Without any wavering, I plant my lips on his and we kiss for what seems like an eternity.

I slowly slide my hand down his broad chest and to his waist where I feel the side of his inner shirt soiled. I immediately pull back from his soft lips, and lift my hand from his side. It's covered in blood. I look down with shocking surprise and find another gunshot wound near his ribs I didn't notice before.

It's dangerously worse than his shoulder wound, and I'm scared for his life now.

"No, no, no . . . don't do this to me, please don't do this," I say, crying uncontrollably. I quickly grab Storm's reins and lead him closer to Matthew. "We have to get you out of here and fast. We'll find someone to help you," I say hysterically.

"Arena . . . Arena! stop. I'm not going anywhere. I can't."

"We'll find someone. We're not far from the southern camps, and they should have medicine, doctors, and—"

"Listen to me! I'm in no shape to move anymore. I've lost too much blood. I can't make it that far, and you know that."

I fall to my knees with my head in my hands, and cry until I have nothing left to give. I wish I were dead right now. Why is this happening to me again?

"Arena, come hold my hand," he says in a soft, fading voice.

I can't keep myself together long enough to move from my knees, nor can I bear to watch him lie there and die, but in a shocking rare moment, I suddenly realize that I love him too much not to hold him again. No other man in my life have I loved so dear in such a short time other than Jacob, and it's all for nothing. I'm drenched in sorrow and anger that I have to live this moment all over again. It is with these two men that will always dwell in my heart forever. It is only but one soul that's torn with misery—mine.

I lie beside him with my head on his chest and his hand caressing my face. He wraps his other arm around my body, and we lie there together until his last dying moment.

"If I'm going to die here, I'm glad that it's with you," he says weakly. I weep on his chest, selfishly wishing I hadn't met him. This is just too painfully discomforting for me to understand, but knowing that his death is imminent, I give him one last kiss. His cold hand relaxes from my tear-covered cheek and his last breath forever releases.

I turn from his blue eyes and bury my face in his chest. I'm cold, alone, and lost, and all that I have left is now shadowed in bane and relentless anguish.

The moon shifts from the dark skies, and the light of the sun glows once again, but it shines differently on my face than before. I discover the warmth of my Father comforting me, as I lie there praying for a cure to this turmoil we've had to suffer.

After an hour of grieving, the tears have all but dried away, and I find myself still lying across Matthew's chest. I unwillingly pick myself up from this painful stupor and search for as many stones I can. I place rocks around his body and stack them to where they slightly rise above him. I cover the rest of his exposed body with small branches and leaves until he is completely enclosed and unseen. To keep wild animals from tearing into his remains, I cover the branches with three flat stones I find near a dry riverbed.

I stand there staring at the rocks, wondering to myself how, if ever, this was meant to be, or if this was just another random misfortune I've come to expect in a wicked and sinful world. Regardless of the reason, another person dear to me has died, and I'm forever stained with his memories.

I fall to my knees once again, but this time I do not mean to leave them. I pull my gun and chamber a bullet. There's a brief, but dangerous void between my conscience and the will to live. I place the end of the barrel inside my mouth and weep. My hand shakes vigorously. I squeeze the trigger half way before I realize how much my brother means to me. In that small wavering moment, I release my finger and drop the gun. I sit there, depleted and broken.

"Just take me, take me from this world now!" I cry. I'd rather be dead than go on like this, but Gabe needs me.

I have no more tears to give, and no more energy to grieve. Though my heart is torn, and my emotions are bruised, I have just enough left in me to say one last prayer. Before I turn my eyes from Matthew forever, I leave a bouquet of white aster and dogwoods I had picked earlier and lay them atop his stony grave.

I pull my exhausted body up on top of Storm's saddle and ride until I can ride no more.

INTOTHEDARKNESS:BOOKII

leave a bouquet of white aster and dogwoods I had picked earlier and lay them atop his stony grave.

I pull my exhausted body up on top of Storm's saddle and ride until I can ride no more.

CHAPTER 33

My eyelids struggle to fully open, but when I see that I'm not on Storm's back anymore they immediately widen with fright. I find myself lying on the ground with my back leaning against an old log in some stranger's camp. I immediately check my wrists, but they are not bound, nor have my weapons been taken. There's a fire that's just barely started burning to my left and another horse tied to a small oak branch.

There's a sudden rustle to my right and footsteps approaching from behind the tree where Storm is tied to. I draw my gun when out walks a young woman carrying a bundle of sticks. She immediately stops with surprise while I hold her at gunpoint.

"Who the hell are you?" I demand.

"Whoa, hold on. I'm not here to hurt you, I've just—"

"Who . . . are . . . you!" I ask again.

"I'm Nadia, First Battalion scout."

My eyes grow stormy and my face is now flushed with fury, but I suddenly realize she's not wearing a military uniform. I draw my gun closer to her head and notice a knife hanging from her belt.

"What army do you serve?" I crossly ask. She pauses for a moment as I watch a bead of sweat run down her forehead.

"I serve no army. I fight for defense under the Southern Resistance," she nervously answers.

I hesitate to believe her, but then I realize no one is stupid enough to leave a prisoner unattended and unbound. I lower my gun and place it back into my jacket. She exhales her nervous breath and sighs with unexpected reprieve.

"How did I get here?" I ask.

"I found you when your horse came wandering in my camp. I saw you laying on your horse and thought you were dead. You didn't budge an inch when I pulled you off, so I laid you down here. I didn't know you were still alive until I saw you breathing."

"How long have I been out?"

"I don't know, your horse's legs still seemed fresh when you got here, maybe a few hours."

"What's today?" I ask.

She digs into her bag and pulls out a small notebook. She flips through the pages before answering. "Sunday."

"Sunday? The date . . . what's the date?" I ask.

She looks back at the notebook and says, "August thirtieth, why?"

I close my eyes; today is my birthday—my sweet sixteenth to be exact. A monumental day in a girl's life only to be spoiled by another tragedy I wish not to remember. It's the first birthday I've had without my brother to celebrate with, and it may be the last.

"Today's my birthday; actually, I share it with my twin brother."

"Did you say twin brother?" she asks with a perplexing sadness.

I stand there pensively wondering why such a strange response, but then a sudden shock overshadows my intrigue when I notice Gabe's horse tied to the other side of the oak branch.

"That horse there," I say, pointing toward Gabe's mare, "where's the person who was riding it?"

She hesitates to answer me, and I can tell that her face hides a sadness I don't know if I'm prepared for.

"Last night, my scouting party came upon a group to the north riding southward. They were attacked earlier in another camp a few miles back. We aided them and led them south for safety. The boy riding this horse refused to go without his sister, so he went back to look for her, or rather, you," she says, piecing the puzzle together. "You're Arena, aren't you?"

I nod my head as a sickening pain fills my stomach. "What happened?"

"We sent a couple of men with him, but they never returned. Not until this morning did I find his horse," she says remorsefully.

I quickly untie Storm from the tree and hop up with a demanding drive and an untamed vehemence.

"He's still alive out there, I know it," I say, ready to ride off.

"Wait! You can't, not like this. It's way too dangerous to go alone."

"Then you're coming with me."

"Just wait. Look, I understand your concern, but this is suicide."

"I've got nothing to lose anymore."

"Well, I do," she says matter-of-factly. "I lost most of my men helping your group, and now I don't even know where they are."

"What do you mean?" I ask.

"We got caught in a fire fight crossing the river, and before I knew it, everyone scattered in different directions. That's how I ended up here. I was about to leave, and then you showed up, lifelessly slumbered over."

"My friends . . . did they know where they were headed?"

"We weren't but a few miles from our base. They probably made it, but I can't know for sure."

"And my brother?"

"Look, Arena, I believe you, I do, but if he is still alive, it's too late for you to find him out there by yourself. You're going to need some serious backup, and we're only going to find that back at the base."

I feel sick inside, and now I'm faced with the horrific dilemma to abandon my brother's search, and an even greater burden of finding my friends.

I stare out into the deep, unforgiving woods, hoping and praying to see my brother's face once again. The daunting task now lies heavily on my decisions and my will to withstand the hell that awaits me. I look back into Nadia's green eyes intently before I decide to turn Storm around toward the south.

"Well, we're wasting time then, aren't we?"

CHAPTER 34

Nadia was right. Not but a few miles out where we were, the land opens into a vast area of flat lands peppered with roads, bridges, and abandoned structure after structure. I'm surrounded by a concrete jungle of desolation. With the hundreds of empty streets spanning the area like a web of asphalt, not a soul walks on them.

Large industrial facilities dominate the landscape, but the sound of industry has ceased to exist in this oil refinery ghost town. I can smell the salt air from the causeways and the putrid odor of death filtering through my refined olfactory nerves. If there are any inhabitants here, I fear they don't cater too well to strangers.

"We're not too far away. It's just on the other side of the port," Nadia says.

I'm not sure our horses are capable of enduring this concrete earth much longer, and the only way I see crossing this mammoth channel is by bridge, and that's at least another mile away, or more.

"This way," she says, bypassing the Sam Houston Parkway Bridge. "We've managed to get a ferry in operation, which makes it less grueling to cross."

The port is filled with weathered and abandoned ships rusting away in this humid salt air. The wide shipping lanes create a difficult challenge for enemy combatants to cross over to the San Jacinto memorial grounds, which is why this remote park makes for a deceivingly yet strategically ideal location for base operations.

Storm doesn't much like the ferry ride over, and it's almost enough to make me sick as well. He stammers about trying to adjust to the moving floor beneath his hooves, while I calmly concentrate on keeping my food from coming up.

The ferry slowly docks on the other side as it gently bumps into the front gates and maneuvers in between the guideposts sticking high out of the water. We leave the boat and ride along a sandy stretch of road that's lined with a short thorny nest of trees. The anticipation of this rumored mystery rebellion has me anxiously waiting, but much of my anxiety is placed in the hope that my friends have made it here safely.

My eyes glimmer with wonder at the five-hundred-foot monument that proudly stands in the middle of the park that can be seen a mile away. When we enter into the main entrance of the memorial, I'm completely jarred with utter incredulity and unexpected fascination. Almost without fail, my expression is dumbfounded with relief that we can now put the rumors of this independent revolution to rest.

Thousands of tents and makeshift structures of all sizes cover the entire grounds of the park. Most of the shelters are sectioned off in regimented rows like corn planted in a field, but some are clustered closely together, almost forming one large structure.

"Arena," Nadia says. "I want you to be prepared when you step onto these grounds for the first time."

"Prepared for what?"

"They won't know you by your birth name, but when they find out who you are, just be prepared for a following."

"And who do these people think I am?"

"The girl who started the Revolution, of course."

"So how did you know?" I ask.

"Mostly by rumors of your description. I knew right away when I saw you lying on your horse."

"So what am I to expect?"

"There's always those few who will curse you for their undoing, but most in the camp will hail you with patriotism."

"Loyalty toward this nation has nothing to do with my agenda. I'm no hero, much less a savior, and I wish not to be treated as such. I'm not here to free people; I'm here to free souls, and I can't do it alone without my brother. So you can have your uprising . . . I just want my brother back."

"The enemy stares us in the face right now, and—"

"The enemy has no more direction than those who are lost," I say. "I do have a taste for blood in this fight, but this is not the time nor the place for God's will to be done. This is just a small taste of what's to come."

"They will need your help, Arena."

"Believe me, I have no remorse for the evil that's tormented your people, and mercy isn't a quality I'm going to strain to use, either."

"I imagine you will sympathize with their plight then."

Before we are allowed to enter into the main area where all the tents are pitched, we have to check in at a gate that's heavily guarded with armed men in plain, gray jackets. The gate is barricaded with a couple of old diesel trucks, while the rest of the base is enclosed by a fifteen-foot fence.

The guard stares at me intently while he checks my weapons and nervously shakes when I place my hand above my gun.

"Ma'am, we can't allow you to take any weapons inside without special authorization," he says uneasily.

I'm not about to remove a damn thing. Contrary to Nadia's prophetic impression of these people's reaction toward me, my suspicion of deceivers is on high alert. It doesn't take much to convince me anymore that spies lurk everywhere, and regardless of their objective, I trust no one anymore.

When I refuse to remove my weapons, the irritated man sighs before he nervously moves forward and attempts to remove them himself. "I can't authorize you to carry these with you in here," he says.

I quickly grab my dagger from its sheath and pull the man against me with the knife buried uncomfortably beneath his chin.

"How about now?" I say.

The two guards behind the gate immediately raise their guns and shout at me to let the man go. Nadia is pleading with the guards to lower their weapons, but they vehemently refuse. The man under my knife fails to persuade these guards to lower their guns at first, but after a brief stalemate, they realize they have no choice. They place their guns carefully on the ground and back up a few paces.

"Okay, Arena, let him go," Nadia pleads.

"You try to touch those guns, and I'll gut him like pig," I say convincingly.

"Okay, okay, there, you see? No guns, now please let me go."

"You have to understand in my position, no one can be trusted, so forgive me if I may seem a little uneasy with guns pointed at me," I say, releasing the man.

"As you should," says a voice from a distance.

"Who are you?" I ask as a man approaches the gate. He is an older gentleman, maybe in his forties, dark hair, dark complexion, and saunters with a confidence that somehow overshadows his short stature.

"A friend who's been waiting a very long time to finally meet the one my people have been praying for," he answers.

"So, are the rumors true, or are you too disappointed?" I ask.

"Rumors are just that—rumors started from some sympathetic soul whose thoughts outgrew their eyes with outlandish embellishment. I don't need to hear it from a trail of gossip to see standing before me the one who started it all."

"I didn't start anything that I wasn't supposed to finish."

"And finish it you will. You are just as Finnegan had spoken of."

Right then, my skin shivers with a fright I haven't felt in some time, and I suddenly become drawn to this man's remarks.

"What do you know of Finnegan?" I ask.

"Funny, I was just about to ask you the same thing."

"Finnegan is dead," I say remorsefully.

"I'm so sorry," he says with a fading voice. His eyes wander to the ground, stunned at the revelation.

"How do you know him?" I ask.

"We worked together for the same cause. He was a valuable asset for the Israeli government working counter intelligence for the militia, but more importantly, he was a good man and a great friend. I'm sorry for your loss, I had no idea."

"Ananiah Shemer?" I say, trying to remember the name of the Israeli militant leader Finnegan had told us about.

After Finnegan had escaped a military coup that killed most of his men, he was taken in by Ananiah where he found shelter and a place to extend his skills for a better cause. While Shemer gave him refuge, Finnegan offered his special-ops services and created a new alliance with the Israelis, and that bond is what brought forth a common covenant. After Finnegan had shared the prophetic visions of our fate to him, Ananiah gave him his promise to lead a nation in prayer for our well-being. I truly believe now that this faithful promise by the Israeli people is what has sustained us through this divine journey.

Ananiah gestures for the two guards to open the gates and clasps his hands together eagerly waiting to formally meet me.

"Ananiah Shemer," he says, extending his hand.

"Shalom," I return with my hand grasping his.

"We are very honored to have you here with us," he kindly says. "Please take the young lady to her new living quarters with plenty of fresh water and food," he tells one of the men.

"Look, I thank you for your kind gesture, but I'm really here to find my friends."

"They would have ridden here on horseback within the day," Nadia adds.

"Take her to the refugees holding," Ananiah says to one of the guards.

"Thank you."

"Don't put too much hope in finding them there though," he adds.

There are so many tents and structures, it's almost too overwhelming to find anyone here. The only distinguishing factor between civilians and militia are their clothes. Many of the people wandering in the endless aisles of tents are wearing the same signature gray jackets as the guards.

"So you're her," the guard says.

"I guess that all depends on your philosophical bent."

"I've just heard stories of you. I never really believed you existed until today."

"Yeah, well that makes both of us."

"I'm just glad you're on our side. I feel much more confident we can win this."

"Win? This isn't some game for a cheap trophy."

"There's always a victor," he says.

"Victory is not in winning. On top of the millions of people who are already dead, millions more are going to surely die. So before you go counting your spoils, I suggest you take a grim look at what's before you, because the only victor in this war is death."

"You started something worth fighting for—"

"Yes," I snap, "but I wasn't sent here to proliferate a war. I've come here to wage a fight for survival and to get my brother back."

A sudden commotion begins to develop behind us back at the gates, and a voice yells out my name. It's Nadia animatedly waving her arms at me, but it's not until I notice Allison's weary face riding in front of the others with Luke nestled in front of her that I understand her excitement.

I rush back with exhilarated eagerness, hoping to see everyone including the possibility of Gabe somehow riding with them. I reach the gates and watch tears of joy flow from Allison's face, but to a much graver affair I notice tears of sorrow leaving Juliana's. It's apparent that Gabe is still out there somewhere, but I refuse to believe he's dead.

Allison quickly jumps down from her horse and squeezes me with elation, while Father Joseph rides near the gates with extreme fatigue and a discouraging disposition. He stares upon my face without a word to speak, and it's all I can do to just mouth the words, "Is he alive?" He pauses momentarily to catch his breath before nodding his head yes. Right then, a rider approaches from the sandy road, and Nadia's face glows bright.

"You made it," she says wistfully to the man. He quickly dismounts and embraces Nadia.

"Arena, this is my brother, Kale."

"So you're Arena," Kale says.

"Where's my brother?"

"The young boy was captured along with a dozen others."

"Where did they take them?"

"They're trucking them to the shipping yards up the coast toward Port Author for the trade market."

"They've started already?" Nadia asks.

"Started what?"

"Shipping us all off. That's what they came here for. Exterminate the waste while the rest of us are taken into slavery to do God knows what."

"Where the hell are these ships headed?" I say as I quickly jump into Storm's saddle.

"You can't possibly believe you can just commandeer a ship. It will be crawling with soldiers," Kale says.

"I'm getting my brother back with or without you. Now, where are they headed?"

"I have no idea, no one does. We just recently discovered they had ships."

"Then we're leaving for Port Arthur."

"You won't make it. They already have at least a half day start on you, not to mention your horses are completely exhausted."

Juliana is a complete wreck listening to all of this useless banter, and her misery is beginning to make me dislike the camp even more.

"Don't worry," I say to comfort Juliana, "we'll find someone who may know where these ships are going."

"Cairo," Ananiah says, sneaking up behind the conversation.

"Excuse me?" Father Joseph asks.

"Cairo, that's where they are headed," Ananiah states. "The Russians have embedded an entire city for slave trade there. Cairo is a city of deceit and wealth. It's about the only thing left the Egyptian government could not afford to lose. To avoid any more political conflict, they've accepted an alliance with China and Russia well before you were even born. The interior ministry has been long crushed and no aid will be allowed by any other nation except under the harsh Russian regime and Chinese rule.

"That passage is a feeding ground for a long-awaited kingdom to rise once again in hopes to take back an unwanted Egypt-Israel peace treaty and regain control over trade routes. Economics is the game here, my friends, and the Russians are willing to roll the dice for world economic diplomacy. And the only way to win favor without destroying everything is to massage it until it feels completely under control. The Russians have already made great efforts to preserve seven nations under their constitutional rule, and three more are on the rise. Before this world completely collapses, you will witness ten kingdoms under one rule, and I don't suspect America will be one of them."

"How long have you known this?" Kale asks.

"Before I came here two months ago looking for Finnegan, our Israeli intelligence have been watching this closely for the past six years, but most of this has been based on recent speculation, up until this this young girl showed up at our gates."

"What do you mean by that?" Kale asks.

"I truly believe God has spoken to me through her. My mind has never been this clear of what direction we are to take now."

"And what direction is that?" Kale asks.

"This country is becoming a barren wasteland. Like Nadia said, extermination is the objective. We need to ready our ships now and leave this place while we still can."

"What ships?" I inquire.

"We've had a few ships in the yard that some of the local barge runners have been fixing in case there was ever a chance we had to flee. It was our only escape plan, but I never thought we would actually use it," Nadia says.

"How many people will these ships accommodate?" Father Joseph asks.

"Enough to transport everyone here."

"There's two problems with that plan. If we do leave, how can you guarantee that we're not going to run into any conflict on the way?" Kale asks.

"I can't, but that's a risk we're going to have to take. It's that, or suffer eradication here. If we can make it to Alexandria, I will guarantee a safe passage to the Israel border."

"So what's the other problem?" Henry asks.

"Convincing the general that this isn't suicide."

"General?" I dare to inquire.

"He's the one who formed this resistance camp. He took us in and encouraged us all when he didn't have to. Together, we created this needed safe haven, but it was him who sheltered us," Kale says.

"And you trust him?" I ask Nadia.

"He has a strong will like you, so yes, I do."

"And a mighty strong heart, considering the near-fatal wound he suffered," Kale adds.

"I guess I'm going to have a little chat with your general then."

"Whoa, wait a minute. We're not going to send her to talk to him, are we?" Kale says.

"Oh, she can be pretty persuasive, trust me," Father Joseph chuckles.

"I've had a little experience with a general before, I think I can handle this," I say, checking the chamber of my gun.

"Look, he's a very wise man who will listen to your cause, but I don't think risking everyone's lives just so you can find your brother will be enough to convince him," Kale says.

"And walking in there dressed with that arsenal isn't going to help your case either," Ananiah says.

I carefully undress my weapons , unlatch the satchel attached to Storm's saddle, and pull out my black cloak that Father Joseph gave me back in the den. I pull the hood over my head and tuck my dagger and Berretta securely behind the cloak to conceal any mystery that would otherwise be a detriment to this negotiation. I'm afraid that if I can't convince him, I will be forced to take unwanted drastic measures to get my brother. This is do or die, and I'm not willing to accept any failure.

Ananiah and Kale escort me into the heart of the camp near the tall concrete monument where many of the tents are much larger. We pass by a row of tents where a few children are resting on the soft sand, one of whom looks like he hasn't eaten in days.

The weary faces that pass by sting deep into the pit of my stomach and make me feel more compelled to free them from this misery. It saddens me to know that many here will die not knowing the true cause of our fight. All I can do is pray for wisdom that they will not have to. The suffering that awaits will be enough for them to endure, and there's nothing I can do to change the coming events.

We stop in front of what appears to be an old circus tent that has been converted into several smaller tents to accommodate for private dwellings. Ananiah walks in to arrange the meeting while I'm kept outside waiting. After a few minutes, he comes back out and asks me to go in.

Though I enter with caution, preparing myself for a senseless debate, I'm encouraged that we will find an agreeable resolution. The inside is dimly lit with orange-scented candles and an unusually ornate oil lamp hanging from the tallest pitch of the fabric ceiling. I realize I probably didn't have to wear this cloak after all, because it's dark enough in here to blend into the shadows.

There's a long table in front of me with two chairs, one of which is occupied by the general's silhouette, and the other waiting for my ass to sit in it. With his face hiding in shadow, I'm overcome by a mysterious sense about the man sitting before me. He doesn't say a word while I stand there, and I can only imagine his eyes are searching me over with questions.

"This won't take long to say, and if you know who I am, then you will understand that what I say is the truth. Your people are in grave danger if they are kept here any longer. I can understand the difficulty to take care and protect them, I sympathize with your cause, but they will die if we don't leave this place. It's only a matter of days until this place is swept clean by the enemy.

"This country can no longer stand by its people without ruin, and it will eventually come to a cruel end. Our only hope lies across the ocean, and Israel will be the last stand for your soul to rest in." He shifts position with intrigue before I continue. "Do you believe God has a plan for you? And if you do, are you willing to follow it if you're asked?"

"A beautiful girl once asked me that before, and I've been reminded of that every day since I last saw her, and yet I have been disappointed in my own convictions to follow. I have no allusions of my future; I just needed someone to remind me."

Without warning, the hairs on the back of my neck stand on end, and I have a sudden lapse in thought while his voice rings with familiar delight. Whatever he is articulating, I'm completely and wholly senseless to it all except for his hypnotic sound resonating deep into my memory.

"Who are you?" I say with a sense of urgency.

"I want no more part of this mystery than you," he says.

"Then show yourself," I demand.

He slowly walks forward as the shadow of his face is gradually uncovered by the hanging lamp. I gasp in utter disbelief while every ounce of life tries to exit me. Not a muscle in my body can hold in my weakness, and my hand, still firmly fitted around my knife, suddenly releases. The dagger is sent flinging to the floor, along with the demons that have been hiding within my misery.

I slowly remove the hood away from my stunned face. His eyes grow bright, and elated tears stream down my face. Have I left myself to grieve for nothing or am I hallucinating?

My brother is still missing, our fellowship is hanging by a thread, and now my haunting memories mock me once again. I don't know what to believe anymore.

Not until his face is fully revealed in the light does my mouth shiver. I'm completely numb and overwhelmed by this shocking revelation that all I can utter from my trembling lips is one word.

Jacob.

THE END

www.ingramcontent.com/pod-product-compliance
Lightning Source LLC
Chambersburg PA
CBHW021059110726
47900CB00007B/1953